CW00693869

TARGET ANTARCTICA

Books by Hammond Innes

FICTION

Wreckers Must Breathe
The Trojan Horse
Attack Alarm
Dead and Alive
The Lonely Skier
Maddon's Rock
Killer Mine
The Blue Ice
The White South
The Angry Mountain
Air Bridge
Campbell's Kingdom
The Strange Land
The Mary Deare
The Land God Gave to Cain
The Doomed Oasis
Atlantic Fury
The Strode Venturer
Levkas Man
Golden Soak
North Star
The Big Footprints
The Last Voyage
Solomon's Seal
The Black Tide
High Stand
Medusa
Isvik

TRAVEL

Harvest of Journeys
Sea and Islands

HISTORY

The Conquistadors

Hammond Innes

TARGET ANTARCTICA

CHAPMANS

Chapmans Publishers
A division of the Orion Publishing Group Ltd
Orion House
5 Upper St Martin's Lane
London WC2H 9EA

A CIP catalogue record for this book is
available from the British Library.

First published by Chapmans 1993

Copyright © Hammond Innes 1993

The right of Hammond Innes to be identified
as the author of this work has been asserted
by him in accordance with the Copyright,
Designs and Patents Act 1988.

Grateful acknowledgement is made for
permission to use the extract from
Antarctic Isle by Niall Rankin.
Copyright © Niall Rankin 1951.
Reprinted by permission of HarperCollins Publishers.

All rights reserved
No part of this publication may be reproduced,
stored in a retrieval system, or
transmitted, in any form or by any means
without the prior permission in writing of
the publisher, nor be otherwise circulated
in any form of binding or cover other than
that in which it is published and without a
similar condition including this condition
being imposed on the subsequent purchaser.

Typeset by Selwood Systems, Midsomer Norton
Printed and bound in Great Britain by
Butler & Tanner Ltd, Frome and London

To
Monty and Maureen,
who, over the years, have
been such good friends.

CONTENTS

I

A BRIDGE TOO MANY

ONE 3

TWO 34

THREE 60

II

FLIGHT INTO FREE ENTERPRISE

ONE 91

III

COW HANGAR

ONE 121

TWO 149

THREE 183

IV

ICE

ONE 215

TWO 244

THREE 269

V

FULL FATHOM FIVE

ONE 287

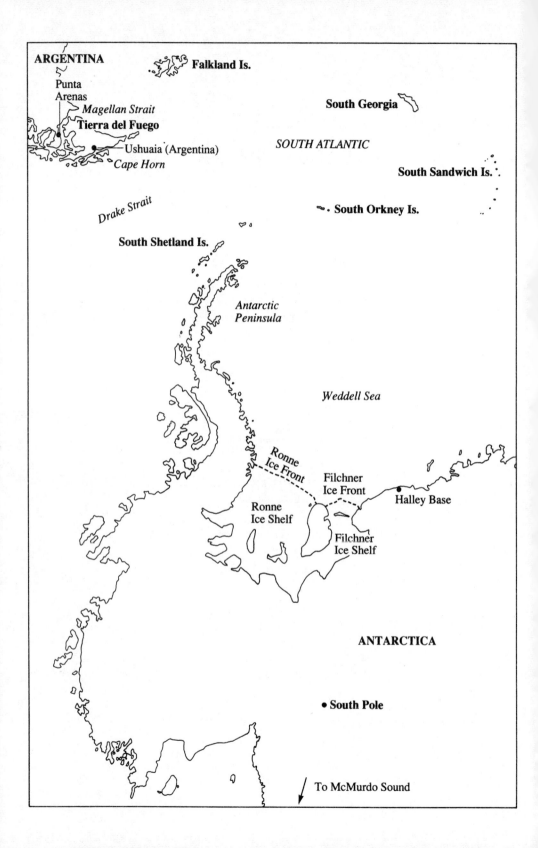

I

A BRIDGE TOO MANY

ONE

I hadn't expected it to be a woman. She came in out of the blazing sun of Greek Street and stood a moment in the doorway adjusting to the gloom and the artificial lighting, her eyes sweeping the crowded bar room. They fastened on me almost immediately and she began threading her way to the table. 'Edwin Cruse.' It was a statement, not a question. 'Kirsty Fraser.' She held out her hand. 'I'm Iain Ward's secretary. He couldn't make it.'

'Why?' I had got to my feet. 'He said to meet him here at noon. It's now almost twelve-thirty.'

'Sorry about that.' She slid into the chair opposite mine. 'Could you get me a shandy please? It's bloody hot outside and I've been on the go all morning.'

'And I've had to slog it up the M4, find myself somewhere to park ...' She wasn't listening and I went on angrily, 'Is he always as casual as this?' She had opened her shoulder bag and taken out a notepad. 'And why Soho of all places? I had to walk almost two miles ...'

'The office we're in now is close by, that's why.' She bent her head, running her eye over a page of notes. Then, 'Please.' She smiled up at me. 'A shandy, mineral water, anything cold.'

I turned abruptly and fought my way through the crowd to the bar. She was about my age, trim, very neat, with a slight accent that had the softness of rain in it. But I hadn't driven halfway across England just for the pleasure of chatting up some unknown female, and now there seemed to be only one man on duty at the bar. By the time I finally got served I was not in the best of tempers.

She smiled her thanks as I handed her drink to her. 'What's that?' she asked, leaning forward to sniff at my glass. 'Whisky?'

'Malt,' I said.

'Do you usually drink spirits in the heat of the day?'

3

'What I drink is my own business.'

'It could be our business too,' she said sharply as I sat down.

'Where's Ward?' I asked her. 'He tells me to meet him here and then sends his secretary. I'm sorry, but it's not you I want to talk to. I've some questions for him.'

She nodded. 'And he has some for you.'

'Then why isn't he here? He phoned me two days ago ...'

'Because he left about an hour ago for Paris. I've just come from Heathrow.'

'He could have rung me.'

'There wasn't time. It all happened very fast.' The smile was back, 'It often does with him. He sends his apologies.'

'I think you made that up.'

She didn't say anything, just gave a quick shrug, concentrating thirstily on the shandy I had brought her.

'What's taken him off to Paris in such a hurry? I mean what does he do? What's his business?'

'He never talks about that, and nor do I.'

'I see.' There was an awkward silence while I tried to think through the implications. 'He said he wanted to talk to me about an interesting piece of flying.'

She nodded. She was really very attractive, but sharp, with a sharp, slightly upturned nose and bright, intelligent eyes.

'He said there was money in it if I could do it. What did he mean by that?' She put her glass down. I had got her a pint while I was about it and she had drunk half of it already. 'What sort of a plane does he want me to fly?'

'I'll fill you in on the details later. First I need to find out more about you –'

'What sort of a plane?' I repeated.

She looked up at me then. 'It's all right. Relax. It's a Lockheed C-130.'

'A Hercules?'

She nodded. 'That's right, a Hercules. That's the plane you've been flying. Correct?'

I nodded.

'And they grounded you.'

I stared at her. How the hell did she know that? Who had been talking? But when I asked her, she just shook her head. 'Iain will doubtless explain it all to you later, but when I research somebody – somebody like you, who is a bit complex shall we say – I do it thoroughly.'

'Who showed you a photograph of me?'

'Nobody. Why?' She frowned, her face suddenly changing, so that she looked older than I had first thought.

'When you came in just now, you walked straight over to me. You knew who I was.'

'A guess. You just looked the part.' And she added, 'I'm good at the parts men play.' She seemed amused about something, her eyes smiling at me. 'I've had a lot of practice. But now –' she was looking straight at me, the whites of her eyes very clear, the irises a startling sapphire blue – 'I'm here to check that we've got it right, so if you'd be so kind, perhaps you could answer a few questions? Then if they're satisfactory, I'll give you some idea of what it's all about. I can't tell you everything, but if my report on you is favourable, I'm sure Iain will be in touch with you again himself.' She glanced down at her notebook. 'Perhaps we could start at the beginning. Your father was in the RAF, a fighter pilot – Hurricanes, then Spitfires, shot down twice during the Battle of Britain, finished up as a group captain giving close support to the Eighth Army in its drive up Italy. Correct?'

I nodded. 'He was shot up and badly burned in the battle for Malta. He didn't do much flying after that.' And I added, the image of him building again in my mind, 'He was one of the great. One of the really great. A wonderful man.'

'His first wife left him, didn't she?'

'What's that to do with it?' I said.

'She left him after the plastic surgery and the skin grafts, and he didn't meet your mother until very much later, when he was having more surgery. A nurse, half-Italian, half-Irish, right?'

I nodded, keeping a tight hold on myself. It hadn't taken me long to learn that life was going to be very different out of the Service.

'Your father, being Welsh, makes you quite a mixture. You speak French, I believe.' She was reading from her notes. 'You had almost a year attached to a French Étandère squadron. And Italian, of course. Any other languages?'

'Some Spanish,' I said, 'and a bit of Arabic. I find languages come quite easily. And, of course, I can swear in Welsh!'

5

It was meant as a joke, but she wrote it all down, her face quite serious. 'Now we come to the difficult bit. I'm sorry. You may find this a little painful. You were very close to your father, weren't you?' She said it softly, and seeing him in my mind's eye again, I was glad of the softness of her voice.

'Yes,' I said. 'Very close.'

'You hero-worshipped him, in fact?'

I nodded. 'I suppose you could call it that.'

'So it was inevitable you would follow in his footsteps and go into the Air Force.'

'I never thought of doing anything else.'

'And now they're kicking you out.'

Where the hell did she get that from? Had she access to the files? Was that what they had put on my Service record? 'I resigned,' I told her.

She nodded. 'Well, yes – that's what they told me. But your background and record doesn't exactly suggest you'd have resigned of your own free will.' She paused there, watching me, waiting. 'What made you do it?'

'Resign?'

'No, the bridge.' A slight shake of the head and again that smile. 'Such a stupid thing –'

'It was in the way,' I said, wondering whether I could make her understand. 'We'd done a tight turn. You can do that with a Herc. But the lead fighter – he was good, that boy – he anticipated, so he was right on my tail as I levelled out with my belly almost skimming the surface of the river. What else could I do? The damn thing was right there in front of me.'

'You could have made another turn, I suppose. It was just bravado, wasn't it? Like the time before, when they took you off Phantoms and banished you to the Falklands. No fighters after that. Bumbling old Hercules and a routine job of flight refuelling.'

'There's nothing bumbling about the Hercules,' I told her. 'They may be slow, but you can throw 'em around, stand them on their heads pretty well ...'

'Then why didn't you twist away when you saw the bridge coming up? If they're so manoeuvrable ...'

'I couldn't. I was too low. I had the Army Apprentice buildings to starb'd, and the other Herc to port, also the Aust service station on its clifftop. I was boxed in.'

'So you went under it.' She was leaning forward, those startling eyes of hers fixed on me, her drink forgotten. 'What about the other C-130? The young trainee pilot. He followed you through, didn't he? It was a crazy thing to do, a man of your experience leading a youngster ...'

'No, he didn't follow me, not then.' I shook my head. 'It wasn't like that at all. We were dog-fighting, two of us, four of them. I hadn't anywhere else to go but under the bridge. Mike banked away and the Phantom that had been on my tail zoomed up in a steep climb, the after-burners full on. No, it wasn't crazy.'

'But then you turned right around and went back under the bridge.'

'Yes.'

She was still frowning. 'But why? You must have known you'd be reported. I've been over the Severn Bridge several times. The traffic wouldn't have stopped to report you. Nobody stops on the M4. It's just a steady stream, trucks, cars, coaches. But they've been practically rebuilding that bridge for years. There's contractors' men, tollgate officials, highway police. To go back and do it a second time –'

'If I'd gone straight on the other three Phantoms would have pounced on me, so I gave the old bus full rudder, flipped her round, and this time Mike followed me.'

She asked me then what I had meant about dog-fighting and I told her it was a training exercise. 'Somebody's got to give the fighter boys some practice, so we play war games with them.'

She was suddenly smiling again, the frown gone, a gleam of excitement in her eyes. 'And that particular day your war game got a little out of hand.'

'I guess so.'

'You could have broken it off.'

'Then we'd have had to buy them drinks. Our time wasn't quite up.'

She sat back, still smiling. 'You goddam silly fool!' she said. 'Your career thrown away for the sake of a round of drinks.'

'Yes. Put like that it does sound rather silly.'

The smile vanished. 'Or was there some other reason? They

7

gave you a medical check, didn't they? A very thorough check that included a brain scan.'

'They didn't find anything,' I said. 'I had a crash, you see. A bad one. I was still at Cranwell then. Concussion. But it wore off and the scan showed nothing, no tumour, no damaged blood vessels.'

'They told you that in the hospital, did they?'

'Not immediately. But I went back later ...'

'What about heart, and arteries – any trouble there?'

'No. All perfectly sound.'

'So why did you do it? And Tower Bridge. Good God! That should have warned you. What are you trying to do, prove something, prove you're a man?' She was leaning forward again. 'Is it your father? Is that what drives you? You want to convince yourself you're as good a flyer as he was, as committed, as daring ...'

'Stop it!' I said. 'Can't you understand? I'm built this way. I can't help myself. Tower Bridge – you mentioned that stupid episode. We were just back from the Falklands and I couldn't resist it. The people in London, Whitehall, the politicians ... I wanted to remind them, show them we were still around ... I wanted to hit the headlines, I suppose. It did that all right. But at the time I didn't think about that. I just put the nose down and went at it. Crazy! But that's the way it is, the way I am.' I was talking too much. I knew that. My tongue always seems to run away with me when I'm not sure of myself.

'And that accounts for all the other things, does it? You break up a mess, leading your squadron against another squadron over the furniture, swinging from the lights, climbing along the picture rails, organising a rugger ...'

'That's not the same,' I told her angrily. 'That's nights off, and only when I'm drunk. Christ Almighty! You have done your homework, haven't you?'

'Yes,' she said. Her eyes remained fixed on me for a moment, a searching, almost speculative look. Then, abruptly, she said, 'I don't know about you, but I'm hungry. Let's go and feed.' She put the notepad away in her shoulder bag, finished her drink and got to her feet. 'I booked a table for one o'clock.' The clock over the bar showed a quarter past.

The restaurant was upstairs where the head waiter greeted her as

Mrs Fraser and showed us to a window table overlooking the street. 'You're married then,' I said as we sat down.

'Divorced.' She said it bluntly in a tone that discouraged any further discussion on that topic.

She had picked up the menu and I could see the fingers of her left hand. No wedding ring. Had she thrown it at him?

'So you can question me about my personal affairs, but I mustn't question you?'

She looked at me. 'It's you who are looking for a job, not me.'

The way she said it got under my skin. There was a hardness about her and I thought she had probably knocked around quite a bit. 'I didn't go to Ward asking for a job,' I told her angrily. 'He contacted me. Out of the blue. Asked me to meet him here, then buggers off to Paris and sends you to find out if I'm mad, ill, or just so bloody wild ...' I shook my head, taking a grip on myself, and suddenly the smile was back on her lips.

'You're certainly volatile,' she said. 'You seem to live on your nerves, a short fuse burning most of the time. Is that a fair summary?' She didn't wait for an answer, but went straight on: 'I've often wondered about fighter pilots. You're really a fighter pilot, aren't you? Is that what happens to them, flying solo, the effect of being alone with death in the cockpit?' And then she suddenly said, 'You mentioned being back from the Falklands. From the Falklands War, is that what you meant? Or was it later, when you'd got switched to the Hercules aircraft?'

'No. I was there for the war. But only briefly. Harriers.' God, it seemed a long time ago! 'I was just a kid.'

'Nevertheless –' she was smiling – 'you made your mark. Quite a story.'

'The Pucará?'

She nodded. 'I read about it. At the time.' So she was about my own age. 'And now, no more war. You're out of the Service. And yet you're just the type. You'd be at your dashing best, collecting decorations, or else getting yourself killed attempting the impossible.'

'Court-martialled, more likely,' I murmured.

She leaned forward, touched my hand. 'We can't give you a war, but I think we may be able to offer you a challenge.' I felt the slight pressure of her fingers and the smile on her face was warm and personal. 'Relax now. I won't ask any more questions. Oh, one more. Are you married?'

I shook my head.

'No little brats lurking in corners? No dependants?'

'None.'

'And both your parents dead. An air crash in Yugoslavia, wasn't it? So now you're pretty well on your own, married to the Service, and in a few days' time you'll be out, your sheet anchor gone, no sense of belonging any more.'

I didn't say anything. She squeezed my hand, then picked up the menu lying beside my plate. 'Just choose what you want now and we'll order.'

But my mind had locked on to her suggestion of a challenge. I didn't look at the menu. I was looking at her. 'What's the job?' I asked her. 'Give me some idea of what the job is, and then I'll –'

'Afterwards,' she said. 'Over our coffee. I've got a couple of photographs to show you, but we'll eat first. Your car all right, is it?'

I nodded. 'I left it in the underground car park off Park Lane and walked from there.' The waiter was hovering and we ordered. And then we began to talk, not about me, but about things in general – the situation in the Middle East, particularly the Gulf, what was happening in southern Africa, America, the IRA. And then, over my crab claw salad, I found myself talking about the Falklands, how attracted I had been to the windswept, treeless desolation of the islands, so indented with inlets that from the air they looked like an unfinished jigsaw puzzle.

We both had roast duck for the main course, and with a bottle of red wine, the talk flowed easily. I liked her. She might have been a nurse. She had that aura of calm, something my mother had always had. It was only after our plates had been taken away that I realised how unobtrusively she had been drawing me out, not questioning me directly, just encouraging me to talk, and all the time those sapphire eyes watching.

We went straight to coffee after that and I began quizzing her about Ward, the sort of man he was. That's something the Services teach you – people, man management, what makes your companions tick. Particularly in the Air Force. Flying, you don't want to discover suddenly that there's one of your crew shitting his pants just at the moment the going gets tough. That way you can lose your life. And if I was to go on flying it would be the same in civilian life. With Ward dealing the cards I needed to be damn sure he wasn't the joker. What was his business? That was the first thing I needed to know. How did he make enough to pay for an office in Covent Garden and this efficient-seeming, very attractive secretary sitting opposite me? But when I asked her she shook her head and smiled. 'You want to know that sort of thing, you ask him yourself.'

'Okay, but at least you can tell me what he looks like – tall, short, fat, thin, handsome, ugly? Come on, give me a clue. What sort of a man is he, how old?'

She shook her head again. 'I've never asked him. He probably wouldn't tell me anyway. He's broad-shouldered, dark-haired, steely-grey eyes, and a nose any Arab would be proud of. He's also got a misplaced hand. You'll see when you meet him. At least you can't fail to spot him in a crowd.' She was speaking quietly, almost affectionately. 'Built a bit like a bull.' She raised her head, the sunlight turning her hair to gold. 'Behaves like one, too.' There was the glimmer of a smile as she added, 'Sometimes.'

'Family?'

She shook her head. 'A wife, that's all.' The way she said it made it clear they weren't living together. Whether it was the wine on top of that pint of shandy, or whether she found me a sympathetic listener, I don't know, but she suddenly murmured, 'She's like a bitch on heat. Know what she does?' She leaned towards me, her eyes fixed on mine. 'Advertises in that London leisure magazine, in the lonely hearts section.' And when I asked her why she should advertise for a husband when she was still married, she gave a snort. 'Don't be silly. She's not advertising for a husband.'

'What then? For company, for sex, or just for kicks? Is that what you mean?'

She nodded. 'Yes, for kicks. She gives her phone number, never her address, and when a man she likes the sound of rings in she gives him a rendezvous.'

'A blind date?' I wondered what sort of a woman she was. 'That could be a recipe for murder.'

She nodded. 'Or AIDS. I've warned her. So has Iain. But she takes no notice.'

'Why doesn't he divorce her?'

'She's a Catholic. Devout on Sunday, in bed with a stranger on Monday. Odd, isn't it? She's half-French and can't seem to leave the boys alone.'

'What's the lure?' I asked. 'What sort of ad does she insert?'

'Quite funny sometimes. He likes to keep an eye on her, so I take the magazine and sift through it for him. He can't bear to do it himself. There's one in this week's issue.' She was smiling as she quoted it. 'I'm French dressing. Shake gently before serving.' She laughed. 'Not bad, eh? No name, just the phone number. That's how we know it's her.'

'Nice sense of humour,' I murmured. 'I might phone her myself.'

I said it jokingly, but she took me up on it straight away. 'You do that and Iain would never have anything to do with you. He's still strangely protective towards her.' She gave a little shrug. 'Forget it. I shouldn't have told you. But if you're fool enough to blurt it out, just watch that artificial hand of his.' She was digging around in her handbag and came up with two photographs which she pushed across the table to me. 'Not very clear, I'm afraid, but the best they could do.' She turned them round. 'They're blow-ups of relevant segments of a Landsat pic.'

They were black and white with a great deal more white than black. 'What is it – ice?' One of them had the dark line of what looked like an ice runway with huts beside it and an aircraft.

'Yes, ice. That was the ice-field camp before a whole segment of the runway split off and floated away. This is more recent.' She pointed a red-nailed finger at the other photograph, which was of a blurred mass of ice surrounded by water. 'This shows the section that calved from the main ice-field. You can just see the outline of the aircraft under its mantle of snow.'

I saw it then, the outline shape of a C-130 that had been slid tail-first into a rough DIY ice hangar. 'And I'm supposed to fly it off, is that it?'

She hesitated, then looked straight at me and nodded. 'If he likes what I tell him about you, then that's what he'll be asking you to do.'

'How long is that bit of a runway?' But she didn't know. 'Where's it got to be flown?'

'That's something you'll have to talk to him about.'

'Well, how far before I can refuel? It's a question of weight on take-off, you see. How far before I can put it down on a real runway and get the thing tanked up?'

'Can you fly it off? That's all I need to know right now.'

'I can't answer that till I know how long that bit of runway is, but a Herc doesn't need all that much. How long has it been there?'

'Since last summer,' she said.

'And when that chunk of ice broke away, what was the plane's condition?'

'It was okay.'

'The engines all working?'

'That's what we've been told.'

'Then why couldn't the pilot fly it off?'

'We did ask that. They hedged for a bit, but then they admitted the pilot hadn't the guts to try it.'

I nodded. 'Good for him!'

'Why do you say that?'

'Presumably he knew his limitations. How experienced was he?' But she couldn't say. Anyway, it didn't matter. The man was hardly likely to admit he wasn't a fully-qualified Hercules pilot. And he certainly wouldn't admit to being chicken. 'When did the ice break away from the main body? Can you give me a date?'

For that she had to refer to her notepad. 'The second of February.'

'Of this year?'

She nodded.

'So it's been there just over seven months. Anybody looking after it?' But of course not. The whole place was deep in snow. And then it dawned on me. Summer, she had said. Summer in February. 'This isn't Greenland, or Spitsbergen, some place like that, is it? This is the Antarctic.'

She didn't say anything and I sat there, staring at her, wondering what the hell I would be letting myself in for if I said I'd have a go at flying the thing out. I was also wondering what it was worth, risking my life down there at the bottom of the world. And, if I could put a tag on it, would they agree my terms? Who were *they* anyway? But when I asked her, she shook her head. 'Just tell me whether you can do it or not.'

'I've told you, I can't answer that unless you tell me where the plane is.' McMurdo had a runway I could land on. I didn't know about the other bases. Or perhaps, if the outfit she and her boss worked for had the right contacts, maybe the flight refuelling unit at Mount Pleasant would tank me up at the halfway mark. 'How do we get down there anyway?'

'That's all fixed. The boat he used before. Quite small, but specifically designed for coping with pack-ice. Right now it's on stand-by and refitting at Port Stanley.'

'In the Falklands then?'

'Yes.'

'Any crew?'

'Three at the moment. Peter Kettil, sailing master and navigator, a Norwegian engineer, Nils Solberg. They are both of them very professional. And there's a woman. Iris Sunderby. I don't know much about her capabilities, but she's the boss.'

'She skippers the boat, does she?'

'No, no. She owns it.' Fraser hesitated, her face reddening as she blurted out between clenched teeth, 'He gave it to her.'

'What do you mean, gave it to her?'

'Just that. He made her a present of it before he left them.' She got control of herself then, sitting back in her chair, her mouth shut tight and her eyes half-closed. I started to ask about the woman and why Ward had given the ship to her, but she shook her head. 'It's not important. But if you really want to know you'd better ask him yourself.' She wouldn't answer any more questions and I got the impression she felt she had said too much already.

She handed me another, smaller photograph. 'This is from the company's files.' It showed a Hercules coming in to land, the runway a flat sheet of ice flanked by heaps of half-melted snow. There was a small, tracked machine with a dozer blade on the front of it parked close by the main hut and the runway began at the top of an ice cliff with open water beyond and pack-ice on the horizon. It had to be on one of the ice-cap edges where the great frozen dome of Antarctica reached down to the sea in shelves of solid ice. But that could be anywhere, for the Met boys at Mount Pleasant had shown me Landsat pictures of Antarctica and told me only about a twentieth of the coastline was rock. The rest was ice, either grounded or afloat, and where the ice was floating it ended abruptly in great cliffs, a hundred, two hundred feet high. The Ice Fronts. It was here, along the floating Ice Fronts, that great chunks, some of them miles in extent, broke off in summer and floated away to form flat-topped tabular bergs. The Hercules they wanted flown out was clearly on one of these. 'Where?' I asked her. 'Where is the damned thing?'

'The Weddell Sea,' she said.

I nodded. It would be right at the southern end. That's where the Ice Fronts were. 'I'll need the dimensions,' I said, turning again to the pictures of the Herc on its floating ice platform. 'What about fuel? Is there fuel in the tanks? And to clear all that snow off the runway we'll need diesel for that little bulldozer.' Innumerable questions, but all she would say was, 'You'll have to ask Iain.'

She looked at her watch then and said she had to go. 'He's probably been on the phone to me already.' She finished her lunch, paid the bill and we went out into the street, the heat coming up at us and the traffic virtually at a standstill, the smell of exhaust fumes reaching down into my lungs.

'Where's your office?' I asked her.

'Just around the corner.' She held out her hand, those brilliant sapphire eyes of hers smiling up at me. 'I've enjoyed meeting you, but I'll see that it's Himself next time and that he comes down to you. Sunday week probably. He'll be back then, I hope with the whole thing buttoned up. As far as I know he's got nothing planned for that day.'

'It's Battle of Britain Sunday,' I said. 'A service, then a reception ...'

'I'll see he makes his number to your station commander first.' And before I could ask her what it was she thought he would have buttoned up, she had turned away, walking quickly to the corner of Old Compton Street, a neat, trim figure, the soft yellow of her shirt almost matching the colour of her hair, her scarf the same blue as her eyes.

I thought about another drink, but it was too hot, and anyway, I had too much on my mind. Walking slowly back to Hyde Park Corner through the tourist-crowded streets I wondered about the new world I would be entering in a few days' time. Kirsty Fraser and her boss seemed somehow symbolic of the change in my life. I would be out on my own then, no longer cushioned by a Service that had been my life since leaving school.

God! What a bloody fool I had been! The RAF had its drawbacks – the sense of being hemmed in by orders, routine, rank, and a loose discipline that sometimes made one feel like a dog on a lead – but it was still a wonderful club: the sense of belonging, the safety net always there.

And I had thrown it away. Why? What was it made me do things that steadier, more sensible men wouldn't dream of doing?

I was still thinking about that as I walked down the slope from Park Lane into the gloom of the underground car park, the smell of concrete and oil lingering on the stale air, the sound of footsteps and engines starting up echoing in the cavernous vaults. My car was parked at the Marble Arch end and soon I was alone except for a young man some twenty paces behind me.

If you have had to pass endless hours waiting for the Met people to clean up the overcast, or ground staff to sort out some electrical fault, you will have seen enough bad American TV for your imagination to get instantly overheated at the echoing tread of somebody behind you in an otherwise deserted parking lot. Twice I turned my head; the second time I actually stopped. He slowed at once, then turned off into one of the bays. But when I went on, there he was behind me again, tall, slim, with fair hair and a beard, and wearing faded jeans.

I had my keys out ready as I walked up to my car. He was close behind me now and moving faster. Should I turn and face him, ask him what the hell he was playing at? And then find it was his car parked alongside mine.

'Can I have a word with you, sir?'

It was the 'sir' that made me pause and turn. That, and the fact that I was parked close against a concrete pillar. Before I could wriggle in behind the wheel he had the nearside door open and was sliding into the passenger seat. 'Greenpeace,' he said, as though flashing some sort of ID card.

'What do you want?' I didn't believe a word of it, the adrenalin running, anger building and my eyes watching for the first sign of a weapon. 'If you want money ...'

'You joking, man?' He grinned at me through his blond beard. 'Don't say you never heard of Greenpeace.'

'Of course I have.' I was into the driving seat now and there was nothing I could do but sit there, still very tense, watching him. There was something about the eyes – 'Well, what is it you want?'

'The answer to a few questions. That is all.' He closed his door. 'I'm going back to the office. Islington Green. If that's on your way, then we can talk while you drive. Otherwise, we just sit here. Okay?'

'Why should Greenpeace be interested in me?' I was still suspicious of him, though he did look the part – fresh, open face, pale blue eyes under the long blond hair, and the slim body bursting with vitality. He had a slight accent. Scandinavian, I thought, and he looked clean and healthy. Only the eyes were still worrying me. There was a wildness about them. 'Come on, what's it all about?' I demanded.

'Giotti Frère. That mean anything to you?'

'No.'

'You sure? KLME then?'

I started the engine. 'I'm headed west, down Bayswater Road.' I started to back out of the bay. 'Either you get out at the exit or you'll finish up in Wiltshire.'

'What about Iain Ward? He a friend of yours, or just a business contact?'

I told him I had never met the man.

'But you have lunch just now with his secretary.'

'So you were following her, then you followed me. Why?'

'Request from our Paris office. They are waiting for Ward when he flew into Paris this morning, followed him to the Giotti Frère office near the Champs-Elysées, then rang us to keep an eye on his Soho office. When his secretary came out I followed her and she led me to you.' He asked me my name and then what I did. I told him, and he nodded as though it made some sort of sense to him. 'So you are a squadron leader in the RAF, and you fly those big four-engined Hercules aircraft.' He smiled, and I wondered how he'd guessed that. 'You going to do it for them?'

'Do what?' I stopped the car.

'Fly that Hercules off.' He had turned in his seat, those pale blue eyes fastened on me, waiting, the wildness in them quite marked now, accentuated by a nearby fluorescent strip. 'That's what Ward wants you to do, isn't it?'

I didn't see what it had got to do with Greenpeace and I said so.

'The Antarctic. Anything to do with the Antarctic ...' He was suddenly very earnest and I switched off the engine. 'A fifty-year ban on mining isn't enough. Greenpeace want the whole continent declared a World Park. We're very committed to that, and Giotti Frère, they're exploiters of the worst type.' He paused, looking at

17

me intently. 'What puzzles me,' he went on, 'is why the RAF should have agreed to loan them a squadron leader to get that C-130 airborne.' He shook his head. 'Something strange here. A decision like that, it is political, not a Service matter at all.' He asked me then whether I had received my orders from my commanding officer. 'Or from the Ministry?' He waited a moment, watching me, but I don't think he really expected me to answer that for he asked me again if I was going to do it.

'That depends,' I said.

'Depends on what?'

I ignored that and began questioning him about Giotti Frère. 'It sounds more Italian than French.'

'Not Italian. Sicilian. The two Giottis, Luigi and Guiseppe, are from Palermo.' And he went on to say they originally operated in the Argentine, their headquarters in Buenos Aires, but then, quite suddenly, they had moved to Paris. 'That was just one year before Galtieri ordered the military occupation of the Malvinas.'

'That was 1982.'

He nodded. '*Ja*, the year you British despatch the Task Force to the Falklands.'

He told me Giotti Frère now had a stake in an oil well off Tierra del Fuego, at the eastern end of the Magellan Strait, that they were active in Cambodia, and through their KLME subsidiary were carrying out seismographical surveys of two areas in the Falkland Islands. Last summer they had begun the construction of a hard-rock runway at the root of the Graham Peninsula in Antarctica, not far from Chile's General San Martin base. 'That was after their camp on the Ronne Ice Shelf had been partially destroyed. They say the work they carry out is for the Argentine Government, but we get no confirmation of that.'

All this time he was staring at me very fixedly, words pouring out of him. He seemed totally obsessed by the Greenpeace attitude to the Antarctic, his mind focussed chiefly on the Giotti company. The crew of their supply ship had been particularly vicious. He described the incident in some detail, admitting he was quoting from a report. He had not been there at the time, but later, when KLME was running geological checks on fumaroles in the Antarctic Peninsula, he had seen for himself how the contractors behaved. They had been levelling rock for a hard-core runway, and, like the French, they were driving it bang through a King Penguin colony, regardless of the fact that they were destroying one of the breeding sites of a rare and important bird. 'To stop them we lay down in front of their bulldozer, and one of us, a young Yugoslav called Janny, nearly got killed. If he hadn't rolled out of the way at the very last moment they would have driven the machine right over him.' He was holding my arm now, his fingers so tightly clenched I could feel them trembling. 'And they were laughing. I'll always remember that. They were laughing.'

He sat there for a moment, completely lost to anything but the picture in his mind. Then, abruptly, he switched back to the present. 'Where are you being asked to fly that plane?'

'I've no idea.'

'Please.' He leaned forward, his voice urgent. 'I need to know. What are your orders?'

He didn't seem to believe me when I said I had no orders, so I told him I would shortly be a civilian.

'A civilian? So it's as a civilian they approached you?'

'Nothing is settled yet. And now ...' I reached for the ignition key, and was about to turn it, when he gripped my arm again. 'Look, man, you ever been down there? To the Antarctic, I mean. No, of course not. There's no RAF station south of the Falklands. But you've been to the Falklands. Was that during the war or since?'

'Both,' I said. 'I was there about a year ago, flying C-130 Hercules.'

He nodded. 'So you are on the South Georgia run, dropping mail and supplies to the garrison there. South Georgia, South Orkneys, South Shetlands, they give you some idea what it's like. But those islands are on the line of the Antarctic Convergence where warm and cold waters meet. That is just the outskirts of the continent. There you are only at the entrance to the Weddell Sea. Flying supply drops to South Georgia you will have some impression of the grandeur, but not the vastness of the huge, ice-bound, endless mass of Antarctica.'

That word Antarctica seemed to spark him off, his voice suddenly eager, full of an almost boyish enthusiasm, as he launched into a flood of words, describing something of what he had seen in the two seasons he had been down there, the impression it had made on him.

I don't remember much of what he said, it poured out of him at such a pace, and anyway half my mind was on how it would be for me if things went wrong and I had to ditch.

What did surprise me, and it stuck in my mind, was how comparatively crowded Antarctica had become, scientists from all over the world wintering over in, I think he said, more than forty bases. Four thousand personnel moving through the American McMurdo Sound base alone, and in the summer months a total of some seventy bases.

I remembered those figures, and what he said about the size of Antarctica – bigger than the whole of Europe. 'The world's largest wilderness.' He used those words, said it contained seventy per cent of the world's fresh water, most of it frozen solid. 'A vast natural laboratory for environmental studies, climate in particular.'

And he went on: 'It's down there, with a lot of painstaking research, year after year, that we learn about the hole in the ozone layer. Now we begin to assess the degree of global warming. We measure thickness of the pack-ice to discover the melt speed. But with temperatures in the centre of the ice dome capable of dropping as low as minus ninety degrees centigrade, you can imagine how fragile the whole ecosystem is, the growth of any surface plant desperately slow.' As an illustration, and as an indication of the impact even the scientists were having, he said the imprint of a human foot on a bed of moss would still be there ten or more years hence.

It was a very emotional introduction to a world that, in prospect, frightened the life out of me. I had never flown in conditions like that. South Georgia had been bad enough, a sea journey of some nine hundred miles there and the same back, glaciated peaks towering wing-tip height at three thousand metres and more. But his description of this huge, white wilderness of a continent . . . And the whole verbal outpouring coming to me quite by chance as I sat there with this strangely obsessed young man in an underground car park in the centre of London.

By the time I got the car moving again and had driven out into Park Lane my mind was in a daze, so full of the Antarctic that I felt as though I were already on my way there. I was going west and Islington Green was up by the Angel, north of the City. I dropped him off by the entrance to the Underground at Marble Arch, but before getting out of the car he found a piece of paper in the glove locker, scribbled a note and handed it to me. 'Phone please when you know more about what you are to do with that aircraft. It is very important that I know. Not only for Greenpeace, but also for me personally. Okay?' And just before he shut the door, he leaned his head in and said, 'We will have the *Gondwana* down there this summer. I think maybe I can be on it. I am studying geology. Postgraduate.' The grin was back, lighting up his face, and then he was gone, his body so full of vitality his feet barely seemed to touch the ground.

I glanced at the piece of paper. No name, no address, just a telephone number with the prefix 081. London. But not central London.

I drove on then, turning down Bayswater, my mind not on the traffic, but far away, absorbed by the picture that wild young man had given me of the Antarctic. A challenge, Ward's secretary had said, and now, thinking of the prospect ahead of me, I became increasingly curious. In Notting Hill Gate I was stopped by traffic lights and there was a W. H. Smith on the opposite side of the road. I did a quick U-turn, parked at the kerb outside and dived in. The magazines were in racks to the left of the entrance and it didn't take me long to find the one I was looking for – and there it was, that ridiculous, teasing ad in the lonely hearts section at the end. And she was so near. It was the proximity that decided me.

I was waiting to pay at the desk when I saw a veteran yellow job approaching my car, her book open at the ready. 'Hey!' I thrust some coins at the cashier and was round the desk in a flash. 'I just stopped for a second to get a copy of *Flight*,' I explained. 'For my boss. An article he wanted ...'

But she had seen the magazine under my arm. 'For your boss, y'say? I've heard that before y'know. I wasn't born yesterday.'

She certainly wasn't, but I didn't tell her so. 'They were out of *Flight* and I'm on the loose in London for the evening. So ...'

'This your car?' She was regarding the battered old Jaguar with an expression bordering on pity.

'No, it belongs to the boss. We share a room at the MoD.'

'Name?'

'Look – please ...'

'Name,' she repeated relentlessly.

'Smith. John Smith.'

'And you fought in the Gulf War, of course.'

I nodded. 'Tornadoes.' But it wasn't Tornadoes, of course, it was C-130s on the supply run.

There was a pause, then she said, 'Funny thing is I believe you.' And she added slowly, 'I lost a son, y'know. In the Gulf. Tanks. A direct hit, they said.'

She stood there a moment, then closed her book. 'Don't do it again. It's a double yellow line, y'know.' The heavy, battle-weary face broke into a sudden smile and for an instant I glimpsed the girl she had been. 'Wouldn't mind a night on the town meself.' She said it so wistfully I almost invited her, but instead I muttered something about a date with a lonely heart, then bent and kissed her on the cheek.

'God bless!' she said as I pulled away from the kerb.

I turned right at the second traffic lights, crossed Kensington Church Street and drove up into Campden Hill Road where I knew there was a telephone kiosk. It was a 229 number she had given in the ad and because I had once had a girlfriend with a studio in Aubrey Walk, I knew Ward's wife must be living in the area.

'What do you mean, you want to shake me?' The voice at the other end of the line sounded startled. I asked her whether she was Mrs Ward, but before I had completed the question she said brightly, 'Oh, that . . .' A sudden tinkle of laughter, then a longer pause. 'Okay. Don't bother about your name. It'll probably be false , anyway.' She sounded warmer now, the voice soft and low with just the trace of a Scots accent. 'Better give me a description of yourself – age, background, that sort of thing . . . Well, go on. Do a bit of sales-manship.'

I told her what I thought she wanted to know, including my real name, adding that I had just the one evening free and would she come and have dinner with me?

'Where are you?' And when I told her, she laughed. 'My God, you're getting warm. You've got a car, have you? All right, drive back almost to Notting Hill Gate, turn right into Uxbridge Street, then park on the corner of Hillgate Place and Farm Place and stand by your car. If you look as nice as you sound, I'll meet you there.'

I did as she said, except there was no slot near the corner and I had to put the car on a resident's parking space at the far end of the street. The sudden decision to phone her seemed less attractive as I stood at the corner waiting. She could be having me on, chuckling to herself at the thought of an unknown man kicking his heels . . .

I glanced at my watch. Ten minutes. I'd give her ten minutes. And then I began to think what I would say to her if she did turn up, a woman I didn't know and asking her questions about a husband for whom she didn't give a damn. And what was it I wanted to know about him?

I was thinking about that, staring vacantly at the little terrace houses standing shoulder-to-shoulder the length of Hillgate Place, when a voice behind me said quietly, 'Squadron Leader Cruse?'

It was the soft, educated voice with the faint Scots inflection I had heard on the telephone. I turned, wondering what she would be like, quite unprepared for what I saw standing behind me. She was neat and compact, dressed soberly and rather expensively in russet colours, only the scarf at her neck showing a touch of flamboyance. But what shook me was her face, so young-looking, so innocent, and the tip-tilted nose, the high cheekbones; I just stared at her, unable to say anything, my mind gone back and full of memories.

'What's the matter?'

I shook my head. 'Sorry. Somebody very dear to me. You remind me of her.' I could see her so clearly, just a kid, built like a young colt with large eyes. 'My younger sister,' I said slowly. 'You look like her – like she would have looked now.' And I added, because it seemed to require some explanation, 'She was killed riding pillion on a motor bike when she was sixteen.'

She turned her head slightly, silent for a moment. 'And I look like her?'

I nodded and her hand touched mine. 'That's the nicest thing . . .' She left it at that. I suppose she was thinking, as I was, that this was a strange beginning to our evening. 'Barbara.' She held out her hand. 'Barbara Ward.' She still kept his name and his ring. 'Why don't we drive out to Marlow, somewhere in the Thames Valley, have tea by the river, then that dinner you promised me?' She flashed me a glance that matched the huskiness in her voice.

'Okay.'

So I took her to the car, threw back the hood and we drove down the M4 as far as the cut-off for Maidenhead. It was hot, one of those sleepy late afternoons. We had tea a little back from the bridge at Sonning, cucumber sandwiches, and a pair of swans at our feet.

We didn't talk much. Not through shyness, or any feeling of nervous tension. We were strangely at ease with one another. That tea on the lawn by the gently-flowing river proved to be one of those rare interludes, a moment of absolute tranquility. And then I said something about our meeting not being a bit what I expected. 'Why do you do it?'

'The ad?' She gave a harsh little laugh and the magic was gone. 'Maybe I'm over-sexed. I don't know. I just like it, that's why.' And she added, 'They're all so different – that's what makes it fun. You never know . . .' She threw the remains of her sandwich at the swans, staring bleakly at a passing motor launch. 'They're paired, those two.' A pause, and then she said, 'Without a mate I get very lonely at times.' She gave a quick little shrug. 'I suppose I should find myself some work, but I like variety, you see. So I don't have a job. Fact is, I suppose, I have a low boredom threshold, and that leads to depression.'

She turned her head, staring at me with big, unhappy eyes. 'Have you ever suffered from depression, from lack of confidence in your-self . . .? No, of course not. You've got the Air Force. But for a woman alone in a big city like London . . .' She gave that little laugh. 'I could have taken to drink, I suppose, or drugs.' She opened her bag and took out a mirror and lipstick. 'Drink, drugs, sex – what's the difference? Fly agaric, hallucinations, fantasy, anything to give the mind a break . . . to stop the endless searching – the heartache – the self-pity –'

'What about your husband?' I said it abruptly, wanting to get her away from her own problems, to switch her mind to Ward.

'Iain?' She seemed to consider for a moment. 'Iain's a bastard, a fucking, straight-out bastard.'

She said it lightly, but there was an undertone in her voice that made me say, 'You're still in love with him, are you?'

It was a mistake, a shot in the dark. She turned on me with sudden fury. 'You've been talking to that Fraser woman of his. She told you, didn't she?'

'Told me what?'

'When you phoned, you asked if I was Mrs Ward. I didn't think about it at the time, but now –' She glared at me, her face flushed.

'It wasn't casual, was it – your phoning me? You had a reason. Well, didn't you?'

'Yes,' I said. 'I had a reason.'

'You want to know about him. So you come to me, digging around in my past, tearing my guts out and putting them on the table here.'

'I'm sorry,' I said, but that only seemed to fuel her anger.

'You're sorry! My God! I don't know you, I've never met you before, what right have you –?' She bit her lip, turning back to watch the swans now headed for the bridge, fighting to control her emotions.

Two women in love with a man. Not everyone, I thought, could be so lucky. 'Perhaps if I explain –'

'There's no need.' She said it coldly, adding as she got to her feet, 'A cousin of mine has a house on the river near Cookham. You can drop me off there.'

I caught hold of her arm as she turned to go. 'Sit down! Please.'

'No.' She was pulling away from me, her face screwed up, and I saw she was on the verge of tears.

'Barbara, please. There are things I need to know.'

'Why? What the hell's it to do with you how I feel about Iain? Some people can live together, others can't ... It doesn't alter the way they feel about each other. Oh, my God! What the hell am I doing telling you how I feel about –'

'Please,' I said again. 'Sit down.' And I began explaining to her how I had resigned from the Service and was in search of a job.

I suppose I managed to tell it to her in a way that made it interesting enough to arouse her curiosity. At any rate, she resumed her seat at the round iron table, gazing stony-faced at the blue of the sky. But she was listening as I told her about Ward having rushed off to Paris, so that it was Kirsty Fraser who had lunched me in that Soho restaurant ...

'He's going ahead with it, is he?'

'With what?' I asked her.

'For some time now he's had a wild idea of making a fortune in Antarctica.' She looked at me, puzzled. 'What are you supposed to do when you've got that Hercules off the iceberg, fly a drilling rig down there in bits?' And when I told her it was more likely to be a mining venture, she nodded. 'Gold, platinum, manganese nodules – he always wanted to dig down for a crock of something at the end of his own special rainbow. But the Antarctic – it's crazy!' She sat there in silence, apparently thinking it over, a frown puckering the clear white skin of her forehead. Finally, she said, almost in a whisper, 'But that's Iain. He's full of crazy ideas.'

'So you've seen him recently?'

'Yes. Why not?' She laughed, suddenly relaxed again. 'What did you imagine – that we were not on speaking terms?' And then, with a sudden switch to her previous mood, 'We can't stand it when we're together, but we can't live without each other, not entirely. You understand?' She stared at me, gave a little shrug and smiled. 'No, of course you don't.'

Silence then, the tranquility returning as we sat watching the sun dip into a bank of cu-nim and the sky flush a livid red, edged with gold. And when the colour had finally been snuffed out we drove on to Marlow and had dinner at the Compleat Angler, a gesture that I knew would be bad for my overdraft, but was, I felt, the least I could do.

All through the meal she chattered brightly about anything other than her husband. Finally, as we sat watching the lights come on across the river and the last of the motor launches tie up to the bank above the weir, I asked her bluntly to describe him to me.

'A big hulk of a man.' That was all she would say, a shut look on her face and staring out at the river. And when I said I wanted to know what sort of man he was, she simply said, 'Impossible.'

'How do you mean?'

'Just that.' And she added, 'With women he's like a bull in a china shop.'

I laughed. We were both laughing, it was such a ridiculous analogy.

The coffee came and when I had ordered a cognac for both of us she turned to me with a nervous half-smile and said, 'I'm sorry. I'm not exactly living up to my ad, am I?'

'I could certainly shake you,' I said.

She gave a little laugh. 'I walked right into that one.' There was a pause, and then she said, 'You were asking about Iain. I hadn't expected that. None of my contacts has ever asked about him.'

'You say he's impossible. Why? Because of his behaviour to you?'

She shook her head. 'It's the way he's made. He's a selfish, egotistical bastard.' And she added, 'He's also an enormously attractive one.'

The cognac came and she sat, holding her balloon glass in both her delicately-shaped hands and staring into space. She was like a piece of Dresden china. 'He's a very complex man, you see.' She said it slowly, reflectively.

'Because of his deformity?'

She glanced at me quickly. 'Oh, so you know about that. Kirsty Fraser, of course. And did she give you a complete CV on him?'

'No,' I said. 'That's why I rang you. I know nothing about his life, what he does, what he is. I need to know the sort of man I'll be dealing with.'

'So you came to me?' Silence again, as though she had gone into a trance.

'You say he's complex, selfish, a brute, and yet you're still in love with him. Why? What, besides the shrivelled arm, tugs at your heart strings?'

The silence dragged on while she sipped her drink. 'I don't know.' She said it slowly, very quietly. 'I suppose it stems from his background. Isn't that what makes us what we are? That, and the genes, of course. And his genes –' Suddenly she was looking straight at me. 'My God!' she said. 'Can you blame him with the sort of start he had in life?'

'How do you mean?' Her mind seemed to be drifting away again.

'Fraser didn't tell you then?'

'No.'

'Well, his mother was a high-wire artiste. Circuses. But she had a bad fall and after that she never trod the high-wire again and earned her living as best she could.'

'And his father?'

'Iain never knew his father. Nor did his mother for that matter. He was a one-night stand and the boy grew up in what the planners had left of the Gorbals, his only parent a prostitute. By the time he was six she was a drunk and he was begging and stealing, anything to get enough for them to eat.'

She paused, her eyes wandering round the restaurant. 'Sitting here, it's hard to imagine what it was like for him, scrounging, stealing, even pimping for his mother, in trouble with the police, in and out of remand homes. He was eight, I think, when he made his escape to London. There he picked pockets and anything else he could lay his little fingers on, even showing off his arm to beg for money in the Underground, fighting off the regulars who took against him muscling in on their pitch. Finally he teamed up with an old man who dealt in antiques, particularly antique silver, stolen silver mostly. He had a dirty little shop off the Mile End Road. And then, after he died, Iain went to Eton.' She said it quite matter-of-factly, as though that was what you did when you'd had enough of buying and selling other people's property, acting as a fence for East End burglars. 'So you see,' she said with the flicker of a smile, 'he's every right to be a little – unusual, shall we say.'

'Are you serious?' I thought she was making it up, like the ad. But no . . .

'Of course I'm serious. It was in the old man's will. Apparently he'd taken to the boy. Not surprising. Iain has a lot of charm when he's in the mood. And, with his background, he must have been very useful at times.'

'And then?'

'After Eton?'

I nodded.

'God knows. Ask him a question like that and he clams up on you. And don't you try it or you'll never get the job.' And she went on, speaking quickly, 'I was curious, of course. We lived quite well, even then, when we were just married, and it's a little disconcerting not to know where the money comes from.' She hesitated. 'I saw very little of him really, but every time I asked him where he'd been, or what he'd been doing, he'd just stare at me or turn his back. Never once did I get an answer. Then one day I persisted. You know what the bugger did? He threw me out of the flat. Literally. My head went through one of the banisters. I can still remember lying there in a daze, my eyes looking straight down the stairwell. Three flights up we were then and I'd come within an ace of pitching headfirst down the well to the concrete floor below. He picked me up, stripped me to make certain I'd no bones broken, then he kissed me all over and we made love on the sitting-room floor, both of us naked in the warmth of the gas fire.' She was smiling, but not at me, her mind back in the past.

A long silence ensued, and then she asked about the plane he wanted flown out. 'Where is it? You didn't say – where exactly. Antarctica is a pretty big place.'

'The Weddell Sea. Right down by the Ice Shelf at the far end.'

She nodded. 'That fits. Did Kirsty mention a ship named *Isvik*?'

'No, only that there was an expedition boat, on stand-by at Port Stanley.'

She nodded. '*Isvik*.' And she went on to say that a few years back her husband had unexpectedly phoned her from a place called Punta Arenas in the Magellan Strait to tell her he would probably be away for some time, maybe a year. He had bought an expedition ship and was going south into the Weddell Sea in search of a two-hundred-year-old sailing vessel. 'Crazy. But then if Iain told me he'd bought a spaceship and was headed for Mars . . .' That little laugh again and the half-shrug. 'So now it's one of those Hercules aircraft.' She was frowning. 'And when you've flown it off, what then? You say he phoned you himself and you arranged to meet him for lunch this morning. Didn't he give you any idea at all what he wanted the plane for?'

'None.'

'And Kirsty, didn't she say anything about mining?'

'No. The only person who has talked about mining to me was a fellow from Greenpeace who accosted me in the Park Lane car park.' And I told her how he had described the people her husband had gone to see in Paris as cowboys, the way the contractor's men had laughed as they drove the bulldozer straight at the Yugoslav lying in its path. 'Giotti Frère. That was the name of the firm.'

Her eyes widened, suddenly alert. 'Giotti?'

'Has he ever mentioned them to you?'

She shook her head. 'No. No, he's never mentioned them.' The denial was too quick, and then she sat there, very still, both hands gripped tight around the brandy glass. 'But something I can tell you,' she went on slowly. 'He didn't winter in the Antarctic. The expedition ship was never iced in. He got himself lifted out by helicopter to a German icebreaker which took him to Port Stanley. It was all in the papers, headline news, and on the box.' Again that slight hesitation, then she said, 'He had somebody with him, an Argentinian. The man died shortly after arriving in the UK.' She reached for her handbag and began to get up. 'You want to know what Iain's up to, I suggest you find out who the man was and why

29

Iain was nursing him so carefully, acting as a sort of minder, even when they had got him to hospital. At least that's how one paper reported it.'

'Do you know the man's name?'

She hesitated, then shook her head. I pushed her almost roughly back into her seat. 'You read about it in the papers, you say. They must have given his name. What was it?'

Her mouth was clamped shut, a tight line. I thought she wasn't going to tell me, but then she suddenly blurted it out. 'Eduardo Connor-Gómez.' And she added, her eyes bright with some sort of suppressed emotion, 'And it's his sister who owns *Isvik*.'

'You say the man's dead?'

'Yes.'

'He died in hospital, I take it?'

'Yes.' She nodded. 'As far as I know.'

I asked her what hospital, but she couldn't remember, and she couldn't describe him to me. The only picture she had seen of him was in the *Express*, and it was out of focus – a close-up of her husband with the blurred face of the Argentinian just visible over his shoulder. I asked her what Ward had said about him, but she shook her head. 'Nothing. He wouldn't talk about him. He wouldn't say what the real purpose of the *Isvik* voyage into the Weddell Sea had been. It wasn't just to rescue Connor-Gómez, I'm certain of that, and how the man had existed alone down there for almost two years God only knows. The papers didn't say anything about that, not even the *Express*.'

'But surely they interviewed him?'

'Eduardo? No. It was most odd. One day he was news, and then the next – silence. Nothing about Iain, or the ship, or the mysterious Argentinian. And there was his sister, the equally mysterious Iris, who had been with Iain in the Weddell Sea. The *Express* ran a story about her having been murdered in the Isle of Dogs. This was long before Iain embarked on his Weddell Sea expedition. And then, a week or so later, they said she was alive and on board *Isvik*. After that, like I say, nothing. They dropped the whole story. So did the other papers. Dropped it bang, like that, all except for a brief paragraph a few days later to announce the death of Eduardo Connor-Gómez in some hospital – I forget which.'

It was all very strange, even the purpose of the voyage wrapped in mystery. 'They were searching for this old square-rigger,' she went on. 'A frigate that had been seen briefly from the air by a man who had died a few minutes later when his aircraft had crashed on the ice. Nothing. Nothing for close on two years, and then a book written by a man who was with Iain on the trek out to the stranded icebergs.'

I asked her the name of the book and she said it was the same as the name of the ship – *Isvik*.

She sat back in her chair, looking puzzled. 'He must have known what was in that hold,' she murmured, more to herself than to me. 'He must have.' She was silent then, thinking about it. I wanted her to go on, but she just sat there.

'What was the cargo?' I asked her.

The silence dragged, her eyes half-closed. Then suddenly she opened them, staring straight at me with an almost startled expression. 'Dead bodies.' Her voice was almost a whisper. 'The carcases of humans and sheep.' And she added, 'Anthrax. They had died of anthrax.'

'Is that why the Government put a clamp on the news story?'

'I don't know.'

'And if they clamped down on the newspapers, why didn't they stop the publication of the book?'

'Learned their lesson, I suppose. All those spy-catcher cases. The media treated it as fiction. Maybe there was pressure, but reading it, it's difficult to tell whether there's any truth in it or not, and if so what is fact and what fiction. It's all so improbable, and yet . . .'

'What did your husband say?'

'Nothing. He won't talk about it. And the young man who wrote it needed the money. He'd lost his job . . .' She got to her feet again. 'It was even described as a first novel on the jacket. Maybe his agent wasn't very good, or more likely he didn't have one. Perhaps they thought it would sell better as fiction. But he was with Iain all the way out there. He was navigator and sailing master, and he was with him on the long trek across the ice to where that old Blackwall frigate lay walled-in by stranded icebergs.' She shook her head, gazing momentarily out at the darkened waters. 'I don't know . . .'

'But surely your husband must know whether it's true .' I hesitated, her face so blank, so devoid of expression. 'You say you see him periodically. Didn't you ask him?'

'Of course I did. I asked him several times. But it was like when I asked him about the trucks he ran to the Middle East before the Gulf War ...' The door to the restaurant was straight in front of her. 'I won't be a minute.'

I thought she was headed for the loo, but when she returned, she said she had rung her cousins at Cookham. They were at home, so she had a bed for the night.

I settled the bill, which was even worse than I had feared, and we drove through Bourne End towards Maidenhead. She wouldn't talk about the trucks she had mentioned, except to say they were big, long-distance vehicles complete with bunk, cooking facilities and chemical toilet.

'What was he running?'

She didn't answer.

'Was it drugs?'

'No, of course not. Whatever Iain is, he's not a fool.'

'Arms then?'

'Could be. It was during the Iraq–Iran War.'

I don't think she knew much more than that, or if she did she wasn't telling me. The picture of the man forming in my mind suggested that he was just the type to be involved in arms dealing. 'Does he speak Arabic?'

She nodded. 'Languages come very easily to him. We went to Egypt once, to the Pyramids and up the Nile to Luxor and Aswan. I don't know what the languages were he was speaking – Egyptian, Sudanese, Somali – but he was able to talk with almost anybody we met, including the French and German tourists who were with us on the boat. And ashore, he'd disappear into the oddest dives and puff away at one of those hookah things. They pass the mouthpiece from one to the other, jabbering away, but he never caught any sort of disease. I tried it once ...' She went on talking about that Nile cruise until we arrived at the De Jongs'.

It was the wife, Sylvia, who was her cousin, a plump little person with large breasts, big teeth and a big smile. She also laughed a lot. It turned out that the relationship was quite close, she and Barbara both having the name Harte before their marriages. The husband, Derek, was of Dutch Huguenot extraction and worked in the City, merchant banking. It was one of those fortuitous meetings that happen once in a while. I liked him and it was to him I turned when I needed to raise a rather large sum of money.

I had intended dropping Barbara off, then leaving, but though I refused a drink, I let Sylvia persuade me to stay on for a coffee. She even offered me a bed for the night, doing it rather discreetly, but with a slightly arch glance at Barbara, who looked at me with what I can only describe as a gamin grin, as though daring me to accept. Whether she really wanted me to stay or not, I don't know – she said later, of course, that she did, but I'm not sure she really meant it. I excused myself by saying, 'I have a meeting with the AOC scheduled for noon tomorrow.' He was new and as he had made a couple of quick jumps up the promotion ladder to Air Vice Marshal, I thought I would probably need my wits about me.

Even so, it was past midnight before I finally left. Derek had got me talking about the Gulf War and it wasn't until I saw Barbara looking at her watch that I realised the time. We stood talking for a moment, and then suddenly the De Jongs had disappeared and I was alone with her.

'Something I think you should know.' She hesitated, and then went on, almost in a rush, 'He's no morals.' We both knew who she was talking about. 'I mean he's amoral.' She shook her head. 'No, that's not the word I want. Ruthless. He's a ruthless bastard, so don't cross him, or try to outsmart him. He's tough, and he's quite capable of killing.'

'You mean he's actually killed somebody?'

She nodded.

'How do you know?'

'I just know.' And without another word she turned and headed for the stairs.

I let myself out and had a perfect, starlit drive back to the station. There was a note waiting for me in my quarters. It was from the CO to say the AOC had a meeting at Bristol University in the morning. He would see me at the Senate House offices at noon. MT were laying on a car for me at eleven.

TWO

He was standing at the window looking out over the city. At the sound of the door closing he turned and faced me. He didn't come forward to greet me, no hand held out in welcome. He just stood there without a word, his eyes staring straight at me. Finally he said, 'So you're Cruse.' No rank, just my name and the hard gaze of his eyes that were so darkly brown they were almost black.

'You wanted to see me, sir.'

He made no attempt to set me at my ease, the round, dark head thrust forward, his feet planted wide as though about to charge. His name was Pritchard and he was Welsh. I moved forward, keeping a tight hold on myself in the face of his evident hostility. 'Good view,' I said conversationally, nodding towards the window. 'You can see most of Bristol from here.'

'Yes, you can almost see your bridge.'

I didn't like the way he said *your* bridge, or the tight little smile on his face. 'That's all settled now,' I told him. 'It's in the past, finished.'

'Is it?' He shook his head. 'I don't think so. Actions are the ultimate expression of a man. Once a thing is done you can't just scrub it out. It's there, like a rope around your neck.' Silence then and the ticking of the clock on the mantelpiece louder than the background hum of traffic. 'Know what I would have done with you? I'd have had you stripped of your commission and sent to the Colchester Garrison glasshouse for six months. Maybe that would have taught you a proper sense of discipline.' He was smiling as he said that so that I wasn't sure whether he was serious or not.

And then he was harking back to the Falklands War, to the day I had flown my Harrier on patrol down towards the ridge line the Argies used to cover their low-level approach to San Carlos. 'You were fresh out of Cranwell, posted to a squadron of jump-jets going out as deck cargo on a container ship. You know what I'm talking about, don't you –'

'The Pucará?' I knew he was serious then.

'Yes, the Pucará. Of all the bloody stupid, reckless . . .' He paused as though lost for words. 'Why? You never gave a thought to what it had cost to get that Harrier of yours all the way down into the South Atlantic, the value of it to a task force desperately short of air cover, and yourself almost as vital as the plane.'

'I was out of fuel,' I said. 'Well, not right out, but I didn't think I had enough to get back to the carrier.'

'So you thought you'd syphon off some of the Pucará's fuel.' He gave a quick bark of a laugh. 'That's what your report says. My own reading of the situation is that the only thought in your head was the bravado idea of flying that Argentine aircraft –'

'No, sir.' I was suddenly feeling hot and angry. 'It wasn't like that.'

'Then what was it like? What the hell did you do it for?'

I started to explain what had been going on in my mind as I circled that stranded plane, seeing the marks of its landing, how the ground there was solid and free of rocks, and no sign of the pilot. But I couldn't put it into words, not so that it would make sense to a senior officer who had never been out there and who wouldn't understand the mood I was in, cooped up in a carrier with the Fleet Air Arm. 'It happened,' I said rather lamely. 'That's all there is to it. The Pucará was there. It was undamaged and it still had plenty of fuel –'

'You didn't know that when you used up more of your own precious fuel putting your Harrier on the ground beside it.'

'It was a gamble,' I murmured.

'It was downright bloody stupid. And then to start playing around with it as though you were a kid with a new toy.'

I suppose he was right in a way. But I was in the cockpit, running through the controls, had actually got the props turning and was trying out the radio when a Scots voice came through, loud and very clear. An attack was coming in. Two Aermacchis flying very low over West Falkland, heading, he thought, for Port Howard, the usual run under the knife-edged ridges that would give them protection right up to the moment when they turned east through the gap into the Sound with San Carlos and the whole beachhead anchorage only seconds away.

I hadn't stopped to think. I hadn't hesitated. This was an old disused sheep station airfield. The ground was firm, dried hard by the wind, and no time to transfer back to my Harrier. I got the Pucará off the ground, a bumpy take-off, but all right, boosting the twin turbo-props to maximum. To avoid 5 Brigade's air defences I took a wide sweep to the north, belly-flat to the waters of the Sound, then through the gap and into the gut, testing the armament as I went. When I picked them up they were already past Fox Bay and coming at me round the shoulder of Blue Mountain. They were into the gut then, so low they were almost brushing the bottom of that steep-sided valley. They were so much faster than the Pucará that I knew I had just the one chance. I came down on them from Mount Moody in a steep dive flat out, opening up on them just at the moment they saw me and began to take evasive action.

'It must have shaken them badly,' I said, my mind full of the vivid memory of that moment. 'One of their own aircraft coming southbound down that gut, diving straight at them with its armament blazing and –'

'I've read the report,' the AOC said tersely.

'They jettisoned, zooming up over the hills, hugging the ridge and tailing it back to their base at Comodoro Rivadavia. One of them didn't ...'

'You were lucky to get away with it,' he interrupted me. 'You should have been court-martialled instead of getting your picture plastered all over the tabloids.' He went on about that, then told me my character was flawed, that I lacked a proper sense of responsibility. 'It's a pity, a great pity, man. An officer with your background ...' And he began comparing my record with my father's.

'I think I should remind you, sir,' I interrupted him, 'that in less that a fortnight I shall no longer be in the Air Force.'

'I'm well aware of that, Cruse.' He started talking about my future then, telling me I was a fool to throw up the Service. 'You could find it very difficult.'

'Not my choice,' I said, feeling suddenly angry.

He nodded. 'I know that.' And he added, 'I'm just warning you, that's all. There are a lot of pilots out there without jobs right now.' He actually sounded concerned about my future.

'I'll be all right,' I murmured.

'I hope so.' He sounded doubtful.

'Fact is, I've more or less been offered a job.' I don't think he believed me, so I told him about the ice-bound Herc floating around on a berg in the Weddell Sea.

It sounded so improbable in that Senate House office high up on the hill overlooking Bristol. He stared at me a moment as though suspecting me of making the whole thing up. 'One thing I can say for you, at least you're original.' I thought I saw the glimmer of a smile, but then he added, 'You go on tilting at windmills like some aerial Don Quixote and sooner or later you're going to get yourself killed, which would be a pity considering what it has cost the taxpayer to train you.'

I told him I owed that to my father rather than the taxpayer, but he shook his head. 'He didn't foot the bill for that Jaguar trainer you wrote off or for the rampage you led through one of our officers' messes. And there was the time you took half the roof off a Welsh farmhouse going through the sound barrier at nought feet.' And then he was holding out his hand, smiling and wishing me luck. 'If you get out of the Antarctic alive, come and see me. By then the ice may have knocked some sense into you.'

Back at the base I checked for any messages but there was nothing. Nothing the following day either, time slipping by and still no word. Then it was Battle of Britain Sunday and very nearly my last day in uniform.

I had been so sure, so very sure, and here I was at the end of my Service career with nothing lined up. 'You'll hear from us in a few days' time,' Kirsty Fraser had said as we parted outside that Greek Street restaurant.

I rang my sister Michelle in Scotland and told her to stand by for a boarding party in a few days' time, and then, as I walked from my quarters to No.2 hangar, where the service was being held, the CO's PA came running after me to say I was invited to lunch at his house after the reception. 'Be there at one-thirty sharp please. He's entertaining the Bishop, also our MP and the Commander of the visiting German squadron.' She was speaking very fast, her voice breathless. 'Don't forget, one-thirty. There are two people from London ...' But she was already hurrying away to greet the Mayor whose car had just drawn up at the hangar entrance.

I was due to read the first lesson so I had an aisle seat in the second row, almost opposite the band which was blaring away at a furious pace. I had never had to read a lesson before and I was nervous. *Remember now thy Creator in the days of thy youth ...* They must have come in while I was thinking about that opening line, thinking about my father and all the Battle of Britain services I had attended – fifteen, twenty? It must be nearly that, my father being one of the *Few*, and I could almost feel my mother's hand on mine, holding it very tight, and Churchill's words, always those same words, rolling out across the hangar.

And now, here I was – for the last time.

The sound of the opening anthem died away, and we rose to our feet as the choir followed the clergy to their seats. The Chaplain moved to the altar, the band started up again and there was the quiet tread of the slow march as the squadron standards were marched in, the bearers with their gilded swords kneeling to hand them into God's keeping for the service that would follow; the steel of the hangar wall behind the altar draped in blue, the ladies of the choir in their long cloaks, the band behind them in uniform. All the men of the station in uniform, myself included. It would be the last public occasion at which I should be entitled to wear it, the uniform that had been a part of me ever since I could remember.

In a few moments the Station Commander would be walking to the lectern to give the opening proclamation, the Battle of Britain Declaration that states what this commemoration is all about. This would be followed by God Save the Queen, then a hymn, some prayers, another hymn, and I would be up there reading the lesson. My eyes, fixed now on the Spitfire replica squeezed in behind the band, visualized my father's face as it had been, not when I knew him, but back in 1940, the face in those two photographs I had of him before he was burned and his features scarred with surgery. One had been taken by a fellow officer beside the Hurricane that had been shot from under him in the early days of the Battle. His squadron had dived on a swarm of Messerschmitt 109s escorting fleets of Dorniers and Heinkels on a daylight raid on the Channel ports. He had bailed out over the sea to be picked up by an RAF rescue launch, and three hours after that he was back at Kenley and scrambling again to head off another bunch of bandits flying in formation towards the Kent coast.

Shortly after that his squadron had been re-equipped with Spit-fires, so that the other picture, taken by one of the ground staff, showed him in his replacement aircraft, just his head and shoulders in the cockpit, features framed in leather flying helmet and one arm reaching up to close the canopy.

If I had had a war like that would it have made any difference? Would that have satisfied my craving for excitement – my urge to show off, as one girlfriend had put it? If I had been in a Battle for Britain, the excitement, the action, nerves stretched to the limit ... I had never had that, never known what it was to live every moment at full stretch with death stalking the sky to the calico-rip of machine guns, tracer whipping past. I could hear my father's voice again, a little slurred as he tried to put his memories into words for the boy who drank it all in. We were so alike, my mother said. And just once in a while she would tell me some of the crazy things he had done, things he would never talk about unless he had a drink or two inside him.

That was when planes were less complicated, pilots less con-trolled. You could beat up the mess, brush the top of a hangar with your wings or try blowing the girls' hats off at an open day; you could even fly under bridges and get no more than a tut-tut, naughty-naughty from the CO.

Well, I had done a couple of bridges and a few other naughty things, no more than my father had done, but I was out, and only now was I beginning to realise how tough it was going to be outside of the Service. The hymn they were singing ended all too soon. The moment had come, and as everybody resumed their seats, I stepped forward and walked to the lectern. The lesson was from *Ecclesiastes*, the final chapter. *Remember now thy Creator* ... It was then, as I read that opening line, that I saw her.

She was sitting in the front row, almost directly in front of me, wearing a little red pill-box hat. And the man beside her was built like an ox, a heavy head, a great beak of a nose and a massive jaw ... *While the evil days come not, nor the years draw nigh* ... I was reading it automatically, my gaze momentarily rivetted on the bulging sleeve of his jacket and the stiff, black-gloved hand that protruded from the cuff. His eyes were fixed on my face, weighing me up, wondering, no doubt, whether I would be fool enough to risk my neck.

Or ever the silver cord be loose ... The magic words rolled off my tongue, and then I was back in my seat again and we were on to the next hymn – *Oh ruler of the earth and sky Be with our airmen when they fly* ... The sermon was short, but I wasn't listening. As I had stepped down from the lectern Kirsty Fraser had caught my eye, smiling and giving me a furtive thumbs-up, so that all I could think of, as the service came to an end and the standards were marched out, was that the job was mine – if I wanted it. If I had the nerve ...

I had no opportunity to talk it over with Ward during the reception. The big mess room was crowded and I had been instructed to look after the German commander. Also there were civilians present, honorary members of the mess who had been good to me, invited me to their homes. It was the last opportunity I would have to thank them. And there was Sylvia Lovebold, who had lived up to her ex-husband's ridiculous name and made life much more agreeable than it would otherwise have been.

'The CO's already left.' His PA nudged my elbow, tapping her watch. It was past one-thirty. 'You had better hurry, the other guests are just leaving.' I saw their cars pulling away as I reached the mess entrance. It was a close, humid day, and walking quickly, I was sweating by the time I reached the house. We went in to lunch almost immediately, so that I had no chance to wash. I was seated between the Bishop's wife, who tried valiantly to change conversational partners as the courses changed, and Betty Trant, the CO's wife, who was a bridge fiend and talked of nothing else. Ward made no attempt to talk to the guests placed either side of him, but concentrated entirely on the Station Commander, seated at the head of the table, speaking in a broad Scots accent through mouthfuls of food.

We had just sent a flight of C-130s out to Bahrain with a small detachment of SAS on board. How he knew about that, I don't know. But he did, and what he kept fishing for, very cleverly, was the nature of the cargo. It was quite evident that he knew the Gulf, and indeed most of the Middle East, exceptionally well, and from the inside, not like our people stuck out on their makeshift airfields. At no time did he mention the Antarctic, or Paris, or mining, nor did he once speak directly to me, though I was sitting right opposite him. I could see the deformed hand moving under his upper right sleeve as it manipulated those black-gloved fingers. There were moments when he sat back, silent, a solid rock of a man with the alert stillness of a trained hunter.

The meal ended. I pulled the Bishop's lady's chair back for her and she glowered at me. 'For a flying officer you seem to have very little in the way of conversation.'

'I'm sorry,' I murmured. 'I didn't think you'd be interested in the mechanics of flying.'

I was spared further embarrassment by a hand on my arm and a soft voice saying, 'Our host has put a spare bedroom at our disposal.'

I turned to find Kirsty Fraser close behind me. 'Just for the two of us? How thoughtful.'

Her face flushed, the wide mouth stretching to a smile. 'Up the stairs, third door on the right. Iain is already there.' She propelled me gently towards the stairs. 'You'll find him a little edgy, so just remember the fingers of that gloved hand are steel. They have a wicked grip.'

'I've got the job, have I?'

'Yes, but wait till you've talked to him.' And she added, 'He's been working on the next stage all week. He's tired and on a short fuse. Just remember that.'

I found him seated by the window, his heavy head framed against a watery gleam of sunlight, the great beak of a nose looking positively raptorial. The room had been converted into a sort of bedsit office. Ward's big bottom overflowed the tiny chair on which he was perched, the desk in front of him one of those reproduction Queen Anne jobs done in some ghastly softwood. 'Come in. And shut the door, will you.' He didn't rise. He was taking some papers out of a flat briefcase. 'This shouldn't take long. Kirsty tells me you're agreeable, that right? Provided –' His raised hand silenced my protest. 'Provided you find the take-off distance practical. She phoned me in Paris after you had lunched with her. So here are the figures. From where the C-130 is parked to the edge of the ice platform is one thirty-seven metres. They reckon another twenty-eight metres can be obtained by towing it back to the eastern limit of the berg. That makes –'

'Who are they?' I asked. 'Giotti Frère?'

'How did you get hold of that name?' The sharp grey eyes stared at me suspiciously. 'Who told you? Kirsty didn't.'

'No.' I hesitated. 'I've been making my own enquiries.' I said it quickly, conscious that he must have noticed my hesitation. 'You don't expect me to go into this blind.'

'Who told you?' he repeated, hitching his chair closer and leaning towards me so that I was conscious of the gloved hand within inches of my knee.

'Never mind.' It wasn't the moment to tell him about that Greenpeace man and what he had told me. 'You realise the C-130 in its cargo transport mode requires a minimum take-off distance unloaded of something around two hundred metres. That's with the aircraft held on the brakes and with only fuel enough for about three hours' flying. A little over seven hundred miles.'

'Everything stripped out?'

'No, not everything. Strip the seats out, the cargo fastenings, all non-essential items –'

'Fuel,' he cut in. 'One hour's flying, that's all you need.'

I stared at him. 'Where the hell would that get me? I'm not flying the thing off just to ditch it in the Weddell Sea, smash into a heaving mass of pack-ice or the side of a berg that's calved off –'

'The Ice Shelf,' he said. 'You refuel on the Ronne.' He pronounced it Ronnay. 'From flubbers Ah'll have had tanked up. So what's that give you by way of distance required for take-off?'

'Depends,' I said, trying to work it out in my head. 'If both the direction and the force of the wind were right, the air cool enough to give a good lift ...' I might just get it airborne. I'd have to fly it off myself, no crew, nobody to help me, nobody to hold my hand, talk to me, give me confidence. 'I'd need a minimum of six or seven hundred feet,' I told him. I'd be on my own, a lonely death. But no more lonely than when I had been flying fighters. I'd faced up to it in the Falklands, and always the memory of my father – with him beside me on the flight deck I had no need of anyone else. 'Okay,' I said. 'It's hellish tight, but it's just possible.' I had turned my head and was looking straight at him. 'How much?'

''Ow much? Wot d'yer mean, 'ow much?' Like an actor he seemed suddenly to have switched parts and become a Cockney dealer in second-hand cars, his grey eyes slitted and sharp as steel.

'Just what I say – how much are you willing to pay me to try and get that crate off the ice and into the air?' Once that was settled, I could start cross-examining him on the accuracy of the information he had got from Giotti.

''Ow much? Me!' He leaned back, smiling and shaking his head. 'I ain't paying ye a thing. Ye buy the plane. Ye fly it off. Then we talk.'

I stared at him. I just couldn't believe it. 'Are you serious?'

''Course I'm serious.' And he started to tell me what it would cost to get me down into the most southerly part of the Weddell Sea. 'That's my contribution. Yours is to fly the thing off the berg and on to the Ronne.'

'And how much do I get paid for doing that?'

'Nothin'. Ah told ye, nothin'.'

'You're mad,' I burst out angrily. The certainty that I had a job outside of the Service was gone now. I pressed down on the arms of my chair, thrusting myself abruptly to my feet. 'You surely don't imagine –'

'Ah'm no' daft, laddie.' The gloved hand shot out, its steel claws biting into my arm. 'Just canny.' He was pulling me towards him, his face thrust forward. 'Ah spend a small fortune getting ye doon there, landing ye on that floating ice platform, an' ye go chicken on me. It could happen. Ye could funk it when ye see that aircraft an' the size o' that berg. Or ye could start tellin' me ye want more cash up front to go riskin' yer neck ...'

I started to say that once I had agreed a thing, I stuck to it, but he shook his head. 'Ye may think ye would, here in England. But doon there –'

'You agree a price, I'll stick to it.'

Again that shake of the massive head. 'Ye've no idea what it's like doon there. Ah've been there. Ah know, an Ah'm no' organising an expedition to get ye there – aye, an expedition, that's what it amounts to. A fuckin' Antarctic expedition just to deliver one pilot body on to that ice platform. Ah want ye motivated. Ye buy the aircraft, then it's yours, ye've got a stake in the venture. Ye'll no' back oot on me then ... Okay?'

The gloved steel of those fingers released my arm and I stood there, staring down at him. I could see it from his point of view, but it just wasn't possible. 'I can't buy that plane. I haven't that sort of money.'

'Oh yes ye have. Apart from what ye'll be getting from the Air Force ye've got an assurance policy. Ye can borrow on that.'

'Don't be ridiculous,' I told him. 'You couldn't replace one of the four engines for anywhere near what I could raise on that policy.'

'Sit doon.' He pushed me back towards my chair. 'We're no' talking of replacements. We're talking aboot the aircraft as it stands. It was insured by a French company, Compagnie d'Assurance Loire Inférieur et Bretagne – CALIB for short. Giotti claimed a total loss. After some argument a figure was finally agreed, and as a result CALIB became the legal owners of a Hercules aircraft stranded on an iceberg.' He was looking up at me, his craggy features relaxed into the semblance of a smile. 'Wot d'ye reck'n that Herc is worth sitting on the tarmac at Mount Pleasant?'

'In the Falklands?'

'Aye. At the Falkland Islands air base. It's no' exactly brand new and it's been stuck on that berg all winter. Wot's it worth, would ye think?'

I shook my head. 'God knows,' I said. 'Quarter of a million. Something like that.'

He nodded. 'That's no' very far oot. And it's yours for ten thousand.'

I sat down, staring at him, not knowing what to say. 'Ten thousand!' I couldn't believe it. 'A plane that's worth –'

'Nothin',' he said.

'But the scrap value alone –'

'Och aye, the scrap value! Scrap on an iceberg down the arse-end of the Weddell, who's going to shell out big money for that? The way things are, that insurance company will be glad to get rid of it, all those damn conservationist conventions. ATS, that's the big one, the Atlantic Treaty System, SCAMLR, AEPA, a whole raft of them. And if the entire continent ends up as a World Park that insurance company could find itself having to send a ship doon there to remove the aircraft in bits or face a hefty fine to cover the cost of an international agency doing it for them. That's how Ah got them to agree a figure of ten K. Ye get that thing airborne, off that bloody ice raft and back on the Ronne, that's a different matter. Then we're in business.' He leaned back, the smile broadening as he rubbed his hands. 'Aye, we'll be in business then and we can talk.'

He really meant it. That's what left me struck dumb and mentally dazed, while he sat there, staring at me, waiting. 'What business?' I asked him. But he wouldn't talk about that. Said it was nothing to do with me. 'Well, what do you say?'

44

'I'll think it over,' I told him finally.

But he shook his head. 'Ah didna come all the way doon here on a Sunday to be fobbed of wi' a vague answer like that. If that's all ye got to say, then ye're no' the man Ah thought ye were. Come on now. Ah need an answer right away. There's a deal of planning to do, people to see, funds to raise.' He paused there, his eyes fixed on mine. 'It's a gamble.' He said it so quietly he might have been talking to himself. 'But then that's life. If ye dinna take chances ...' He leaned suddenly forward, the gloved fingers gripping my knee. 'Ye think ye're goin' to find a nice cozy job – nine-to-five with a fat salary an' safe as houses ... Well, Ah tell ye this, laddie, if that's what ye're looking for ye're in for a shock. It's cold out there in the civilian rat race. As for flying, there's a milling mob of pilots hollerin' for work. Ye haven't a hope.'

'So why have you come to me? If there's such a wide choice –'

The claw fingers tightened their grip. ''Cos Ah need that plane off the berg and on to the Ronne in one piece, an' ye're fool enough to have a go and good enough to succeed. Okay? Will ye do it?' And then, to my astonishment, he said, 'Please. I need a transport aircraft at a price I can afford, and that Herc is sitting there, just waiting for me.'

I think it was that word *please*. He was so obviously a man who didn't normally plead with people, and the way he said it ... I hesitated a moment longer, but he was right about the flying prospects. With the USSR disintegrating, the Cold War at an end and the Gulf War over, there didn't have to be a slump in the airline industry for there to be over-supply of pilots. 'So what do I get if I land it on the Ronne Ice Shelf for you?'

'We'll talk about that when ye've done it.'

'No, we'll talk about it now.' I was thinking hard, wondering what his game was. 'I want a hundred thousand.'

He shook his head.

'Then forget it,' I said. 'I'm not risking my life for less than a hundred grand.' He was getting to his feet. So was I, and we stood there, glaring at each other. 'You agree it's worth somewhere around a quarter of a million. I'm doing the salvage operation, and doing it more or less on a Lloyd's form basis. If I don't get it into the air or I crash into the Ice Front cliffs you won't have to pay me, will you. I'll be dead. So before I kill myself I want ten thousand down, the rest when and if I succeed. I'll give you details of the account I want it paid into when I've decided where I'll be making my base. The Channel Islands, Luxemburg, maybe Andorra. One of the havens, anyway.'

I thought I'd blown it then. He stood there, glowering at me. Then he began clearing up his papers, packing them into his briefcase. He didn't offer me his hand. Just turned towards the door, the silence in the room almost audible. 'I'm sorry,' I said. 'I've never had to value my life before and put a price-tag on it.'

He didn't seem to hear me. But then, when he had the door open, he paused, turning his head and staring at me. I thought for a moment he was going to try and beat me down again. Instead, he suddenly smiled. 'Ah'll no' argue wi' ye about the value ye put on yer life. The first ten Ah can manage. It's the rest of it that's a wee bit of a problem. Maybe Ah can mortgage the aircraft. Either that, or else persuade you to take a share in the venture in lieu.'

He stood there for a moment longer, his sharp little eyes searching my face, looking for some sign of weakening on my part. Then abruptly he closed the door again. 'Ye'll do it then?'

'Yes,' I said. 'You pay me what I ask and I'll have a shot at it.'

He nodded, coming back to the desk, opening up his briefcase and pulling out a folder. 'Joining instructions,' he said, passing me a typed sheet of paper. 'Also some background information. The ship's name is *Isvik*, the registered owner Mrs Sunderby, sailing master and navigator Peter Kettil. The vessel is periodically under charter to KLME, the mining subsidiary of Giotti Frère operating in the Falklands. She is normally anchored off Port Stanley. Ah've arranged for her to be at my disposal from first November when she'll start taking on stores for the Weddell Sea, prepared to winter over if necessary. From the moment you go aboard her Ah'll be responsible for yer general cost of living, everything. All ye have to do is get yerself doon there. The RAF has a TriStar service out of Brize Norton. Ye'll be ex-Service then, but they have a certain number of seats for paying passengers. Alternatively, ye can fly to Buenos Aires, then on to either Montevideo in Uruguay or Punta Arenas on the Magellan Strait. There's a cargo-passenger ship does the circuit of those two ports and Stanley twice a week.'

He passed me another sheet. 'Ah had Kirsty type out the itinerary and a list of contacts. If ye have any difficulty in getting the visas ye need Ah have somebody who can fix it for ye at short notice. His name and address is there.' He pointed to it with the index finger of his left hand. 'Great Windmill Street is near Piccadilly Circus, off Shaftesbury Avenue.'

'I know where it is,' I told him.

He nodded. 'That's it then.' He closed his briefcase and turned to the door. 'When d'ye reck'n ye'll be joining ship? Shall we say early November? Ye'll need time to settle in, get to know the ropes.'

'I'll need an engineer,' I said.

'There's a Norwegian on board, and he's good.'

'I'm not talking about marine engines. There are four big Allisons on that Herc. I want them checked and double-checked by a qualified aero-engineer. Somebody I know and can trust.'

'My information –' he was leaning over me – 'is that all four are in perfect running order.'

'Maybe they were –'

'Ye doubting my word?' His tone, his whole manner was suddenly changed, almost menacing, as he dabbed his finger at the information sheet I was still holding in my hand. 'Look, man, there's the name and address of the engineer KLME employed. Ye can check wi' him, or with the pilot. Ah've even given ye their telephone numbers.' He glanced at his watch. 'Ah got to go now. Ring Kirsty at the office, let her know where Ah can contact you. Meanwhile Ah'll fax Iris Sunderby she can expect you on board *Isvik* early November. Right?'

'Me and an engineer,' I insisted.

'No. Just yerself.'

I shook my head. 'Sorry. That aircraft has been locked in the ice all winter. Either I have the support of an engineer of my own choice or the deal is off.'

He didn't say anything for a moment, staring down at me. Then suddenly he nodded. 'Ah guess ye're right. But ye'll pay his fare out, all his expenses. Ah'll fax Iris to expect the two of ye early November. An' Ah mean early. Ye've got a deal of sail and ice training ahead of ye.' He held out his hand. 'Ah'll see ye in Port Stanley.' And with that he left me.

I stood there for a moment, thinking over that astonishing interview. The Antarctic, that was challenge enough, but I had lived with the idea for the better part of a month now. I had accepted it. But owning an aircraft ... That was much more difficult to accept. It was hard to believe that for as little as ten thousand I could have one of those great big lumbering four-engined beasts I had been driving for the past three and a half years.

I sat down again, studying the two typed sheets he had given me, reading them through again and again. Compagnie d'Assurance Loire Inférieur et Bretagne (CALIB), and he had given the address of the Paris office and both telephone and fax numbers. There was no information about Giotti Frère on the first sheet, but at the bottom of it, very faint, were the letters *KLME (B. Phuket)*, then a line impossible to read followed by two words that looked like Pebble Bench or Birch. The writing then went off the page. Clearly Ward, or somebody, had been making notes on paper that had a built-in carbon facility.

The other sheet contained background information on both Giotti Frère and KLME which I skimmed through quickly, surprised to find the mining subsidiary was run by a Chinese woman, and somebody had scribbled a pencilled note above the typing: *BP – watch it if your paths cross*. Details of the pilot who had refused to try and fly the plane off were also given, and a phone number where he could be contacted. His name was Horace Travers and he lived with his wife and two little girls in a cottage on the river just outside Weybridge. His flight engineer was now working in the Gulf, the only point of contact a hotel in Dubai.

I suppose I sat there, staring down at those two sheets, for ten minutes or so, the outline of what I needed to do gradually forming in my mind. To rely on Ward's information about the state of the aircraft, the amount of fuel in the tanks, the length of ice available for take-off was out of the question. I would need to confirm his figures, and that meant talking to Giotti Frère. Then, if it still looked possible, I could see the insurance people and settle the whole thing personally instead of having to do it all through a fax machine. But first I needed to sign up an engineer. Charlie Pollard, who had shared the flight deck with me for almost two years, was the obvious choice.

He was one of those men who look a good deal younger than they are, bright, open features full of fun and a boyish enthusiasm for life. I wondered where he was now; still at Leuchars? He had been posted there more than a year ago. Leuchars is a big RAF

48

station on the east coast of Scotland just north of Dundee and not much more than three hours' drive from Michelle's place at Lennoxtown.

When I rang Leuchars later that afternoon, I discovered Charlie had left the Air Force some six months ago to run a small factory near Stirling that supplied specialised alloy parts for Rolls Royce. I had hoped that the RAF might release him on extended leave to experience the cold weather conditions I would be offering him, but a factory didn't sound promising. I phoned them next morning, but the line was dead, and when I got through to the exchange, I was told the factory had closed. I had better luck with Horace Travers. He was working for a small airline flying out of Gatwick and I arranged to see him the following weekend.

Friday was my last day in uniform. That morning the Station Commander's PA sent me a note to say I was to report for final duty at the officers' mess at 19.45 sharp. I guessed something was up, but I couldn't discover what. The CO himself was waiting for me in the mess entrance. A stiff, formal greeting, and then he was leading me down the main corridor to the big room we use for special occasions. 'Bunny' Leverett, a retired wing-commander with marvellous handlebar moustaches, was on duty at the closed doors. 'Good evening, Sah.' He had sprung to attention and now gave me an exaggerated parody of a salute, then flung the doors wide open. 'Gentlemen, our honoured guest.' And then, in a stentorian voice: 'Bridge-busters, atten-shun.'

I couldn't believe it. The whole Mess must have been there, certainly all of my squadron and everyone of them with a paper cap cut-out of the Severn Bridge on their heads and standing rigidly to attention. 'Pre-sent Hercs!' And suddenly all their arms were extended and, like boys playing at aeroplanes, they began circling and wheeling, dipping and rising, a practised ballet to the accompaniment of the rudest of engine noises.

And when that was finished, the mess staff wheeled in an iced cake fashioned most delicately as a replica of the Severn Bridge with a model of a C-130 hanging from the central span, while across the iced waters below was the legend: A BRIDGE TOO BLOODY NEAR.

And then Joss, my radio operator and navigator, produced a squeeze-box and they were all singing:

A bridge too near, too bloody near,
And Mickeymas is out on his ear.
A bridge too many, too bloody many,
Oh dear, oh dear, oh dear.
A bridge too much, too bloody much,
The brass are wetting their pants and such,
And yelling like hell it ain't in the book,
So we'll fire the bugger,
Before there's another.
And that gets us off the hook.

God! That was one hell of a piss-up! They were dining me out, all the Station silver and a five-course meal. The port going round and round, cries of 'Speech', and after the tables were cleared, the evening went on and on. God knows when I got to my bed. They carried me there – *A bridge too near, too bloody near, We shan't see his like again. A bridge too many, too bloody many, Do you think he'll make the train? Or do we have to fly him again, write off a Herc and ditch him in pain* ...

I can't remember any more of it, nor could they. But when they dumped me on my bed, there on the chest of drawers was a perfect replica of the bridge, just as the chef had done it in icing, but this was meticulously engineered in some bright alloy.

They saw me off on the Saturday morning, the CO and most of my squadron, and there was a lump in my throat as I drove out through the main gate. In fact, I was very near to tears, thinking about my father and wondering how he was feeling about it, seeing his son virtually drummed out of the Service. But what the hell! I had had a wonderful send-off. *A bridge too much, too bloody much* ... I found myself mouthing that ridiculous piece of doggerel. Where had they got it from? And the tune ... Was it from a musical? A hymn perhaps?

It was a beautiful morning and I had the hood down, belting it out at the top of my voice and the sound whipped away by the rush of the wind.

I had arranged to meet Travers at a pub called The Goat & Compasses, which he informed me, rather pedantically, dated from Commonwealth days when it had been the God Encompasseth Us. He was already there, waiting, when I drove up ten minutes before noon, a very serious-looking man with large, round, steel-rimmed spectacles and an irritating habit of scratching at the backs of his hands. But over a couple of pints of Abbots Ale he gave me what I had come for, a first-hand account of the calving of the runway KLME had bulldozed out of the flat surface of the Ronne Ice Shelf.

He had been bunked in a newly-erected prefab when it happened. Time: 03.17, the early hours of 5 January. He had checked his watch and entered it up in the notebook he always kept handy. What had first woken him was a strange grinding, grumbling sound deep below the floorboards. His immediate thought was some sort of submarine disturbance, a tremor or quake below the earth's crust that was shaking the seabed. Others thought it started with a violent electrical storm.

'My engineer, who admitted he was scared of bunking down in a prefab that had been erected on floating glacier ice some twenty miles from shore, and had lain awake for some hours, said he heard what he took to be a clap of thunder away to the east, then a whole series of minor bangs that were repeated a few minutes later, to the westward, followed almost immediately by the grinding sound of the ice below us tearing itself apart.' He paused a moment, his eyes staring past me, seeing only what was in his mind.

'This went on for more than a minute,' he added slowly, 'perhaps two minutes, then it was suddenly overwhelmed by a much louder, much nearer noise, the sound of ice breaking up, followed by a clap like thunder and the whole hut shaking, a crack opening up at the far end and moonlight flooding in as the whole north end of the prefab splintered and fell away.'

He had rolled out of his bunk. He didn't remember doing so, but he was suddenly standing with his torch switched on, and there were dark shadows moving, the beams of other torches as sleeping bodies came alive, reaching for their cold-weather gear. The odd thing was that the hut was still intact, all except that north wall – 'I shall never forget the sight of that empty wall space, a great gap opening up, and the ice beyond, and all the seaward end of the Shelf slowly drifting away with blocks of ice the size of houses peeling off it and sliding down into the black abyss of the water below.'

Half the runway had gone. It had become a great flat-topped berg carved off from the Shelf and swaying very slowly to the movement of the sea as it was thrust into the howling, gale-swept darkness that was intermittently lit by an almost full moon eerily peering between piled-up banks of jet black cloud.

He might look like a rather dermally-diseased owl, standing there at the bar, peering at the vivid memory of that night through his big glasses and desultorily scratching at the back of the hand that was gripped tight around his tankard, but he was clearly a sensitive man who, even now, almost a year later, could relive an experience that was so deeply etched on his mind, so vivid, that he almost convinced me I was living through the terror of it myself.

'And the plane?' I asked when he had finished. 'You could see it, could you?'

'Of course not. But it was still there all right, snugged down in the ice hangar we had blasted and bulldozed out for it.' And then he was back to the picture in his mind, the way it had looked when the cloud had suddenly uncovered the moon. 'It was very dramatic then, like a film set. The moon was low to the north-west of us. Oddly-shaped, not a complete round, and yellowish. It threw a weird sort of light that came and went as it raced in and out of the clouds. It was the moon that seemed to be moving rather than the clouds. I remember that most distinctly, the clouds like a giant shutter opening and closing, and that jaundiced orb, a deformed lens peering down at the disaster that had struck us. Out there, beyond the end of the hut, half our runway, the aircraft, the bull-dozer, all our machinery and most of our stores, were slowly reced-ing into the pack-ice, the whole scene backlit by those ghostly glimmers of yellowish light. It was the weirdest night . . .' He shook his head. 'Nothing we could do. Nothing at all.'

And because of that it hadn't seemed real to them – 'more like a nightmare, all of us just standing there in a daze.' And he went on, still speaking slowly, reflectively, 'I even thought I glimpsed a small vessel, a lifeboat, something like that. In a shaft of moonlight it was, there one minute, gone the next. And a whale. I could have sworn I saw a whale. Others saw it, too. The whale, I mean, not the ship. I was the only one who saw that.' He thought about it for a moment, then shook his head. 'An hallucination. I must have been hal-lucinating – wishful thinking, the desire to be rescued from what appeared certain death. The whole thing was so terrifying, so cata-strophic – so absolutely incredible – you could imagine anything. One fellow began talking to his wife, as though she was right there in the hut beside him. Another kept calling for Rupert, who wasn't his son, but the teddy bear he had had when he was a child. It was that weird, the whole thing beyond belief, the wind and the cold blowing through us.'

I didn't say anything for a moment, the image he had created so awe-inspiring I found myself seriously considering abandoning the whole project. That would have been the most sensible thing to do, and there were times later when I wished I had. Instead, I began questioning him about his Service career, what experience he had had of the C-130, the number of hours he had put in.

He had been almost ten years in the RAF. From Cranwell he had done a Shackleton course. Eighteen months as Junior Pilot had been followed by AWAC training. More courses, then the Gulf, and after that he had been posted to a C-130 squadron at Lyneham. He had been flying Hercules for just over a year when he left the Air Force to take up charter work. That was how he came to work for KLME.

I asked him what it was going to be used for, but he didn't know. 'Bit of a mystery like. We'd no mining equipment, no seismological gear. The general view seemed to be that we were the advance party of an operation planned for the following summer.'

'But what about the plane?' It was the Herc I was interested in. 'Had you flown it in purely as an exercise?'

'Aye, I think that was it – to see whether it was feasible to fly back and forth between the Ronne and Ushuaia at the bottom of Tierra del Fuego. She was fitted with extra fuel tanks. Carried internally, in the fuselage, so there wasn't much room for equipment, not heavy equipment.'

A bit of a mystery, as he said, and looking at the man, and bearing in mind the short experience he had had as a pilot in charge of a Herc, I could well understand his reluctance to stick his neck out trying to fly one of the things off a berg in the Antarctic. He was a Yorkshireman, very practical, very down-to-earth. Both his experience and his temperament made him quite unsuitable for such a risky operation. And, of course, his attitude of mind was undoubtedly conditioned by his memory of what it had been like in that hut when half the airfield they had constructed out of the ice broke off and drifted away. 'A right bugger of a night, that was. Some of the boys had lost their clothes, and with the days shortening and ice beginning to form, it was getting right cold, 04.00 by then and blowing a full gale out of the south.'

I left him as soon as I decently could, fearing my own confidence would be undermined if I stayed with him much longer. But before we parted I did get confirmation of Ward's length of take-off figure. When the icebreaker arrived from Halley Bay to rescue them from their camp on the Ice Shelf, KLME had arranged for the ice-breaker's helicopter to land Travers on the berg so that he could check the C-130. He found it just as they had left it the night of the disaster, undamaged and still secure in its ice hangar. The half-runway was covered with a light dusting of snow, but it would still be usable once the bulldozer had ironed out the few patches of drifting.

He had paced out the length of runway available and his figures were the same as those Ward had given me. The ice platform had by then drifted some three and a half miles to the nor'-nor'-west and had swung slightly clockwise, so that the runway was now facing 208° magnetic. He had also had the sense to check the tanks, and since his estimate of the maximum hours' flying at the most econ-omic turbo-prop speed was three and a quarter hours it was obvious all the figures Ward had got out of Giotti Frère were based on Travers' report.

Walking with him to the car park I asked about KLME itself. The company was of no real interest to me, the question more to break an awkward silence than a need for information. He shrugged. 'Just a mining company.'

'Ward said there was a Chinese woman running it. Did you meet her by any chance?'

'Once.' He was suddenly silent. Then he said slowly, 'A very attractive, very strange person.' Silence again and I had the feeling his meeting with her had not been exactly cosy.

I was thinking then of the notes Ward had given me and the name in brackets. 'B. Phuket. Does that mean anything to you?'

'Yes, that's her name. Belle Phuket.' He pronounced it Pooket, but then he spelled it out to me, adding, 'Looks funny, I know, but you get used to that in South-East Asia. I had a tour in Singapore two or three years back, and at one stage, to pass the time, we began making a list of all the oddest names we came across. Quite hilarious some of them.' He looked at me, and he was actually smiling at the memory. 'It's an island really, on the west coast of the Kra Isthmus about seven hundred miles north of Singapore.'

'What's that got to do with it?' I asked.

'That's where they found her, busy organising a fishing co-operative. And because she hadn't a clue what her real name was, they called her after the island. She had found her way there from Cambodia, which the Khmer Rouge called Kampuchea. Her mother had been ill with dysentery and the family were resting in a village when the Khmer Rouge overtook them. She had been the only young girl in that village, and when the Khmer Rouge thugs finally pulled out, they set light to the whole place, and having no further use for her, flung her into one of the huts and then set fire to it. She couldn't remember her name. She couldn't remember anything much about her past, the arrival of those Communist thugs and what they did to her family blotting it all out – but not her knowledge of the Chinese language and all the things she had been taught. Just the personal memories had gone. Funny, isn't it, the human brain?'

'So Phuket isn't her real name?'

'No. She'd no idea what that was, so, like I say, they named her after the island, and because she had such a beautiful figure, and the features below the burn scars were good, and her eyes so full of vitality and intelligence, the cameraman, who was French, called her La Belle Pookay.' And he added, with a nervous laugh, 'Little did he know!'

'Know what?'

'The sort of woman she was, or rather the sort of person she had become. Not her fault, I suppose. Not altogether.' And then, with no prompting from me, he told me something of her story, how the family had been caught up in the aftermath of the French departure from Cambodia, her parents killed in front of her by the Khmer Rouge, and herself raped and raped again. At least, that was what Travers had been told by the French member of the Australian television outfit that had found her on Phuket Island.

Travers had met up with Louis, the cameraman, at the Upland Goose Hotel in the Falklands. He thought some of what Louis had told him was probably exaggerated, possibly even fabricated, but the circumstances in which they had found her, and what had happened to her, to her family, to the whole village, that he believed to be factual. 'And from my own experience of her I can tell you this, there's nothing wrong with her brain. Aye.' He nodded. 'Two and two always makes four with her. She's as full of cold-blooded logic as a Jesuit priest.'

'You don't like her?' It was the way he had said it. And it didn't sound as though he liked the Jesuits either.

'No, I certainly don't. She's a bitch, but a most extraordinary one.' Apparently La Belle, as he called her, had walked all the way from Phnom Penh to the coast, where she had stolen a small fishing boat and sailed it across the Gulf of Siam to Surat Than. Then she had walked on across the back of the Kra to Phuket Island where she was hoping to stow away on a vessel sailing south through the Malacca Straits, and because of the way her brain worked she had immediately started to organise the fishing community. She had almost succeeded when the TV boys found her. Louis said she led them a hell of a dance. In the end they took her on the strength and airlifted her to Singapore, where in no time at all she had got in with what he described as 'the Triad set'. She had left for South Vietnam shortly afterwards and within months was deep into the Boat People racket, queening it over a bunch of Chinese thugs. 'They say she made a fortune out of it.'

We were standing by my Jag then. There was no reason why I should meet the woman, but it was such an odd CV, if you could call it that, I couldn't help asking how she had come to be running a mining and engineering company.

'Money,' he said. 'That's what the boys at the Ronne Ice Front camp told me.' Their story was that Giotti had acquired KLME from an Italian company, a leveraged buy-out that went wrong because the parent company found themselves over-extended at a time when the oil price was falling, and they couldn't find a big company backer for the discovery well they claimed they had drilled in the Gulf of Siam just offshore of the west coast of Thailand. 'She came to their rescue.'

'Alone?'

He shrugged. 'I don't know.' He shook his head. 'The story is she virtually guaranteed their bank loans, and for that she had their subsidiary KLME transferred to her, lock, stock and barrel.'

'She owns it then?'

'Maybe. I'm not sure. For all I know she may own the parent company as well by now.'

'It all sounds very complicated,' I said as I got into my car and started the engine, thankful that it was the insurers, not Giotti, or KLME, I had to deal with. 'If I meet Miss Phuket I'll give her your love, shall I?'

I thought he looked suitably appalled as I drove away, but I was looking ahead and it never occurred to me that I should have questioned him more closely about the Chinese lady and her reasons for going to the rescue of a company with a mining and exploration subsidiary operating in the Falkland Islands and the Weddell Sea.

It wasn't far to the London Orbital intersection and once I was on the M25 I knocked off the next thirty miles or so at a steady ninety, stopping at the South Mimms Service Station, where I had a quick lunch and phoned my sister. She and I were twins, both born on Michaelmas Day, hence my nickname Mickeymas. God! The fights I had had over that: Mickeymas was okay, but any blundering idiot calling me Mickey Mouse ... It was my sister's fault. She never could pronounce Michaelmas properly as a child, it always came out as Mickeymas, and this was accepted by everybody in the family. She had popped her head out ahead of me, so she was Mickeymas One, and I was Mickeymas Two, but our nice old vicar wasn't accepting that, so Mickey One was christened Michelle Belinda and I got the names Michael Edwin. We weren't in Wales then, you see, otherwise it would have been Ellwyn.

We took no notice, of course, always referring to each other as Mickey One and Mickey Two. That was between ourselves. With strangers I stuck to Eddie. I told her I would sleep the night at an old inn I knew in Rutland and be with them at about drink time the next day. 'That's a Saturday,' she said. 'We'll be down at the boat.'

They had a Swan 32 which they kept down the Clyde at Gourock. They were both of them lawyers, so they lived in some style, a yacht during the summer and skiing during the winter. They were shacked up together for the best part of six years, only thinking in terms of marriage when wives were recognised by the Inland Revenue as a separate entity for tax purposes. There was another reason, too. She was pregnant, and after she had produced the twins she insisted on legitimising them. And just to make sure we all remembered the occasion, she insisted on the men wearing full penguin outfit, something that isn't exactly regulation dress for a registry office wedding. They had then grabbed a full month's leave and taken their tots roller-coastering down the west of Ireland to spend a lazy fortnight cruising the Scilly Isles.

When I reached Lennoxtown, which was under the Campsie Fells just north of Glasgow, there was a note to say they had left the house key with their neighbour. After dumping my things and freshening up, I rang Charlie's number. He was in. And he was on. It took him just two minutes flat to make up his mind. He was bored stiff, no wife, no living-in girlfriend, and no job. His was a frustratingly lonely existence in a couple of rooms rented to him by a nice, solid Lancashire couple.

We went out to the pub and got thoroughly pissed while fantasising about the Herc and what we would do with all that money. 'Piece of cake.' Charlie kept on saying that, said it so often I almost came to believe it myself by the time I staggered out to the old Jag.

Back at Charlie's quarters his landlord took one look at me, got in behind the wheel and insisted on driving me back to Lennoxtown, his wife following in their Renault Cinq.

Phil and Mickey got back late Sunday evening, having had a good windward thrash down the Clyde and through the Kyles of Bute to leave the boat at Castleton with the intention of making it through the Crinan Canal to the Western Isles the following Saturday. 'Why don't you stay the week and sail through to Crinan, maybe Tobermory with us?' That was after I had told them what my plans were. 'Give you a chance to brush up on your sailing.' And Phil added, 'Lucky bastard! Wish I were in your shoes. Wouldn't mind a go at the Antarctic myself.'

'Why don't you then?' Mickey said.

'You see – now she's got the brats she's trying to get rid of me.' They were like that, full of quips, but I could see he meant it about wishing he were in my shoes.

So I stayed the week with them, exploring the Highlands north of Callander, and on the Friday night we motored through an endless twilight to Castleton and slept on board. The weather that weekend was perfect, bright sun and a good, stiff sailing breeze. Saturday we motored through the Canal and that evening, after a meal ashore at the Crinan Hotel, we took the tide westward through the Dorus Mor, then into the maelstrom of the Corryvreckan on the slack, Phil at the helm, myself at the chart table and Mickey breast-feeding her twins.

It was a wonderful break for me. I had never been offshore before. All the sailing I had ever done was dinghy racing in a Kingfisher on the East Coast when I was a kid.

Those two days' sailing with the McEwens were the perfect culmination to a week of hard walking and climbing in the Highlands north of Callander. Driving south on crowded motorways, I was down to earth with a bump. Charlie would join me at Paddington, en route for Brize Norton, but first I had to fix it with whatever branch of the RAF handled the Falkland Islands flights. Something else I had to do, find out more about that Argentinian Ward had brought back with him from his Weddell Sea expedition. All week it had been at the back of my mind. Now, on the long drive south, with the memory of Barbara's words nagging at my mind, the need to know more about the whole mysterious affair became increasingly urgent.

THREE

Eduardo Connor-Gómez. That was about all a visit to the *Express* office the following day yielded. But reading between the lines, I got the impression Ward's rescue of the man must have been something of an epic. He and Peter Kettil, just the two of them, had sledded him out, three days across the ice, back to the relative safety of *Isvik*, a vessel that was little more than a yacht with strengthened bows. For twelve days they were feeling their way east through the pack-ice, keeping as far as possible to the clear water close in to the floating ice shelves of first the Ronne, then the Filchner. After that it was north, seeking out lanes through the pack to their rendezvous with a Royal Fleet Auxiliary-based helicopter. This landed Ward and the Argentinian on an icebreaker heading back to the Falkland Islands, and almost as soon as they reached East Cove, the port just south of RAF Mount Pleasant, an army ambulance had whisked them away to the flight terminal building, where an RAF TriStar was being held ready to take off for the UK.

The *Express* ran the story for three days, a lot of it repetition, and then, after the 15 March issue, nothing. The only new piece of information I gleaned from all this was that two other members of *Isvik*'s crew had been involved in the search, both Argentinian, and both dead. It did not say how they had died, and their names were not given. There was no mention of the old square-rigged sailing ship that Barbara Ward had said was the original object of the expedition.

I had tried to get hold of a copy of the book she had referred to, but it seemed to be out of print. At any rate, I tried three bookshops without success, though *Books in Print* still listed it. I did try one public library, but the only copy they had was out on loan. Anyway, my main concern was to find out what had happened to Connor-

Gómez after the TriStar had landed the two of them at Brize Norton.

According to the *Express* he had been taken straight to the big hospital at Swindon. This was reported in the issue of 15 March, and the following day there was a news paragraph announcing that he'd been transferred to another hospital, but it didn't say where. The stories were all by-lined Frank Baldwick and there was a note to the news item to say his enquiries had been met at first by the extraordinary statement that the hospital did not know where he had been sent, and it was only after he had insisted on being put through to the Senior Administrator that he had finally been able to wring out of them the statement that they were not at liberty to say where Mr Connor-Gómez was being treated, or for what.

There was nothing in the next day's paper, nothing until the 23rd, when the index led me to a very brief announcement of Connor-Gómez's death under the heading *Argentine Ice Survivor Succumbs to Ordeal*. The cause of death was given as heart failure. He had been cremated. It did not give the name of the crematorium and the only member of his family present had been his sister, Mrs Iris Sunderby, who had been flown in from the Falkland Islands at the expense of the Foreign Office. By the time Baldwick had tracked her down to a hostel for foreign students in the Bayswater area she had already left for Montevideo en route to Port Stanley.

My brushes with the upper echelons of the RAF had given me experience of the workings of the Establishment mind and I felt fairly sure the lack of information was deliberate. I asked the security officer on duty at the desk whether Frank Baldwick was in the office, and if he was could I speak to him. After a short wait I was handed one of the phones and a Yorkshire voice was asking me why I was interested in the Connor-Gómez story.

I suppose I was a bit naive. I could see it from his point of view. He didn't want to waste his time on some casual enquiry, and when I said the whole thing smelt of a cover-up, there was a long silence. 'Do you know what a D-Notice is?' He didn't wait for an answer, but began cross-examining me about my interest in Connor-Gómez. As soon as I mentioned KLME and the Herc that had been lying out there in the Weddell ice all winter, the tone of his voice changed, a note of excitement creeping in as he said, 'Stay right there. I'll be down.'

He was a small, intense man in shirtsleeves with a moustache and thick-lensed glasses. I asked him why he thought a D-Notice would have been issued.

'The reference to anthrax, I imagine. It killed the story stone dead.' But he wasn't really interested in that, only in my involvement with KLME and their C-130. How was I going to get down there? '*Isvik*, you say? That was the name of the vessel Ward took down to the Weddell Sea in search of an old square-rigger. There was a book, too.' And he added, almost breathlessly, 'Do you know Ward? Have you talked with him?' The man smelt faintly of garlic and tobacco.

I shook my head and after that he seemed to lose interest. He hadn't been at the funeral, or at the cremation, and all I really got out of him was that if I wanted more information I should go and talk to Woodward, Les Woodward of the *Telegraph*. The supposed murder of Iris Sunderby had occurred in Dockland, quite close to the *Telegraph* building. The police had apparently arrested a young student, but only temporarily. When they discovered that the Sunderby woman was alive and in Peru, and the body in the dock was a local tart who had committed suicide, they had let him go. 'That wasn't the coroner's verdict, of course,' he said, 'but there was no firm evidence of foul play. The *Telegraph* ran the story quite fully, it being on their doorstep. We didn't touch it.'

That was that. I stayed two nights with an old mate of mine, who was now an air commodore at the MoD with an RAF pad in West London, then flew to Paris. By then I had sorted out my finances, fixed TriStar flights for Charlie and myself, and had had a word with Ward on the telephone.

'Good,' he said. 'So ye're all set. The man ye want to see at CALIB is Maurice Gautier. He has all the details, and if he tries to up the anti above ten thousand ye start walking out on him. Okay? But don't mention a figure to start with, just talk about the difficulties. That way ye might frighten the old Frog into letting ye have it for a wee bit less.' He chuckled to himself. 'That machine represents environmental pollution, evidence of KLME's intentions to rape the virgin Antarctica, if ye follow me. As long as CALIB own that C-130 it's their responsibility to see that the carcase is got out of the area. At least, that's the way Greenpeace, WWF an' all the rest o' the World Park pack see it.'

It was roughly what he had told me at our first meeting. 'So you

62

mean they really could be forced to send a ship down there to break it up and cart it away?' It still seemed to me a bit far-fetched.

'Tha's exactly wot Ah do mean. Once Antarctica becomes a World Park ... But that will take a wee while yet.' Again the chuckle. 'Och aye ... Don't reck'n Ah need tell ye how to play it. Wot Ah seen o' ye leads me to think ye're pretty streetwise.' And then he added quickly, before I had a chance to ask him about Iris Sunderby, 'Ah got to go now. Kirsty'll fix an appointment for ye wi' old man Gautier.' Then he was gone and the voice on the line was his secretary's.

She wouldn't discuss Iris Sunderby with me, or the death of Connor-Gómez. 'You talk to Iain. If he wants to tell you he will. If not ...' The soft Scots voice left it in the air as she asked me when I would like her to fix the meeting with Gautier and where she could contact me. I told her to fix it as soon as possible and ring me back.

She came through again about twenty minutes later. She had fixed a meeting for the following day, 15.00 hours French time, but not with Gautier, with another member of the firm, André Lesparre. She thought he might be their adjuster. 'And I've booked a flight for you, Heathrow, Terminal Two, noon tomorrow. That's time of take-off. The travel agents are Hogg Robinson. They'll have your tickets waiting for you. You'll need your passport and you pay at their office. Okay, Mr Cruse?' And she rang off.

It was almost the first time in my life I had been called Mister and it came as a shock, emphasizing as it did my severance from the Service.

Perhaps if my father hadn't died when he did he would have talked some of the wildness out of me. But hell, he'd been just as wild in his way. I was thinking about that, and about what the future held in store, as I drove out to Heathrow the following morning. If I could get the aircraft off the ice and into the air, if I could find out what Ward was up to – if, if, if ... Too many damned ifs; if I was able to buy it from the insurers for next to nothing and could arrange for refuelling at the US base at McMurdo Sound ... the possibilities would then be endless. I could fly it on to any country in the world and sell it on the open market to the highest bidder.

But that would leave Ward sitting forlornly on the Ronne with his bulging flubbers. Hardly fair. And he wasn't the sort of man to just sit there. He'd come after me. God! The world I was into now was certainly very different to the RAF. My brain was going round in circles, turning over all the possibilities. But it was no use. So much depended on other people.

In the end, to give my mind a rest, I switched on the radio. I was tuned to the LBC station and I just caught the tail end of a news flash ... something about Greenpeace and the Uruguayan police. I turned up the volume, listening for a fuller report. That was when I got his name, Bjorn Lange. He had been booked out on the Falkland Islands supply vessel, but though he had arrived in Montevideo by air and had gone straight down to the port and boarded the ship, nobody had seen him after it had sailed. His things were in his cabin, but no sign of him, and the possibility that he had slipped back ashore was now being explored with the active co-operation of the Uruguayan police. The newscast ended with the statement that some concern for his safety was being expressed at both the London and Amsterdam offices of Greenpeace.

At Heathrow I bought two or three newspapers, searching through them while waiting for the Paris gate number to come up on the nearest flight indicator, but I could find no mention of it. And after I had boarded the plane my mind switched to consideration of how best to handle my interview with André Lesparre.

Now that I was in the air, and that meeting not much more than an hour and a half away, I was filled with a growing excitement, my mind leaping ahead, relishing the risk, the stupid bloody risk I knew I was going to take. I was so wrapped up in the prospect ahead, so full of a wonderful sense of elation, that before I knew it, we were on the glide path, whispering our way over Paris.

I had coffee and a cognac at the airport and just over an hour after landing, was being shown into Lesparre's office looking across the Avenue Hoche to the Faubourg St Honoré. The windows were open and the faint roar of traffic filled the room. '*Monsieur.*' He had risen to greet me, a small, neat man in a grey suit brightened almost incongruously by a pink shirt with a bright green bow tie with white spots. 'You are the man who flies bridges, yes?' There was a sour glimmer of humour and with that bow tie I wondered about him.

I took the seat he offered me and there was an awkward silence as we faced each other across the pile of paper that littered his desk. A fax machine began chattering away in the outer office. He seemed to think it was up to me to open the discussion, so I began to explain in technical terms the difficulties and dangers I would be facing if I attempted to get the machine airborne.

'*Oui, oui, d'accord.*' He gave a dismissive wave. 'But you wish to buy it.'

I shook my head. 'I was under the impression that your insurance company would pay me for risking my life.'

'*Non, non.*' He shook his head violently. 'When your friend Ward is here ...'

'Ward is nothing to do with it,' I said. 'He's not the one who's risking his life, and in any case, he doesn't know the first thing about the Lockheed C-130.'

'But it was agreed between us that you would purchase the plane from us. The C-130 then becomes your responsibility –'

'That's the point, isn't it?' I said. 'You need to be rid of it. You want it off your books. And if I buy it and then fail to get it off the ice, or decide it's too damned risky, then I'm stuck with it.'

He began telling me there were plenty of other pilots available, but I told him those experienced enough to have any chance of succeeding would know the risks involved. 'You get some other idiot to have a go at it – if you can.' I got to my feet, telling him to make that abandoned, ice-bound plane over to me and pay me my costs in advance, or I'd have nothing to do with it. I glanced at my watch. 'It is now fifteen twenty-four. What time do you leave your office?'

'Fife o'clock, *environ*.' He was on his feet now, his eyes hard behind their glasses, his face set.

'I'll come back at sixteen forty-five,' I told him. 'That will give you time to make up your mind.' It was a gamble, but what the hell? I didn't like him, you see. He was a money boy, hard-faced and bland.

I turned, moving slowly to give him time, and the little bastard let me get right through the doorway before he said, ''Ow much for the expenses?'

I stopped, then swung round, staring at him. I'd got it! That was my first thought. The bluff had come off. 'Difficult to say,' I murmured. 'But I did a rough calculation last night and I would think a hundred thousand would just about cover it. Provided, of course, nothing goes wrong.'

'So. You do not know the real cost. You are just guessing.' He hesitated. 'Then per'aps you will allow me to guess also.' He was actually smiling now. 'You see we 'ave considerable experience of costing air catastrophes. My guess, speaking, as you would say, off the top of my head, would be somezing in the region of forty thousand. We are talking francs, you understand.'

I nodded, walking slowly back into the room. I tried a compromise figure, but he wasn't having that. I think he really did know a good deal about air hull salvage costs and I wasn't prepared to argue. I had got what I wanted, the plane for free and something towards my expenses.

He had picked up his phone. '*Ma'mselle Phuket, s'il vous plaît.*' He pronounced it Pookay, but I guessed who he was contacting. There was a moment's pause while he was connected, and then he went into a flood of French that was much too fast for me to follow. Only the repetition of my name made it clear that he was discussing the proposal I had just made. A long silence was followed by a quick nod of the head. '*Bon. D'accord, d'accord, je le lui dirai.*' He put the phone down. 'She wish to see you before we decide.'

'Where?' I asked him.

'At her office, which is quite close, in the rue du Faubourg St Honoré. She will send her car.'

I asked him why he had referred to her, why the hell he couldn't make up his own mind. But he didn't answer that, turning down the corners of his mouth and giving me a somewhat exaggerated Gallic shrug.

'Is she a director of CALIB then?'

He hesitated. Then, with another little shrug, he muttered something about her being a major shareholder. '*La Belle Phuket . . . Alors*, you will see. She is a vair forceful little madame with her finger in many pies, is that 'ow you say it?'

I nodded. 'You mean you have been taken over by her?'

He nodded. '*Oui.* It was the big gale.' His dark, sardonic features were glum with the memory of it. 'All insurance companies, Lloyd's of London even, who handle much of our excess of loss, were in trouble. That is when she strike. She always buy when things are at their bottom.'

'It was the same with KLME, was it?'

He looked at me sharply. '*Oui, exactement.* Pierre Lange, he had over-extended the company. Too much borrowings, you see, so the *banque –*' He stopped, his lower lip folded under his slightly rabbity teeth. 'But that is all vair boring for you.' He had got to his feet and was turning to a filing cabinet that stood between the windows.

'When was that?' I asked.

'*Comment?* Oh, about three years ago.'

'Before she took you over?'

'*Oui.* Before – '

The phone rang and he picked it up with obvious relief. 'The car waits for you below, in the street. You come and see me again when she is finish with you. Okay?'

I glanced at my watch. It was already past three-thirty. 'Will you still be here?'

'Of course.' he nodded. 'I stay 'ere for you.'

The car waiting for me at the kerb was a big gold-painted Roller with fawn leather upholstery and two telephones. It was the sort of car a sultan might own, solid enough to be bulletproof, and the immaculate chauffeur holding open the door for me had the quick, hard eyes of a bodyguard. God knows what race he was, a mixture, I think, with Chinese predominating. I got in and he closed the door so quietly I heard the auto-lock click into place.

The interior was air-conditioned and we moved off in almost complete silence, the sound of the engine no more than a faint purr, the noise of the Paris traffic barely audible. 'You go straight to Ma'mselle, yes monsieur?' It was the driver, but I couldn't see where the voice came from.

'Yes,' I said and leaned back. I'd never been in such a car before, and cocooned like that from the outside world, I had a chance to think about why she wanted to see me. I was also worrying about whether I had overplayed my hand. I had taken a chance, gambling on their need being greater than mine. But I knew bloody well it wasn't. With the void of unemployment ahead of me if I didn't take the risk and clinch the job, it scared me that I might have blown my chances by insisting they hand it over to me for free. Perhaps I should have bought it. After all, it's not every day you're given the opportunity of buying a huge crate like a Hercules for a paltry ten K, even if the scales are weighted with your own life.

I had the experience, of course. And the nerve. Surely to God that would balance things out ... But what if I got out there, and

67

when I was on the broken-off section of the Ice Shelf and was able to get down to the entombed Herc, I found that the whole thing was totally impractical?

The car was slowing to a stop outside an ornate stone building that looked like a part of the great Haussmann rebuilding period. The chauffeur was round at the door in a flash, and as he opened it for me, I could see his little eyes darting here and there as he automatically checked people walking the pavement, coming out of doorways, and the traffic along the Faubourg St Honoré.

Inside the building the décor was a glitzy red and gold with a huge flower piece on a central table of Siena marble. It was all very Italian baroque with a bored security guard standing by the lift and another uniformed attendant seated at a big, flat-topped reception desk of palest ash or sycamore, a bank of telephones at his elbow and the mike of a broadcast system in front of him. I asked for Mademoiselle Phuket and gave him my name. He flicked a switch and, having announced me, and after checking my passport, told me to take the lift to the eighth floor where Monsieur Chan Li would meet me.

The lift was smooth and fast, yet in the brief space between the doors at the entrance hall level closing and their sliding silently back at the *huitième étage* my mind raced through all the possibilities of my first meeting with the young woman who was to prove the most extraordinary, vital, and I should add dangerous, I had ever met. And if she hadn't been scarred by burn marks, one of the most beautiful.

No, beautiful is perhaps not the right word. It wasn't her beauty that struck one. It was her vitality, her sheer sexual emanation, and the eyes, those dark, almost indigo pools that stared at one from beneath the slanted lids with a fixity that made one wince. It was only gradually that I came to appreciate the cold, calculating intelligence behind their unblinking gaze. And then the other side of her nature, the warmth.

The eighth floor was the top of the building. Above that, Chan Li told me, there was a flat roof with a small garden beside a helicopter landing pad. He was very definitely Chinese, smiling and bowing as he took me through a large open-plan office with about a dozen people in it, mostly women. It was full of the sound of word processors and fax machines chattering away. There was a door at the far end. He didn't knock. He just opened it and announced me.

She was seated at a beautifully-polished oblong table, her back to a wide picture window that took in an enormous sweep of Paris from the Madeleine to the Louvre. I caught a glimpse of the Seine and thought I could just see the twin towers of Notre-Dame. She looked very small against the vastness of the Parisian background. 'Please sit down –' She hesitated, not smiling, but her voice was gentle as she asked whether she should call me Mister or Squadron Leader, and when I said I had resigned from the RAF, so was now a civilian and plain Mister, she nodded, looking down at a sheet of paper laid out flat on the desk in front of her. She indicated a chair to her left and I sat down.

She didn't rush straight into a whole series of questions. In fact, for a moment she just sat there, staring at me fixedly and not saying anything. It was unnerving, but I realised she was giving herself time to check out the man himself after reading up on his background. And for my part, I took advantage of the opportunity to try and form some impression of her, which wasn't easy, her face being heavily made-up so that there was a doll-like quality about her. This was emphasised by the surround of the almond eyes being painted a deadly nightshade, almost indigo blue.

Then suddenly she smiled and the roundness of her face was split by a flash of very white, very even teeth between lips that were like the scarlet edges of a wound folded back. She sat back in her chair, no longer watchful, and I realised she had made up her mind about me.

'Did André let you have sight of the deed of sale?' Her voice was quiet, barely a trace of any accent.

I shook my head.

'Do you know anything about business, Mr Cruse? No, of course, you have been flying aeroplanes. Why should you?'

Evidently she had pressed a bell, for the door behind me opened and Chan Li came in. 'Here are two copies,' she said, taking the documents he held out to her and passing them across to me. 'You realise,' she added, smiling at me again, 'once you have signed the deeds, that is it. You are committed absolutely to all the clauses. So you read them. You read them very carefully. Anything you do not understand you discuss with me this evening. There are two copies.

Make certain they are identical. Tomorrow André sign one for you to keep and you sign the other for him.'

She turned to Chan Li, her voice almost twittering as she spoke to him quickly in Chinese. He nodded and left the room. 'He is confirming the room we provisionally book for you at the Tour d'Or. At eight o'clock we will meet at the Dragon Rouge. It is almost directly opposite your hotel. So you have only to walk across the road. I will tell Wu to expect you.' She glanced at the gilt travelling clock in the centre of the table. 'Shall we say eight o'clock? I think I can be with you by then.'

I nodded and thanked her, my mind on something else now, for there was a covering letter clipped to the documents. It was in French, on KLME notepaper, and it referred to the need for reinsurance cover on an XL basis for the *MV Kanut Lange*, no limit on latitude. Lange! Doubtless a common enough name in Norway, but for a French vessel to bear the name *Lange* . . .

'Mr Cruse.' Her voice was suddenly sharp and imperative. 'I was saying I hope you like Chinese food.'

'Yes – very much.'

She leaned forward, her eyes on the letter. 'That is for André, nothing to do with your aircraft deeds. It should have been in a separate envelope.' She reached across and took it from me as I asked her if the *Kanut Lange* belonged to her company.

'Yes. Why?'

'So that is what the letters KLME stand for – Kanut Lange Minerale et Exploration?'

'Of course. Why do you ask?'

I shook my head. Stupid of me. It would surely be too much of a coincidence. And yet . . . 'Just somebody I met,' I murmured. 'He had the same name.'

'Kanut Lange?'

'No. Bjorn. Bjorn Lange.' I was watching her as I said his name, but it seemed to make no impression. The door behind me had opened, Chan Li interrupting us again. '*Bon*,' she said. 'It is all fixed. I have a table reserved for us. You see André Lesparre again now. The car will wait and take you on to the Tour d'Or.'

I thanked her again and got to my feet. Why exactly she wanted to spend the evening with me I had no idea, but it would give me a chance to get to know something of the KLME set-up.

70

I had almost reached the door when she said, '*Moment, Monsieur.*' I turned to find her smiling at me. 'I think perhaps you will like to know before you see André again that I have agreed your terms in general, but not in the amount you originally asked for. You put your estimated costs at a hundred thousand francs. André say it should be forty thousand, not more. Because I like what I have seen of you so far, and think you may have a better chance of getting that machine in the air than any of the French and German pilots we have been considering, I have agreed a figure of fifty thousand francs for your expenses, half to be paid to you on arrival in the Falkland Islands at Port Stanley and the other twenty-five thousand to be posted to you in the form of a cheque on completion of the assignment –' She hesitated. 'Or to your next of kin in the event of your losing your life. *C'est ça?*'

I nodded. I wasn't going to argue. I had got more than I could possibly have hoped for. 'Yes, I agree,' I told her.

'Of course.' She was still smiling, but already her pen was hovering over a thick wad of papers. 'We will celebrate the future and a happy association tonight.'

She was taking a lot of trouble over me and I wondered why. The car waited while I went up to Lesparre's office. He didn't waste any time, holding out his hand for the documents and signing both copies. 'Now it is only for you to sign. Here and here.' He showed me. 'And initial each page, please, at the bottom right and also the figures for your expenses which have been written in.'

He obviously wanted me to sign the documents right there in front of him, but I told him I would read them through first so that I could discuss any points of detail over dinner with Mademoiselle Phuket.

'As you please.' He was looking at me with sudden interest, his expression one of wariness. 'Where are you dining?'

'At the Dragon Rouge.'

'Ah, so!' He nodded, an undertone of respect in his voice as he sat looking at me as though seeing me for the first time. 'You are vair honoured. It is one of the most expensive places in Paris.' He didn't say restaurants, he said places. 'Many decisions are made there that affect the Bourse, the banks, the politicians. You are staying at the Tour d'Or?'

'Yes.'

'It is a new hotel on the Rive gauche. You will be very well looked after.' He got to his feet and saw me to the door, wishing me a happy and successful evening. 'I will see you tomorrow. Shall we say about half after ten? Then if you find there is anything to be changed . . .' He nodded at the envelope containing the documents and left it at that.

I read them through before I had my bath, and as far as I could see there was nothing that needed altering. They were even agreeing to my retention of the first half of the expenses if I crashed the Herc or even if I decided, once I got there, that the whole thing was too dangerous. The second half would then be at the discretion of the CALIB management. The main body of the Agreement concerned the transfer of ownership of the hull and my acceptance of the entire responsibility for it once the sale was concluded. The cost of purchase was now set at a nominal thousand francs, something I could hardly complain about. Nor could I really complain at a paragraph stating that legal fees would be shared between the two parties to the Agreement. There was even a note to indicate that they were not expected to exceed the agreed cost of the aircraft.

My room at the Tour d'Or was on the third floor looking down the rue de Bec to the Seine, and sitting there, with the slanting sun shining on the roofs of the buildings opposite, I had the feeling one gets before a combat operation, a tightening of the nerves and the adrenalin running. But it wasn't the ice and the problem of converting my thousand franc purchase of an ice-bound Herc into an airborne fortune that occupied my mind. It was the woman who had arranged that I spend the night in this very lush hotel and who was taking me out to dinner at a restaurant frequented by the South-East Asian equivalent of the Mafia.

If I leaned forward I could just see the Dragon Rouge across the street, the sign blood-red, but discreet, against the black glass front. Already there was a doorman on duty. He was Chinese and built like a wrestler, the folds of his chin running into the huge column of his neck, his body so cumbersome it seemed to have been forcibly stuffed into his uniform.

To unpack, all I had to do was turn my canvas holdall upside down and empty the contents on to the bed. I had nothing to change into except a rather flashy bow tie which I had tossed in at the last moment, thinking that if I did have to stop over I might take in a nightclub, forgetting of course that Paris is not like other cities and tends to close down early.

A hot bath has the effect of giving very free rein to one's imagination, and the Delamain on ice I had mixed from the room's fridge acted, as cognac always does on me, as an aphrodisiac. Did she expect me to sleep with her? Was that what the dinner was about? But somehow I couldn't see her as a Chinese nymphomaniac. What then? She wanted something. Of that I was certain. The cost of the meal wouldn't matter to her, but I couldn't see her wasting her time on a man she had never met before just for the pleasure of male company.

My cognac-induced arousal went limp on me as I remembered her background. A woman who had been incessantly gang-banged by the Khmer Rouge and then virtually torched, who now wore heavy make-up to hide the scars, would hardly be desperate for the sexual pleasure of a man. So what – what the hell was it?

Sharp at 20.00, and wearing the bow tie and a rather colourful matching shirt, I strolled across the road and was confronted by the doorman, who looked even larger at close quarters. '*Vous avez une réservation?*'

'*Non.* I want Mr Wu.'

He looked a little surprised, then switched to English as he told me Mr Wu would be busy right now, but if I had a message he would phone it through. His manner altered abruptly when I told him Mademoiselle Phuket had a table reserved and had instructed me to ask for Wu.

'*Ah bon.*' He was very light on his feet as he moved his bulk quickly to the door, opened it for me, at the same time pulling a cordless phone from inside his uniform and talking into it very fast in Chinese.

The interior of the restaurant was dimly lit, lamps behind beautifully decorated paper screens and concealed coloured lights shining on painted columns. The effect was soothing and at the same time strangely menacing, as though the dimly-lit interior was designed to hide something quite different going on behind the screens. There were no tables set for dinner, nobody sitting around having a pre-prandial drink, yet there was the soft murmur of voices and

73

waiters moving discreetly through swinging screens, all beautifully painted.

Wu appeared suddenly at my side, a small man, bustling with vitality, his eyes full of quick intelligence. 'You are Mr Cruse? Mademoiselle has not yet arrived. She will make her entrance, I think, about ten minutes after the time she say.' He showed me a mouthful of very white teeth and ushered me to the back of the room, pushing back a screenful of birds to reveal a perfectly appointed table set for two. 'A drink, Monsieur?'

I hesitated, my eyes still taking in the intimacy of the cubicle. The whole restaurant must be like this, a series of quite small, very intimate little cubicles. 'Do you have a Bloody Mary?'

'But of course, Monsieur. The waiter will be here with it very shortly.' He turned to leave, but then paused. 'Here is Mademoiselle now.'

I don't know what I had expected, but certainly not the apparition that made her entrance through the painted screen. In place of the simple dark blue suit with the white collar she had been wearing in her office, her slim body was now sheathed in emerald silk, the sheen of it glistening to her every movement. But it was the face that had me staring at her. The doll-like look was gone. She was wearing almost no make-up now, the burn marks nakedly revealed like some monstrous accident of birth. They covered half the forehead and stretched down across the right cheek almost to the mouth, which was no longer a red wound, but softer, more feminine, in a sense more vulnerable.

Wu pulled out a chair for her and she waved me back to my seat, smiling and ordering champage. A waiter came in and lit the candles. 'You look worried – because I show you my real face, or because of the privacy here?'

'Neither,' I said. 'It's because I don't know what you're up to.'

'Up to is very colloquial.' She smiled. 'But I understand.'

The wine came and she watched me, still smiling. '*Santé.*' She raised her glass. 'To the future that will open up before us. *Si nous avons de la chance.*'

I hesitated, wondering what she meant by that. But when I asked her, she shook her head. 'Later. Now we will enjoy our meal.' The champagne was cold and chalk-crisp on the tongue. 'So, you are out of the Air Force and on your own, no wife, no children, no job. You have a girlfriend? A serious relationship?'

I didn't answer that. It was no business of hers. The waiter appeared with two menus, but she waved him away. Her hands, I noticed, were blunt-fingered. They looked very workmanlike, the nail varnish uncoloured.

'You would not know what to order in a place like this. Every dish is cooked and served separately, each of them complementing the others, both in flavour and in texture.' And she added, 'You may not know this, but the texture of food is very important. I hope you like what I have ordered. There is lamb, duck, chicken of course, and fish, and some intermediate dishes. And while we drink French champagne now, we will have a very special rice wine with our meal. I hope you are not allergic to anything I have ordered.' She smiled. 'You do not look the sort of man who is allergic to anything.'

Her emphasis on the word allergic had me wondering. 'No, of course not.'

We smiled at each other, and I waited, the silence lengthening and becoming a little awkward. 'Suppose, when you get down to the Ronne Ice Front, you don't like what you see of that aircraft after a winter cocooned in the Antarctic ice, what then? Do you have other employment you can take up?'

'That's something I haven't considered. I left the Air Force barely a week ago.'

'Yes, of course. But you must have given it some thought. Conditions are not of the best, and the break up of the USSR is still a relatively unassessable factor in the global economy.'

Shortly after that the waiter appeared again and filled our glasses. It was then that the real purpose of this intimate and expensive dinner emerged. It was Ward she was interested in. She wanted to know what he proposed to do with the plane when I got it back on to the Ice Shelf.

'If I get it back there,' I said.

She smiled and raised her glass to me. 'Now that I have met you I am very sure you will.'

I wished I could be as confident. She reached for the bottle, which she had told the waiter to leave with us, her second glass already empty. It seems I was faced with a woman who could drink like a man. The first course arrived, not a meat dish at all, but a mixture

75

of vegetables and a sauce so delicate I had no idea what had gone into it. 'So what does he propose?'

I told her about the only meeting I had had with him. 'But don't you ask him?' Her tone was impatient. 'Weren't you curious?'

'Of course. But I wanted the job.'

'So you don't ask. You don't know what he proposes to do with the Hercules when you deliver it to him. You don't even settle a price. You are like a babe. You land it on the Ronne, at the camp my company build, where there are two flubbers full of aviation fuel and he can tell you to fuck off.' Her matter-of-fact use of the word took me by surprise. 'He can even charge you a fortune to get you back to the Falkland Islands. Have you thought of that?' She shook the black mass of her hair. 'You are a fool.' And then in an impulsive movement she reached across and squeezed my hand. 'I don't mean that unkindly. You fly planes. That is your expertise. Why should you know how to handle a businessman as complicated as Ward? And you don't even take the trouble to find out about him!'

She had, of course, and not just his background. She had tried to visualise what the progression from remand homes to Eton had done to him, his mother a drunken prostitute who didn't even know who his father was. Two or three dishes came and went as she told me the details of the years he had spent in and out of remand homes, finally jumping a truck on the Carlisle road and hitching his way south to disappear among the homeless street kids of London. 'My people learn about him again when he is two years or more older. He is then no longer stealing. He is dealing in bicycles, radios, TV and stereos. All stolen, of course. He is arrested and sent to a Borstal, where he develops a good business in tobacco, possibly drugs as well. I don't know. That is his education. And then the solicitors catch up with him and he is whisked away to a special school.' She was laughing quietly to herself. 'Finally he is sent to Eton in accordance with the old man's will. Just imagine it. Eton!'

'He still has his Glasgow accent,' I said, wondering why she had gone to such lengths to dig back into his origins, whether her Oriental mind was planning to make some use of the information.

'Why should he lose his accent?' She leaned towards me as though imparting some secret. 'It is an asset. It is the audible difference that marks him out.' And she added, 'He was an actor. Did you know that? For almost two years after he leave Eton that is how he earn

76

his living.' She reached for her glass, smiling. 'You like this rice wine?'

I hesitated, but, since she was not considering the cost of the meal, I said, 'I hope you won't think it rude of me, but I'd much rather have a malt whisky.'

There must have been a bell under her side of the table, for a waiter appeared almost at once, and after a brief discussion, she turned to me and said, 'They have only two malts – Glenmorangie and Glen Grant.'

I chose the Grant and with it came another course. Shark this time.

The actor in Ward she regarded as perhaps the most important part of his make-up. That and Eton. 'You will be seeing more of him, so just remember acting and Eton may be the soft underbelly of the man.'

I doubted that. What I had seen of old Etonians in the upper echelons of the Services and the bureaucracy didn't suggest any softness in their education. 'Did he go on to a university?'

She shook her head. 'My information does not cover that. But two years after he leave Eton he set up his own business, running long-distance vehicles down through Turkey to Iraq and Iran.'

That seemed to be the limit of her knowledge of him, except of course what I had read in the papers, the *Isvik* expedition to the southern limits of the Weddell Sea and the strange story of some Flying Dutchman of an old wooden ship – a Blackwall frigate, the *Telegraph* had said – stranded down there in the ice. 'What about the Argentinian they rescued and brought back to England?' I asked.

'So!' she said, looking at me with sudden interest. 'You *have* been making enquiries.'

I told her what little I had discovered, but when I tried to find out what she knew, she slid away from my questions, talking instead about conditions in the Antarctic. She had been to the Falklands and she had persuaded some RAF officer to let her ride down on the mail delivery Herc to South Georgia, a seven-hour trip that can be about as uncomfortable a ride as any the Air Force has to offer.

Visibility had apparently been good that day, and after the mail and supply drops had been completed, they had moved her up to the usual look-out position behind the pilot's seat, flying north-west along the coast as far as Prince Olaf Harbour. There they had made the standard 90° turn to port to cut across the narrow neck of land to the south-western coast, then port again to hug the steep slopes of the Three Brothers, Sugar Loaf Peak and Mount Paget, which at over 9,000 feet, is the highest point of the great frozen waste of the Allardyce Range, and indeed of the whole of South Georgia.

It was the old security check tour that I had done so many times myself, searching the bays and inlets for any vessel that had no clearance from the Falklands Islands Government, also the seaboard slopes in case interlopers had landed and set up some bogus scientific camp full of surveillance electronics, or just hoisted some other national flag, the very thing that had sparked off the Falklands War.

But though she said conditions had been good, I knew damn well that the whole exercise is hard going. Having complimented her on her fortitude, and got a warm smile in return, I made the mistake of asking her point blank what KLME had planned to do with a C-130 operating out of an ice-field on the Ronne. She closed up on me immediately. 'I never discuss company affairs with anyone but my associates,' she said coldly. 'You have finish your whisky. Do you want another?'

I shook my head and didn't ask any more direct questions. She surprised me then by talking about her life before the Australians had found her. 'You know about my burn marks so I take it you know most of the story?'

I nodded.

'From Travers?'

'Travers and others.'

'Ward?'

'No. Not Ward.'

'Who then?'

'Lange maybe.' I shook my head. 'No, I don't remember, but Travers certainly.'

'It does not matter. You know about me, how that film outfit find me on Phuket Island, so I can talk freely with you. Though I am centred in Paris now, I have many contacts in Laos. Even with the Khmer Rouge. That is one reason I come to this restaurant. It is the one in Paris where the Triad people come, not only from Singapore, but from all over South-East Asia. This way I keep in touch.' And then suddenly – 'What is it that Argentinian bring back from the two years he spend in that frigate ship?' And when she realised I didn't know, she said, 'You ask your friend Ward. There were stones, in a satchel. He can only have got them from around the ship. And he is let through Customs at Mount Pleasant just like that.' She snapped her fingers, leaning forward and adding, 'What is Ward, do you know?'

I shook my head.

'He is connected with your government in some way, otherwise how would he have been able to arrange for a Royal Navy Fleet Auxiliary vessel to be diverted and have himself and the Argentinian lifted off in a helicopter. And two tourists are thrown out of first class on a TriStar flight, which is then held till he arrive with this Eduardo somebody.'

'Connor-Gómez,' I said.

'So you look it all up – where?' I told her and she said, 'Okay, then you know there is what your people call a D-Notice covering the whole episode so nothing can be published about it. Why?' And when she realised I did not know, she said, 'There is something on board that ship, still there, electronic equipment maybe. They had every bit of iron and metal stripped out of her, everything duplicated in plastic, so the original idea was probably to use it as a spy ship. But then, after the Falklands War, which is over so quick, they strip everything out of her, this at Ushuaia, then she is hidden away in some kelp-infested inlet, all very secret. At the Pacific Ocean end of the Beagle Channel there are many subsidiary channels encumbered by rocks.' And she added, 'Nobody knows when she finally sails. She must have had a crew on board, but they have disappeared completely, no bodies found.' She leaned forward. 'So what is it? What terrible thing is hidden away on that ship?'

The coffee came and the waiter placed balloon glasses beside our cups and produced a bottle of what looked like a very fine old cognac. She pointed to the table and waved him away, pouring the drinks herself – very large drinks. '*Isvik* was stopped by the pack over a hundred miles to the south of where the ship is supposed to be locked in the ice, according to Peter Kettil, *Isvik*'s sailing master. He and Ward went on by sled. But an Argentinian member of the crew, a very colourful character – Mario Ángel Connor-Gómez – yes, Connor-Gómez. It all gets very complicated because his half-sister was on board *Isvik* and now owns it, and she says his real name is Borgalini and he is not her half-brother, is no connection. And also on board is another Argentinian, a student named Carlos Borgalini. These two head out on their own, ahead of Ward and Kettil, taking the Sno-Cat with them. So there are two pairs and they make a sort of race to it, as though what is on board is some great prize. The Argentinians are never heard of again. Not either of them. And a few days after Ward and his Connor-Gómez companion get back to Britain, everything is hushed up. Why?'

She had been talking very fast, as though by repeating the story she could conjure up a solution to the mystery. We talked round it for perhaps half an hour, the level of cognac in the bottle lessening with frightening rapidity. She could certainly hold her liquor, so that at times I felt there was something strongly masculine in her make-up. At one point she began talking about the landing strip they had constructed on the Ronne. She had visited it in the C-130 on one of its supply runs. The camp was nearing completion then, the ice hangar completed so that the Herc could be slid down, tail-first, protected from the wind.

It was while we were talking about the camp, and I was trying, in a roundabout way, to fathom what the object of the exercise really was, that she returned to the matter of the stones brought back by the ship-marooned Argentinian. Talking about that, and the mystery of the ship itself, I got the impression she suspected the British Government of being in some way involved. 'You think somebody got at Travers?' she asked me suddenly. 'He was willing to fly the aircraft off. But then, suddenly, he cools off, says it is too dangerous.'

'I take it that was after he'd been on the ice island and seen the situation for himself.'

'He did not have to go there to see what the situation is. He could see it from the Ronne. They could all see it, and anyway he had already measured off the length that had been subtracted from the original shelf runway. My base manager said he was still willing to fly. I offer him a good fat fee, you see. So why does he change his mind?'

'Delayed reaction probably,' I told her. 'You think about an operation and gradually fear builds up. Not always. But sometimes. Don't forget, he had been through a very traumatic experience.' And I repeated what Travers had told me of that night when he had woken up with the prefab heaving about like a ship in a storm, the claps like thunder, the grinding noise of the ice, and then the northern end of the hut falling away into the black void, how, in flashes of moonlight, he had seen the calved-off ice island floating away, the wind howling and his mind suffering from hallucinations, so that he thought he saw a small ship dancing on the waves and the moon racing across a black-cloud sky. 'I think if I had been through all that –'

She wasn't listening. She was suddenly sitting very still, almost frozen, those jet black eyes of hers boring straight into me, all her muscles gone rigid. 'Ship? What ship? Travers never mention a ship in his report.'

'On reflection he probably realised he was hallucinating. He thought he saw a whale too.'

'I did wonder,' she murmured.

'About what?'

'It is like what happen on the Filchner. And all so convenient. A great slice calves off the Shelf along the line of an old crevasse.' She shook her head. 'Greenpeace warned us. No mining in the Antarctic for fifty years. But the countries in which we are registered are very positively not signatories to the treaty. In any case, Greenpeace is a non-violent organisation. They would never go sailing around the Southern Ocean with a ship full of explosives.'

'Bjorn Lange was Greenpeace.' And as soon as I said it I wished I hadn't.

'Lange? You mention him before. Who is he?' She was leaning forward, her eyes, her whole body, suddenly tense again.

I told her about that one meeting with him. I felt I had to, though I knew I was getting into deep water. I could feel the tension in her building, waves of anger, and something even worse, growing all the time as she stared at me with extraordinary fixity. 'Ward. You say they were tailing him, following him to the CALIB offices?'

'So I was told.'

'Did you ask Ward why?'

'No, of course not. It was no concern of mine, and anyway, my one meeting with him was strictly business, to agree the terms on which I was prepared to fly the plane off.'

'But that secretary of his, you lunched with her.' I hadn't told her that. 'Does she say anything about Greenpeace? Does she refer to the hostility of Australia, France, and all the rest of the World Park countries, to mining in the Antarctic?'

'No, I don't think so.'

'Ward,' she said again, speaking the name softly to herself. She reached for the bottle. 'Will he go out this time, do you think? In that ship – with you?'

I thought it quite likely, but I didn't say so. 'There's the British Antarctic Survey base at Halley. If they have an icebreaker there this season, he could go out with the relief personnel and supplies and then get BAS to fly him on to the camp on the Ronne. That is, if they have re-established it by then. I presume they will.' I put my hand over my glass as she leaned forward to top it up.

'You sure?' She seemed disappointed. The low cut of the emerald silk gaped to show the swell of her breasts. They were small, very neat, very firm, just the size that would fit the palms of one's hands.

I don't know whether she guessed what I was thinking, or whether the amount of drink she had consumed was beginning to loosen her tongue, but she began telling me about the things that had happened to her at the hands of the Khmer Rouge, her memory oddly patchy, so that I recalled Travers saying how strangely the human brain could behave. She couldn't remember her childhood, her name, her parents, or where she had come from, but she could speak both Chinese and French, and she was well educated, so I presumed she was almost certainly from Phnom Penh; and her family must have been well-off, since they had had to flee from the advancing Khmer Rouge. What had stuck indelibly in her memory was the Communists bursting into the hut where her mother lay on a mattress on the earth floor.

Her father – at least she had presumed it was her father, and she definitely knew it was her mother lying on the floor – her father had tried to protect her. They had run him through with their bayonets, pressing him back against the hut's centre support until one of them pinned him to it, pulling his Kalashnikov clear by firing a fusillade of shots into the jerking body. Another, the leader, a taller, more powerfully-built man, laid his gun carefully on the dirt floor, pulled a machete from the bedroll strapped to his back, and with two criss-cross strokes virtually disembowelled her mother, and then with one wild sweep severed the writhing woman's head from her body. There had been two others in the hut, both men. They shot them. 'Then they look at me. I don't know what age I am then, but I am old enough to know what their looks say, the grins and the sucking sounds they make as they giggle.'

It turned out that there were only three or four women left in the village. All the others had fled with their children. Of those that were left, she was by far the youngest. And then she told me in explicit and horrific detail all that had happened to her at the hands of those men. How they had used her night after night. She was speaking very softly, very emotionally, not looking at me at all, her tendency to pronounce the letter S as TH becoming increasingly strong as the tide of her emotions mounted with the dreadful nature of her story.

If I had been a doctor or a midwife she couldn't have given a clearer, more intimate picture of a gang rape. She said there were twenty-four of them under the command of an officer named Tan Seng, billeted in the village and they had used her continuously. And I remember these words of hers – they stick inescapably in my memory: 'Their steaming pricks, their gaping mouths.' Her lips were trembling and she was snuffling quietly as the tears began. 'It went on and on and on, one after another, endlessly, night after night. And in the day, too. The pain and the blood as they tore my insides to pieces.' There was a long pause, and then – 'I can never have children now. Never. Never, never, never.' Her small fist beat the table. 'Do you understand what that means to a woman?' She shook the black hair lying in a fringe across her eyes. 'No, of course you don't.'

Feeling her need of comfort I put my hand out and gripped her arm. 'I'm sorry,' I said.

Her head jerked up. 'What fucking use is that? It's done. It's happened. Like a bullet, a bomb, a road accident, all the things that happen to one in life – when it's done, it's done, and it cannot be undone.'

'Why are you telling me this?' I took my hand away, but she reached for it quickly, her fingers gripping tight, her dark eyes staring at me from under the fringe of her hair.

There was a long pause then, neither of us saying anything. She was shut away in the past, and I just sat there, appalled. Finally, slowly, almost unwillingly, she began telling me what had happened when the Khmer detachment pulled out, how they had set fire to the village that had been their refuge for – she couldn't remember how long. But first they had ordered the villagers into their homes, then barricaded the doors. She had been with one of them at the time. He was their leader and ... She buried her face in her hands, almost whimpering as she mumbled, 'He stripped me and take me, right there on the track running through the village as they burn the houses ... Oh God! The burning of their flesh! I can still smell it.'

There was a long pause, then she muttered, 'And I can't find him.' Her head came up, her face contorted, the eyes streaming with tears. 'I can't find the bastard,' she repeated. And then, banging the table so that the glasses and crockery rattled, 'I can't find him, I can't find him ... All the others. I have account for all the others, every one of them. Five are dead, three so badly injured they will never do anything again – and the rest ... I know where the rest are. I can get them. All except that one man who is responsible for everything.'

Her head, bowed down to the table, rested on her arms, and in the long silence that followed I heard myself ask again why she had told me all this.

She didn't answer at first. At length she dried her eyes and raised her head. 'I am not quite sure.' It was said almost in a whisper. And then, 'I think because –' She shook her head, the black mop falling across the scarred cheek.

Her eyes, staring at me so despairingly through that fringe of hair, seemed to express the need for understanding, sympathy, some affection even. 'Of course,' she murmured, 'it comes to an end finally. Everything comes to an end some time.' Her fingers were gripping mine again. 'Why do I tell you? God knows ... I think because you are different. You come from a different world, and now I have reach a point when I must tell someone, or I go mad. There is nobody here, nobody to whom I can expose my feelings the way I have to you. They are all wanting money. Nothing else. Money and women.'

Her face, the movement of her hands, the tone of her voice – she was speaking with total contempt; but whether of the human race in general, or those around her, the world she knew, I could not be sure. 'How can you understand?' There was a sort of despair in her voice. 'How can anybody?' Then very softly, so softly I barely heard her – 'There is nobody. I have nobody.'

She took a grip on herself then, straightening up and reaching into her bag. 'I must go now. I have to be in Rome tomorrow. Ten o'clock, a meeting with some Italians. It is very important, so I must look my best, huh? That is the worst of being a woman. A man does not have to worry about how he looks. And I must brush up my Italian. I do that on the aeroplane.' All this was said very lightly and in a great rush. She glanced at her watch. 'Yes, definitely. The car is coming for me at seven, so now I must go.'

'You haven't told me how you escaped.'

'Escaped?' She was collecting her things. 'Oh, that. The roof collapsed, almost on top of me. That was how I get burned. The flames are licking all round me, the wood of the roof snapping and crackling. My hair – ' She stood still for a moment, remembering – 'It is burning. I can still sometimes smell my hair burning, hear the sizzling of my skin as it curls away from my flesh . . .'

She was very still then, lost in recollection. 'And then there is a hand on my ankle, somebody pulling me.'

That somebody, who saved her life, was an old man who had been left behind when his son fled with his wife and children. He had been hiding in the drainage channel at the back of the hut, a shallow trench full to the brim with effluent. He had dragged her into it and pushed her body right down into the filth, half lying on top of her. And when Tan Seng had ordered his men to check that nobody was left alive anywhere in the village, he had forced her face down into the evil-smelling softness on which she lay, so that she was totally immersed in the filth. 'I think perhaps the shit that covered my raw flesh acted as a sort of dressing, like a mud pack that has healing properties.'

Her hand touched the right side of her face, the fingers stroking down the scar tissue towards her neck. 'It could perhaps be worse.' When I didn't say anything, she smiled brightly and said, 'At least I do not feel pain any more. Not physical pain.' She held out her hand. '*Au revoir, Monsieur Michel.*' She hadn't liked the name Eddie. 'And please, if you wish to have a few days in Paris, you stay on at the Tour d'Or as my guest. Okay?' She squeezed my hand slightly and with a flash of white teeth and a shimmer of emerald silk she parted the curtains and was gone.

I sat down again and reached for the bottle. There was about an inch of cognac left in the bottom of it, that was all. Yet she had been perfectly steady on her feet as she slipped out of the room. I emptied the bottle into my glass and sat there, going over in my mind all she had said. The truth of it I did not doubt. But the way she had told me, the emotion, the tears – and coming out to this restaurant without any make-up, the burn marks so lividly exposed . . .

Well, I had got what I wanted. Tomorrow I would sign the contract, in front of Lesparre – yes, it would be best to sign it right there, in his office. From that moment the huge, snow-bound plane at the bottom of the world would be mine. *And it'll be your responsibility, mate, yours entirely,* whispered a still, small voice somewhere at the back of my brain.

But I had got it virtually for nothing. Also fifty thousand francs towards the cost of shifting it. I could hardly complain. I knocked back the rest of my drink and got to my feet.

Wu was by the door as I left the Dragon Rouge. His smile was conspiratorial as he said, '*A bientôt, Monsieur Cruse.* We see you 'ere again, yes?'

I slept like a log till dawn, then lay awake, my imagination leaping to the Falklands and south into a world of ice that I only knew as far as the glacier-bound mountain ranges of South Georgia. Just two days from now our TriStar would be approaching Ascension Island in the South Atlantic for refuelling and instead of the rain and wind that was now battering at the windows of my room, the sun would be shining out of a hard blue sky and it would be blazing hot.

I tried to push all thought of the Herc out of my mind, but, however hard I tried, it was there, the problems of getting it off that tiny platform of a berg looming larger the more I thought about it. I hadn't read the RAF's Cold Weather Operations booklet since my Falklands days. Produced for conditions ruling in the Arctic North, it was a deadly little pamphlet of do's and don'ts. I would have to get hold of a copy somehow. No way could I remember the check-list of survival equipment to be carried, and all the de-icing routine, the dire warnings if you didn't understand how important the time factor was after all snow has been brushed clear of the fuselage, the procedure for landing on iced-up runways. Contaminated surfaces, that was the jargon. And there were dire warnings about keeping the PT2 probe clear of ice and freezing snow. I remembered that one, too.

So much to remember, and the next I knew the telephone was sounding off in my ear and the sun was shining in my eyes from the edge of a very black cloud.

II

FLIGHT INTO FREE ENTERPRISE

ONE

I had little more than a day in which to complete the arrangements for Charlie and myself, pack everything I would need and purchase anything extra, stupid little things like razor blades, a new shaving brush, arctic underwear, and gloves, several layers of gloves, sunglasses to replace the ones I had lost on Campsie Fell, and sun lotion, the waterproof Vitamin F (15) type. I made a list in the plane flying back to Heathrow, and when I got to the flat I found a message from Tony, my air commodore pal, to say that a Mrs Fraser had phoned. Would I ring her back as soon as I got in? And Charlie had phoned twice, nothing to worry about, but could I have my contacts at Lyneham provide him with an up-to-date C-130 engine manual?

'Christ! You could have thought of that before,' I said when I got back to him. On the flight over I had almost filled the backs of two envelopes with things I had to do or get. I added the manual to the list and scrubbed out the note I had heavily underscored to check that he would be on the train to Brize Norton. At least he was in London now, packed and ready to go. And he sounded cheerful as hell, not a care in the world and nothing to do but go and watch Arsenal play at Tottenham.

I think it was talking to him that helped me unwind. And then Kirsty Fraser telling me, when I rang her, that she had the expenses money waiting for me. I had forgotten all about Ward's advance payment. And it was a glorious day. Indian summer weather, and I felt suddenly light-hearted.

It was in this mood that I climbed the stairs of the dingy office block in an alley off Neal Street. Third floor, she had said, above an artistic glass-blower's shop. There were two doors and both had heavy steel grilles across frosted glass with no indication of the nature of the business. I pressed the bell-push on the one that had a safety lock device and a metallic female voice asked me my name. I told her and there was the click of the catch being released.

To my surprise the office I entered was bright, cheerful and very modern. A vase of pale, spiky dahlias stood on what looked to me like a valuable Georgian side-table set beside a big settee covered in a warm tapestry material. Kirsty came round from behind her desk to greet me, and because I was feeling on top of the world, the office so bright and the sun shining in, and the girl herself, with the freckles all gold, her straw-yellow head of hair glinting and those brilliant sapphire-blue eyes, I took the hand she was holding out and carried it to my lips. I can't remember what I said – something stupidly endearing that produced a little laugh of embarrassment as I had intended – and then I reached out for her shoulders, pulling her towards me and kissing her on both cheeks.

That was when I noticed the half-open door to an inner office. There was a man standing there and behind him I caught a glimpse of heavy leather chairs and bright steel furniture with a black desktop littered with electronic equipment. The door slammed shut.

'Was that Ward?'

She pulled herself free of me, stepping back behind her desk. 'He's waiting for you.' She picked up an envelope, handing it to me. Though it was addressed to me and marked 'Private', somebody had slit it open. The note inside was handwritten, a single sheet with no date, no address. I turned it over. No signature either ... 'Did you open it?' I asked her.

She shook her head. 'No. Iain.'

Ward! Was that part of his world, opening other people's letters, listening at doorways? 'Why?' I asked.

She didn't answer and my eyes went back to the letter. It was short and the handwriting large, almost a scrawl, as though he had scribbled it in a hurry. He hoped to meet up with me in the Falklands. He was flying out to Montevideo the following day, then taking a ship to Port Stanley; would I try to find out from Ward what his plans for the Antarctic were? Was it oil he was after, or something else? The last paragraph read: *And if you are at Goose Green look out please for a man named Barratt – Ferdinand Barratt. That is not his real*

*name. I don't think so. He is booked in, I believe, to stay at the boarding
house by the shearing sheds. He will go with you most probably to the
Ronne.*

*If you find some news leave a message poste restante at Port Stanley
Post Office. Do not use my name. Just address it Greenpeace. Somebody
will collect it and get it to me.*

I looked at the envelope again. It was addressed to me care of Iain
Ward at Neal's Yard and marked *Urgent Please Forward*. 'How did
he know where to contact me?' I asked Kirsty.

'They rang up.'

'Who?'

'Greenpeace. A man's voice. He asked me whether I would be
seeing you again before you left. I said I thought it likely. He
wouldn't give his name, but said to tell you the man you met in the
Hyde Park underground car park hoped to be at Cow Hangar
House, East Falkland, around the end of the month.' She reached
across the desk and handed me a slip of paper. 'Here, I've written it
down for you.'

I glanced at it, and a voice behind me said, 'Ye'd best steer clear
of Greenpeace.'

He had the door to his office wide open and was standing there
again, large and untidy, his shirtsleeves hanging loose, no tie and a
smile on his heavily-boned face. 'They're an organisation Ah've got
a lot o' time for, s'long as it's other people they're harassing.' He
nodded for me to come into his office. 'Right noo Ah'd rather they
kept well clear of me.' He took my arm. 'We've got business that's
best kept to ourselves, eh?'

'You mean the Herc?' But I knew it wasn't that.

'No, no.' He shook his head. But when I asked him what he did
mean, he laughed and muttered something about all being revealed
in time. 'Ah'll maybe talk aboot it when we're safely away to sea.
Not before.' He waved me to the black leather chair across the desk
from him. 'So you saw La Belle Phuket, huh? What did you think
of the little lady? Did she scare the living daylights oot o' ye?'

'No, not really. Fact is I found her –' I hesitated, searching for
the right word – 'a little sad in a way. You can't help feeling sorry
for her.'

'Och aye. So ye felt sorry for her.' He was chuckling to himself.
'She gave ye her life story, did she? Told ye in pornographically gory

93

detail all that had happened to her in that village in the highlands to the north of Phnom Penh.'

'She's told you, has she?' I asked. 'About her father being bay-onetted to the hut's main support, her mother disembowelled, herself gang-raped night after night?'

'Oh, sure.' He nodded. 'An' aboot how Tan Seng, the officer in charge of that particular guerilla detachment, fucked her while his men were setting light to the village, burning those that were still alive in their huts. Was she crying when she told ye? Did the tears roll down her cheeks? An' her own burn scars exposed, no make-up?' He gave a fat chuckle. 'So she gave ye the works, eh? Ah wonder why.' And he added, staring at me hard, 'Quite a little actress La Belle.'

'Are you saying it wasn't true ?' I couldn't believe that. She could never have spoken with such intensity if it hadn't been true .

'No, no,' he said. 'It's all true . It happened to her, an' the scars it's left her with will never heal, the ones inside of her I mean. Ah guess she just has to go on telling aboot it time and time again.' He paused, looking at me with a funny little smile on his lips, as though he was savouring something he found peculiarly appealing. 'Ah don't imagine, though, she told ye the end of the story.'

'How do you mean?' I had a feeling of resentment, but whether at the callousness of his reaction, or because it hadn't been to me alone she had told her story, I wasn't sure. 'So what's the end of the story?' I asked angrily. 'Is it so funny she can't have children now?'

'No. An' that's no' what I was referring to.' He was suddenly serious. 'Did she tell ye she had been tracking down the Khmer boys who had raped her?' And when I told him yes, that four of them were dead and five others were so badly injured their lives were finished, he nodded. 'Aye, but what aboot the other fifteen? Did she tell ye aboot them? They've all been accounted for except for the man called Tan Seng and two of his henchmen. And what she'll do to them when her agents find them Ah shudder to think. Blind them perhaps, or ram a red-hot poker up their backsides, the way the poachers do to the poor bloody leopards.'

I stared at him, wondering what sort of a man he was.

'Ye don't believe me, do you?' He had sat down and was leaning forward, his elbows on the black formica desk top that was crisscrossed with scratch marks. 'It's like that Christie play – An' then there were three.'

'She's killed them? Is that what you're saying?'

He smiled and shook his head. 'That wouldn't be fitting the punishment to the crime, would it? Och no, that little madam had them tied up, their legs pulled apart, an' then she cut the balls off them. Makes sense, don't it? They'll never gang-bang a girl again, never ever again. Nature doesn't enable man to grow replacement testicles, an' hospitals haven't got around to issuing spares yet.'

'How do you know all this?' I asked him.

'Never ye mind. But it's true all right. Five o' them were still together, a guerilla cadre. The other seven were hunted down individually.'

'How do you know? Have you been out there?'

He shook his head. 'Not recently. But Ah've contacts.' And then he went on, speaking slowly, 'It was the verra first place they sent me. Cambodia. The Khmers called it Kampuchea. Quite a time back, that was. An' in all the years, an' all the places Ah bin to since, all the things Ah seen, nothing compares with the horrors Ah witnessed there. Ah was still just a kid, but Ah'd experienced more than most youngsters at that age.' He paused there, his eyes glazed with the memory of what he'd seen. 'But it still came as a shock, a ter-rible shock. Ah'd seen people blown apart by bombs – not just men, women and children, too. Ah wasn't squeamish about blood an' shattered faces, bodies torn to tatters. But Kampuchea in '75–'76 ...' Again the shake of that heavy head. 'That was the year the French finally pulled out, the year Pol Pot and his Khmer Rouge swept into Phnom Penh an' the rice paddies of the meandering, lazy Mekong had another name given them – the Killing Fields. Jesus Christ!' he breathed. 'In that one year it's reckon'd more than a million, mebbe two million, died – driven to their death on the land and the paddies through overwork, starvation, beatings, shootings, rape. An' it was the Americans, with their indiscriminate bombing five years earlier, that turned the country away from Sihanouk's successor, Lon Nol, an' paved the way for Pol Pot and his bloody Khmers.'

He was leaning that heavy head of his on his one good hand, silent now and sitting quite still. A fax machine clattered into life. He took no notice, lost in the past. 'The skulls,' he muttered. 'The burned bodies. The smell. An' people dying in their hundreds of disease – cholera, malaria, dysentery. Thank God I was only there that one year. But it was the year for horrors.'

'Who sent you?' I asked as he fell silent again.

He stared at me as though he couldn't believe I had asked such a stupid question. 'The people who employed me.' That was all the answer I got, and then he was talking about Pol Pot and the Khmer, telling me how the current regime in neighbouring Vietnam had finally had enough of it. 'That was in 1978. The Khmer were pushed back into the forests of the northern uplands, Pol Pot overthrown an' what looked at first like a more sensible Communist military regime took over with the return to power of General Lon Nol.'

'Have you been back since then?' I asked.

He shook his head. 'No, Ah left Kampuchea in November '76.' He got up and walked to the fax machine, which had now stopped its machine-gun rattle, the room silent as he stood peering down at the print-out. I think he only did it to take his mind off it all. Reliving that first experience of the filthiest of all forms of warfare cannot have been easy for him. I wondered why he had bothered to tell me about it in such detail.

But then he turned slowly, and, walking back to his desk, he said, 'Ye can mebbe understand now a little of how Ah felt, listening to that young woman pouring it all out to me with her burn marks and the tears streaming doon her face. She seemed then, and she still does, the embodiment of all that ghastly, senseless, stupid, fucking war.' His teeth were clenched tight as he spoke those words. 'It must have been late '76 when it happened to her. The French had gone, Phnom Penh had fallen, an' the refugees from that once-elegant city were streaming northwards. It would have been there, in one of the forest villages, that her parents were slaughtered before her eyes. Ah reck'n she would have been about eleven then. She said her breasts were only just beginning to bud up when she was left for dead, and then she began the trek westward to the sea.'

He paused a moment, and the effect of that pause was to bring it all back to me, the Celtic emotion with which his words, his whole being, was imbued, infecting me with the intensity of his feeling, so that I saw the scene in that hut again in my mind's eye as visibly as when she had been leaning towards me across the table, the tears forming in her eyes and her scarred features set with a terrible anger. 'If it had been me,' he said, his jaw set, 'Ah'd 've left the bastards cockless in Gaza as ye might say.' Then he laughed and shook his head. 'Ever bin to Gaza? No. Well, ye'd no' wish to be in tha' part of the wor-rld wi' all ye wedding tackle gone. The girls wouldna' understand. As Ah 'collect they're possessed of a verra imperative libido.'

He went on to talk for a while about Cambodia as it must have been before its name was changed to Kampuchea, before Pol Pot and his 'merry men' was the way he put it, marched into Phnom Penh. 'When they marched oot again they left it virtually empty. Then they went on to kill off by one means or another a good third of the country's population.'

Then, suddenly switching the talk to practical matters, he said, 'Here's the money Ah promised ye. Cash. Ah reck'ned ye'd prefair it in cash, eh?' He passed a thick envelope across to me, and since I was sitting a little to the right of him, he did it with that black-gloved hand. It was done with such an easy, natural movement that, if his hand hadn't touched mine, so that I felt the steel of the fingers beneath the tight-stretched plastic, I would have thought it a perfectly ordinary hand. 'An' Ah've got somethin' else for ye.' The gloved hand passed me a sheet of paper with a drawing on it and some figures.

'What's this represent?' I asked.

'Yer cargo. The dimensions an' weight o' the cargo Ah'll want ye to lift off o' the Ronne when we've got the ice strip fit for take-off as well as landing.'

I stared at him. He was serious. He had some sort of a container, something solid and big – the figures leapt out of the page, millimetres presumably . . . Evidently this was what the C-130 operation was all about.

I threw the paper back on to his desk. Jesus Christ! He wasn't thinking of the sheer enormity of the difficulties facing me just to get the Herc airborne. 'Don't you understand?' I had got to my feet. He must be out of his mind, letting it jump ahead like that, ignoring all the immediate problems. 'Can't you get it into your head that this is something that's never been done before. Not as far as I know.' And I began detailing the difficulties that lay ahead, a big, complicated machine with four bloody great engines, and this stupid idiot of a jumped-up Glaswegian boy . . .

Thank God I didn't put it in those words. He'd never have forgiven me, and if I was to get that bird airborne, I'd need his co-operation, and lots of it.

He smiled, his face suddenly relaxing, a little amused even. 'Och, do sit yersel' doon, laddie, fur God's sake. Ah appreciate yer problems. Ah really do. But reopening that ice strip, gettin' equipment an' stores doon there, funding the whole –' He shook that massive head of his, still smiling. 'It all costs money, a hell of a lot of money. Somebody's got to be thinkin' ahead. That somebody is me, an' that's what Ah'm doing.'

His sudden change of mood, the charm switched on, I began to simmer down. Anyway, he had given me the opening I needed. 'Just what is it then, this cargo of yours?' I asked him as I sat down again.

He hesitated. 'A piece of machinery,' he said slowly, apparently reluctant to reveal even that much. 'Ye've got the figures there.' He indicated the rough drawing lying on the desk. 'Ah've given ye the outside dimensions for the prototype they're building for me right now.'

'And this is what you want my Herc for, to pick up a piece of machinery and deliver it – where?' *My* Herc! It sounded good, it had a nice ring to it. 'Where?' I repeated.

He shook his head. 'A step at a time.' And then, tapping the desk with his gloved steel fingers: 'But Ah can tell ye right noo it'll be waitin' for ye on the Ronne.' And he added, 'Hell of a lot o' use it would be to us if we got it doon there, and ye flew that C-130 off the berg and on to the Ronne ice strip, and then we found we couldna' load it 'cos the bloody thing was a few millimetres too large. The weight, as ye see, is not excessive.'

He pushed the piece of paper across to me again and I saw there was a figure given for deadweight. He was right. It wasn't excessive. In optimum conditions the Herc could have lifted two of the machines.

'It's well below the maximum payload,' he said. 'Ah've already checked that. It's the dimensions Ah'm concerned aboot.' He sat there, watching me, but there was nothing I could say. 'Ah could mebbe get the engineers to knock a few millimetres off here and there so as we could squeeze it in. But Ah would rather talk to them noo, while they are still building it. So the sooner Ah have the plane's interior dimensions, the better.'

'What mark is it?' I asked. 'The C-130 is getting to be quite an ancient workhorse. The only comparable transport plane in the world is the DC-3, and like that old Dakota, the Herc has already been through several modifications. Not as many, of course, but a good few all the same. It was the C-130H I was flying most recently.'

He nodded. 'That's okay then. It's the H ye've just bought.'

I shook my head, frowning down at the figures. Trouble was, of course, I didn't carry the internal dimensions of the fuselage in my head. 'If you'd told me earlier ...' I dropped the sheet of paper back on his desk. 'Depends what that particular Herc has been used for – before KLME acquired it. For instance, if it has been a tanker and used for flight refuelling, then –'

'Yes, that's what they told me had been its main duties before they bought it.' He said it quickly, with virtually no trace of an accent.

'There you are then,' I said.

'Wot'yer mean, there ye are then?'

'Have you ever been inside one of the Hercs that's been converted to tanker duties?'

'No, of course not. Why should I?' And he added, 'Ah don't see that it makes any difference. Anyway, they dismantled the tank part of the refuelling equipment, so the fuselage is stripped oot already. All ye need to find oot is the internal dimensions.'

'It's not as easy as that,' I told him. 'Imagine a Heath Robinson drawing brought to life by a mad mechanic, who then squeezes it into the fuselage, bolting it to the brackets he has had welded to the airframe. You start flinging a fully-loaded C-130 tanker around in the air, or worse still, hit maximum turbulence in a real bad storm, the strain on those brackets ...'

'So what do ye need?' He was suddenly impatient. 'Detailed drawings of a tanker conversion?'

'If they haven't cut the brackets out, yes. Do you know if they have?'

'No, of course I don't.' He yelled for his secretary. 'MoD (Air) should be able to produce what we need. There's a couple of boys I know ... Kirsty!' He pushed himself up out of his chair. 'Bugger, the girl! Gone to the loo Ah s'pose.' He moved to the connecting door with remarkable agility for such a large man and flung it open.

She was at her desk, the telephone to her ear and jotting something down on a notepad. He started to say something, but she waved her pen at him for quiet, her voice suddenly quite clear as she said, 'Hold on a minute, will you, and I'll see if he can manage it.' She put her hand over the mouthpiece. 'It's Greenpeace,' she said. 'They want to know –'

'Well, tell 'em ter –' He hesitated.

'Fuck off?' She gave him an impish smile. 'Is that what you really want me to say?' She shook her blonde mop of hair. 'I don't think that would be wise.'

'Why the hell not? Ah'm buggered if Ah'll have some young student, straight back from the Wall of Death an' barely oot of his wetsuit, telling me wot Ah can an' canna du. Or is it one of those intense young women –'

'Relax, for God's sake, Iain.' She was still smiling. 'It's not any of those. It's the top man at their Islington headquarters. He wants to talk to you personally.'

'Wot aboot?'

'He won't say. But I'm pretty sure it's the Antarctic.'

'World Park, eh? Well, Ah suppose Ah'd better see him. Tomorrow sometime.'

She shook her head. 'He wants to see you now, right away. Says it's urgent.'

'Right away?'

She nodded.

Ward stood there, thinking it over.

'What's his name?'

'Stunnard. Arthur Stunnard.'

He glanced at his watch. 'Eleven-thirty, tell him. An' when he comes, say Ah've got somebody wi' me. Ah'll give it two or three minutes, then when Ah slam my outer door –'

'Okay, the usual routine.' She turned back to the phone.

'An' then get MoD (Air) for me. O'Higgins.' He slammed the door shut and turned angrily back to his desk. 'Greenpeace! Wot the hell do they want?'

O'Higgins came through almost immediately. 'Sean.' He spoke softly, getting up and walking to the far end of the room, at the same time waving me to stay where I was. As a result, I heard very little of the conversation, but his manner, and the few words I did hear, also the fact that they were on Christian name terms, made it obvious they knew each other quite well. What department he had got through to, or what the pull was that he had, I couldn't gather, but in the space of a few moments he had been promised the information we required. 'In sub-arctic conditions,' I called to him. 'And see if they'll give you a minimum runway figure for a stripped-out airframe taking off in low temperature conditions from an ice-contaminated strip.'

He nodded, and a moment later he returned to the desk and put the phone down. 'That's settled then. He'll send the information direct to me here an' Ah'll either get it to ye at Brize Norton before ye take off or Ah'll have Kirsty fax it oot to ye via Sid Mackenzie at Mount Pleasant.'

I stared at him. 'Sid Mackenzie! What's he doing there?'

'Station Commander.'

'At MPA? So he's a group captain now.' How did Ward come to know him? Two contacts in MoD (Air), and now – 'How come you know these people?' I asked him. 'What's your job?'

He smiled. 'Never ye mind. None of yur business. An' right noo –' He leaned towards me across the desk – 'Right noo Ah'm workin' fur mesel'.' He was smiling then, quite relaxed. 'First time Ah ever did that since Ah was a wee bairn workin' the pitches on the Underground here in London.' He reached for the piece of paper with the pencilled drawing on it, screwed it up and threw it into the waste-paper basket. 'When ye get oot there, ye'll probably find Mac has all the necessary information right there on the spot. How many Hercs has he got?'

'Two,' I said, 'maybe three. It depends. There are only four C-130 H Mark Is in the Air Force.'

'Okay. Anything else?'

'That machine,' I said. 'Just what's it for?' He stared at me as though I was a fool to ask. 'That's the purpose of this whole exercise, isn't it?'

He nodded slowly, 'Ah s'pose ye could say that.' The admission was made reluctantly. But when I asked him again where he wanted it delivered he closed up on me.

'Is it mining?' I persisted.

He shook his head and pushed himself to his feet, waiting for me to go. But I sat there, persevering with a few more questions. One thing I did get out of him, he admitted the snout contraption he had drawn to illustrate the dimensions was a mole-type excavator, and the machine was tracked, the power hydraulic.

'Then it's for mining,' I murmured. 'Under the sea?'

'It can operate anywhere, except in quicksand. Or so they say.' Apparently the engineering firm had already completed three of these machines, all much larger, and all operating in different parts of the world, and now they were working on the prototype of a much smaller mole. He had been down to their factory in East Anglia and they were prepared to tailor it to his specifications. He said it smugly, as though he had won some sort of a battle.

He saw me to the door then and shook my hand, using his left. 'If all goes well, we'll meet next in Port Stanley.'

'*Inshallah*,' I said.

He smiled and clapped me on the shoulder. '*Inshallah*. An' *bien viaje*.'

Kirsty jumped to her feet as I crossed the outer office to retrieve my raincoat. She even tried to help me on with it. 'So I won't see you again before you go.' She was standing quite still, the lips of her large, mobile mouth slightly parted and those astonishing sapphire-blue eyes fixed on mine. I bent to kiss her on the cheek. The next thing I knew her arms were round my neck and her lips were on mine. Through the halo of her hair I could just see the door of Ward's office still open and the man himself standing there, watching us. I tried to draw away, but she had tight hold of me and she was saying, 'Somebody has to wish you luck, so it may as well be me.' Her body was pressed against mine, her head on my shoulder. 'I hope everything goes well for you,' she murmured. 'I have been looking again at those satpics –'

'He's watching us,' I said.

'I know.' His door slammed shut and she gave a little laugh, her breath warm against my ear. 'That'll fix the bugger.' And she added, 'After that he'll be eating out of my hand for the next week or so.' She let go of me then, smiling and her eyes alight with something, I don't know what – devilry, excitement, something. 'Take care,' she breathed. 'I'll be thinking of you come December. And of him. He'll be down there with you.'

She turned away from me, going to her desk and picking up her bag. 'Just a moment,' she said as I was moving towards the door.

'This came for you today.' She handed me an envelope with a French stamp on it and the letters CALIB. Inside was a cheque for 30,000 francs. 'And something else. Something from me I'd like you to have.' She pulled out the blue scarf that so nearly matched her eyes. 'You admired this, remember? When I first met you and you were so angry because it was me, not Iain taking you to lunch. So here it is – for luck. Wear it when you take off from that island of ice.' She pressed it into my hand. 'Good luck!' And she turned quickly back to her desk.

I stood there awkwardly, murmuring my thanks. I was deeply touched. But her fingers were already rattling away at the keys and she didn't look up.

I turned then and went out, closing the door behind me, still holding the scarf in my hand. I was feeling strangely elated, conscious that, with the closing of that door, I had crossed some sort of a Rubicon and was now started on my long journey down into the ice.

I found a branch of my bank and arranged for Ward's bundle of notes, all fifties, to be paid into my account. That, and the CALIB cheque would take care of my overdraft, leaving me plenty to spare, and I was able to buy almost everything I needed personally at just two department stores in Oxford Street. It was raining by then, but my luck was in, there was a cab drawn up at the kerb disgorging its fare as I came out loaded with parcels. I was walking on air by then and when the driver asked me where to, I said, 'The RAF Club in Piccadilly.' I wasn't a member, but I had been a guest there on several occasions, and the Jag was stabled very close in the garage behind the Park Lane Hotel. Also the Club was handy for the ships' chandlery in Albermarle Street.

Unfortunately, the man on duty was not one I knew, but I was in the grip of an adrenalin-fuelled, pre-take-off high. It was almost twelve-thirty. I wanted a drink and I was hungry. Without stopping to think I said I was lunching with a member. He wanted to know who, of course, so I took a chance and said, 'Air Vice Marshal Pritchard.' I banked on his being a member and still down in the West Country. It worked. I was able to leave my things, and when I said it was my last day before going out to the Antarctic, I was even allowed into the bar on my own.

It was when I was into my second Bloody Mary that I had the

bright idea of ringing Barbara Ward. She was in, but she had a date that evening. 'Put him off,' I said. 'It's the only time I've got. I'm flying out tomorrow.' I didn't give her a chance to refuse. 'Expect me around four-thirty,' I told her and rang off. Then, as I was leaving the phone, I ran straight into a man I hadn't seen since the Falklands War. He was working now at the MoD and was on his own, so I spent an enjoyable lunchtime going over that very strange campaign, the Islands and the vessel I was joining seeming much more real now, and very near.

After coffee and a couple of large brandies, I spent a happy hour in Captain O.M. Watts just a few blocks up Piccadilly in Albemarle Street. It was a little after four-thirty when I turned off Notting Hill Gate and backed the Jag into a conveniently empty residents' parking slot right outside Barbara's little house in Hillgate Place. As I went up the steps to the front door I saw there was an Omo packet in the basement window. Now in the old days, when I was training to be a fighter pilot, an Omo packet in the kitchen window of a married quarters meant only one thing – On My Own. If she knew the drill, then she had ditched her date.

She did, and she had – she was ready and waiting. The rain had stopped and the roads were steaming in the warmth of the sun as we drove west to the place on the Thames where we had fed the swans. We held hands most of the way, behaving like a couple of kids on a joy-ride.

'How many of my breed have you chalked up so far?' I asked her at one stage.

'I don't know what you mean.' She said it archly.

'The packet in the window. That dates you.'

'How kind you are.' She was looking at me out of the corners of her eyes, smiling. 'I found that packet at the back of my draining-board cupboard.'

'How many?' I persisted.

'Oh, I don't know. I've lost count.' She giggled, still with that provocative sideways look. 'Pilots mostly. They seem particularly prone to sexual enthusiasm. I suppose it's driving those big, beautiful, high-powered machines. But it doesn't seem to do their love tackle much good. Smaller than average. G-factor, I'm told.' And she lapsed into silence.

'It's the stomach that is affected by G,' I muttered angrily.

Feeling flush with money, an unusual sensation for me, I had decided to take her to the Compleat Angler again. But she had other ideas. After watching the sun disappear into a red inferno of cloud she said, 'We'll go to that place by the bridge at Sonning.'

'You'll go where you're taken,' I told her.

'Drive on. And set a course for Sonning.'

I told her where I was taking her, but she was absolutely adamant. 'You're my guest this evening. Or rather Iain's, in a roundabout sort of way.' And she gave that attractive little giggling laugh of hers.

So we had a table in the window looking out over the river, and afterwards we drove back to her place in teeming rain. Maybe it was the cognac she had insisted on ordering. It always reacted on me as a mild aphrodisiac. But not this time. Instead, I found myself limp and useless thinking of La Belle Phuket, the brandy she had drunk that evening, the terrible story she had told me. We were in bed then, and Barbara was being as nice to me as any woman had ever been. But it didn't work, that part-Chinese face coming between me and the woman I was with, the tears in her eyes, the husky voice that found some of our consonants difficult.

'What's the matter?'

She might well ask. I sensed her mounting frustration, her anger. 'What's the matter?' she asked again. 'I thought you of all men, with your background, showing off at every opportunity – I thought you would be Macho Man personified. Instead –' She pushed me away, swinging her legs over the side of the bed and reaching for the kimono she had laid over the chair.

She was leaning forward, her small breasts beautifully shaped. I felt ashamed. 'I'm sorry,' I murmured. Not being able to satisfy a woman was something that had never happened to me before.

'Why couldn't you?' she demanded, standing over me, the kimono wrapped round her nakedness. 'I never failed to rouse a man yet. So what's wrong? Why couldn't you?'

'It wasn't your fault,' I muttered.

'Of course it wasn't my fault. And you're not impotent. Something came between us. What?'

She was very upset. And so was I. 'Come on, what was it? A woman?'

I got out of bed and she handed me my clothes, item by item like a valet. No attempt at further seduction, her eyes fixed on me curiously, and all the time the scene in that hut when they had raped La Belle in front of the mutilated bodies of her mother and father vivid in my mind.

'Well, was it?'

I shook my head, remembering how I had felt as I had seized hold of her naked body. Lust. Nothing but lust. And I had seen myself then as one of the Khmer Rouge, the same universal male urge driving me. That's when the excitement in me had died. She must have repeated the question, a certain wildness in her voice, and I realised how much I had hurt her pride. She was taking it as an insult to her womanhood.

'Your mind was far away. You weren't thinking about me. You had your arms round me, but I didn't exist. I was a nothingness. Are you in love with somebody?'

I remember staring at her without any real comprehension – except that I knew she was deeply hurt. 'Sit down,' I said wearily, tucking my shirt into my trousers.

'It was another woman, wasn't it?'

'Yes,' I said savagely. 'It was another woman. But not what you think.'

'What then?'

'Sit down,' I said again. 'Sit down and I'll tell you. I owe you that. But you won't like it.' And I pushed her into the chair, seeing the anger die out of her eyes, her emotions responding to my changed mood.

She sat in absolute silence, her eyes grown large in the shaded light, while I told her the whole dreadful story. It was only when I had finished that I realised I was sitting on her bed. There was nowhere else to sit and I felt drained. I had always tried to steer clear of emotions. Get involved emotionally with a woman and it interferes with your flying, comes between you and the split-second reactions needed to handle a fighting machine through the barrier and into the Mach numbers. I had got emotionally involved once, and only once. As a result I had nearly taken a hangar out. We had been on target practice and my Phantom was fully armed.

The silence in the room was broken by a sound that almost shocked me. It was Barbara crying. She was actually in tears, the kimono front flopping open, her shoulders shaking slightly. 'Will you see her again?'

'I don't know. Probably. When they get the Ronne ice strip back into commission. Depends on transportation, but she's been out there before.'

'And Iain. Does he know about this?'

'Yes. Apparently she's told quite a few people. Can't get the details out of her mind.'

'My God! Can you blame her? And it'll stick in my mind now. Just as it's obviously stuck in yours.' She got up and came across the room to me, taking my head in her hands and pressing my cheek close against the warmth of her breast. 'Thank you for telling me.' She spoke very softly, almost a whisper. 'I understand now.'

We stayed like that for quite a time not saying anything, just holding each other. My arms were round her waist and she kept hugging me to her. Once or twice she kissed me on the top of the head.

Finally we released each other and I took my leave of her, kissing her gently on the mouth and then walking out without looking back. As I closed the bedroom door I thought I heard a whispered 'Good luck!' But I wasn't thinking of Barbara as I drove through the late-evening quiet of Kensington. I was thinking of La Belle sitting across the table from me, her cosmopolitan Chinese face framed by a painted wall-screen and the tears catching the light from the candles. Within the space of twenty-four hours I had been closely involved in the two faces of sex and I began to realise it had affected me deeply, changing, in a way I did not understand as yet, my attitude to women.

I phoned Charlie Pollard at his hotel first thing in the morning, but the porter said his key was still in its pigeon-hole and he didn't think Mr Pollard had returned to his room since going out the previous evening. I might have expected that. It was typical of Charlie, but it was annoying all the same as I would have liked to check over with him the list of requirements we had worked out together in case there was anything we had forgotten. I left a message for him to meet me on the train and got on with the things I still had to do, the most important of which was disposing of the car which meant driving out to Greensted-juxta-Ongar in Essex.

It was raining again by then and the traffic bad. A farming friend of mine had offered me the use of a barn. This turned out to be little more than a corrugated-iron shed literally within sight of the oldest wooden church in the world. He showed me split oak uprights that dated back to the seventh century and then took me into his ranch-type farmhouse for a whisky-mac. He then drove me to the Underground station. I had all my gear with me so I made sure I arrived at Paddington in good time for the train. No sign of Charlie, of course, and I paced up and down on the platform, fuming.

It would be just like Charlie to miss the train, and then what did I do, fly out to the Falklands on my own and hope he would be able to talk himself on to another flight? But I was fairly certain Air Movements wouldn't play along with that. Places on the TriStar flights were a high priority, the seats reserved by the various Services weeks in advance.

In the end I went back to my seat, having decided I would go without him if I had to and hope that somehow he would manage to join me. But of one thing I was certain, if Charlie didn't turn up there was no way I would attempt to get that kite airborne without him there to check and double-check the engines. Everything depended on those four Allison engines transmitting maximum power to the turbo-props.

He turned up in the end, a bare two minutes before departure, red-faced and full of apologies, a bag in either hand, a loaded rucksack on his back. He was followed by a grumbling porter heaving a bulging bedroll and an old blue kitbag on to the topmost luggage rack which already had two suitcases on it. He had barely sat down before the platform began sliding away from us past the window. 'Got any money?' he asked. 'Had a whizz time of it on the town, but I'm just about skint now.'

It was typical of Charlie, always late, always in a rush, everlastingly broke. The man was a pain in the arse, but I wouldn't have changed that round, fat, florid face of his for that of any other engineer. He was just so good at his job. 'What was the woman's name?' I asked.

'Sandra.' He beamed at me. 'Oh boy! ...' The smug grin on his face was as noticeable as the whisky on his breath. 'Twenty-two she said she was. More like seventeen, with the neatest little ...' I told him to shut his mouth; heads were lifting as his drink-loud voice penetrated down the length of the coach.

'You'll have to make do with penguins from now on,' I told him.

'Chrissakes, Eddie, what the hell you mean by that?' He had never served in the Falklands.

The coach laid on for us at Oxford filled up very rapidly, squaddies returning from leave or going out to replace men who had finished their tour, a sprinkling of RAF personnel, several women, two of them with young children. Everything was sodden with wet, the rain coming in cold gusts and the windows steaming as we cleared the last of the houses and headed west into the gathering dark of the storm clouds.

It was about fifteen miles to Brize Norton and at the gates to the base we were stopped by an armed guard, figures in camouflage jackets moving alertly, rifles at the ready. 'Look like SAS,' Charlie whispered out of the corner of his mouth. 'Or else there's a panic on. Never seen the RAF Regiment looking as sharp as this.'

A woman in front of us turned her head and said, 'You'd look sharp if you'd just come back from Northern Ireland. They lost almost a dozen of their pals in a car-bomb attack two weeks ago.'

The sergeant appeared in the open door. He had a notepad in his hand. 'Lance-Corporal Feathers?'

'Here, Sarg.' The man jumped up so smartly I almost expected the crash of boots.

'Message for you.' And he read it out. His brother's wife had just given birth to a baby girl. And there was another message, for a Pilot Officer Briggs to report to Air Movements immediately on arrival at the terminal building. 'Anyone here of the name Cruse? Mr Edwin Cruse. Is he on board?'

It was so unexpected that for a moment I didn't say anything.

'Mr Edwin Cruse. Is he on board?' And when I acknowledged my presence, the sergeant said, 'Would you come with me, sir? There's somebody in the guard post wants to see you.'

'Who?' I asked. But he had ducked out of sight. Maybe it was somebody I knew at the station. I told Charlie to look after our things and went out into the rain. 'This way, sir.'

'Who is it?' I asked again as I followed the sergeant through a great pool of water to the guard post.

'Name's Stunnard,' he said. 'Says he's from Greenpeace.' That was the man who had so urgently demanded to see Ward the previous day. There was a company-type car in the holding bay. Inside the hut the warmth hit one in the face. There was a counter with an RAF sergeant behind it, two khaki-clad figures leaning against the back partition which had various notices pinned to it, and a civilian sitting on a bench by the door. 'Mr Cruse?' The man got to his feet, his hand held out, the look on his face showing the relief he felt at seeing me.

I turned my head at the sound of the coach moving off and the sergeant said, 'It's all right, sir. There'll be transport laid on to take you to the check-in. There's no hurry. Word is the TriStar flight is delayed.'

'What's the trouble?' I asked.

'Weight, I imagine. It usually is. They'll start taking two or three spoonfuls out of the fuel tanks, and if it's more than that, then they'll reroute via Dakar. That cuts out Ascension and they won't be able to pick up the mail that some idiot dumped there last week.'

Stunnard was tallish, balding, very slim, with a clipped moustache and round, bulging eyes, the whites very pronounced. 'It's about Bjorn Lange,' he said as we settled on the bench. 'He's missing.'

I nodded. 'I heard it on my car radio.'

'You met him, I believe.'

He hadn't been able to get hold of my address in London so he had driven down to Brize Norton, having been told, presumably by Ward, that I was flying out that night. He hadn't been allowed into the base. The regulations about entry and permits were much stricter than when I had last been here, so he had decided to wait in the guard hut. He had been there over an hour, his object being to persuade me to see if I could locate Lange for him. 'He's a good lad, but he's got a certain amount of money and as a result shows a degree of independence that's a little disconcerting at times.' He thought perhaps this was just a show of independence.

It was now apparent Lange had been on board the Falkland Islands ship when she entered the Magellan Strait, but had totally vanished by the time she docked at the Chilean port of Punta Arenas. 'We received a fax report from the *Gobernador Marítimo* that his cabin had been found just as it would have been had he left it to take a stroll round the deck, but the bunk had not been slept in. His clothes were still there, his suitcase, everything, even his razor, and his passport and money had been left in a drawer. The report ended with these words: "It was as though he had just walked out and gone down the passage to the toilet." But the ship, including the toilets, everywhere, even the hold, had been thoroughly searched. No trace of him had been found.'

'So what do you think happened to him?'

He didn't answer that, and when I asked him how rough the passage down the coast had been, he said, 'It's nearly always bad in the entrance to the Magellan with the prevailing westerlies funnelling out of the Strait.'

'He could have jumped. Have you thought of that?'

He shook his head emphatically. 'He just wasn't the type. Suicide? Out of the question.' And he added, 'He had only recently finished a spell at the Halley Base. BAS thought a lot of him. I was talking to them this morning. The Antarctic meant a great deal to him.'

'You think he was pushed?'

'He looked puzzled.

'You said *meant*. You were talking about him as though he were dead.'

'No, no, I didn't mean that. I've no reason to think he's dead.' He said it slowly, working it over in his mind, toying with the idea as though such a possibility had only just occurred to him.

'If he went overboard,' I said, 'then there are only two possibilities – either he jumped or he was pushed.' An accident was something I had ruled out. The way he had walked cat-like on the balls of his feet. He was far too athletic a man to be thrown off balance by a sudden movement of the ship.

And then Stunnard surprised me by saying, 'I understand you were in Paris the day before yesterday and saw the French insurers of that Hercules you're going to try to salvage. Afterwards Mademoiselle Phuket sent her car to pick you up, so I take it you saw her.' I wondered what he was getting at. 'You do realise, don't you, that her takeover of KLME was a hostile one. Bjorn Lange's father founded that company and Bjorn himself regarded the takeover as directly responsible for his father's death. He's no reason to love her, you see.'

'Are you suggesting she is responsible for his disappearance?'

'Of course not.'

'Then what are you suggesting?' He could have shaved off his beard and gone to ground, I suppose. I was thinking of the letter he had sent me via Ward's office, trying to remember my impression of him. But it had been such a brief meeting, and in such odd circumstances, that I had difficulty in recalling even his features. What I did remember very vividly was his enthusiasm for the great white landscape in which he had worked for the better part of a year.

'You were at the Tour d'Or,' Stunnard went on. 'It's a very expensive hotel and I don't imagine you settled the bill yourself.' A pause, and then he said, 'The doorman at the Dragon Rouge opposite said you dined there with Mademoiselle Phuket.'

The door beside us swung open in a rainswept blast of cold air and an aircraftman ducked in, forcing the door shut against a violent gust. He went up to the desk and I heard my name mentioned. The sergeant looked across at me. 'Your car's here, sir.'

Stunnard was saying how greatly Bjorn Lange was regarded – 'not only by me, but all of us at Greenpeace had a high regard for him. KLME have a seismographical team working the islands. I'm sure that's where he's gone.' He wanted me to use my contacts to see if I could track him down. And he added, 'You've done at least one tour of duty there. You know the country. You must have a lot of contacts.'

'They're all Air Force contacts. I hardly got out into Camp at all.' It was always hard for people to understand how cut-off one was at the Mount Pleasant air base. The world outside, what the natives called Camp – the sharp-edged ridges, the mountains that were only just mountains, but looked big, humped up out of the bare desolation, the rock-runs, the lakes and peat bogs – it was all so totally different. In the main our only contact with the people, the Kelpies, was in the bars of places like the Upland Goose in Stanley, and Stanley was over thirty miles down a bum-breaking gravel road.

'Excuse me, sir. Would you come right away please.' It was the driver and he sounded urgent.

'Okay, I'll be right with you.' I got to my feet. 'I'll do what I can,' I told Stunnard. 'But the Falklands are as big as Wales. If he is there and for some reason he's lying low, and he has friends ...' I gave a little shrug.

Stunnard had also risen. 'KLME is operating in the north-west of West Falkland. Onshore and offshore of Pebble Island, if that's any help. And here's my card. If you do get news of him either telephone or fax me at the Greenpeace office or my home. That card gives both numbers, and as I'm sure you know, communications with the UK are excellent.' He shook me warmly by the hand, thanking me quite effusively, saying how much he appreciated my co-operation. 'We really are very concerned for Bjorn's safety. He's not only quite exceptionally dedicated, but he's also very likeable. We're all of us very worried about him – about what he might do.' The way he said that, the depth of feeling in his voice, made me understand why he had driven all the way down from London in the pouring rain on the off-chance of being able to make personal contact with me.

'I'll do what I can,' I said again. I left him then and went out with the driver to the waiting car. He held the door open for me as though I was still in the Service, and then, as I stepped in, a voice from the far corner said, 'So it really is Eddie Cruse.' A hand reached out. 'George Saddler.' He was in evening dress. 'Wattisham, remember? I'm Wing Co Eng here.'

The car started to move through the heavily-guarded entrance to the station. 'You expecting a terrorist attack?' I asked him.

'No, just routine precautions. We get quite a few targetted VIPs passing through, also the occasional odd politico who is either nursing his ego or trying to hide the fact that he's scared.'

As far as I could recall we had not seen each other since the year we had spent together at that East Anglia fighter base. He had been alerted to the fact that I was in the guard post just as he was about to leave for a civilian party. He handed me a bulky brown HMSO envelope containing the engine maintenance manual Charlie had asked for. His opposite number at RAF Lyneham had sent it over that afternoon. 'Who's your engineer on this lark?'

'Charlie Pollard.'

He nodded. 'You couldn't do better. If anybody can get you airborne, in the sort of circumstances that I hear you're going to have to contend with, he will.' I asked him how he knew what I was planning to do, and he said, 'Good God, man! I should think just about everybody from air marshal right down knows about it, and about your playing miss-the-bridge with a Herc in the Severn estuary.' He shook his head, laughing softly to himself. 'You've quite a reputation. That Pucará. I remember that. The war gone momentarily quiet and your escapade the only thing for the Press to latch on to. I thought you'd have a swollen head by now, but you still seem much the same, oblivious to the stir your peccadilloes create.'

He didn't just drop me at the terminal, but came to check that

Charlie and I had our seats allocated and would be looked after. He had a word with Air Movements, then told us we would be leaving on time after all. 'No point in transferring you to the VIP lounge here. You'll be embarking in a moment. But I'll have Mount Pleasant alerted to look after you properly. Okay?'

He left and shortly afterwards we boarded the TriStar. Ten minutes later we were airborne, the lights of the Wiltshire towns and villages vanishing abruptly as we climbed into the rain cloud. By the time we had been through the safety routine and crossed the coast Charlie was asleep. I got the bulky packet Saddler had given me down from the luggage compartment and opened it. In addition to an engine maintenance manual, the Lyneham Wing Co Eng had included *The Plain Man's Guide for Hercules Co-pilots*, and there it was again, that wretched little pale pink booklet headed *Winter Is Here*, and below a crest the words COLD WEATHER OPER-ATIONS. I opened it at random and was riveted by nice little line drawings of a snowblock and parachute shelter.

The plane droned on, my eyes closing and a picture of that Herc stashed away in its winter tomb of solid ice forming in my mind, the berg, with its flat top, the sea all black beyond its edge marking the appallingly constricted limits of the ice runway. And then I was on the flight deck, my hands on the wheel and the ice streaming white under my landing lights, the black void ahead looming and no lift to the wings. A hand touched my arm and my eyes opened to the softly-lit interior of the TriStar.

It was the warrant-officer. 'Squadron Leader Mackay's com-pliments, sir, and would you care to join him on the flight deck? He said to tell you there's something like a bridge ahead.'

'A bridge?'

'That's what he said, sir.' And he permitted himself the ghost of a grin.

'Right.' I followed him up front, past the toilets and through the door to the flight deck, everything dark, except for the luminosity of the instruments, and hanging in the sky ahead the misshapen gourd-like form of a three-quarters moon. There were stars too, and beyond the moon a huge mountain of cloud towered up from the distant horizon. It was very black, very dense, a dreadful backcloth to the lit night above.

Squadron Leader Mackay, sitting in the pilot's seat, turned his head, looking up at me with a taut little smile. 'Did Mr Morgan give you my message? That thing's going to hit us in about ten minutes' time, and when it does it's not going to be at all nice. Rather bigger than any of your bridges. Thought you'd like to see what the overspill from a Caribbean hurricane looks like before all hell breaks loose.' He turned to the warrant-officer. 'What's the state of the passengers, Mr Morgan? Are they fastened up yet? Better check, will you. Tell your people to check each belt personally.' He reached for the mike that was wired through to the fuselage broadcast speakers:

'May I have your attention for a moment please. This is Squadron Leader Mackay. I shall be flying your aircraft for as long as I think necessary. We will not be on autopilot. We have a rather unpleasant-looking storm ahead of us. It's too large for me to go round it, too high to climb over it, and I have a report from a bulk carrier steaming a little ahead of us – cloud down to the deck, visibility nil in rain and spray that's being driven horizontally by the strength of the wind. In short, we've got to go through this beast and the turbulence may be considerable. When that happens, put your head down to your knees, your hands laced across the back of your neck, and stay that way until I tell you we're through it. If you have any questions the cabin staff will be available to answer them.'

He hooked the mike back on to its bracket, glancing quickly round at me. 'What do you think, Mr Cruse?'

The cloud mass was getting near now, a hellish pile with something of the shape of a nuclear explosion, and it was no longer totally black, but shot through with great, jagged tongues of electric brilliance.

Mackay looked up at me again. 'This thing was pupped by that hurricane that's been milling around in the Caribbean for more than a week. Three days ago it was building into quite a storm. It passed just north of Bermuda, swinging eastward and moving very fast. At that point the Met boys were saying it was filling and would be no more than another Atlantic low by the time it reached the Azores. This morning they changed their tune and said it was building again.'

'What's the most recent satrep you've got?'

The last one we got was 22.36 hours, a massive cloud area extending almost a thousand miles across from the Azores as far as Gib.

It's not deep through, thank God, but I've no information about the barometric pressure we'll encounter as we go into it. There could be thermals, or we could encounter a vacuum and drop right through to sea level. What do you think, sir? Do I start climbing, or would it be better to take it at a lower altitude?' He sounded unsure of himself, his voice a little too high. I wondered if he was scared as well as nervous. The cloud mass was reaching up towards the moon now, blacker than ever at the fringes, but shot through in the centre with electricity so that it was beginning to look as though the inside was a gigantic hell's kitchen. 'You're going straight through it, are you?' I was trying to match what I was seeing with other storms I had flown through, my imagination building a picture that had me beginning to be scared myself, for it looked so much bigger than even the monsoon storms of the Indian Ocean.

He nodded, pushing his hand up through his corn-coloured mop of hair. 'We'll go straight through. No alternative now.'

'No.' It was time I left him to it. 'Good luck!' I said.

He nodded again, perfunctorily this time, his mind already bracing itself to cope with the unknown forces that were stabbing electrical charges through the bellying monster that was about to engulf us.

I went back into the subdued lighting of the 'A'-category cabin and hurried to my seat. It was at that moment Ward turned his head, looking straight at me. He was seated at the back, on the port side. He stared at me a moment, no smile of recognition, the heavy-boned features immobile, and then he had turned back and resumed his discussion with the small, dark-featured man beside him.

Why hadn't he said he would be on the plane? Why the secrecy? He could so easily have had a word with me after we had boarded. And who was the man next to him who was now arguing some point with urgent concentration? Charlie asked me about the storm, but my explanation was drowned in the thunderous roar of it, my mind wondering at the same time why Ward should have suddenly decided to go out to the Falklands. But if it had been a last-minute decision how had he got a berth? Somebody would have had to be jettisoned, and at the last minute, which meant he had a high priority.

I was still puzzling over the reason for that when we entered the mass of cloud. But we didn't just enter it, we hit it, for they weren't clouds in the normal sense. They were a solid wall of air that was so hard the whole aircraft juddered under the impact and then began to shake. Everything inside of that fuselage was shaking as though it had taken on a life of its own. And then, suddenly, the seat under me was no longer there. It just fell away from my bottom, leaving me sitting on air, my stomach, my lungs, everything trying to force a passage to freedom through my gullet.

Charlie was bent almost double, his head virtually between his knees as though he was being sick, his hands clasped to his neck. 'What are the chances, Eddie?' The question seemed to explode out of his mouth, and before I could answer we hit solid air. It was like a belly-landing on salt water, my seat slamming up into my bottom. After that the plane was like a lift going up with about 4G thrusting all the organs of my body against my pelvis and the other bones of the lower part of my trunk.

I don't know how long the up-and-down movement of this crazy lift went on. A long time it seemed. No way of counting because my mind was numbed by the shock.

Finally, when we came out of it, and the movement ceased, there was this extraordinary impression of a deathly silence. It was the abrupt switch from the shattering noise of vibration and everything loose being hurled about in a demented cacophany of sound, to this stillness, this utter silence, only the steady hum of the engines still audible to my numbed senses. Nobody moved, nobody spoke for a long time. Finally Mr Morgan sent his stewards round, first with sweets to suck, then with mugs of hot coffee.

After that I slept.

A little over four hours later we were seated at a table outside the terminal building on Ascension Island, drinking cold lager with the TriStar being refuelled and checked over only a few hundred metres away. The sun blazed down out of a blue sky, and the single mountain standing up like the boss on a shield of burnished sand in the centre of the island. It was so hot we had to cover our heads and arms to avoid skin burn. I don't know what happened to Ward. I searched all the tables and the interior of the terminal. Even the loos, but there was no sign of him. Yet, when we re-embarked, there he was in the same seat, his gold pen moving over the open page of a notebook. Presumably he had stayed on board.

We took off at 08.43 local time, the expected duration of flight to Mount Pleasant another seven and a quarter hours.

III

COW HANGAR

ONE

I had almost finished the copy of *Isvik* I had brought with me and was sitting back in my seat, staring down at the sundance pattern of the waves some thirty-seven thousand feet below me. But my brain did not record what my eyes saw. I was thinking about that ice-bound, wooden frigate, stranded barely three hundred miles from my C-130's position, wondering whether it would still be there. It was an almost unbelievable story, yet I was absolutely convinced it had happened. All those bodies battened down below decks, the dead sheep, and that half-demented Robinson Crusoe character, Eduardo Connor-Gómez, who had survived alone for two years and more, living off ship's stores and contaminated flesh. Nobody could write it the way this man Kettil had if he hadn't been there, certainly not someone writing his first novel. It had happened, and it was Ward who had found Connor-Gómez and got him out of Antarctica and back to Britain.

I glanced back again at the two men seated at the rear on the port side. Ward had been asleep when I had last looked, but he was awake again now, his head turned away from me, talking animatedly to the man with the little beard and the dark hair streaked with white. Were they planning to go back to the frigate and if so what were their feelings? Was Ward recalling how he had opened up that hold, ignoring the risk of disease?

'Excuse me, sir.' The warrant-officer was bending over me. 'Flying Officer Skelton said to tell you he's just sighted land, so if you'd care to come up for'ard ...'

'Thank you, Mr Morgan.' I had requested permission to watch our approach from the flight deck. 'What's the cloud cover situation for landing?' I nodded my head in the direction of the window. 'Something brewing out there to the west by the look of it.'

'I think it's okay, sir. Forecast is for about three-tenths cloud at touchdown, ceiling five or six thousand. That's not bad for the Falklands.'

Ward's head was still turned away from me as I rose from my seat. He was leaning forward now, staring intently out of the window, his face set, as though the thoughts passing through his mind called for total concentration. He and *Isvik's* sailing master, Peter Kettil, had trekked more than a hundred miles across the pack from the point where their ship had finally been halted by the ice. They had been following the trail of two Argentine members of the crew. Both those men had died, one of bullet wounds on the ice, the other shot in that ghastly graveyard of a hold.

None of my business, but I did wonder who his companion was as I pushed my way between the toilet and the galley to find Squadron Leader Mackay standing beside his navigator, looking down over his shoulder at the Series 1501 Air Sheet I knew so well. He looked up at me quickly, a brief smile, and then: 'See what you think, sir. Is that Mount Kent just coming up over the horizon, or are we looking at the nearer height of Salvador Hill?'

Peering ahead through the windshield it was difficult to tell, little patches of sun-whitened cloud drifting across and the shadows they threw on the corrugated surface of the sea looking like rocky outriders. Then suddenly there was the glint of sun on water just to starb'd of our course, smudges of grey showing at the edges, and beyond, straight over the nose, a distant pointer of land. 'Looks like you're coming in over Standing Man Hill,' I said. 'And that's definitely Mount Kent –'

'Right on course!' Mackay's voice sounded jubilant. I thought he was still elated by his success in coming through that storm front in the North Atlantic without any visible damage. It was the first opportunity I had had to compliment him. 'We were lucky,' he murmured, a flush of pleasure on his face. 'Mount Kent!' He clapped his navigator on the shoulder. 'Good show, Philip! Bang on target.' And then he explained to me that they had been carrying out a navigational aid breakdown exercise. 'We've been flying DR and sextant ever since leaving Ascension.'

'I didn't know that.' No wonder he was flushed with excitement at the landfall.

He went back to his seat then and took over, while I stood behind the co-pilot watching the well-known features becoming more distinct as we slipped quietly down towards our base. The land we had first sighted was the ragged peninsula separating the two great inlets of Port Salvador and Berkeley Sound. Soon we were flying almost over it, the narrow Green Patch isthmus that connected it with the main body of East Falkland laid out before us like a topographical map. We flew right over Mount Kent with a magnificent panorama of rock-runs and ridges spilling down from the mountainous range of jagged rock that forms the backbone of East Falkland. And on the southern side, the heights that had featured so much in the newscasts of June '82 slid away to port – Two Sisters, Mount Longdon, Sapper Hill, and further south still, Fitzroy and Bluff Cove.

We were quite low as we swung in over Cape Pembroke lighthouse, the brick cathedral, Government House, the wharf and the old three-masted hulk of the *Lady Elizabeth* lying to its moorings at the far end of the inlet, all the familiar details of Port Stanley picked out in a shaft of sunlight away to our left. But no sign of *Isvik*, the little schooner with its squares'l-rigged foremast that Peter Kettil had described in such loving detail. She wasn't lying alongside the wharf or anchored off, nor could I see her in Fort William or up the Murrell River.

The sunlight was suddenly snuffed out by the black bulk of cu-nim piled above us. A flurry of sleet hit the windshield, great splodges of wet snow clinging to the glass, visibility momentarily cut to nil. Then it cleared, and ahead of us the TriStar hangar poked its box-like structure above the top of the quarried hill where the eastern Rapier battery was sited. Moments later the runway appeared as a great slash of wet tarmac across the flat, stony upland that some wag of a long-dead Kelpie had named Mount Pleasant. My eyes went automatically to the Met Office. As usual, there were two of them sitting at readiness on the nearby pad, big, lumbering creatures, their bellies so low-slung they looked like a couple of fat sows about to farrow instead of the finest transport aircraft since the old Dakota.

The TriStar hangar is the only blatantly conspicuous building in the whole military complex. The terminal, mess and NAAFI centre, all the quarters, everything else, is crouched low into the shallow folds of the plateau. Whether or not that monstrous hangar is really primed with explosives I have never discovered, but there is no doubt that, in the event of a resumption of hostilities, the first job the sappers would have to do would be to blow the thing up.

By the time we had taxied to our disembarkation point, the rain had stopped and there was a gleam of watery sunlight. Somebody's hat went whirling across the apron. 'Hold on to your skirts, boys.' The navigator grinned cheerfully. 'Wind speed thirty-two knots outside.'

'Par for the course,' Skelton muttered. 'Wind and sheep. That about sums it up.'

'There's some squid too.'

'And krill.'

'Albatross,' somebody added.

They were all unwinding after the long flight. I went back to my seat, and as soon as the door was open, we began gathering up our hand luggage. A blast of cold air engulfed me as I stood by the exit waiting for Ward. The slight, dark-featured man was close behind him. 'Ah came over to have a word wi' ye,' Ward said, 'but ye were fast asleep. Ye'd been reading *Isvik*. Barbara said she'd told ye to read it. Fiction,' he added. 'Not all of it. The names are real enough an' the trek across the pack-ice Pete and I made.'

He didn't seem in the least concerned that I had been seeing his wife. What did seem to worry him was that I might take Peter Kettil's book literally. 'Fiction,' he said again. 'But the ship, that damned frigate, that's real enough. Ah tell ye that because ye'll see her fur yersel', if things go according to plan.'

'Why didn't you tell me we were booked out on the same flight?' I asked him.

'Because Ah didna' know. That's why.'

'You mean your secretary didn't tell you?'

He hesitated, his face reddening, his cold, grey eyes full of sudden anger. 'Aye,' he admitted. 'Ah mean just that. There are moments when that stupid little bitch displays the oddest sense of humour. But at least it saves me hunting round for ye.' He pulled a slip of paper out of the zip pocket of his anorak. 'There's the number of the laddie in Goose Green. He'll know where to find me. But don't contact me unless you have to. Ah'll contact ye. Okay?'

I nodded, my eyes fixed curiously on his companion. He was younger than I had thought. It was the black hair thinning on the top and the little beard prematurely shot through with white that aged him. Also, the dark features were drawn and lined, and the brown eyes had something of a haunted look, constantly shifting their gaze. There was a long silence, then, almost reluctantly it seemed, Ward said the man's name. 'Ferdinand Barratt. He'll be sailin' to the Weddell Sea wi' ye.'

We were moving forward now, out on to the mobile platform, where we met the full force of the wind, and the warrant-officer told Ward there was a message for him. 'The Station Commander will give it to you.' He held up the queue of passengers, letting Ward and Barratt go ahead. 'He's waiting for you at the bottom of the steps.'

As a result, it wasn't Sid, but the Wing Co Flying, who greeted Charlie and myself and took us to the VIP room for coffee and sandwiches while our papers were dealt with. No sign of Ward, or his friend. I don't know why, but I was suddenly thinking of Eduardo Connor-Gómez, who had been one of the Argentine 'Disappeareds', and whose sister, Iris, ran the boat that would take me down to the southern limits of the Weddell Sea, to the Ronne Ice Shelf, and my appointment with that abandoned Herc. But Connor-Gómez was dead. Cremated, according to the *Express* account.

My mind went back to *Isvik*, impatient now to get on board, see what the vessel was like, get to know the people who would be sailing with me. But the Wing Commander confirmed that she was not in Port Stanley, nor was she in East Cove, at Mare Harbour, which was the port nearest the air base through which all the MoD supplies and equipment came. He had been in Stanley two days ago, down on the jetty talking to the Harbour Master. He could not tell me where the ship was, only that she had sailed the day after Iris Sunderby had come in on the boat from Punta Arenas. 'She sailed with just the two of them on board, Mrs Sunderby and Peter Kettil. Their engineer, Nils Solberg, is lodging somewhere in Stanley. He's Norwegian, but speaks passable English. Doubtless he'll be able to tell you where *Isvik* is.'

I had just been handed a cup of coffee when Sid Mackenzie came bustling in, still in his flying suit and the same as always, a short, compact dynamo of a man with a tousled mop of ginger hair and a little brushed-up ginger moustache, his cap at a rakish angle and those prominent blue eyes casing the room as though in that quick glance he could command everybody's attention. And it worked.

125

The old magic was still there. He not only had that ability to make an entrance, but in greeting people, he could kid them they were the ones above all others he wanted to talk to. 'My God, it's good to see you, Ed. No temptations here, eh? Ha-ha!' That same guffaw of a laugh, the head thrown back and the eyes sparkling with vitality.

'Coffee or tea, sir?'

He checked at the mess steward's query. 'Tea, I think. Yes, tea. Talking to our would-be political overlord – thirsty work, eh?'

We shook hands briefly and I introduced Charlie to him. 'What did you mean, no temptations here?' I asked him.

'No bridges in the Falklands. At least, none you can fly under.' The eyes were full of fun as he put his head back again and laughed.

He would have put me up at his house, but they had had a pompous bore of a visiting politician wished on them. 'Wendy is furious. She refers to you as Eddie the Bridge Basher and it seems she'd prefer your company at breakfast to the Right Honourable Member for the Opposition, who is clearly out to close us down. A pack of school kids playing with expensive and dangerous toys, that's his line, and they're threatening to make him Minister of Defence, if and when they're in power again.'

Sid had been one of my squadron at Wattisham. That was shortly after the Falklands War and I had just been reprieved following my low-level misdemeanours along the Thames. I hadn't actually buzzed the Palace of Westminster, but there had been some sort of a function going on on the Members' Terrace with a whole pack of MPs and Lords gathered there. That was what had really given me the idea, and I had certainly shaken their glasses for them as I roared past at about fifty feet above the deck and literally only a biscuit-toss away. We had been flying Phantoms then and Sid had followed me down, and on along the Embankment to halt the traffic at Tower Bridge.

It was schoolboy stuff, but we had made our point. We had reminded them about air power when their minds were being brain-washed by the Navy, who were in there, batting for a larger slice of the Defence Budget, and claiming they needed more ships, a new carrier, better torpedoes and an expansion of the Fleet Air Arm to provide cover for the next Task Force, if it was to be capable of fighting what could well be a much more powerful adversary.

Sid had learned his lesson. He had never tangled with the Establishment again. So here he was, newly promoted Group Captain, commanding not only our most southerly air base, but playing landlord to both the Army and the Navy, so that, in effect, he was military supremo. And I was out of the Service.

I should have envied him. But somehow I didn't. The politician he had been landed with was a reminder of how quickly flying gives way to administration as you go up the ladder. It might be a lot safer, but out here in the Falklands I was sniffing the rarer air of excitement and danger. No, I didn't envy him. A few more years and he would be grounded, flying a desk at the MoD, and later he would be out of the Service with a pension and a small financial pat on the back. Or he might be dead, shot down peace-keeping for an Eastern State about which he knew nothing and couldn't care less. Whereas I was free to choose. I could accept a risk, or I could shrug my shoulders and walk away from it.

Nobody any more could order me to do anything.

'Well now, what's the game?' Sid asked me as he finished his tea and called for a refill. 'You're not posted here. Not this time. You're here of your own free will. Why?' And then, as I opened my mouth to explain, he held up his hand. 'No, don't tell me now. I can see by your face it's a long story. And anyway, word is that you're after that Herc that's gone adrift on an island of ice calved off from the Ronne Shelf. Working for that mining company, are you? What's the name, K-L-something?'

'KLME,' I said, and he nodded. 'But I'm not working for them,' I told him. 'I'm working for myself. You see, I own it.'

'You own it? Own what?' He stared at me. 'What do you own?'

And when I told him, he said, 'I don't believe it. You really own the thing?'

I assured him I did, and he said, 'How? How can you possibly –' He glanced at his watch and downed the second cup of tea in one long gulp. 'Got to go now. You can tell me the whole improbable tale as we rattle our way down the M1 to Stanley.' He brushed the wetness from his moustache and started for the door. 'You're booked in at the Upland Goose, both of you,' he said over his shoulder.

Somebody called my name from the doorway. They had got our baggage out of the TriStar.

'That the lot?' Sid paused, standing over it and eyeing the pile as though he would like to retract his offer of a lift.

Seeing our gear, all in one heap for the first time, there did seem rather a lot of it. I began to explain it included our sailing gear and cold-weather clothing, but he cut me short. 'We'll squeeze it all in somehow.' He clapped me on the shoulder, saying he'd be back in ten minutes. 'Got to change and tell Wendy where I'll be. That damn politician! She'll have to cope on her own, and she isn't going to like it.' And with a grin he was gone.

Looking round the room, I could see no sign of Ward or his companion. The steward knew nothing about him, nor did the warrant-officer, who suggested that perhaps he didn't rate VIP treatment. 'It's only for senior officers, important people, or guests of the Station Commander like yourself.' He offered to check with the warrant-officer in charge of the main arrivals hall. He came back a few minutes later. 'Mr Ward and his friend left a few minutes ago in an old Land Rover.' And he added, barely able to conceal his curiosity, 'Their baggage was almost the first off the aircraft and one of the Air Movements officers looked to their clearance ahead of everybody.'

One of the Secretariat had been among the passengers, a man named Simmonds. I had met him at one or two parties while I had been posted here. That was just after the Mount Pleasant base had been completed. I thought of asking him whether anything was known about Ward at Government House, but he had been button-holed by a woman journalist, who had also been on the flight. She looked to be in her late thirties, a long, dark face with rabbit teeth that had been badly capped and were so jagged they might have been used exclusively for cracking nuts. She wore civilian khaki with the two top buttons of her shirt undone so that the swell of her rather ample breasts was provocatively exposed.

Jack Simmonds introduced me to her as soon as I went across to have a word with him, then he drifted smartly away, calling over his shoulder, 'Sorry. There's a bit of a flap on. Anything I can do to help ...' A brief wave of the hand and he was hurrying out to a car that had just pulled up by the Argie gun mounted on the apron, presumably as a cut-them-down-to-size gesture for the benefit of any visitor from that country.

Cynthia Snedden was one of those very determined newspaper women, no beating about the bush, one question after another, and straight to the point. Why was I here? What company did I represent? Who had sent me? And when I said I was just a simple tourist doing the Falklands, she looked at me with her head on one side and a knowing little rabbit-toothed smile. And then she laughed and I was looking right down her throat to the uvula waving up and down at the back and all her dentures exposed. 'How come you greet the Station Commander as an old friend? Anybody would think ...' She stopped there, a thought dawning and her eyes suddenly filled with suppressed excitement. 'Cruse. Edwin Cruse!' She put her arms across her breasts, hugging herself. 'Now I've got it. The dashing Eddie who eats bridges for breakfast and stirs up politicians with sonic bangs. What the hell are you doing down here?'

'A holiday,' I said. 'I'm out of the Service now and having a well-earned break.' I cast my eye round the room, looking for someone I could pass her on to.

'You're staying at the Upland Goose, I take it?'

I nodded, without thinking. But of course she was staying there too. Would I have dinner with her?

Thank God, Sid returned at that moment. 'Sorry, but you know how it is. The after-flight clings. Flying suits,' he explained to Cynthia Snedden, 'are self-heating.' He grinned at her, and then to my relief he said, 'Okay, let's go. They're loading the gear now.'

It had taken him just over a quarter of an hour to alert his wife to the conference down at Government House, have a shower, change and get back here ready for a full evening's work. That's how it is in the Service, suddenly the heat's on and everything goes at double the speed of sound, showering and changing down to a fine art, like scribbling your name on a flight form.

Snedden pounced on him immediately. She had seen our baggage being loaded into his car. 'Can you squeeze me in? Some questions –'

But he shook his sleeked-down head, telling her quite blatantly that she was in the Falklands to write a piece on Service personnel and all information would be channelled through Fred Morse, the civilian PR man, who already had her transport to Port Stanley organised. 'You stick with Freddie.'

'That's just for my local paper,' she said. 'I'm also a stringer for Reuters and for one of the weeklies –'

'Not my department.' Sid tore his eyes away from the gaping

shirt front. 'You talk to Freddie.' His voice was abruptly official. 'He'll look after you. That's his job.' And he turned away. 'Sorry. But I'm in a hurry.' She wanted to know why of course. 'Governor's Conference,' he told her tersely.

'What's it about?' And she was now almost trotting to keep up with him as he made for the car.

He turned on her then. 'This is an MoD station, Miss Snedden. Just do what you're told and you'll get our co-operation. Otherwise ...'

'You're threatening me.'

'I have full authority over everybody on this base. Go through the proper channels – in your case Fred Morse – or I'll put you on the next TriStar flight home. Understood?'

She stood there, speechless, watching as he crossed the apron, her breasts heaving as though she had been running and a cold fury in her dark eyes.

'You've made an enemy of that little woman,' I told him as we settled into the seats and drove off.

'So what? They come out here, start trying to stir things up ...'

'She was only doing her job.'

'We have a perfectly good civilian public relations chappie to answer her sort of questions. I've enough on my plate without being badgered by half-exposed female journalists.'

'Okay,' I said. 'But I'm just as curious. What is this conference about? It's past five, your time. What's the hurry? Why doesn't he call it for tomorrow morning?'

That started him off. 'Exactly what I told Jack Simmonds. But somebody's radioed in from Goose Green to say he saw a man put ashore from a rubber dinghy just before first light this morning. This was over in Low Bay, Adventure Sound, the east side of it. The dinghy then made off towards one of those foreign fishing vessels, which he could dimly see, anchored across the Sound by Mutiny Point at the entrance to Barrow Harbour. He thought the Governor should know, so all hell breaks loose. I have to fly off the Sea King which is on stand-by for SAR, to fly a search pattern over the area while I spend a bone-shaking two hours driving to Stanley and back for a meeting at Government House called to consider ways of tightening up on the Conservation Zone.'

'Is that what used to be called FIX – the Falkland Islands Exclusion Zone?'

He nodded. 'C-Biffy's house first,' he told the driver. 'Then Stanley.' He reached for his car mike and cleared with the control tower to use the short north-east/south-west runway.

Petrel Crescent, Krill Lane, Sheerwater Lane, Sandling Road and Griffin Road, the old familiar road markers flashed by, and then we were crossing the main runway, which faces into the prevailing westerlies and at the 6,000 marker seems to touch the horizon so that it is almost like an aircraft-carrier. Flying a Phantom you take off on the hump.

C-Biffy's house stands on a rise slightly removed from the rest of the senior officers' married quarters. The three Services take it in turns to supply the Commander British Forces Falkland Islands. Currently it was an admiral. Sid had already had a brief word with him on his way back to pick us up and was gone only a moment. By chance the Navy had their destroyer patrolling off the south of West Falkland Island, covering with their radar for the big installation on Mount Alice, which was temporarily out of action for servicing and repairs. The admiral had already ordered it to proceed at speed to a point south of the entrance to Adventure Sound. 'They won't find the ship, of course,' Sid said as he flung himself back into the seat beside the driver and we drove to the perimeter road. 'Not a hope. It will be clear of the Zone before they get there. My Sea King is the only chance, but it's a big area to search and the weather is deteriorating. Forecast is ten-tenths cloud at two thousand by nine or ten this evening.'

The massive build-up over Tierra del Fuego I had seen from the TriStar was now closing in on us, the cloud already thick and the light fading. We had barely reached the end of the paved roadway before sleet was driving almost horizontally past us. It turned to hail as we reached Macphee Pond, which is quite a large lake with the highway cutting across the middle of it. Ice pellets big as sugar cubes were flung past us on the wind, drowning the rattle of stones on the mudguards, our speed cut to a bare 20 m.p.h.

There were none of those mysterious rock-runs here, of course, but the road was built up like an embankment, with almost sheer stone drops either side. Sid was in full spate about the size of the station he had to run, the complications of dealing with all three

Services with a South American time bomb ticking away hardly more than three hundred miles across the Roaring Forties to the west. We passed the spot where Alastair Cameron met his death, pressing his luck and driving too fast to attend just such a hastily-called meeting at Government House. 'Did you ever meet him?'

'Once,' I said.

'They say he would have been the first Falkland Islander to be appointed Governor if he'd lived.'

'So I heard.'

The hail stopped abruptly. The wind dropped and I listened to Sid going on about the C-Biffy appointment being a two-rank promotion for the other Services, but only one rank up for the RAF. 'Fact is, I've got almost as much responsibility and I have to fly the bloody aircraft as well, and a fine gloat the youngsters have if they can pinpoint me in their target camera lense. Now this crops up. I can guess what the Governor wants. So could C-Biffy. Patrols. More patrols. Sometimes he doesn't seem able to get it into his head that fuel, spares, everything has to be brought in across eight thousand miles of ocean. Poor bugger's overstretched, of course. Physically, I mean. This appointment used to be the end of the road for the FO, the place where a worn-out old bureaucrat could put his feet up and relax. Not any more. Now he finds himself in the hot seat with more despatches to read and decisions to make than most senior ambassadors working with the benefit of a large staff. He's got the FO breathing down his neck by satellite, and the Argies and the Kelpies don't help, both sides still beating their chests.' That laugh again. 'No, not quite that, but it isn't exactly cushy for a Governor down here now. Or for me either.'

Rock-runs were now either side of the road, grey rivulets of stone. 'How do you think you're going to get it airborne?' He had turned his head, leaning on the back of his seat and looking at me curiously. 'Not relying on me, I hope.'

The switch in his line of thought was so sudden that for a moment I did not realise what he was talking about. 'That Herc,' he said. 'Down the bottom end of the Weddell. I've seen a satpic. You don't surely expect to fly it off?'

And when I told him that was exactly what I intended to do, he wanted to know how I planned to do it, every detail. I told him I didn't know. That I'd work it all out when I had seen what the situation was on the spot.

'How are you going to get there?'

'Boat.' And I explained about *Isvik*.

He laughed. He had been on board the vessel. 'Jesus Christ! Even if it gets you there, it's not big enough to lift in fuel and spares, and I reckon you'll need both.'

It took me some time to convince him that there was even a fifty-fifty chance that the operation was viable. Running over all the problems, answering his questions, was a useful exercise, reminding me of all the things that had to be dealt with before it came to the moment when the four turbo-props were building up to maximum revs and I coarsened the pitch and slammed the brakes off.

'You're mad.' He had taken off his cap and that untidy mop of ginger hair was waving in the breeze from his partly-open window as he shook his head at me. 'You'll never do it, Ed. Once you let go the brakes there'll be no turning back. When you fly that big beast off the end of your tiny little runway, the nose will dip, you'll have no lift. If it's water you hit then it'll be so bloody cold you'll only have a few minutes. And if it's ice . . .' He left it at that.

He didn't believe me at first when I told him what the minimum take-off distance was. And even when I had finally satisfied him that a stripped-out Herc needed only 500 feet of runway, all he said was, 'In theory, Ed. In theory.' He had always called me Ed, or Edwin, never Eddie. I think out of respect for the fact that on the occasions we had served together he had always been one step below me in rank. 'Pity I can't fly a Chinook down to you, give you a lift-off, the way I heard you got that Harrier of yours airborne. Or is that just part of the hype your name seems to attract?'

I thought if I didn't answer him he'd let it go at that, but he persisted. 'You'd had a dog-fight with a Learjet, hadn't you? You were low on fuel. Then this God-given Pucará turns up, abandoned on the ground, and you set yourself down beside it in the hopes of topping up your fuel tank. Then suddenly you change your mind, swop planes and go off joy-riding in a two-seater twin turbo-prop. To cap it all you end your little spree shooting up a couple of Aermacchis. Right?'

I didn't say anything.

'I was at Wattisham then,' he went on, 'getting myself accustomed to Phantoms. I remember reading about it in the mess. *Father and Son Both Heroes.* That was one headline that sticks in my mind.'

'The tabloids got hold of it,' I muttered defensively. Odd, but I still felt embarrassment at the way they had embellished a rather stupid episode done on the spur of the moment. 'It was just after the *Atlantic Conveyor* was hit and all 5 Brigade's helicopters went up in flames.' God! I could remember it so clearly. That was when the Guards and all the rest of them began walking. They should have been lifted up to the battle zone in a quick, violent assault. Instead, they had to march seventy deadly miles, yomping all their equipment and ammo. It was in this desperate period, when the whole attempt to win back the Falklands was in the balance, that I had flown that Pucará and seen off a couple of Aermacchis.

I started to explain this to Sid. Of course, the tabloids had grabbed at the story. They were desperate for something to point the way towards victory.

'So that much was true then. But what about the rest of it?' he asked. And he added, 'They still talk about it out in Camp, particularly up by Green Patch.'

'The Kelpies?'

'Aye. There are still the burnt-out remains of the Pucará you crash-landed on the way back. I've flown over the charred skeleton of it myself.'

'So what do the Kelpies say?'

'That you whistled up a Chinook loaded with fuel, topped up, and then, failing to get vertical lift-off, you borrowed a long mooring line from a Kelpie fisherman, slipped it round the Harrier's fuselage and had the Chinook lift you off.'

'Good God!' I said. 'Was that in the Press?'

'Something like it, I believe.'

I hadn't seen it. No wonder the AOC had called the whole thing downright bloody stupid and had started to read me a lecture on the value of aerial hardware down in the South Atlantic.

'True or false?' Sid asked.

I laughed. It was so nearly true. 'I didn't whistle the Chinook up, as you put it,' I replied. 'The thing was suddenly there, right over my head, flattening the grass and making a hell of a din.' The whole episode had been very dicey and I didn't want to talk about it, never had talked about it. 'The silliest piece of flying I ever did and that bloody great Chinook hanging over my head ...'

I told him then what had really happened, how it had been flying fuel up to helicopters operating in close support of 5 Brigade's spearhead attack on the Stanley defences, how it had passed right over me and I had flagged it down. 'The pilot had the sense to realise that topping up a Harrier's fuel supply was of paramount importance, so I'm afraid a heli up for'ard went light of fuel and I made it back to the carrier.'

Charlie had heard it all before and his mind was still concentrated on minimum take-off limits for a Herc in ice conditions. 'When you've quite finished seeking the CO's admiration for a suicidal piece of showmanship, perhaps we could get back to the problems of the moment.' He wanted to know what I would do if the brakes failed to hold as I revved up for take-off. 'What experience have you had of contaminated surfaces?'

'Canada,' I told him. 'I've flown a C-130 in near-blizzard conditions up in the Yukon.'

'Okay then, so you know the drill.' And he went on to remind me that surface conditions of impacted wet or dry snow, ice, water or slush, all imposed limitations, and that take-off was to be abandoned if there was either a tail or cross-wind in excess of 10 knots, or if contamination exceeded 3mm, in dry snow 10mm.

Sid nodded. But I don't think he had taken it in. This was the sort of detail he left to others. He was a flyer, not a flight-deck bureaucrat. I could almost hear him saying in that funny, clipped voice of his, 'You fly by the seat of your pants, boy, not by the rule book.' But if he had stuck to those early principles, he would never have made the rank he held now. No doubt he had learned from what had happened to me after the Tower Bridge incident.

The sky cleared as we swung north over Fitzroy Ridge, then east by Bluff Cove with a whole series of rock-runs coming down like dark rivulets from the southern flanks of Smoke Mountain, Mount Challenger, Two Sisters and Longdon.

Over several miles I fired questions at him, trying to discover what it was all about. But he didn't seem to know. Government House had been unable to give him any more information than just the bare fact that a semi-rigid inflatable had been sighted beaching in Low Bay. There had been two men in it. One had been seen to land, a pack on his back, and had started walking. As it was barely four miles to Walker Creek across the long neck of land separating Choiseul and Adventure Sounds, enquiries were being made at the settlement to see if any dinghy or small boat had been taken.

The inflatable that had landed him had been seen to disappear in a flurry of rain, heading south-west, back across Adventure Sound. Government had had no information about why the man had been landed, his nationality, or the nationality of the vessel that had anchored briefly in Barrow Harbour on the west shore of the Sound.

I was thinking, of course, that it could be Bjorn Lange who had been put ashore. But then what was the point of his landing surreptitiously? As a Greenpeace representative he could have come into the Falklands quite openly. I suggested that Sid contact Government House on the car radio, but he assured me his Sea King pilot would report to him the moment he sighted anything.

The flight, the change of air, the sense of being on the threshold of something I might not be able to handle ... I half-shut my eyes, feeling suddenly tired. Charlie was talking again, fishing for the Station Commander's authority to quote him if at any time he was in desperate need. 'Nothing big, sir. Just the odd spare. Down here even a little thing, the want of the right washer, something like that, can stop you in your tracks. Don't want to have to tell Eddie here he's got to abort the operation just for want of a washer, if you follow me, sir.'

He still clung to his Service habits, but perhaps the 'sir' helped, for Sid didn't refuse outright. Instead, he turned to me. 'Up to you, Ed. You had close on two years with the C-130s at Lyneham and elsewhere. You're bound to know some of the boys in our squadron.'

'I may, or I may not,' I murmured. 'They change so often. Every four months, isn't it?'

He nodded, turning back to Charlie. 'Okay. If Ed can't wheedle what you want out of them, you can say you've talked to me and they're to give you what help they can. But you'll have to pay. Everything, down to the last lousy nut and bolt, is accountable.' He turned back to me. 'I think I'd better tell you this right now, whatever sort of a mess you get yourself into, I'm not authorising a C-130 flight down to the Ronne.'

'Why not? You've got two tankers here. Either of them could make it there and back, no trouble.'

'I suppose.' He nodded reluctantly. 'But that's not something I could do off my own bat. I'd have to have MoD clearance, and by the time they understood what it was all about, you'd probably be dead. Just think of the faxes, the phone calls – my God! I sometimes think it would be worth laying a cable between here and Whitehall just to cope with all the things that require their clearance. And a lot of it has a political element, so we send in code. It all takes time.'

Another squall overtook us, a wild flurry of rain and wind that stopped as suddenly as it had started, and there, as we topped Sapper Hill, was Stanley itself, the dumpy spire of the cathedral standing very stark against the leaden waters of the harbour. The new hospital stood bright blue and conspicuous away to our right as we came down on to the waterfront, but the Upland Goose was still the old original building, a low, rambling place almost opposite the dock-yard and wharf. And inside there was the same smell of stale beer and cooking, the hard-used furniture and fittings reminding me once again of the frontier-type hotels you still find in the Canadian outback.

Sid dropped us there with our baggage and drove straight on to Government House. It was the last I was to see of him for quite some time. The room they had booked for me was at the back of the hotel with a view, if you could call it that, of clapboard, box-like houses, and across their roofs to the hospital and the prefab litter of the military HQ establishment called The Lookout. This was the most likely source of information, for the officers' mess was the focal point for the doctors and nurses from the hospital and they would be the best source of local gossip. There was also a military PR major and an officer in charge of bomb-disposal, but he might have been posted home now. When I had last been here the auth-orities had virtually abandoned any hope of clearing the Argentine minefields around Stanley and up by the old airport. There were too many of them, and even when they had been marked, the mines shifted in the peat, and if they surfaced the sun soon bleached the paint so that they looked like small, round boulders just lipping the dark soil.

There is a four-hour time difference between London and Stanley and I had already put my watch back during the stopover at Ascen-sion. It was still only just after five. I had a quick wash and hurried out, across the road to the wharf and the Harbour Master's office, but they couldn't tell me where *Isvik* had gone, nor could any of those I spoke to on the quay. An old man walking his dog, a Welsh-type collie, said *Isvik* had left the day before yesterday. In a hurry, he thought, as there were just the two of them on board, a man and a woman. 'Engineer'll tell 'ee 'spect.' A short, broad hunk of a man was the way he described him, and he told me I would probably find him in the bar of the Goose some time during the evening.

There was nobody answering to that description anywhere in the public rooms when I returned there. The man who ran the bar said *Isvik*'s engineer was back and would likely come in fairly late in the evening, around half-eight or nine. Yes, he was Norwegian, name of Solberg. Nils Solberg. So he was the same man Kettil had referred to in his book.

I had a bath, changed and went down to the bar. Charlie had gone off to have a look round the town. Also he wanted to send some letters. He had a list of almost a dozen people who wanted first-day covers for the latest issue of stamps. 'Sailing ships, you see. Everybody seems nuts about sailing ships. Don't get it myself.' Charlie was interested in nothing much but aero engines, the bigger and more complicated the better, that's what made him so good at his job.

I got myself a jar of the local brew and took it to a vacant chair. There were four men standing at the bar. None of them answered to the description I had been given of *Isvik*'s engineer. An Australian family were sitting by the window, two grown-up daughters, one with her boyfriend, their accents strong, their laughter loud. The men at the bar were talking about wool shipments and the price a bale of fleeces would fetch in Bradford.

I was tired and hungry. At home it would be getting dark now, but here they were moving towards the longest day and a rift in the cloud cover showed the sun still riding high. I wondered what was for dinner. Mutton or goose probably. Never anything else, except if it was out of a tin. The woman from reception came in, looked around, then walked across to me. 'For you,' she said and handed me a folded slip of paper torn from a notebook with my name on it and marked *Urgent*. The fold was held together by a piece of stamp paper. I broke it open to find the message consisted of a single line: *22.00 by the war memorial – please*. There was no address and in lieu of signature he had simply written – *Hyde Park car park*.

Bjorn Lange! I left my beer and went in search of the woman who had brought it to me. But she could tell me nothing. She had been talking to the cook and when she came back the note was lying there. I returned to my beer, wondering what he wanted. And when I had finished it I went in to dinner, which was the same sort of meal I remembered from previous visits to the Goose. I had asked the barman to let me know if the *Isvik* engineer turned up and I had just finished my main course when the waitress told me he had arrived.

Nils Solberg was standing with a small glass of clear liquid in his hand, smiling broadly at the group that had been holding up the bar when I had gone in to dinner. They had been joined by a man looking very neat in black, well-creased trousers and a spotless white shirt. He had a little brushed-up moustache, pale hair, and sideburns that curved halfway down his freckled cheeks. I remembered that face, a South African who flew for FIGAS, the Falkland Islands Government Air Service. He was showing the others a piece of paper and they were all laughing, their faces shining with the beer they had drunk. 'A rose by any other name ...' one of them said and there was another burst of ribald laughter. Asked about the destination, I thought I heard the pilot mention Port Howard, but by then the engineer was holding out his hand. '*Ja*. Nils Solberg. That is me.' The hand that gripped mine was big, creases and nails begrimed with long years of diesel and engine oil. 'They tell me you vill join us for the voyage south, you and an engineer, not marine, air engines.' He wore a grey polo-neck sweater, his head round like a cannon ball and one of the nicest smiles I have ever seen on a man with such a time-worn, craggy face. 'They go two days back. I am away fishing, so I get their message only today when I am at the harbour office.'

I ordered myself a whisky, and when I asked him if I could buy him another, he said, '*Ja. Tak.*' He put his head back and poured the contents of his glass down his throat. 'Vodka plees. They don't have Akavit.'

He showed me the note they had left him. It simply said they had been offered a short-term charter and were leaving at once for Port Howard. I knew Port Howard. It was in West Falkland, one of the largest sheep stations in the Islands with tourist facilities and its own grass airstrip. 'Ah t'ink they like to be alone some time.' His little blue eyes twinkled at me as he said it, adding that he was booked out on the first FIGAS flight in the morning.

He told me quite a lot about the charter work they had managed to secure in the two years since that extraordinary expedition to the southernmost limits of the Weddell Sea. Peter Kettil he described as a good sailing man, good navigator, too, but engines ... He shook his head. 'Ve haf big diesel, pumps, vinches, outboards and there is a skidoo.' He was one of these men who, given an engine to look after, will treat it as though it were his own child. You meet them in RAF workshops and maintenance hangars, and when you do, you thank your lucky stars, and reckon you'll live a little longer.

He thought a lot of Iris Sunderby. He pronounced her name Eeris, saying she was a good businesswoman, a good ship's house-keeper and also a very charming young woman who always seemed able to get what she wanted from the ships and dockyard officials in Punta Arenas or Montevideo on the occasions when they had sailed across the three hundred miles of stormy waters to the mainland of South America. 'A very strong girl, strong stomach, and almost as good a sea cook as me – she can even make good omelette with eggs of upland geese!' She was part-Irish, part-Portuguese with a temperament that was very '*flytig*'. And when I asked him what that meant, he frowned and shook his head, smiling gently to himself.

He knocked back the rest of his vodka, still smiling as though at past recollections. 'Like a volcano,' he said and insisted on buying me another drink.

There was a sudden flurry of activity along the bar. The FIGAS pilot was leaving, the group breaking up. I remembered his name now, Johnnie Van Loeden. He passed quite close to us, but either he didn't see me or else he failed to recognise me, and I didn't say anything. I wasn't in the mood to make conversation with a man I knew only slightly. I was tired and it was almost ten o'clock. My meeting with Bjorn Lange seemed more important.

Before leaving the warmth of the bar, I asked Nils Solberg what the short-term charter was that had been booked for *Isvik*. But he knew only what the note had said. 'Ah don'know 'ow long is for, vhere they go or who order it. But Port Howard is on the vest side of the Sound, so per'aps is somewhere in Vest Falkland we are to go. They vill let me know ven I am to join them.'

Outside it was very dark, a fine drizzle falling that was more like a very thick, very wet blanket of mist. There are three war memorials in Stanley. The ordinary one is down by the shore below the water-front and is seldom visited; then there is the Battle Memorial, which is topped by the model of a Navy ship under full sail and commemorates the defeat of the German squadron in December 1914, offsetting our defeat at Coronel off the Chilean coast; finally, there is a larger one to the Task Force in the war of '82 with the names of all the units and all the ships in a sweeping half-curve of marble with plaques to each of the three Services. This is only a couple of blocks away from the Goose and it was here that a shadowy figure stood waiting. He had no beard now and his hair was no longer blond, but I recognised him by his walk as he came to meet me.

'You've changed your appearance,' I said. 'Have you changed your name too?'

He checked, his hand half-held out in greeting. Clearly he did not know how to answer me and he just stood there.

'Are you still Bjorn Lange or not?'

'How do you know what my name is? I never tell you.'

'Your boss at Greenpeace. Arthur Stunnard. He came to see me at Brize Norton just before we took off.'

'Why?'

'Look,' I said, 'you can't just disappear without questions being asked. I heard about your vanishing act on LBC Radio in my car. And then that note you left at Ward's office. He opened it, incidentally. Did you intend that?'

'No, of course I don't intend it. I needed to tell you where to find me if you have any information. I knew you were coming out to the Falklands and that you had been to Paris – to see that woman.'

The slight hesitation, the way he avoided her name . . . 'You don't like her.'

'No.'

'Have you met her?'

'No, I don't meet her.'

'So your dislike is based on the fact that she purchased the mining company your father founded.' It was too dark to see his eyes, but I remembered the wildness in them as he had thrust himself into my car.

'She kill him.' He said it with extraordinary intensity. 'My father

141

not only found KLME, it was his life. He is a mining engineer. Also a diviner. He has a sixth sense for metals, precious metals in particular. Also water, and oil, anything that is marked by changes in subsoil configuration.'

'So why are you here?'

His hand reached out, gripping my arm. 'I am here because Ward is here. And that Argentine man. Also she is coming.'

'La Belle –'

'*Ja*, La Belle Phuket.' He pronounced it the way a Frenchman would, so I guessed he was multilingual. 'And you?' he asked. 'Do you know vhy you are here? That aircraft is only the first step, y'know. He needs it to fly in equipment. You get it on to the Ronne, then you will know what is the true reason. That is why I ask you to meet me. I wish to explain to you. Come, sit down please, for a moment.'

The drizzle was dying now. I could dimly see the far side of Stanley Harbour, could even begin to make out the shapes of the two beacons marking the narrow passage to Port William inlet and the sea. He led me to a bench where he had dumped his gear. It consisted of a bulging backpack, a thumb stick and a high-powered torch. 'How far have you trekked?' I asked.

'I have a lift from East Cove. A fuel truck.' He was looking north across the still, black waters of the harbour. The lights of a small vessel had appeared between the entrance beacons. It looked like a fishing boat and the thought crossed my mind that it might be coming in to pick him up. I asked where he planned to spend the night, but he didn't seem to hear.

'Your ship is at East Cove, is it – the ship you came on?'

'Why do you ask?' He had turned his head, his voice sharp as he said, 'I don't come here to answer questions.'

I accepted that. A man doesn't change his appearance and then start back-packing in the wild emptiness of a place like the Falklands without he's got some secret reason. 'Stunnard was worried about you,' I said. 'I think you should try to contact him. He needs to know you're safe. If only so that he can inform the authorities in Uruguay and Chile.' And I added, 'He thinks very highly of you.'

Lange gave a little shrug, as though he didn't care, as I began telling him in some detail about my meeting with Stunnard in the guard post at Brize Norton. He seemed to be listening, but then he suddenly said, 'You don't understand, do you?' The words burst out of him on a rising note. I began to realise then the degree of tension he was under, like a pilot who has come face-to-face with fear for the first time. The drizzle had started again and in the cold darkness of fading visibility I began to recall the irrational behaviour of some of the servicemen I had had to deal with.

'No,' I said. 'I'm afraid I don't understand.'

He turned on me then. 'What don't you understand? You've met that woman. You must have formed some idea of the sort of person she is. She took the Giotti brothers, their company, to pieces. I don't care about them. They were financiers, company gamblers. She caught them with their trousers down, unable to meet the interest on their borrowings. Now they do what she tells them. But my father. He would never do what a woman like that demanded of him. He fought her, and he lost. His bankers pulled the carpet under his feet. He woke up one morning to find he was broke. What do you do then if you have your pride? She want him to use that gift of his –' My arm was gripped again, urgently – 'Do you know he could take a topographical map, put on those Japanese clickers he had, put them on his fingers, then the faraway look come into his face as he moves his hand across the paper, very slowly, following some line, following it involuntarily, the fingers shaking of their own volition –' He gulped for air. 'There was always something, an underground water channel, a vein of mineral, something ... He had that gift, you see. And she want him to use it for her and her alone. Instead, he take the small fishing boat he loved to sail and goes straight out from the Morbihan where he keep it, straight past Belle Île into the Atlantic and we never see him again. A lifebelt. That is all. Nothing of the boat. The lifebelt is recovered by a tunny fisher. It is out by the edge of the continental shelf where the seas break heavily. The Météorologique say there is a strong wind out there that night. So – now per'aps you understand something of how I feel.' All this spoken very jerkily and at great speed.

But while it told me a little of his relationship with his father, even explained his almost paranoid dislike of La Belle, it did not account for the covert manner in which he had arrived in Stanley. 'When did you reach the Falklands?' I asked him. 'Was it this morning?'

'*Ja*, this morning.' He said it hesitantly. 'Why do you ask?'

'There's a search been mounted for a man seen landing this morning in Low Bay. Was that you?'

'So what?' There was a note of defiance in his voice. 'What if it was me? It is not a crime. I am a British subject –'

'You have a British passport?'

'Of course.'

'Let me see it.'

But he shook his head.

'You haven't got a passport, have you? Not in your new identity. You've entered the Falklands illegally.' And then I remembered the other man. 'Who is he? There were two of you. You had an inflatable and you came from one of the foreign fishing vessels –'

'They give me the chance of a direct passage.'

'From Montevideo, or was it Punta Arenas?'

'Montevideo.'

'Who is he?' I asked again. 'And who are you, if you are no longer Bjorn Lange? What do I call you?'

He shrugged. 'Does it matter?' His tone was sullen.

I hesitated. I didn't want to ride him too hard. 'Perhaps not. But the other man. What is his name?'

'I don't know his name. He is from the ship.' His voice had risen on a higher note and he burst out suddenly – 'I come to you for help, not to answer so many questions. You are not in authority here.' Then on a quieter, but still urgent note, he said, 'Please. Will you tell me when she is arriving here? And where she is going, what is the purpose of her visit? Also, if possible, what she and Ward are arranging between them. Please. I need to know. They are planning something. Why else should he go to Paris? And the two of them coming here at the same time. It is to do with that aircraft. Once he has that C-130 he can fly equipment in, anything he want. But where? And to do what?' He seemed to run out of steam then, sitting there, staring at me, very still and suddenly silent.

So much I didn't understand. Why had a foreign deep-sea fishing vessel given him passage to the Falklands, dropping him off on a remote beach in Low Bay. And then 'borrowing' another inflatable at Walker Creek and so getting himself across to the north side of Choiseul Sound within reach of the fuel terminal at Mare Harbour? 'You must be tired,' I said. 'You've had a long day.'

He nodded.

'Do you have friends in Port Stanley?'

'No.'

'So where are you spending the night?'

'Oh, somewhere.' He was being deliberately vague. 'It don't matter. I have a sleeping bag.'

'What about the other fellow, the man you came ashore with, where's he?'

He looked at me quickly. 'Why do you ask?'

'Just curious,' I said.

After that I didn't say anything for a while, sitting there, trying to think the thing through. Nervousness I could understand. Uncertainty would cause that. He must be worried about the possible repercussions of his very odd behaviour, and about his future. He had every right to be nervous and on edge. But it wasn't that. It was more than nervousness. He was scared. 'What's the trouble?' I asked.

He stared at me dumbly.

I let it go for a moment, but I knew I had to get it out of him somehow. 'You're scared. Why? What are you scared of?'

'Nothing. Nothing.' He had turned his head away, his face catching the streetlight. It was almost contorted, the skin reddened and a vein pulsing in his neck. 'I don't come here to be questioned by you.' He was almost shouting at me. 'You are not Police or Immigration. You don't have a right to question me.' And then, lowering his voice, 'I come to you for help and all you do is ask questions.'

'If I don't know what the problem is how can I possibly help?' I kept my voice down, speaking to him quietly, hoping to soothe his nerves. 'Now just relax. You've told me about your father. I understand that and how you feel about the company being taken over. You have a resentment of the woman who arranged the take-over and she is due in Port Stanley any day now, you say. You have come here to meet her. Why? What will you gain by a meeting with her? You could have seen her any time, during the take-over and after. So why do you come to see her here?' I leaned forward, speaking to him very softly. 'Is it Ward you're scared of?'

I half expected him to deny he was scared. Instead, he said, 'No, not Ward.'

'Who then? Belle Phuket?'

He shook his head.

So it was the man he'd come ashore with. It had to be. The man who had probably persuaded him to change his identity and switch from the Falkland Islands cargo-carrier to the fishing vessel. But when I asked him again who the man was, he clammed up on me. 'Where is he now?' I persisted.

I had to repeat the question twice before he suddenly burst out – 'I don't know. I don't care.' He was wide-eyed, his hands, his whole body, trembling. So different from the brash, confident youngster who had accosted me in that London car park. And after that sudden outburst, I could get nothing out of him. He wouldn't say what the man's name was, refused even to describe him to me. Exasperated, I asked him once again where the man was now, but he shook his head. 'I tell you I don't know.'

'Where did you leave him?'

'On the beach.'

I gave up after that. It wasn't really important. A ground search would soon flush him out. The topography out in Camp was much the same as the Shetlands, except for the sharpness of the ridges, and a man on the run would find very little cover. He would be a stranger in an area the size of Wales with barely five hundred people outside of Stanley. No way they wouldn't spot him sooner or later.

However, my first priority was Lange. What the hell was I to do about him? The obvious and most sensible thing would be to persuade him to give himself up to somebody in authority. I told him about the conference that had been called. 'All because of you,' I said, and I suggested he came with me now to Government House. If I could get hold of Jack Simmonds I might be able to arrange legal entry for him.

But he seemed to be in some sort of mental block, obstinately refusing to get involved in any way with the authorities. 'Not until I have seen Mr Ward. That woman, too. I must see her. I have to warn her. Whatever I feel for her she must be told.' All this in a sudden flood of words that tumbled over each other.

'Told what?' I asked.

He shook his head. Then suddenly he was asking about *Isvik*. He wanted to know where he could find her, asking me if I could arrange for him to be taken on as a member of the expedition. I could just imagine how Ward would react. 'I have been crew on board the *Gondwana*,' he went on. 'I also sail with friends who have a one-ton ocean-racer they keep in Limfjord, and I have been one winter at the BAS base at Halley Bay. I would be a good crew if they could have a place for me.'

The last of the sunset showed for an instant through a gap in the cu-nim, so that in contrast the whole great cloud mass loomed black and menacing, and I sat there looking up at it and thinking perhaps it wasn't such a ridiculous idea after all.

'Please.' The urgency was back in his voice. 'She is coming out here to see the KLME manager where they are working on Pebble Island. I think now they are to move their seismological equipment across the Sound to West Falkland close by Cow Hangar House, which is a sheep station. It is when she is at Cow Hangar –' He stopped there.

I must admit I was beginning to think of him as a mental case, near the borderline anyway. He was very excited, very het-up. 'Please,' he said again his voice reaching towards the high note of hysteria. I tried to calm him, but he went on and on, until finally I agreed to see what I could do about getting him a berth on *Isvik*. Also I promised not to tell anybody I had seen him. Why I did that, God knows. At least I could contact Ward and see what he had to say. 'Will a message addressed to Greenpeace still find you if I leave it at the Post Office?'

'*Ja.*'

'How? Somebody will go there and pick it up?'

He nodded.

'So you do know somebody here in Stanley.' I hesitated. But there was no point in pressing him further, and I was tired. 'I hope they'll have a bed for you,' I said. 'It looks like being a wet night.'

He shrugged, thanking me and shaking my hand, holding on to it as though to a lifeline. 'Please.' The urgency was there again. 'Let me join *Isvik*.'

'I'll do my best.' I left him then, a solitary, lonely figure standing by the war memorial, the wet bronze of the plaques catching the light, the stone half-curve giving it the atmosphere of a Greek Odeon. A grumble of thunder sounded out of the great bank of cloud to the west, a jagged flash highlighting the tension in his face, the memory of it staying with me as I walked back to the Upland Goose. It wasn't just that his nerves were on edge. He was scared.

Fear is something we all experience at some time in our lives, flyers more than most. But with us things happen so fast it's the reaction afterwards that leaves one's muscles out of control, so that limbs, sometimes the whole body, start shaking uncontrollably. What I had seen on Lange's face was a glimpse of a boy beginning to lose control. There was an immaturity there, as though, if stretched much further, he would break. And when that happened . . .

I was tired, desperately tired I realised as I turned into the hotel. I went straight to my room and tumbled into bed. But, tired though I was, I found sleep evading me. I lay there, on that strange bed, remembering the war, the exhilaration of driving that Pucará flat out down the gut between the hard, serrated grey of those knife-edged ridges, the Aermacchis coming at me, and then wheeling away. The elation I had felt, the sheer fantastic exhilaration that had gripped me, my mouth wide and pumping out the Battle Hymn of the Republic – *Mine eyes have seen the Glory of the coming of the Lord.* That's what I had sung – at the top of my voice. And then I had crash-landed beside my Harrier, stumbling out of the Pucará, my limbs trembling so uncontrollably I just collapsed on the ground. That was when the Chinook had arrived.

I could hear the sound of distant thunder, my mind drifting. War! But what they had experienced here in Stanley was different, a hard, bloody grind, day after day living with a growing mass of dangerously scared conscripts. It was very quiet in the hotel after they had closed the bar, and flickering through my mind were the stories I had been told, some good, some bad, young Argentinians screaming with the pain of torn flesh, others moaning with the cold as they huddled against the walls of the houses, the naval shells sighing overhead. At times I thought I heard voices. That must have been just before I drifted off to sleep, imagination working overtime and the ghosts of a beaten army wandering the streets outside.

TWO

The problem of Bjorn Lange was still with me in the morning and I lay there for some time trying to resolve it. I could, of course, push it into the background, forget all about him and say nothing. But that wasn't very sensible. Sooner or later he would be picked up and they would want to know why I hadn't reported his presence in Stanley. I thought about taking a FIGAS flight to Goose Green and contacting Ward, but that wouldn't absolve me from the duty to report the fact that he was one of the two men who had entered the Islands illegally.

I was accustomed to making split-second decisions and it annoyed me that in this case I was finding it so difficult to make up my mind. I thought a bath might help and flung out of bed. The room was cold, the light in it startlingly brilliant. From the window I looked out on to a world miraculously transformed, the drabness gone, the roofs, the gardens, the whole hillside, everything covered in a light dusting of snow, and the frozen sleet that had caused it was being blown eastwards by a storm-force wind.

The squall thickened, snow swirling in the yard immediately below my window, piling itself like icing sugar against the out-buildings, and beyond the outbuildings there was the black gash of a lane in shadow, then gardens and the first of the roads with houses glimmering palely white, terraces following the contour line of the slope – St Mary's Walk, Allardyce, Moody, Brandon, and away to my left Fitzroy, Davis, Callaghan, Endurance – streets and roads I had walked, an age ago it seemed now. Away to my right, to the east, I could just see the bulk of the drill hall almost lost in the grey curtain of the driving snow.

But the squall didn't last, of course. By the time I had had my bath the wind had dropped and the dusting of snow was rapidly disappearing, drabness returning. I found a can and finished up, as I usually do, with a douche of cold water, pouring it over my head. By then I was fully awake and had made up my mind. I wrote a short note to Ward, and, after taking it across to the Post Office, I walked east along Ross Road, which is the waterfront road, as far as the Public Jetty and the neighbouring Falkland Island Company Jetty with its storage sheds now dripping with melting snow.

To the west, beyond Sapper Hill and Two Sisters, the sky was lightening, the clouds thinning, and I felt suddenly as though I were riding on air, the adrenalin pumping and my heart light with a sense of exhilaration born of expectation. Looking north, beyond the FIC sheds and across Stanley Harbour, I could see The Narrows with port and starb'd lights on beacons either side. That was our gateway to the Southern Ocean. Turn right, to starb'd, down the open waters of Port William, past the unlit lighthouse on Cape Pembroke, and we would be away, eastward, then southward into the ice.

That would be the day I would really slough off my Service skin, going out into the wild of an unknown world, owner of a great four-engined workhorse. I would become part of a two-masted schooner and go fighting my way down into the ice of the Weddell Sea. Just thinking about it filled me with intense excitement, the danger of getting that plane airborne adding a further zest.

As soon as I had finished breakfast, I phoned FIGAS and booked out on an early afternoon flight to Port Howard. Having done that, I walked along the street to Government House. The Governor's Residence has a conservatory, and as I walked past it to the offices, I could see the blaze of colour that filled it. A scribbled note to explain my presence resulted in Jack Simmonds seeing me almost immediately. 'You should have told me last night. We've a new Superintendent and he isn't going to be pleased to learn his lads could have picked Lange up last night right here on Ross. Now we don't know where he is. You can't even give me the name of his contact here. Didn't it occur to you to ask who was going to call for messages at the Post Office?'

'Why should I?' I was annoyed by his words, and even more so by the sense of being sucked back again into the system. 'Your police surely know who the local Greenpeace representative is. At any rate, the Post Office should be able to tell you who collects their mail.'

He nodded, waving me to the seat opposite him while he made a couple of phone calls. 'If you care to go down to the Police Station,' he said as he put the phone down, 'Detective-Inspector Brawdy will see you right away. As I thought, he'd like to hear it from you direct, and no doubt he'll have a few questions.' And he added, 'Alec Brawdy is an islander, born in Stanley. You'll find him very conscientious, very thorough.'

My reluctance to mention Reynolds and the Cow Hangar address Lange had given in that note, or to reveal his presence in Stanley was, as I had feared, amply justified. A Greenpeace operative gone missing, with police enquiries in Uruguay and Chile, it was inevitable that the whole thing would be blown up out of all proportion to the actions of a young man in a confused state of mind. Simmonds would have to write a report for the Governor to fax by satellite across 8,000 miles to the FO in London, the Falkland Island Police Superintendent would need to make a full report for his records. Endless complications.

The sun was shining, the water of the harbour sparkling with the ripples of a light breeze. The Police Station was on Ross Road, a block east of the Upland Goose, almost opposite the Town Hall and the Post Office. The meeting with Brawdy took even longer than I had expected. Things moved rather slower in the Falklands and by the time he had interrogated me, very fully, and I had made my statement and it had been typed out, corrected, retyped and signed, I only just managed to finish my packing and catch my flight. The trouble was Brawdy had checked up on my background and refused to believe that I didn't know where Lange was holed up.

The Norman Islander was already boarding when my taxi finally deposited me at the old Stanley airport. It had a new terminal building, small, but neat and functional, a new windsock waving its nylon trunk in the wind. Otherwise, nothing had changed, still the rusting barbed wire guarding the Argie minefields amongst the burrows of Penguin Walk and the worn concrete of the runway stretched out towards the white tower of Cape Pembroke lighthouse. The tourist population had clearly grown considerably since my posting here. The Islander is not a large plane and every seat was taken. The pilot was not the one I had seen in the Goose the previous evening. This was a large, round-faced Welshman, who perspired heavily and was tiresomely curious, his questions incessant as soon as take-off formalities had been completed.

Most of the planeload was bound for Goose Green and it did not stop at Mount Pleasant. The clouds that had given Stanley the thin mantle of snow I had seen that morning had been almost totally dispersed. It was now one of those wonderfully pristine days you get down on the edge of the Southern Ocean. The sky was a lightish, washed-out blue, the remnants of the storm showing as a scattering of white cloud galleons reaching in long lines of battle to the horizon. With a total absence of pollution the clarity of the air is such that visibility is virtually infinite and the MPA base, seen from the low level at which we were flying, presented so sharp an image that, if I had been stationed there, I'm sure I could have recognised most of the tiny figures moving around the dispersal points and the terminal. The RAF Regiment was standing to at their Rapier battery, some of them in shirt-sleeves.

Soon we were able to pick out the islands and rocks that littered Choiseul Sound and the pilot wanted to know if I had any news of the man who had landed there. 'They say he hitched a ride in a fuel truck from East Cove into Stanley. Bloody nerve of the man! Did the police say anything about that?' Apparently the police had rung the airport terminal just before take-off to say I was on my way and would they hold the plane for me. His information was that the driver had given them a description of the man he had given a lift to. 'Tall, athletic and clean-shaven with dark hair and a funny way of talking.'

Like most of the Camp airstrips, the one at Goose Green was grass. A little knot of people were standing around the pick-up truck with its fire pump hitched on to the rear. We made a good landing, the grass dried by the wind and the ground hard as concrete. We had a short pause there while the baggage was being unloaded and the new lot sorted out and stowed away. This gave me just enough time to walk up to the memorial erected to the dead of 2nd Para who had died following Colonel H in his desperate dash over open ground. This at night, against prepared positions manned by a force almost five times larger.

There were flowers there. It was the colour of those flowers that had drawn me to walk up the grassy slope to the simple stone cross standing stark against the blue of the sky. Flowers after all this time. Mostly they were from local people, the ink of the simple messages beginning to run. A few were from relatives come halfway across the world to say goodbye.

The names on the grey stone plinth were not numerous, but down the slope the Argentine graveyard was massed with the white of simple wooden crosses. Dead conscripts, the unknown buried one on top of the other, sometimes three to a cross. And no flowers, no visitors from their homeland, the burials, the crosses, the tending of their resting place left to the British. I had been there once before, and as on that previous occasion, I found myself close to tears as I walked back to the plane. Their loneliness, the way they had been abandoned here, I found it deeply moving.

Back in my seat beside the pilot there was a woman crying close behind me, her eyes fixed on the hilltop memorial as we taxied to the grass limits of the airfield. She was still staring fixedly at it as we took off, tears rolling unchecked, her sobs heart-rending. She wasn't young, and it was her son who had been killed there, the only son she had been able to have. Her husband was dead and she was travelling alone, the first visit she had been able to afford.

We were over the great sea slash of Falkland Sound when she told me that. We could see San Carlos Water quite clearly away to the north, and when I pointed it out to her, she said, 'That's where he landed. And then they walked. He called it Yomping and he wrote me a letter. They found it in his breast pocket. He hadn't finished it, and when they gave it to me, it was all covered in dark, red-brown stains.' And she added, 'It was as though he had been crying blood.'

As she told me this I was looking northward up the Sound, remembering the burnt-out remains of bombed ships in San Carlos, the bodies laid out for burial, prostrate soldiers pale against the black peat earth seen from just below the cloud base as our small formation powered over the Sound to head off another attack into what had become known as Bomb Alley. And those Argentine pilots, flying so crazily low they almost brushed the water, loosing their missiles and hitting their targets, but achieving so little for such brave determination, the missiles in some cases going right through the hulls without exploding because they were released so low the fuses had no time to detonate.

'Port Howard.' The pilot pointed to a scattering of houses straight ahead of us with a jetty and line of storage and shearing sheds.

There was a small coaster alongside, but no sign of *Isvik*. The airfield, a mile or more away from the settlement, was on the brow of a hill, a long green sward of grass with a dirt track snaking up to it. The Station Manager's Range Rover looked like a toy model as it breasted the rise and approached the fire-pump housing and its attendant windsock. The radio was crackling incoherently, then the pilot banked. 'Gaggle of geese on the flight path. He's going to drive them off.'

The Range Rover swung away from the windsock, heading upwind, away from the box-like hangar where they kept the station Cessna. The geese rose in untidy batches, wheeling uncertainly, reluctant to leave their grazing ground, and we circled while the Range Rover ran back to the shelter and two figures manhandled the pump into position, hitching it on to the back. Looking eastward, I could see the entrance to Bold Cove and the ridge beyond that formed the last rock screen before Many Branch Harbour and the gap where the attacking aircraft had had to bank sharply to the right and face the firepower of the Task Force vessels sitting anchored and vulnerable off the beachhead.

We taxied up to the little group of people standing by the tin shed and the pilot shut down the engine. 'Did you see her?' he asked, switching off the radio and taking off his earphones. 'In Bold Cove. The ship you've come to join.'

I shook my head. My mind had been on other things.

I could have stayed the night at the tourist lodge. They had a room spare and I was offered it. But now that I was within so short a distance of the ship, I wanted to get on board as soon as possible and meet Peter Kettil and Iris Sunderby, the two people I should be living with on the first leg of my attempt to get that C-130 of mine into the air. 'Thank you, but no,' I told the manager. 'Could you arrange for somebody to take me out there?'

He nodded. 'Dyfed Evans. He's the boy will take you out to her.'

It was late afternoon and nothing to do after the Islander had taken off, flying north to its next port of call which was Elephant Bay, Pebble Island Beach. Evans was away in his boat with a handful of tourists, headed for a tussac island where there were usually some seals hauled out. Nobody seemed to know when he would be back – ten minutes, an hour, two hours; time didn't seem to have any relevance for people out in Camp. While it was summer time in

Stanley now, here they had not altered their clocks, so Camp was an hour behind Stanley, which gave them even longer daylight evenings.

I hadn't had anything to eat since breakfast, and as soon as it was known I was hungry, the kitchen produced some cold mutton with warmed-up greens and potatoes, and, heaven be praised, a good, old-fashioned treacle tart to finish.

Clouds were gathering again, darkening the sky. 'Forecast says rain.' This from a guest who was doing duty as barman and serving the first drinks of the evening. I dozed for a while in an armchair, then went for a quick walk and had a look at the little museum of Argentine war equipment that had been fixed up in an outbuilding. It had grown considerably since I was last at Port Howard, weapons and clothing, gas masks, basic rations, examples of the wretched footwear, every type of ammunition, all of it either handed in to the manager or found nearby.

I had just returned and was sitting nursing an Aberlour malt when a short, stout man with a great bush of a beard that made him look like some figure out of the Bible walked in. 'Somebody here wanting a boat to Bold Cove?' I said it was me and offered him a drink. He didn't answer. He just stood there, staring at me hard, the silence dragging. 'Isvik, is it?'

I nodded. Either his mind worked very slowly, or else he was trying to decide if it was worth his while to take me. At length he said, 'Better get going then. There's a deal of wind behind this lot of cloud I wouldn't wonder.'

He had a pick-up outside. I flung my gear into the back of it and we rattled our way down to the sheds and the concrete jetty where his high-bowed fishing boat lay alongside. It was a sturdily-built boat with a solid box of a wheelhouse. 'You can cast off right away. I want to get back before this lot breaks.' He jerked his head at the lowering clouds, jumped on board with surprising agility for so large a man and had the engine thumping away before I had managed to free the straining stern warp.

There was a stillness hanging over the flat, pewter surface of the harbour inlet as we motored out, no breath of wind. Albatross were everywhere, gliding effortlessly in search of the little ilex squid and wheeling to seek out shifts of almost indiscernible air currents. There were other seabirds, skuas, terns and cormorants. I could identify the cormorants, of course, the albatross, too, on account of the huge wingspan, but I had to ask Evans about the others.

There is a certain shyness about these island people. He would answer questions, but that's all – until we had motored through the narrow entrance passage into Falkland Sound, gradually turning the point of the Gut's inner rock ridge to enter Bold Cove itself on a bearing of roughly 40°. I didn't see her at first. She was a good three miles away, the black of her hull and her white masts blending into the background. That was when Evans, for the first time, volunteered a question of his own.

'You going with them?' he asked, shouting to make himself heard above the racket of the engine. I was looking at her so intently I barely heard him. 'The Weddell Sea, man,' he yelled. 'That's what I hear. They're going down into the Weddell. Round South Georgia, way south. You going with them?'

'Yes,' I shouted back, my eyes still glued to the black-hulled vessel, so small and fragile-looking under the rock-strewn ridges. There was something of a void in my stomach at his words. Over two thousand miles, and the last thousand virtually due south, straight down into the frozen heart of Antarctica where the central ice dome rises two and a half miles above bedrock. I had done my homework, and looking at *Isvik*, I didn't like what I had learned.

The C-130 was suddenly more and more of a wild dream.

I think it was my silence that encouraged Evans to be less taciturn. 'Well, I bin whaling down to the Ross. Two seasons I had with a Salvorsen outfit, the crew all sorts, but mainly Norwegians. Open water most o' the time, but the Weddell now, that's different. I wouldn't go in a little boat like that in among all that ice.' He nodded his beard at the open window of the wheelhouse and the ship lying bows-on to us, shouting at me with great vigour, the sound of his voice merging with the engine which echoed back from the rock ridges that hemmed us in.

I tried to tell him that *Isvik* had been adapted for wintering over, that her hull was wedge-shaped, so that, under pressure, she would pop up like a cork, but he shook his head, that massive beard opening to show his teeth in a great guffaw. 'You tell that to the marines. Bad enough marching across East Falkland Island at the start of winter, like the poor buggers done in eighty-two, but where we are now is on the same latitude south as London is north, fifty-one degrees thirty near enough. So there you are then. That gives you some idea, eh? Is cold down there, boy. Bloody, sodding cold. You get past South Georgia, an' that's bad enough – storm-force winds, hurricane-force at times –' The beard opened again, that loud guffaw. 'Not me, boy. Had two seasons, like I said. Tha's enough for me.'

A flurry of wind darkened the water ahead and the ship faded ghost-like behind a rolling curtain of rain. 'Hold the wheel, will you, while I get my gear on.' He handed over to me without apparently a thought as to whether I knew how to steer a boat. 'Four-O, near enough.' He made a vague gesture at the compass with a large, calloused hand, and taking some grubby oilskins down from a peg beside what I took to be the echo-sounder, he got into them with a speed born of years of practice.

The rain lifted as suddenly as it had started, the wind taking off and the ship appearing again as though by magic. She was quite close now and I realised she was bigger than I had thought. 'Get into some oilies and go up for'ard. You'll find a warp lying ready coiled. I go alongside on her port quarter. You hitch on, then get yerself on board.'

I asked him how much I owed him, but he just laughed. 'I heard tales about you. Next time you pass through Port Howard throw me a bottle of Scotch and we'll get drunk together, eh?' The beard opened up and his great paw slammed into my back. 'Be seeing y'boy.'

He was throttling back as I went for'ard, picked up the thick, coiled rope and stood there in the bows watching the masts grow taller, the vessel taking on a hard-worn, much-travelled personality of its own. The throb of the prop against the soles of my feet died, the bows touching with only the slightest jar of wood on steel. No wind now, no rain, everything quiet again as I hauled myself aboard and made fast.

'Ahoy!' I called. 'Your new crew. Ahoy!'

There was no reply, the ship lying still and very quiet.

'Ahoy there! Anybody home?' The echo of my voice came softly back from the tops of the ridges on either side. The door of the wheelhouse was half-open. I slid it right back and saw that to the left of the helmsman's chair was the opening to a companionway that led to a saloon, the table littered with the remains of a meal, bottles too. 'Anybody there?' I called again. 'Ahoy!' Still no answer, the silence leaving me with a feeling of anticlimax. I went out again on to the deck to find Evans had moved up into the bows of his boat, the big, bearded prophet's face peering above the guard rail. 'Looks like they've gone ashore,' I told him.

He looked up and down the deck, then shook his head. 'Inflatable's still on board.' He let out a great bellow – '*Isvik*! You got a visitor.' He looked up at the clouds, which were now settling over the tops of the ridges. 'Got to go now. You gonna come, or you want to stay on board and wait for them?'

'I'll stay,' I said. No point in going back to the hotel. I was here and there'd presumably be food on board, and a bunk. I got out of the oilskins I'd borrowed and tossed them down to him. He nodded, his eyes searching the shore. 'That cairn there, family and friends of a good man called Alastair Cameron. They put it up as a memorial and to mark the spot where Captain Strong of the *Welfare* went ashore in 1790 to claim the Falklands for King George.' He looked at the sky again, gave a sort of growl, and scrambled aft, coming back with all my gear and tossing it on to the deck at my feet. A brief wave of the hand, and then he was back in his wheelhouse, shouting at me to cast off.

I walked the warp aft, coiling it as I went, and cast it down on top of the anchor in the bows as he dropped astern, swinging in a wide arc to head back down the cove. I stood, leaning against the back of *Isvik*'s deckhousing, watching the broad arrow of water receding, the sound of the diesel gradually fading, stillness closing round me. Thunder sounded, faint like distant gunfire, away to the west.

I was conscious then of loneliness and a great sense of space around me. There was a broad slot in the stern for the propellor to be retracted, presumably to protect it from ice damage, a reminder that I was on the edge of another world.

Isvik was anchored just outside the kelp line, opposite a channel of weed-free sand caused by the fresh water from a stream that flowed from the western ridge to a flat area of brilliant green that looked like part of a golf course. In the centre of this was the cairn monument of grey stone Evans had referred to. Two hundred years ago a man had anchored his ship in this very spot where nobody had anchored before. I wondered how he had felt about the land to the south that he barely knew existed.

The gunfire sound of thunder was getting nearer, the first drops of rain beginning to fall, big drops that spattered the flat, pewter water surface with broadening ringlets. I slung my gear inside the wheelhouse, the sound of the raindrops merging into a solid hissing. I could still just see Evans's boat starting to round Bold Point. Then it was gone, the faint sound of it abruptly cut off, everything suddenly very quiet, just the splashing hiss of the raindrops. The light was fading all the time, clouds creeping in a pale miasma down the ridge slopes on either side.

A stabbing flash, the crash of thunder close above, and then the wind came, a sudden wild burst of fury, the strength of it so great you could lean against it. I felt *Isvik* shy away under the impact. The anchor chain gave a tremendous jerk as it was stretched out, bar-taut. I dived back into the shelter of the wheelhouse as the ridge above the cairn was wiped out by a solid wall of water driven almost horizontally. The noise of it against the steel of the deckhousing was shattering. It wasn't rain any more. It was hail, lumps of ice as big as sugar cubes.

I leaned over the open cavity of the companionway. 'Anybody there?' Maybe my voice was drowned in the cacophany of sound. I threw my gear down, then followed it into the warmth and relative quiet of the saloon. It was a big comfortable place, the table in gimbals, broad settles that could be used as bunks and curtained apertures to the starb'd cabins. The curtains and the wood panelling gave a sense of comfort and warmth to the interior and there was a galley on the port side with a big, oil-fired stove that gave out plenty of background heat as well as having ovens and hotplates.

Having located the switchboard and turned the lights on in the saloon, I called out again. There were two after cabins and these had sliding doors. A strip of light showed under the starb'd one and a voice called out, 'Who is it?' The voice was male, and he sounded only half-awake.

'Edwin Cruse,' I replied.

'What do you want?' He was shouting to make himself heard.

I called out my name again and the door of his cabin was flung back with a crash. 'What the hell?' He erupted into the saloon, still hauling on the belt of his trousers, his red hair standing on end like the hackles of an infuriated fox. 'Cruse?' The freckles were startlingly evident against the pallor of his skin and his eyes stared, his expression one of sullen exasperation. 'Why do you come out here? We had a room booked for you at the Upland Goose.'

'I stayed there last night.'

'Then why come out here? We left a message for Nils, to explain –'

'I thought it more sensible to come out to the ship as soon as possible.'

He glared at me, his face getting whiter. 'Better get this straight. I run this ship. For the voyage south you're crew. Understand? You do what I say.'

The man was strangely distraught. 'I'm sorry,' I said. 'I would have asked Mrs Sunderby's permission to join ship if I had known how to contact you. I was expecting to join you in Stanley. When I found you'd gone . . .' I gave a little shrug. 'What did you expect me to do, sit on my arse, waiting for you when I'd come eight thousand miles to meet up with you?' And I added, 'I'm only just out of the Air Force. I'm used to running a squadron of Hercules transports, and running it my way. I'm not prepared to accept orders that don't make sense. Do we understand each other?'

I think he was about to let fly at me. His face was beginning to flush now and there was a sulky look to his mouth. That redheaded temper of his would have burst out had a voice behind him not said, quietly, but very clearly, 'For God's sake, Pietro, let it be.' It was a feminine voice, but behind the softness was a decisive quality that I was to learn to respect. This was Iris Sunderby.

She was quite small really, but that was not the impression she gave, for she held herself very erect. Her eyes were fixed on mine as she came towards me, the olive skin of her rather Latin features puffed and slightly flushed, a line of perspiration showing beneath the tousled helmet of black hair. 'Welcome on board.' She held out a hand and I swear there was a little devil of laughter in her very dark brown eyes.

She hadn't bothered with the top buttons of her shirt and the dark tan of her breasts was visible down to the nipples. It was very obvious to me now why Peter Kettil had been so put out by my unexpected arrival. Nils Solberg's words, 'they like to be alone some time,' came back to me. There was a glint in her eyes as we shook hands, so very formally, and I realised she knew that I knew, and she didn't give a damn, her lips mirroring a sort of Mona Lisa smile.

There was even the flicker of an invitation in the way she looked at me, but perhaps I was imagining that. The fingers tightened on mine, just the faintest movement of the muscles. Then she let go my hand and looked at her watch. 'Hungry?' she asked.

I nodded.

'Fish stew,' she said, 'and Chilean wine. Will that do? And *brebis*, sheep's cheese. I have found a woman just outside Stanley who makes it. I'm Eeris, by the way, and the surly one here is Peter, or Pete for short. When I want to be nice I call him Pietro.' Again that glint of laughter. 'I'm half-Portuguese, as Iain has probably told you. And you are Edwin – is that how you like to be called?'

'Eddie,' I said.

'Eddie – the diminutive. That's very nice.' She turned to the stove and stood a heavy, blackened cast-iron pot on it. 'We use given names on board because sometimes things happen a little fast and it is quicker to call out just the one name. Also, it is more friendly, yes – more relaxed? We shall be together for quite a little time, the conditions sometimes not very good. So we have to be friends, no?' She had been speaking very fast, as though to cover for the manner in which I had been welcomed on board, but this last was said hesitantly, and I understood. She was remembering the previous voyage down to the Ronne Ice Shelf, the two Argentinians and how they had died.

'Christian names do not necessarily mean friendliness,' I murmured.

She glanced at me quickly, pushing back the straight fringe of her almost jet black hair. 'No.' She nodded. 'I see you know what happened.'

'Yes.'

She nodded again, and this time she smiled. 'Good. Then we can forget about it now.' She sounded relieved. Another shrapnel burst of heavy rain or sleet, the ship giving an almost convulsive leap, then coming up hard with the chain at full stretch and heeling to port quite significantly. She turned to Pete. 'Will the anchor hold, do you think?'

'Should do. We're in good holding.' The boat shivered to a particularly fierce gust and he ran up the companionway to the wheelhouse above. I followed him. His face was glued to the starb'd window, a small plastic compass in his hand. No sign now of the rough green slope of the westward ridge, even the cairn wiped out by the sweeping curtain of sleet. Rain and wind were like a solid wall pushing relentlessly at the ship's side. 'Every now and then I get a glimpse of it. Still the same bearing.' He sounded relieved. 'If we do drag ...' He glanced at me speculatively, then shook his head. Clearly he didn't relish the thought of it. 'I've never dropped the hook in Bold Cove before.' This in explanation of his nervousness, and to take his mind off the possibility of the anchor dragging, he pulled up a trapdoor in the wheelhouse floor and showed me the engine, a whacking great Merc diesel, also the battery charger and bilge pump. He then introduced me to the engine control panel in front of the steering wheel, also the Brooks & Gatehouse masthead information dials – wind speed, boat speed, apparent wind speed, course information automatically adjusted for magnetic variation, tidal effect, everything slotted into the computer. The wind speed indicator was now steady on four-two, direction six-O. Every now and then he picked up the compass to check the bearing. Finally, after he had shown me the echo-sounder and instructed me on the handling of the VHF and single sideband radio equipment, also the satnav, he started on man overboard drill.

I really think if Iris hadn't called us to feed he would have had me out on the deck checking the marker buoys, lifebuoys and inflatables. He was a good instructor, and with the storm raging outside I appreciated the way he concentrated on the essentials of survival. I just hadn't expected to be pitchforked into the rough side of life in the Southern Ocean quite so soon.

Just as we were going below he stopped me. 'You know who the charter party is, do you?'

I turned, one foot already on the companion ladder. 'Yes, Ward,' I said. 'Ward and another man.'

'No. His charter doesn't start till first November.' He was looking down at me, I remember, and that freckled face and the brush of red, almost ginger hair, was caught in the sudden glare of a great streak of fork lightning that hit the ridge above us like a thunderbolt. He might have been a ghost, just the disembodied head leaning over me, the red hair and the freckles, and the face white in the flash.

'Who then?' I asked. But in that instant I think I guessed.

'A woman,' he said. 'Iris had a fax from Paris. In French, of course. Why can't the buggers communicate in English? Everybody else does.' And he added, 'We had to go to Government House to get it translated, so now every islander knows. The telephone system is HF out in Camp. They all listen in, so nothing's ever private.'

'What did it say?' I asked. 'That she's coming out here?'

'Tomorrow. She'll be with us tomorrow.'

'La Belle?'

'Yes. Mademoiselle Belle Phuket.' He pronounced it the French way. His hand reached down and gripped my arm. 'Don't talk about it to Iris.'

'Why?'

'She doesn't like the thought of another woman on board, that's why. Nor do I. Could be a clash of temperaments, Portuguese and Irish on one side, Chinese on the other, and both of them strong personalities. You've met her, have you?'

Iris's voice called up to us – 'It's on the table and getting cold, so shift it, both of you.'

'Coming,' I said and slid down on the handgrips, almost falling into her arms.

'What were you talking about?'

'Man overboard drill,' I said.

And when we were seated, she said, 'What's your normal drill, gybe round and drift down on the body, or sail hard up on it, then turn into the wind and come up all standing?'

She was testing me out. I knew that. 'It depends,' I said, smiling, my eyes on hers.

'That's no answer.'

'You can't give an answer till you know the precise circumstances.' I changed the subject. I was too damned hungry to start crossing words with her on a subject I knew little about. We had never bothered much about man overboard technique on Mickey One's boat.

The fish stew was good – 'Nils left us with a great pot of the stuff' – and the talk was all of the Islands, the wildlife that had no built-in fear of man, and the islanders themselves, some 1800 in Stanley, the remainder, about 700, scattered thinly through an area of water, rock and peat the size of Wales. That made the ratio about one human to each individual island, communications with the northern hemisphere quicker and easier than with the next settlement. And while I was summing the two of them up, they wanted to know about me, so there was plenty to talk about. And all the time the wind outside battering at the hull, the flapping of the rigging like the rattle of machine-gun fire, occasionally tempestuous floods of rain. And Pete running up the companion ladder in the heavier gusts to check the bearing, until it was too dark to see the cairn.

I excused myself then. It was almost eleven. I had had a lot to drink, for in addition to the Chilean red, they broke out of a bottle of malt, the big, peaty, Islay brew called Laphroaig. In spite of all the coffee I drank, it saw me off the instant I was in my sleeping bag and my head touched the pillow I had made of my clothes.

It seemed only a moment later I was suddenly wide awake, wind and hail hammering at the steel plating close by my ear, and the black dark of the cabin filled with a grumbling, abrasive sound, as though a bulldozer were shifting piles of rock. I hadn't a clue where I was. In fact, I thought for a second I was in an aircraft that was breaking up around me. Somebody shouted, a female voice. A shaft of light showed a curtain at the cabin entrance stretched out almost horizontal. There was the sound of a starter motor, then the deep throb of an engine. My whole world trembled and the bed gradually assumed a more sensible position, so that I was no longer lying with my feet in the air.

I knew where I was then. The curtain was pushed aside and a light came on. 'Eddie!' It was Iris. She was fully clothed and in oilskins. 'Oh, good. You're awake. We're dragging and Pete could do with some help.' No panic, her voice quite calm.

I was out of the bunk in a flash, pulling sweater and trousers over my naked carcase, grabbing my oilskins. Up in the wheelhouse Iris was steering, and through the snow-plastered windows I could see a vague, yellow, oilskinned figure crawling around the steeply slanted deck in the beam of spotlights fixed to the foremast crosstrees. 'Can you give him a hand? We need to drop a second anchor.' She was holding the ship into the wind, using the engine to take the strain off our one anchor.

Out on deck it was bitterly cold, but I soon built up a sweat under my oilskins as we worked to cast the spare anchor over the starb'd rail.

'Katabatic,' Pete yelled in my ear. 'Hold tight – all the time – if Iris loses control and we turn broadside ...' He must have seen I didn't understand what he was talking about, for he put his mouth close against my ear and yelled, 'Wind katabatic. Down draughts. Knock us on to our beam-ends if she can't hold *Isvik* bows-on. Understand?'

I nodded, and we got to work again, one hand for ourselves and one for the ship. We worked non-stop, and at times Pete was literally dancing about the deck, one minute directing Iris through the open door of the wheelhouse, the next back at the windlass, letting out chain and waiting for the moment when he could signal me to heft up the stock I was holding and tip the spare anchor over the side.

Even with the three of us, it took the better part of an hour before we had done, the two anchors set well apart and taking the strain evenly, the ship steady and riding bows-on to the storm, which chose that moment, of course, to start easing off.

Dawn was breaking as we finally went below, sitting, dazed with weariness, warming our hands on scalding mugs of coffee laced with rum. I remember, when I finally returned to my bunk, I glanced out through the cabin porthole to see the clouds had lifted off the eastern ridge and the rocks were limned by the first light of a sunrise that was still below the earth's curve. And as I fell asleep, I was thinking the storm had achieved something ... I had had a rude baptism, but at least the three of us now knew we could work together and survive a crisis.

I woke to sunshine and the sound of an engine. It died and a voice hailed us. I sat up, taking in the tiny cabin, the sleeping bag and my crumpled clothes, oilies and seaboots strewn on the floor, a shaft of sunlight from the small porthole acting like a spotlight. Footsteps sounded on the steel deck above my head, the murmur of voices. I unfastened the canvas leeboard that had held my body in place during the first part of the night as the ship heeled to the wind. Now there was no wind, everything very still and the sun shining.

I glanced at my watch. Seventeen minutes past ten already. A door banged, the sound of metal on metal as somebody shifted pots on the stove and a voice from the wheelhouse calling down to see if we were awake. The broad Glasgow accent was unmistakeable.

My cabin curtain was whisked aside. 'Tea?' It was Iris, wearing a faded dressing-gown and no make-up. Even so, she looked fresh and alert. She thrust a steaming mug at me. Her nose wrinkled. 'Smells like you got quite a sweat up last night.' She stood there, looking down at me, and I grabbed my sweater, realising suddenly that I was stark naked. 'Sounds like him,' she said, ignoring my state of undress. 'I knew he had arrived, but I wasn't expecting him so soon. What is it he is wanting, do you know?'

I shook my head. The sweater was cold and damp against my loins.

'You say he had a man named Barratt with him? Why? What does he do, that man?'

'I've no idea.' I was beginning to shiver.

'Surely he tell you something?' She waited, but when I didn't answer, she said, 'Drink your tea up and get dressed please. We will be moving round to the quay at Port Howard as soon as I find out what it is Iain is here for.'

Pete was already with Ward in the wheelhouse. I could hear their voices. I dived for'ard to the starb'd heads, relieved myself, had a quick shave, a flannel wash and a hard rubdown, then scrambled into my clothes. Ward was standing by the stove, warming himself, with a mug clutched in that black-gloved hand. He looked big, his body bulked out by a thickly-quilted anorak, an old seaman's cap rammed down on that massive head of his, and yellow oilskin trousers stuffed into seaboots that had once been white.

He nodded to me and smiled. 'Ye've no' let the grass grow, have ye? Ah got yer message, by the way. The boy should be at Cow Hangar by now. Josh will take care of him.' He turned to Pete. 'Yer not to say anything' aboot Ferdinand Barratt to Iris. Do ye understand? Not yet.' He spoke in a whisper.

So he had brought his friend with him. I wondered why. And he was strangely nervous, standing there, not saying anything more than he had to and darting quick glances every now and then at the door to Iris's cabin. In the end, he said, 'Canna keep the bugger waiting indefinitely up there in the cold.' And he called for Barratt to come down. 'Ye've met our friend here?' He gave a nod in my direction. 'We flew out from Brize Norton together. An' this is Peter Kettil. Pete doubles as navigator and sailing master.'

And after he had said the man's name, there was an awkward silence as we stood around, waiting for Iris to appear.

She took her time, and when she did come out of her cabin into the saloon I understood why. She was dressed now in light blue slacks, white boots and a scarlet polo-neck jersey. But it was her face that had me staring. She was in full war paint. That's what had taken the time, and the big, dark eyes, fastened on Ward, made it perfectly clear that it was done for his benefit.

He stepped forward and she lifted her face to his, but all she got was a peck on the cheek. 'Ah've brought somebody to see ye,' he said, a little hesitantly. 'His name is Ferdinand Barratt.' He indicated the silent figure standing at the foot of the companion ladder. 'He'll be sailin' with ye.'

Iris held out her hand, but the man made no move to take it, standing there, his mouth open and his eyes devouring her. 'Welcome on board.' She said it perfunctorily, turning almost angrily on Ward. 'You realise your charter does not commence till next week. In any case, it is for me to decide who sails with us. Eddie I can take. He's a quick learner and to pick up that aircraft it is right for him to get ice experience. But I know nothing about your friend here.' She turned to Barratt. 'I'm sorry. I do not wish to be rude . . .' Her voice trailed away, her eyes widening to a stare.

'Iris.' He took a step or two towards her, said her name again, 'Iris.' Said it in a voice trembling with emotion.

I was watching her then as, first disbelief, then hope, flickered across her face. 'Eduardo?' She said it doubtfully. Then, as he gave just the slightest nod of his head, she repeated it in a tone of wonder. 'Is it really . . .?' She shook her head. 'It cannot be. I was there. At the church. And later at the crematorium –' Her voice choked.

I glanced quickly at Ward. He was standing absolutely still, as though transfixed by the drama of the scene he had engineered. The man was actually smiling as though he were enjoying the build-up of tension between the two of them.

'I don't believe it.' Iris's voice was almost out of control and I was shocked by the expression in her eyes, her mouth open and her breath coming in quick pants.

'*Sì*. Eduardo.'

I suppose it was the way he said it, for the doubt was suddenly wiped from her face, her eyes lighting up with the excitement of a child. It shocked me, for she wasn't a child, and what I was seeing as she flung herself into his arms was the blatant, unadulterated passion of love.

They stood there, clinging to each other and murmuring endearments, quite oblivious of us.

Pete was the first to move. He started up the ladder to the wheelhouse, muttering something about seeing to their boat. I could guess what was going on in his mind. When I had come on board he had been in bed with this woman. Now she was in the arms of another man. Not any man, but – her brother.

They stood like that for perhaps a minute, probably less, but it seemed a long time. Nobody spoke, the ship so quiet I could hear the slap of small, wind-whipped waves against the steel hull. Her face was buried in the rough wool of his sweater and she was making little whimpering sounds. I don't think she was crying. I think it was the outward expression of the tide of emotion that was sweeping through her as he stroked her hair. For that moment they were lost to the world, their bodies pressed against each other.

And then she raised her head, her eyes opening slowly, bright with tears, but still with that blank look of a woman in a trance. For that moment her face had a Madonna-like quality, yet at the same time her body was literally trembling with the emotional storm that had engulfed her.

The position of her head was such that she was looking straight at Ward, recognition coming gradually, her gaze hardening, passion changing to anger.

'You.' She said it in a long-drawn-out whisper full of accusation. And then she said it again, much louder – 'You.' She pushed herself clear of her brother's arms, stepping back. 'You fucking, sodding bastard! You never tell me. You left me, all the time, thinking –'

'It was for his own good. The Argentinians ...' Ward shook his head, raising the palm of his left hand in a placating gesture. 'There were still men of the Escuela Mecánica –'

But she wasn't listening. She was mouthing a torrent of Spanish at him; curses, or obscenities, I couldn't tell which, but the beauty of her face was gone, the wide mouth a gaping hole through which the fury that possessed her expressed itself in sounds that were barely recognisable as words.

'Ah tell ye, Iris, it was necessary.'

'Balls!' She flew at him, her arms reaching out, fingers clawing. He seized hold of her, the gloved steel fingers clamping down.

'You're lying. You dirty, rotten bastard, you never did anything for anybody in your life, it was always for you – you –'

She cried out at the pressure of his hands bending her arms back. 'Ye would have told somebody. Ye may think ye wouldn't, but Ah couldna risk it. If Ah had written ye –'

She didn't let him finish. She was screaming at him, in Spanish, needling him about his parentage. *'Tu madre era una puta, tu padre un desconocido, tú eres un ladrón, un asesino –'*

He stopped her there, his hand lifted against the torrent of words. 'Och aye.' He said it mildly, still quietly smiling. 'Me mother was a whore, a drunken slut. Ah admit that. An' ye're right aboot me havin' done some thievin'. But Ah'm no' a murderer.'

'You are, you are.'

'Tha's not true .'

'What about Ángel?'

'Ah'm no' a murderer,' he repeated. 'Ah've never killed a man in cold blood. Is that understood?' The tone of his voice, everything about him, was suddenly impressive.

'Ángel,' she said again. 'You kill him, don't you?'

He gave a little shrug. 'If that's what ye want to believe.'

'You kill him.' Her voice was rising again. 'You kill him, you kill him.' Her hands were tight closed, the knuckles white, her face quite contorted. *Like a volcano.* I could hear Nils Solberg's heavy Norwegian voice. And then suddenly she turned with lightning speed, reached to the stove, picked up a stainless steel saucepan and hurled it at him.

She wasn't more than ten feet from him, and she couldn't miss. If it hadn't been for his gloved right hand and that metal forearm, he could have been badly injured.

The crash of metal against padded metal, the clatter of the saucepan and its lid falling to the floor, seemed to bring her to her senses, for her shoulders suddenly sagged and she burst into tears, muttering something about Pete and Eduardo being there in the frigate's after cabin. 'They hear the shot. And you weren't there. Ask them.'

I looked at Ward. There was an almost frightening intensity about the man now, his eyes gone cold and his mouth a tight line. 'Seems to me, girl, ye're still hankerin' after yer dead lover.'

It was a cruel thing to say in front of her twin brother. She gave a sobbing gulp, staring fixedly at Ward for a moment, then turning and rushing into her cabin. The slam of the door echoed through the ship.

Ward turned to Barratt. 'Does that bring it back?'

The man shook his head.

'Ye still don't remember?'

'No.'

'But ye've read Peter Kettil's book. Ye an' he, ye were in the *Santa Maria*'s after cabin and ye heard the shot.' He turned to me. 'Ye've read the book, too. What do ye think? More to the point perhaps, what would ye have done if ye'd been thrown into the lower deck wi' the bodies of the men ye'd caused to be infected with anthrax, a mass of daid bodies preserved in ice like they'd been refrigerated in a morgue. An' ye had a gun. The hatch slams shut an' no light. But ye know what is there. What would ye have done?' He paused for breath, then said slowly, 'If anybody's a murderer, he was. How many of the *Desaparecidos* died because of him, God knows.' He turned to Barratt. 'An' that silly little bitch of a sister of yours goes an' falls in love wi' him. Not once, but a second time, up there in the Andes at his ranch near Cajamarca. Not only lets him use her, but lets him fill her up wi' coke.' He looked round, suddenly conscious of Pete standing on the companion ladder just behind him. 'Ye heard that?'

Pete nodded.

'So what d'ye think happened?'

'God knows.'

'He shot himself. That's what Ah was tryin' ter tell that silly woman.' He nodded towards the closed door of Iris's cabin, then turned again to Barratt. 'Ye don't care to believe what Pete wrote, do ye? Ye don't want ter think aboot a situation where she falls in love wi' a beautifully handsome monster who is evil, thru' an' thru', an' who, at that same time, she believes to be her half-brother.' He shook his head. 'Wimen. My God! Who was it who said ye canna live wi' them, an' ye canna live wi'oot them?'

'Adam, I imagine.'

He looked at me, but without any hostility, both of us, I imagine, thinking of his wife and her amoral behaviour.

'Time we got under way,' Pete said. 'What about your boat, Iain? Do we tow it?'

'Aye. Tow it.'

'Okay, but if you've left anything in it that'll spoil get it out now. Could be a wet tow. The wind's getting up again.' He turned to me. 'Better get some warmer clothes on. It'll be chilly when we get under way.' He yelled for Iris to take the wheel, then started up the companion ladder, pausing halfway to look back at Barratt. 'What's your Christian name, did you say?'

'He didn't,' Ward said. 'Ah did, an' it's Ferdinand. Ferdinand, as in Ferdinand and Isabella, the two monarchs who finally kicked the Moors out of Spain an' started Columbus on his way.' He said it loud enough for Iris to hear him beyond her closed door, and I got the impression it was he who had thought up this alias for a man who had been baptised Eduardo Connor-Gómez.

It took us the better part of an hour to get under way, the main anchor having dragged into the edge of the kelp. It meant winching the ship up to it, hoisting it into its housing, then winching out to the second anchor. Quite an exercise since Pete wouldn't use the engine until we were well clear of the kelp for fear of wrapping the weed round the prop. 'Take quite a time to disconnect the shaft and swing the prop up clear of the water.' This, and other pieces of information, were tossed to me in between giving directions to Iris, who was manoeuvring the ship from the upper steering position on the flat top of the wheelhouse.

I had no need of warmer clothes. Fetching those two anchors proved hard, exhausting work, even with power winches, and I was sweating by the time we had the second anchor stowed. I stood there for a moment, looking up at Iris, now muffled in a thick, padded anorak.

The way she and Pete worked the ship between them, no orders given, just a few hand signals. It was a joy to watch them. At no time had I felt we were in any danger of getting tangled up with the great lianas of weed rising from the seabed and sprawled out in a lazily-moving quagmire of glistening brown fronds.

We were under way now, driving straight into the breeze as it funnelled up the cove. In an instant my body's refrigeration system turned the sweat ice-cold. I dived into the wheelhouse and grabbed my oilskin jacket. I heard my name called, and when I went out on to the deck again, I found Ward and Barratt winching the mains'l up, the slat of canvas almost drowning the noise of the engine.

It was Pete who had called to me. He was up in the bows, clearing the tie-ers from the fores'l ready for hoisting. He wanted me to wind it up with the foremast winch. He joined me almost immediately, tagging on the hoist, the tail end of which was rope spliced into wire.

We then moved to the winches aft, sheeting the main in hard, then the fores'l. Bold Point was already almost abeam. Pete stood, his slim body balanced like a ballet dancer, watching the rocky shore sliding by. 'Okay. You can bear away now.' Suddenly all was peace as the breeze filled the sails and Iris cut the engine. For a moment the five of us just stood there, relaxing. Everything had gone so smoothly. 'You, what do I call you? We use Christian names on board.' Pete had moved to face Barratt. 'Do I call you Eduardo?' He shook his head. 'No, that won't do. We already have an Eddie here.'

'His Christian name is Ferdinand,' Ward growled.

'On board ship? With his sister here?'

'Ferdinand,' Ward repeated. 'Get used to it. You, too, Iris. If ye don't, sooner or later somebody will hear ye and the word will be out. When we come back from the Weddell will be time enough to think about a passport in his rightful name.'

'Okay.' Pete nodded. 'But I'm not yelling Ferdinand in an emergency. Too much of a mouthful. Ferd. It'll have to be Ferd. Right?' He didn't wait for Barratt to reply, moving off along the deck and calling for Iain to release the catches on the forehatch. 'Come on, Ferd. Give me a hand up for'ard. You, Eddie – you go below and help Iain pass up the warps. Bow and stern warps,' he called as Iain's bulk disappeared back into the wheelhouse. 'Springers, too.'

Iris stayed at the upper steering position. It was all so like sailing the Outer Isles with Mickey and Phil, except that *Isvik* was so much bigger, so very much more complicated than their Swan 32.

The breeze, funnelling up Falkland Sound, was strengthening, the ship leaning to it close-hauled as Iris held her with the two sails just shivering. It was colder now and I went into the wheelhouse. Ward was on the HF radio, talking to the Alexander Towing tug normally stationed in Mare Harbour, East Cove.

Listening to their conversation, I gathered the tug had left Elephant Bay, Pebble Island, just before sunset the previous evening. It was towing a string of three barges loaded with KLME's seismographical gear and accommodation unit. The disembodied voice of the tugmaster informed Ward over the loudspeaker that his present position was approximately two miles south of the entrance to Many Branch Harbour. He was making eight knots through the water, between six and seven over the ground, and he refused absolutely to slow down or wait for us off the Port Howard entrance. 'If the little lady wants to come aboard for the last part of the tow, you'll have to make the transfer before nightfall, eh?'

'She's the one who's payin' ye,' Ward said bluntly.

'Right. But only to deliver these three chicks to Cow Hangar Cove. There's a window in the weather right now which, pray God, will last till we clear the end of the Sound. I should be through Eagle Passage as dawn breaks and round Porpoise Point and through Bleaker Jump into Cow Hangar all in daylight. If she really wants to come on board she's welcome, but I'm not hanging about for her, so better shift ass, boy.'

Ward didn't reply. He didn't even sign off. He just hung up, switching frequency and calling the FIGAS flight, which had just left Goose Green. The pilot confirmed that Miss Phuket was on board, and he gave his ETA at Port Howard.

I'd been following the conversation on the chart, which was laid out flat on the chart table. The narrow gut of an entrance to the long arm of Port Howard inlet was still nearly three miles away and we were barely making three knots under the small amount of sail we had hoisted. 'What about a genoa, instead of that jib?' I suggested. 'Have you got one?'

Pete was in the wheelhouse now and he vetoed the suggestion. 'We've got one, but it's a pretty big sail. By the time we've lugged it up on deck, flaked it out and hanked it on ready for hoisting, we'll be just about into The Narrows, and I'm not wearing that amount of canvas when we turn downwind with the wharf and the sheds only a couple of miles away. Could be blowing hard between the ridges.'

By then Ward was actually talking to La Belle on VHF, trying to get her to drop the idea of transferring to the tug. 'The weather's deterioratin' an' since he refuses to stop for ye it could be a wee bit hazardous. Ye'll have all the time in the world to talk to your people at Cow Hangar.' But apparently she was insistent, and though he tried to argue her out of it, he finally said, 'Your funeral then. It'll be an uncomfortable transfer. Tell the Port Howard people to drive ye straight down to the quay, and fast.'

Just as he replaced the hand mike, we caught sight of the Islander, a glint of sunlight on its wings as it swept in over the Sound from the direction of Shag Rookery Point. We could see it dropping towards the hill with the airfield on it, and ten minutes later, with the wind building up in gusts along the outer ridge of West Falkland Island, we entered The Narrows, the ship sheering wildly, the speed indicator showing seven knots. Away to the north we could now see the tug and its attendant barges growing rapidly larger. We were back on deck then. 'You can start easing off on the mainsheet now.' Pete was already easing off the fores'l as Iris began the turn to starb'd that would take us down to the quay.

It never occurred to me that we would go alongside under sail. The airfield Range Rover was already parked there as we roared past the end of the quay. I had a glimpse of La Belle, small and very elegant in a beautifully-cut navy suit, and then all hell broke loose, the winches humming as we hauled in on the sheets till the sails were hard as boards. We had turned completely about and were now sail-shivering our way quite slowly up to the end of the quay. I took the after warp for'ard to the bows, outside of both sets of standing rigging, and stood there with the end of it held coiled in my hand. I wouldn't have believed it, all the weight of that big ship and Iris touched the bows so gently against the wood covering of the concrete piers that I felt no more than the slightest judder and was able to step ashore. Moving quickly aft, I got several turns round the farthest bollard, slowing her forward movement, while Pete ran the bow warp out and made fast.

It was all over so quickly, Iain virtually lifting La Belle on board. Her baggage followed, the Vuitton cases flung into the scuppers, and then I was loosening off the after warp and clambering on board, Ferd Barratt backing the fores'l, the bows swinging, the ship moving away from the quay. 'Let me know when you get tired of roughing it, Miss Pooket.' It was the Station Manager, a last plug for the comforts of Port Howard Lodge as we lowered the fores'l and began motor-sailing on the main to get back to the Sound and catch up with that tug.

'You'll not get anything as tricky as this down in the Weddell,' Pete said. We were coming out of The Narrows and the wind was down-draughting, the ship heeling heavily to port. 'It'll just be colder. That's all. Nothing to worry about, and always an island of ice to hitch on to.' He was grinning at me.

Motor-sailing, we managed to make eight knots plus against the wind, and with the tug, and its train of barges, only about two miles ahead of us, Pete reckoned we would be able to make the transfer at about 1900 hours, well before dark.

'Are ye sure that's what ye want?'

Either she didn't hear, or else she deliberately chose to ignore him. She just stood there on the port side, a little for'ard of the mainmast, with her arms folded across her breasts.

'Forecast's no' verra good. Could be a wee bit rough.'

It made no impression on her, the expression on her face quite blank as she gazed across the bows towards the south. The way she held her arms, it was almost as though she were hugging herself, in anticipation of some excitement to come, or was it just because she felt a thrill at being back here in the Falklands?

She stood like that for quite a long time. Then, suddenly, she turned, 'I'm going to the cabin now. Tell the tug I will wait until we are in the shelter of the Speedwell Islands. And do it on VHF. You understand please?'

'It will be dark by the time we're in the lee of the Speedwells,' Ward said.

'I know that.' She said it flatly, her tone making it clear that her decision was final. Even so, Ward persisted. 'Are ye sure ye really have to go across to the tug? Why not wait until we get to Cow Hangar?'

'Yes, quite sure.' She walked quickly past him into the wheelhouse, adding, 'And when you speak to the tug remember please, speak on VHF.'

The significance of this request was not apparent to me at the time, nor I think to Ward as he watched her trim, neatly-suited little body disappear down the companion ladder.

I asked Ward what he made of her insistence on going across to the tug. He shook his head. 'She probably feels the need to assert herself.' He nodded. 'Aye. Ah reck'n it must be that. But Ah don't understand why she needs to prove she's a tough little lady. Ah know that already.'

It would be nearly midnight before we came under the lee of

175

Speedwell Island, but it made sense to postpone the transfer. Conditions were steadily deteriorating, the wind already force 4 and increasing, the moon lost behind banks of black cloud.

Those few hours, when we were all together on *Isvik*, gave me the opportunity to familiarise myself with the personalities involved in what I was beginning to think of as the Weddell Sea venture. What else could you call it? An expedition? But it wasn't that. Whatever Ward was financing, it wasn't research or exploration. He wasn't that sort of man. Nor was the slim little Chinese lady, the scars showing through her make-up. She had changed into trousers and looked quite dumpy in bright red oilskins, standing out on the deck, regardless of the little gusts of cold drizzle the wind periodically flung at us, her face impassive, quite oblivious of the weather.

Contrary to what Pete had suggested, she and Iris Sunderby seemed to have hit it off. They had never met before, but they took to each other, Iris showing her over the ship, then taking her below, where the two of them produced mugs of very chilli-hot goose stew, which we ate in the wheelhouse.

It was as Ferd and I, under Pete's direction, prepared *Isvik*'s semi-rigid inflatable for launching that I heard La Belle say, 'You know, I think is more interesting, the trip you make.' She and Iris were standing watching us. 'I prefer this to a big icebreaker. Is more –' she hesitated for the word – 'companionable.'

The icebreaker had apparently just arrived in Mare Harbour. 'When are you sailing?' Iris asked.

'In two days. Is loading now. I have talk with Iain Ward.'

Iris laughed. 'You want to check the inventory at your old base on the Ronne, is that it?'

'*Oui*. But it is not so much the inventory. It is the condition of everything.'

'Don't you trust him?'

'Of course – if I am there.' And they both laughed.

It was a reminder of what lay ahead, and what the value of the equipment was that KLME had been forced to abandon on the Ice Shelf. And if another section of the Ice Front had split away from the main body of the Shelf during the winter, the huts and equipment might no longer exist. It was a gamble Ward was taking, and a very expensive one. For what? What was the lure that had brought him all this way from home, banking on the KLME equipment still functioning and the C-130 being serviceable? Before we got to Cow Hangar Cove I would need to know, otherwise I would be going into it blind. Did La Belle know? I should have asked her while I had the chance, but when Pete and I had finished getting the semi-inflatable ready for launching she was back in the wheelhouse with Iain.

I did mention it to Barratt, who was standing by the rail, breathing deeply, but he just stared at me and shook his head.

'You're coming with us, aren't you? On *Isvik*.'

He still didn't answer, his face pale and his eyes oddly bleak. Then he turned abruptly and went into the wheelhouse. The clouds were lower now and the wind was stronger, blowing a thin veil of drizzle across my face. Iain was in the helmsman's seat, steering with his gloved hand, looking at the chart and making notes with his left. The last of the barges was only just visible, the tug itself completely hidden by a curtain of wind-blown drizzle.

'This place Cow Hangar,' I said as he tore the page he had been writing on out of the pad and stuffed it into the breast pocket of his blue denim shirt, 'is it a settlement?'

He looked at me quickly. 'Ye want ter know Belle's new location, that it? Where they're goin' to run their shots.' He pulled the chart round so that I could see it. 'There's Cow Hangar. Old cattle country in the days when there were no sheep and the islands were peopled by gauchos from the South American mainland.' He was pointing to a deep inlet on the south-west shore of Adventure Sound just west of the Bleakers. 'They'll be surveyin' over towards Cattle Point.' And then he added with a sly little smile, 'Ah'm guessing there. She's much too fly to volunteer that sort of information. But all will be revealed once they start moving their equipment.'

'Is that why you arranged for Lange to stay at Cow Hangar?'

'What d'ye mean?'

'So that he could monitor her operation for Greenpeace.'

He didn't answer immediately, just sat there as though thinking it out. Finally he shook his head, and, looking straight at me, he said, 'Ye know Ah'm not sure. Ah only spoke to him very briefly, in Brawdy's office. Ah got the impression he was worried sick aboot somethin'. Wouldn't talk about it. Something personal to himself that was eatin' into him. Know what Ah mean? Ye met him. Ye had a talk wi' him, night before last.'

I nodded.

'Well then, ye'll understand how Ah felt. The puir little sod was scared. Ah could smell it. But scared of what he wouldna say. Ah just felt sorry for him, tha's all. Somethin' on his mind, an' nowhere to go. So Ah gave him a note to Josh, told him to find his way to Cow Hangar and they'd look after him.'

I asked him whether that was the only reason.

He shrugged. 'Does there have to be a reason? It was done on the spur of the moment. As Ah say, Ah felt sorry for the puir wee laddie.' He laughed. 'Don't know that Ah'm usually that kind-hearted. He wanted to join *Isvik* for the voyage into the Weddell. Ah said he'd have to talk to Iris, or Pete, one of the two. What d'ye think? He's experienced. He's got a good physique.' He stared at me, waiting for a reply, and when I didn't say anything, he nodded. 'Okay. So he's got something gnawing at his guts, something that's eating into him. And we don't know what. Ah've seen boys like that. He's still growin' up, and faced with somethin' that's too big for him, he could suddenly crack.'

We were now meeting the first of the Southern Ocean wave trains deflected up the Sound. They were coming at us on the starb'd bow, so that *Isvik*'s movement through the water had become a twisted roller-coaster ride that was liable to catch one off balance.

Iris's head appeared from the saloon below. 'All you're concerned about,' she said to Iain, 'is keeping him off your own back.'

'What the hell d'ye mean by that?'

She reached for a handgrip and hauled herself up, balancing with ease as a wave rolled under us. 'Focus his mind on Belle's operation and he'll be too busy to monitor yours.'

'Ah told ye, he wants to sail wi' ye. Think aboot it, Iris. He'd be a useful hand.'

'You want him where you can see him, I think.' She laughed. 'Then you know what he reports to Greenpeace. Isn't that it?' And she added, 'How do I know whether he makes a good hand on board or turns out to be as sick as a dog and no bloody good?'

Iain turned to me. 'Ye're the only one of us who's really talked with him. What d'ye think? Will the laddie fit?'

'As a hand on the voyage down to the Ronne, yes,' I said. 'But once we're there . . .' I began to explain about his father's death and his attitude to Belle, but I was interrupted by the tugmaster's voice on the VHF saying he agreed with Miss Pooket's suggestion that the transfer be postponed until we were under the lee of Speedwell Island. 'The wind's got up and if we do it now she'll likely get an ice-cold bath.'

We were closing the last of the three barges with the Tyssens to starb'd and Great Island dead ahead. It would be dark by the time we were into the shelter of Eagle Passage. But it made sense and Pete agreed. 'We'll go into watches right away.' Anything to do with the ship he was very sure of himself, very much in command. He split us up into two watches. Iris and I would take the first, he and Iain the second. La Belle was already stretched out on Iris's bunk and Ferd was only too happy to get his head down. He looked quite white.

We cut through The Pass, south-east of Great Island, and came out into the open again, west of the Wolfe Islands. The ship was beginning to pound. 'You all right?' Iris asked me.

'Fine,' I said. But I wasn't so sure. The movement was very peculiar and my eyes tended to blur when pencilling in our course on the chart. I envied the others stretched out on their bunks down below.

'Why don't you flake out on the settle in the saloon?'

'No.' Damned if I was going to fade out in front of this young woman who appeared to have a cast-iron stomach and ran the ship with such ease and confidence.

'Okay. Then tell me about your flying.'

It was kind of her, for it took my mind off my insides and enabled me to ignore the way my body was breaking out into a cold sweat. She seemed really interested, asking all the right questions, and as I talked I found myself balancing in harmony with the movements of the ship.

We kept watch together for almost three hours, and by then I was my normal self again. It was very dark now, and the big swell angling up from the Horn was being broken by Stinker Island and the Elephant Cays. Another half-hour and we were past Phillip's Point. As we came under the lee of Speedwell Island the tugmaster called us to say his boat was in the water and would be with us shortly.

For most of our watch we had been sailing at the same speed as the tug, holding a position about two hundred metres off her starb'd side. I took the wheel and Iris went into her cabin to rouse our passenger. She came up almost immediately, wearing a heavy sweater under her red oilskins, a black beret on her head. 'Have you seen any other boats?' She peered out at the sea beyond the red glow of our port navigation light. There was a long, low swell coming up through Eagle Passage, otherwise the water was fairly calm. She seemed nervous, her face very pale, her body tense. 'Anything for me on the radio?'

Iris shook her head. 'No. Nothing.' She took the wheel from me again.

'Are you sure?'

'Of course I am sure. Why?' She was watching the other woman with a slight frown. 'Were you expecting something?'

'No, no. I just wonder.'

On instructions from the tugmaster Iris was allowing *Isvik* to drop back. We were just abreast of the last barge when a small light showed under its stern. 'Here is your boat now.'

Belle hesitated, as though suddenly reluctant to do what she herself had been so insistent on. Then she lifted her head and I could almost see her square her shoulders. 'Is okay. I go now.' She glanced at Iris, smiled briefly, then slid back the wheelhouse door, letting in the sound of the sea. 'You give me your hand please.' This to me, and I followed her out on to the deck. The boat roared alongside, a semi-rigid inflatable, the painter snaking through the air to fall at my feet. I made it fast, then helped her over the side into the boat.

Holding her arm, I could feel her trembling. 'Nothing to worry about,' I said. 'You'll only be in the boat a few minutes, then you'll be on the tug.'

'You think I care about making passage across this little water?' She was looking up at me, her feet searching for the plastic bulge of the inflatable's side. Her eyes looked enormous, almost unnaturally bright, as though she had taken some sort of a drug. She said something in Chinese, said it very quietly through teeth clenched tight, then she let go my arm and collapsed like a limp puppet into the bottom of the boat. The man in the stern, a big fellow, his features lost in the hood of his oilskin jacket, raised his hand. I dropped the painter into the bows and he gunned the outboard engine, steering a quick half-circle and heading back under the stern of that last barge.

I returned to the warmth of the wheelhouse, and time passed. Ten minutes by the clock above the control board lengthened to a quarter of an hour. We were forging ahead now, for there was no longer any point in staying with the tow. We would meet up with it again at Cow Hangar Cove. We passed quite close to the tug. It was then that her skipper came on the air to ask why we hadn't sent his boat back. 'Is the little lady still with you?' The note of exasperation in his voice indicated an attitude to women that caused Iris to tell him quite sharply that his boat had left us a good fifteen minutes ago. 'If it has not returned to you, then the engine must have broken down.'

Iain erupted into the wheelhouse. 'She's not arrived back at the tug, is that it?' Iris nodded, and he bent his head, listening intently to the exchange between her and the skipper of the tug. 'Are ye clear enough to cross his bows?'

'I think so. Why?'

'Then let's go. We need to be on the other side of those barges.' His voice was urgent. 'Something's happened.'

'How d'you mean? What –'

'Put the wheel over, woman.' He was across the wheelhouse in a couple of strides, making for the engine controls and switching to maximum revs. The roar of the big Mercedes diesel filled the night.

We crossed the tug's bows with only a few metres to spare, the voice of her skipper coming over the radio with information about a small blip seen on his radar away to port shortly after they had passed Phillip's Point. 'Difficult to tell with the land so close behind it, but it looked like a fishing boat paralleling our course. Then it seemed to move out towards us.'

'Ye sure about that?'

'Of course I'm not sure. It was against the land, I tell you.'

'Can ye see anything of it now?'

'No. The barges blocked it out.'

'It came astern of ye then?'

'I'm not sure. Why?'

Iain didn't answer. He was staring down at the chart. Then he turned to Pete. 'Ye got John Smith's map of the Falkland wrecks? Ah thought Ah caught sight of it in one o' the chart drawers. It's a

181

yellow map o' the Islands, the wrecks drawn in meticulous detail, names, history, everything.' His urgency was reflected in a broadening of his accent. 'Ah seem to recall –' He stopped there, the voice over the loudspeaker saying, 'If something happened to our boat and that blip was a fishing vessel ...' The tugmaster was suggesting it might have gone to their boat's assistance.

'Mebbe.' Iain said it doubtfully. 'We'll know soon enough, eh? Call ye back as soon as Ah've anything to report.'

We had been running down the black slab sides of the laden barges. Now, as we closed the last of them, Pete went to the upper steering platform above the wheelhouse, swinging the beam of the big spotlight across the lazily heaving swell as we zigzagged back along our course at reduced revs.

We found the tug's semi-rigid inflatable about three miles astern of the last barge, the outboard still ticking over and the driver slumped in the stern. There was no sign of Belle.

THREE

By the time we had got the man on board he was beginning to come round. He had an ugly scalp wound and was babbling incoherently. 'Somethin' metallic,' Iain said as we laid him out on the saloon settle. 'Pistol butt probably.' He told Nils to look after him and ran back up the ladder to the wheelhouse, ordering Iris to the radar and Pete to get him the wreck map he had asked about earlier.

I think we were all in a state of shock, all of us that is except Iain, who snatched the map Pete held out to him, laid it on the flat top of the chart table and moved the adjustable lamp so that it was right down on the paper. 'There's a couple o' wrecks, but they're both sunk. The nearest that's above water ...' He glanced up. 'Ha' ye got him yet?' he asked Iris.

'I'm not sure. I thought just for a moment ...' She had her eyes glued to the radar sweep. 'It could have been a rock. It was close against the land.'

'Bearing?'

'About nine-O.'

'Can you see it still?'

She nodded. 'I think so. But it could be another rock. It's moved position.'

'The direction, for God's sake. Which way has it moved?' The impatience in his voice mirrored his urgency. 'South-east?'

'Yes, south-east. But it's so close inshore ...'

'Och aye.' He was no longer listening, his pencil fixed on a point on the chart. 'Looks like he's headed for the *Suzie Whittaker*. That's the only wreck shown lyin' above water in this vicinity. It's round Porpoise Point, up across Bull Roads, sheltered from the westerlies. Just where Ah would have expected him to hole up.' He peered down at the map, reading with the aid of the chart table magnifying

183

glass: '*Iron barque, carrying a cargo o' teak an' ivory from Rangoon to Liverpool, beached in a gale, 1885.* And there's a nice little picture of her too.' He threw the pencil down and turned to Pete. 'Put the revs right up to maximum. Ah want all the power we can get. If Ah'm right ...' He hesitated, frowning down at the map and murmuring to himself, 'Ah should've guessed. That boy – the bugger had scared the life out of him.'

The others didn't hear that and Pete started to ask the obvious questions – the same questions that were streaking through my own mind. Iain turned on him then, his voice suddenly harsh. 'Give me full power for Christ's sake.' He had hold of the wheel now, turning *Isvik*'s bows back towards the tug's towing lights. 'Then work out courses for Porpoise Point.'

I saw Pete hesitate. Accustomed now, I suppose, to running the ship himself, he resented being ordered about. But the urgency in Iain's voice got through to him. He reached over for the rev-control lever. 'I take it you know what you're doing.' He began pressing for the big spotlight to be manned again and a search pattern worked out. 'You're just guessing, aren't you?'

'Guessing?' Iain shrugged. 'Mebbe Ah am. But take a look at the chart. Lange told me the boat he came ashore in was an inflatable with a very powerful outboard. The bastard daren't come out into the open water of the Sound. We'd pick him up. And the nearest shelter is round the corner of that big peninsula.' He tapped the long promontory running down from The Black Hill and finishing in what looked like the skeletal shape of a sea horse. 'If there's a hole in the hull of that wreck it's the perfect hide for him, and once round Porpoise Point ...' I lost the rest of it in the crash of a wave bursting against our starb'd side. And then: 'A hell of a ride she'll be having out there.' He was shouting now, the roar of the big diesel loud in the night, vibration hammering at the soles of our feet and the bows slamming as we hit wind-whipped chunks of breaking water.

I, too, was thinking of that poor wretched woman out there, slammed to hell and drenched with spray. All the horrors she had been through, and now this.

My thoughts were interrupted by a cry from Iris. 'I think I've got him now.' And she asked Iain for his heading.

'Almost due south,' was his reply.

'And the bearing on the next headland?'

'The same. Ah'm steering to run between Mid Island and the jut of land by Speedwell Settlement.'

'The blip I'm picking up is close in to the land on the eastern side of the Passage. And its position is changing quite rapidly. If it is him, and not the break of waves, he is moving fast.'

Iain handed the wheel to Pete, glanced quickly at the chart, then pushed Iris aside. 'That'll be Flores Harbour he's off, with Butler's Hill behind it.' He was standing with his feet apart, hands gripping the ledge in front of him, his eyes glued to the radar. 'He's hugging the East Falkland shore, hoping we won't pick him up. An' ye're right. He's movin' fast.' He turned to me. 'That boy – ye say it was an inflatable he came ashore in?'

I shook my head. 'That's right.'

He straightened up, staring intently for'ard, the moon showing through a ragged black hole in the cloud cover. 'Reck'n that's Peat Bog Ridge, that high land bearing green three-O. Soon as it's abeam we'll start crossin' over to the east side of the Passage.' He told Iris to take the wheel. 'We're going to have our work cut out to hoist the genoa. When ye're masked by Mid Island switch off all lights, everything. Understand?' He didn't wait for an answer, calling on me to follow him and sliding back the wheelhouse door. Once outside, he moved quickly for'ard, bent almost double against the wind.

It was cold on deck. The near ten knots we were making, plus the force of the wind funnelling up Eagle Passage made the wind-chill quite nasty. What it would be like sitting immobilised in an inflatable powering along a lee shore I shuddered to think. It was different for us. We were on the move all the time and we soon warmed up, for it was hard work getting that bloody genoa on deck from the forepeak, hanking it on to the forestay, then hoisting it, and there were all the ropes. I found it very confusing, and just as we had got the sail hoisted, and Pete was yelling at me to go aft and sheet in on the port winch, Iris pulled the switch and the deck lights, everything, went out.

It must have taken us the better part of half an hour to get that sail up and drawing properly. By then the tug, with its three barges, was way astern of us. We had radioed the master that his man was warm and reasonably comfortable, and that we would probably have him back on the tug in Cow Hangar Cove around lunch time. 'An' wi' luck,' Iain added, 'we'll also have your little lady charterer.'

The tugmaster had also picked up the blip, but could do nothing about it with the three barges in tow, only swear. This he did, giving in some detail the things he would do if he ever got his hands on her kidnapper. To which Iain replied, 'Wi' any luck Ah'll be doin' it for ye. Okay? See ye in Cow Hangar. Over and out.'

All this time Pete had been up for'ard, his safety harness clipped to a ring in the deck, staring up at the foremast and feeling the tension on the starb'd stay, which on our present tack was taking a great deal of strain, particularly when *Isvik* fell off the top of a wave. Suddenly he unclipped his harness and came scrambling aft. Back in the wheelhouse, he told Iain he was taking a hell of a risk with that genoa. 'You could lose the foremast. When we clear George Island we'll have only the low Barren Island between us and the full force of the wind –'

'There's a woman's life at stake,' Iain cut in. 'To hell wi' the mast. We'll be runnin' almost downwind by then.'

'On to a lee shore,' Pete reminded him. 'And round Porpoise Point we'll have to gybe. If that mast goes then –' A gust hit us. I could feel the boat straining and Iris cried out that she could barely hold her.

'Give her to me.' Iain took the wheel from her. 'An' go back to the radar. See if ye can pick the bastard up again.'

'There'll be too much broken water, the surf piling in –'

'Well try, damn ye.'

It was going to be a long, hard night, and no sleep for anyone. The waves were growing larger as we moved over to the eastern shore, breaking now and slamming against the starb'd bow, white water pouring across the deck, the ship heeling so violently I felt sure something must give. The speed indicator showed sixteen knots in the surges and Iain was using all his strength at times to hold her from broaching-to. 'You've got to reduce sail.' Pete had to shout to make himself heard above the noise of water and wind.

'That means lying-to, wasting time.'

'Your fault. You insisted on the genoa.'

Iain stared at him, his eyes gone suddenly hard. 'Ye scared, laddie? 'Cause if ye are, ye'd best go to your bunk. It's my ship an Ah'm sailing it as is till that sail splits or the mast goes. Okay?'

Pete was white-faced as he yelled, 'It's not your ship. Not any longer. You gave it to Iris. It's all we've got.'

'Fuck that! There's a woman out there with a wild beast –'

'How the hell do you know?' And he added, 'You do know, don't you? You know who it is.' He turned to me. 'It's the man who came ashore with Lange, isn't it? Who is he, some sort of a pirate? From a Korean ship. Didn't you say it was a Korean ship?' The deck heaved under our feet and the four of us held on to whatever was handy as the wheelhouse lay on its side.

'*Por Dios!*' Iris was sprawled on the deck at my feet, grabbing at my legs as she slithered across to the port side, her nails scrabbling at the brown teak of the boards.

'Another half-hour,' Iain said as the wheelhouse righted itself. 'That's all. We'll be running eastward then with the sheets eased, and when we're round Porpoise Island –' Another wave hit us.

'I'm going to get that sail off.' Pete's voice was suddenly calm and quite decisive. 'She'll ride better and probably make just about the same speed.' He told Nils to take over the engine controls and hold her into the wind while we lowered the sail and stowed it, then he dived down the ladder to the saloon, yelling for Barratt.

We were a long time struggling with that sail, bundling it up and pushing it down the for'ard hatch. By then we were half across the Passage and Barratt was being sick. As we came out of the lee of George Island, we were into the uninterrupted flow of the wave trains rolling like downland hills beneath us. They were not breaking quite so much and I noted that Pete had been right, we were going almost as fast.

Iain turned to me in the sudden quiet as another wave rolled under us and *Isvik* slid down the back of it. 'Wonder if he'll try for a ransom before he kills her. What do you think?' It was said in such a matter-of-fact tone that it was hard to believe he was talking about the murder of a young woman we both knew and who had been here on board only a few hours back.

'Who?' I had to shout as an extra large wave picked us up and flung us forward. 'Who are you talking about?' I was holding hard to the corner of the chart table, the wheelhouse reeling.

'Seng,' he replied. 'The last of that Pol Pot patrol, the one she ha'na' dealt with yet. Tan Seng.'

I was remembering the look on her face as she had let go my

hands and dropped into the tug's inflatable. 'The patrol leader. That who you mean?'

'Aye.' He nodded. 'The man who had her parents slaughtered before her eyes, who raped her while his men burned the huts with the village people locked inside and who threw her into the last of the huts and torched it over her head.'

He was looking at Iris as he said that, and she stared back at him open-mouthed, her eyes wide with the shock of what he was telling her. Pete was looking at him, too, the expression on his face one of disbelief and horror. 'The last of them,' Iain added. 'All of them dealt with except –' He staggered to the slam of a wave breaking astern, the ship shuddering as it hit the back of the wheelhouse, white water roaring along the deck. 'I wonder ...' He was thinking aloud, his voice barely audible. 'She could have planned it. She could have planned the whole thing. And if that's the case ...' He was staring at me hard. 'What do you think – will he go for a ransom? Is that what she's banking on?'

I was thinking back to that scene in the Dragon Rouge in Paris, her account of what had been done to her and her family, and Iain telling me later, his tone quite dispassionate, how she had administered her own form of justice. Could she really have laid a trail that had drawn their leader to the Falkland Islands and this strange incident in the dark of the Eagle Passage? It didn't seem possible, and yet ... 'You really think ...?'

'Aye. But it's no' what Ah think. It's nothin' to do wi' logic. It's just a gut feelin' Ah have.'

'And it's just a gut feeling you have that he's taking her to this wreck the other side of Porpoise Point.'

He didn't answer that, muttering something about being miserable. He was staring out at the night, and then, quite clearly, I heard him say: '*Which way shall I fly Infinite wrath, and infinite despair?*'

I looked across at Pete, wondering what the hell he meant.

'*Which way I fly is hell; myself am hell; And in the lowest deep a lower deep Still threatening to devour me opens wide ...*' Pete was at the wheel now and he gave a little shrug, then leaned over to me and whispered, 'Milton. *Paradise Lost*, I think. He and I, we share a love of poetry.' And he added, 'I remember, when we were trekking back across the ice from that wooden graveyard of a wreck, Iain suddenly started

188

quoting from *The Rubáiyát of Omar Khayyám*. Fitzgerald.'

A wave hit, water flooding for'ard, the whole deck submerged again in a flurry of foam. We were running almost free now on a course of one-one-O degrees logging ten knots, and more at times. 'Why the *Suzie Whittaker*?' Iris asked in the quiet that followed the sea draining off the deck.

Iain told her then about the SAS men who had holed up in the SS *Garland*, a 600-ton iron barque condemned in 1900 and beached in Choiseul Sound south-east of Goose Green. 'Ye've been in the Falklands long enough surely to have heard the story, how they warned the San Carlos beachhead of Argentine air attacks in time for the Navy to lock their missiles on to them or call the Harriers down.

'Just a couple of our boys living it up in that Godforsaken hulk with a short-wave transmitter, nothing but cold rations an' the water rising an' falling with the tide. Bloody awful.'

I had moved to the radar, the sweep now showing in close-up the low-lying peninsula that finished at Porpoise Point.

'With this wind we'll be round the corner inside of half an hour,' Pete said. He was peering over my shoulder. 'Not much shelter from the wind as we run north across Bull Roads, but the sea will be a lot easier. What's that?' He leaned closer. 'There. Down by Tussac Point.'

It was a blip. No doubt of it now, and right at the bottom of the peninsula and moving position with each sweep. On a rough calculation it looked like we were a good half-hour behind. All Iain said when I told him was, 'A lot can happen in half an hour wi' a man like that. Let's hope he's hungry for cash.'

The blip merged with the end of the land. 'It's gone now,' Pete said. 'It's round the corner.'

'How long before he reaches the *Suzie Whittaker*?'

I had already worked that one out. The peninsula was shaped like the head of a very battered Iron Age axe. It was about three miles long and another five miles from Bull Point and Porpoise Island to the wreck. The sea would be quieter then and he would make better speed. 'Forty minutes,' I said. 'Maybe a little less.'

He nodded, leaning forward and peering intently at the chart. 'We'll make it in *Isvik* as far as Bull Island. Ah'll go in from there wi' the inflatable. Eddie, ye'll come wi' me. The others stay wi' the ship.' He didn't ask us, just presumed we would agree. Pete remained at the wheel, Ward telling him to let him know when we were abreast of Porpoise Point and ready to turn north. 'Gi' me a shout. Ye'll need to gybe then.' And to me he said, 'Better get your head down too. A wee kip will freshen ye up.'

I followed him below, wondering how he was going to play it. If it was Seng, and if he had holed up in the old barque, then it could be tricky. 'Oilskins, seaboots and a lifejacket,' he said. 'An' Ah hope ye're fit. We'll likely have a long paddle.' He stood for a moment looking down at the man we had found alone in the tug's inflatable, then stepped through the curtained entrance to the cabin next to mine and curled up, fully clothed, on the bunk.

I did the same, but I couldn't sleep, thinking all the time of that poor wretched woman. Perhaps she was dead already. But if not, they would now be very near the beached hulk, and then what? The things he had done to her previously, and what he might do to her now, were there in my brain, picture flashes, all imagined, all feeding adrenalin into the urge that was growing in me, the dreadful, over-powering desire to kill. I'd never felt that before. And trying to analyse the whole situation, my strange involvement with her, it gradually dawned on me that I'd never felt like this about a woman before. I had never had this protective feeling. My mind running dreamily back over the women I had known, some of them I couldn't even remember clearly, I realised it had just been excitement, fun, straight sex and the desire to dominate. Not this. This was different.

I was still thinking about that, my mind engrossed in fantasies that shook me to the core, for they were all about killing and vengeance, when reality stepped in with the steely grip of a hand on my shoulder. 'Come on. Time t'go.' Something hard and cold was pressed into my hand. 'Ever used one o'these?'

I swung my legs off the bunk, looking down at the gun Iain had put into my hand. 'Only in practice,' I said. But that had been the ordinary Service hand gun. This was smaller, a light automatic.

'Aim for the legs an' ye'll probably hit him in the stomach. The tendency is for it to jerk upwards as ye fire.' He showed me the safety catch and the single shot lever, then he was gone and I sat there for a little while, looking down at it, realising that the man I was going with to that wreck was a professional. But what sort of professional? An undercover agent, SAS, Intelligence, or just a very dangerous private operator ...? He could be any of them. I didn't know. I was suddenly not certain of anything, except that I had a gun in my hand and the night's expedition was for real. I was a flyer. The only killing I had ever done was at long range with cannon or machine gun, or that deadly Sidewinder missile. I had never come face-to-face with the man I was trying to kill.

There was noise suddenly above me, feet padding on the deck, the slat of sails, then the crash of the booms coming across. The ship's heeling angle changed abruptly, almost flinging me across the saloon. I stuffed the little automatic into the pocket of my oilskin jacket and clambered up the ladder to the wheelhouse.

We were on port tack now, the sheets eased and the ship on an even keel, the engine humming almost happily now that we had land between us and the march of the Southern Ocean waves. Iain was on the radio to the tugmaster. Iris joined me at the chart table. 'Less than three miles to go.' There was tension in her voice and in the feminine smell of her. The speed indicator was steady at just over twelve. Another quarter of an hour and we would be across Bull Roads Bay and transferring to the tug's inflatable. My mouth felt suddenly dry.

I went over to the far corner of the wheelhouse and stood there, looking out across the port bow. No sign of land, everything very black and the moon hidden behind cloud, the sea only visible as lines of white formed by our bow wave.

I was wondering what this beached hulk would be like. What would we find there? The young Chinese woman disembowelled by a makeshift machete? A scarred head nailed to a beam? All sorts of horrors chased through my mind, imagination running riot. And such a waste! Such a bloody, senseless waste! Her manner, the way she had looked in that emerald sheath of a dress, so beautiful even with the scars bared to my gaze. And so clever. So determined. Why the hell had she dined me with all the scars showing? What had she been trying to say?

I felt almost sick with anger, and only a few hours ago ... A hand gripped my shoulder. 'Ah forget you boys are so busy drivin' your flyin' machines ye don't normally have time to think about the fight ye're headin' into. Stop thinkin' about it an' get this inside ye.' He held a steaming mug out to me. 'A Nils special. Ah've had it before, down in the Weddell. Do ye a worrld of good.' It was a cross between soup and stew, and it was heavily laced with rum. He handed me a spoon. 'Five minutes to go. Nils has got the engine pump ready so we won't have to bale the water out and now he's seeing to the outboard.'

'That gun,' I said. 'Have you got one?' I was thinking of what it would be like if we had to fight it out in the dark of that hulk.

'No. Ah don't like them. Too noisy. But if things begin to go wrong ... Ah like to be covered, that's all.'

We had barely finished our fortified soup when Pete announced he could actually see Bull Island. Iain slowed the engine and as soon as we were under the lee of Black Rincon, we rounded to, dropping all but the main, while Nils pumped the water out of the inflatable we had been towing. Paddles, torches, a spare can of fuel and a packet of biscuits just in case ...

Nobody said anything as Iain and I dropped into the boat. Nils must have primed the outboard, for it started at the first pull of the cord. Pete dropped the painter into the bows, and that was that. We were away, leaving the four of them standing there at the guard rail watching us, and no doubt thinking what I was thinking, that they might never see us again. I tried to kid myself the man wasn't as dangerous as I feared, but then Iain said, 'Put some of this on your face and the backs of your hands.'

He was holding a tin out to me, only the whites of his eyes showing in a face masked with blacking. God knows what the stuff was, but it smelt like shoe polish. I smeared it on, thinking how we would board the hulk, taking the bastard by surprise. But what then? I presumed Iain had some sort of plan, but when I asked him, he simply said, 'We play it by ear. On an exercise like this, if ye plan it, it don't ever work out that way. You just follow me, an' don't use that little toy Ah gave ye unless ye have to.' And then he suddenly switched to questioning me about the Pucará I had found abandoned on that grass airfield back in '82. He wanted to know where it had come from.

'Pebble Island,' I told him.

'No, not Pebble. We dealt with those.'

'Pebble Island,' I repeated. 'I made enquiries, found out the pilot's name, and his address, so I was able to write to him. I had several letters ...' I stopped there, the significance of what he had just said suddenly dawning on me. 'You were on that raid?'

'Ah had a trip there afterwards. They were all immobilised, all the aircraft that were there. Eleven o' them.'

'So you were SAS,' I said. 'That was an SAS raid.'

He hesitated. 'Aye, Ah was there when they went in.' And he added, 'It was aborted, ye know. The first night. Bad weather. Too bad for the choppers. An' when they did go in –' He shrugged. 'It was no' very nice. Wet. Bloody wet. An' windy.'

It was strange talking about that particular episode of the Falklands War, sitting in an inflatable, almost in the water, and shouting to make ourselves heard above the racket of the engine. And that hulk, and the unknown, ahead of us. I had a feeling he had asked about the Pucará episode just to keep my mind occupied, so that I didn't dwell on what lay ahead. He must have known I was in a state of tension, every nerve in my body strung taut. 'The boys would have got yer pen friend if he had been there when we landed.'

'He wasn't there then,' I told him. 'He flew in later. He hadn't enough fuel to make it back to the Argentine, so he turned north and landed at the Pebble Island base. It was deserted. So he flew on in the dawn and landed at the occasional airfield where I found his plane. I think he had already decided to give himself up.'

Looking back, it seemed strange we should be talking about the Pebble Island raid and my subsequent flight in that Pucará – not really talking, virtually shouting at each other – all in the dark, powering our way towards that hulk, with no idea what we would find, if anything. Even stranger perhaps was the fact that I couldn't quite figure out Iain's part in the affair. My impression was that he was already on Pebble Island, but I may be wrong about that. What he said was, 'Ah was scared they wouldna' come at all. The weather was foul an' Sea Kings are not expendable items when ye're eight thousand miles from base.' And he added, 'Nor are forty-five of the best we've got.'

He was referring to the SAS then, saying it as though they were his own crowd. But when I asked him straight out whether he was SAS, he side-stepped the question. 'Ah had somethin' t'do wi' them, tha's all.'

The cloud was thinning now in patches, moonlight filtering through, and I could see he was smiling to himself as he recalled that night. 'The wind was southerly, gale force. It was so strong they had difficulty spreading the rotor blades. Three out o' the four

Sea Kings had to be taken below, engines started up, blades spread and rotating. That's how they got them airborne. It all took time so the raid came in a bloody sight later ...' He stopped there. 'Christ! I can see it now.' He cut the engine. 'It's nearer than Ah thought.' Then in his normal voice, the night suddenly very silent without the noise of the engine, 'This is where we start paddling.'

I was kneeling in water on the bottom of the boat and by the time I had turned to face for'ard the opaque light of the moon was fading. I caught a glimpse of it, bows on to the shore, the stumps of three masts and the deck dipping till the stern disappeared under the water. I had just that glimpse, nothing more, but it remains very clear in my mind. A paddle was thrust into my hand and I saw Iain had tipped the outboard up on its bracket.

'How far do you reckon?' We were both of us kneeling, tentatively synchronising our paddle strokes.

'Half a mile. Probably less.' I felt the steel grip of that right hand of his on my shoulder. 'Silence from now on,' he whispered in my ear. 'No talking. Sound carries over water.'

It was very quiet with Black Rincon to our left, sheltering us. We could only just hear the wind overhead, the water relatively smooth, no waves, and the night pitch-black again. Every now and then Iain missed a stroke as he checked our bearing with the luminous compass strapped to his wrist.

It was probably not more than ten minutes we were paddling into the black darkness, but it seemed an age. The ripple of the water from our bows and the wind overhead were the only sounds. And then suddenly there it was, a vague shape straight ahead of us that was blacker than the darkness. It gradually materialised as the hulk's half-sunken stern. 'We'll beach on the deck,' Iain whispered to me. 'Just for'ard o' that rear mast.'

The whole ship now had form, for we were very close, the stumps of the three masts standing like gantries against the black of the clouds. I could even make out the bows rearing steeply up out of the sea. We began manoeuvring to position ourselves over the sunken stern so that we could beach on the slope of the open deck, and then something like a shriek sounded above the noise of the wind in the masts.

'What's that?' My exclamation was quite involuntary, but the only answer I got was a whispered, 'Shut up!' Our boat's rigid keel touched the iron of the deck plates, a soft, scraping sound as it ploughed through rust. We were close inshore now, but even so the sea had enough movement in it to keep lifting and dropping the inflatable. Scrapes and thumps, and then that shriek again, muffled this time and dying away in a sort of gurgle, a wavelet slopping on the deck. Iain was already out of the boat, feeling with his feet for safe standing and moving silently towards the remains of a hatch. I followed him. Either it was a night heron or else there was somebody down there in an agony of pain.

We had come to rest just above the second mast. Ahead of it was the remains of a companionway shelter leading below. Iain was already halfway down the iron stairway, a shadowy figure feeling his way. At the bottom I was right behind him. The sound that had so appalled me was not repeated, all we could hear now was the drip and slop of water. An iron walkway slung above the hold led for'ard. Most of the wooden floor had rotted away and the metal cross pieces that had supported the planks were so degraded with rust that we were in imminent danger of falling into the black void below. There was a smell of salt damp and weed.

My outstretched hands touched Iain's back. He had halted where the catwalk went round the cylindrical iron bulk of the foremast, and beyond the mast there was the ghostly glimmer of a light filtering up from a lower level. He was standing quite still, listening. 'Fo'c'sle,' he breathed. But all I could think of was the way that agonised cry had gurgled into silence. I could see her face, the scars, and now the same man inflicting more pain, raping her again, his hands on her throat and slowly squeezing her to death just for pleasure ... I was suddenly in the grip of something I couldn't control, her face so white and desperate in the darkness, and the faint glow of that light ahead.

I gripped Iain's shoulder, pushing past him. I felt his hand reach out to stop me, grabbing at my oilskin jacket. But I wrenched myself free, and hardly caring whether I missed my footing on one of the catwalk's rotten iron supports I almost ran for'ard, shouting something, I can't remember what, shouting at the bastard to let her go. I had the automatic in my hand, thumbing the safety catch, intent now on killing him. What did it matter? What else could you do with a man so full of depravity? It would be like putting down a mad dog.

I dropped down a short ladder that was held only by a single rusted bolt, and then I stopped.

I was in the forepeak, sails piled against the wet iron plates of the hull, and for'ard of the sails was the chain locker, coiled hawsers green with slime. There was a makeshift bed and a table, the place lit by several old food cans filled with oil with lit wicks floating in them. The cans were wired to the iron frames of the hull and the naked oil flames gave a weird glare to the place, the air so still and dank it was a wonder they burned at all.

My eyes must have taken it all in and imprinted it on my mind in the split second of seeing it as I staggered at the foot of that crazy ladder, for my memory of the details of that place remains extraordinarily vivid. Yet I wasn't looking at the place itself. I was looking at the human tableau for which it was the setting, and I just stood there, my blood running cold at the sight.

He was lying spreadeagled on a disintegrating canvas heap, the remains of a big squares'l green with mould. I can see his face, the dreadful grin of the bared teeth, the blank stare of his slanted eyes. His clothes had been ripped from the lower part of his body, his genitals smashed to a pulp, half his stomach hanging out.

And she was standing there as though in a trance. Standing quite still, not looking at him, not looking at anything, her eyes as blank as those of the man she had killed.

'You stupid, fucking bitch!' Iain had caught hold of her shoulders and was shaking her so that her head, with its straight black hair and scars on the cheek, wobbled like a grotesque latex effigy. Then he swung her round and slapped her. 'Come on, snap out of it! This isn't Cambodia. This is British territory, with a Police Superintendent, a Governor, all the trappings of law enforcement. An' that man's dead.' Understanding was coming back into her eyes. 'Ah can see it from here. He's dead. Ye've killed him. In the eyes o' the law that makes ye a murderess. Do ye understand?'

She nodded her head slowly, still in a daze. And then with a sudden vehemence: 'He deserved it. Jesus Christ, if any man deserved to die –'

'So ye're a Christian?'

'What difference does that make?' She was coming alive again, coming out of the trance induced by the fury and hatred that must have eaten into her the last few years and that had suddenly been transmuted into fearful action.

Iain shook his head, smiling. 'Ah don't know. But it must make some difference.' He was actually smiling. 'It does to me anyway.' He was looking down at the jagged piece of iron ladder that lay at her feet. 'Is that what ye used?'

She nodded.

The rusty end of it was smeared with blood and pieces of the man's entrails. 'Well, we got to get rid o' that. An' of yer Pol Pot friend.' He moved over to the motionless mess of a body lying on that sodden green relic of a sail and bent down, feeling the heart. Then he closed the eyes and straightened up, looking down at the pale, scarred mask of a face staring impassively up at him. 'Ye can forget him now, Belle. Put the bugger right out o' yer mind. Ye've killed him, and that's that. As ye say, he deserved it.' He seemed to shake himself. 'But right now we've got to think what we can manage by way of a cover-up.'

She didn't answer, her eyes half-closed, her arms hanging limp. She seemed barely conscious of our presence, locked in on herself and what she had done here in this dimly-lit iron tomb of a place, where the only sound was the slop of water. I think she was totally wrung out with the climactic end to the fear and the hate, all the emotion that had built up to the storm of hitting and hitting at that supine body.

It was Iain who put my thoughts into words. 'How did ye do it?' he asked her. 'Was it a drug, an injection . . .?' He waited, his question hanging in the dank air. 'Ye planned it, didn't ye? Ye planned the whole thing, baiting the trap with yer own body. For God's sake, girrl, ye took one helluva risk.'

He might not have spoken for all the response she made, her body limp like a Chinese doll with the sawdust dribbling out of it.

He took her by the shoulders and shook her again. 'So what was it? What did ye use to knock him out? An injection?'

She nodded, an automaton movement of the head. 'Yes, an injection,' she breathed, her face still chalk-white against the dank black of her hair.

'What injection? The man was screaming. We heard him scream as we came aboard. So it was a short-term knockout drug. What was it?' He shook her again. 'What was it? Ah need to know, just in case.'

'Thai,' she muttered. 'It is an old Siamese distillation from a rainforest plant.' She started to talk then, seeming to find relief in telling us, for she went on, the words suddenly pouring out of her: 'I pretend to be frightened. I don't struggle. I let him tie me to the ring in the bow of the inflatable. Is very wet and I am lying in water, the waves breaking over. We go very fast. I am cold, cold and frightened. He is sitting in the stern, steering with the handle of the engine, and I am wondering if he will give me the chance I need. You see, I don't know where he is taking me.' The words tumbled over each other. 'Then we were here. There is a hole in this ship, down near the water. He use his paddle and when we are inside, and the boat is tied up, he make me climb an iron ladder. Then we are here and he begin to light these tins of oil, also my arms are free.' She was looking straight at Iain, her eyes very wide now. 'That is when I –' She faltered, searching for the word, and then she made a jabbing movement of her hand.

'And afterwards?' he prompted.

'Afterwards.' She stared up into his face. 'Afterwards I find that piece of iron lying there. I just want to kill him.' She caught hold of Iain's arms. 'To kill, that is all. But then –' She shook her head wonderingly. 'Then something take hold of me. All those people, a whole village, the smell of them burning, and that man ...' She was trembling, her voice almost out of control.

I started forward. I had a need to comfort her that was almost overwhelming. But it was Iain who reached out, taking her in his arms and saying, 'It's all right, Belle. It's over now. Ye can forget the whole thing.'

She shook her head. 'I can never forget.' Reaction had set in and she was sobbing almost uncontrollably as she tried to tell him of the terrible passion to destroy that had overtaken her, to hurt, to disfigure ... I can't remember the words she used, only the impression they left on me. For those few minutes I was looking into the soul of a woman and seeing the fearful force of vengeance in its rawest and most primitive form. And then abruptly the outpouring was over, her body going limp again as she pressed her face against Iain's oilskin jacket.

Once more I found myself wondering at their relationship, a pang of something akin to jealousy overcoming me for a moment. Stupid of me, but I felt resentment that it was to Iain she had turned for comfort, ignoring me.

'Now. What happens now?' She had lifted her head, gazing up at him. 'You said about the law. Will they arrest?' She was suddenly being practical, but the tone of her voice was one of resignation. It was as though, having done what she had planned, a mood of resignation had taken hold.

But then her manner changed again. She was suddenly coquettish, like a child, using her feminine wiles to gain the support of a favourite uncle. 'We get rid of Seng's body, then we say he ran away – in the boat. It is down there –' She pointed to the hold aft of where we stood '– and he could lose his balance, anything. You say he disappear into the night. That is all. You cannot know what makes him go overboard. They find the boat, drifting, and it is empty. That is all. You do not have to know anything about what happened to him.'

The transition from a state of almost total paralysis to that of a clever woman planning a pack of lies to cover her actions shocked me, it was so sudden. I remembered Travers describing her as a bitch, yet the provocation was overwhelming. She had taken a terrible revenge, but it was done now. Why should she have to go on paying for the sadistic cruelty that had possessed him. The man was a monster.

'We cannot take him out into the proper ocean in case *Isvik*, or some other ship, pick us up on radar. So, we have to sink him quite close.' She was thinking it out as she talked, planning with clarity, and all the time working on Iain, that coquettish, little-girl-in-trouble, look in her eyes. I think I was shocked more by the blatancy of it than the fact that what she was proposing was his complicity in murder. Or perhaps it was the certainty that when he had agreed she would turn to me, and I would agree. I would be taking a hell of a chance, so would Iain. We both would.

'Ye realise what ye're asking?' Iain didn't wait for an answer, his voice strangely soft as he said, 'Don't worry.' His left hand moved to her head, stroking her hair and holding her to him. 'S'long as we stick to our story.' He was looking across to me. 'You agree?'

I nodded slowly.

He let her go then and came across to me. 'Ye realise what ye're doing? The four of them on *Isvik*, the tugmaster, probably his crew too – a dozen or more people, they know what happened back there in the Eagle Passage. They know she was kidnapped, one of the crew knocked out, and that the kidnap boat ran down the east shore of the Passage and round Porpoise Point. They'll have followed its movements on radar. But that's all they know. What happened afterwards is what we tell them. Just the three of us – Belle, ye an' me. We agree the story and we stick to it. Okay?'

I agreed. What else could I do?

'We'll be interrogated, by Brawdy, possibly by the Governor himself. They won't necessarily believe what we tell them. They don't have to, so long as we stick by our story. They'll want to be shot of the episode with the minimum of fuss. All we have to do is make it easy for them.'

I hoped he was right.

'What about ye, Belle? Think ye can manage?'

She looked at him, her face impassive now, her gaze steady. 'Of course.'

'It won't be a hostile interrogation. They'll know, of course, that we're hidin' somethin' – they'll know that from the fact that our stories will be so exactly similar – but they won't know what we're hidin'. Not unless ye break down or get confused.'

'I don't get confused.'

'Good girl!'

He was still treating her like a child, but there was nothing childish in her mood now. 'You tell me what to say.'

'Okay. We'll work it out between us, between the three o' us.' He turned to me. 'Then we go over an' over it until there is no chance of one o' us slippin' up.' His eyes were roving round the dimly-lit forepeak. 'Where's that gun Ah gave ye?' He held out his hand for it and I pulled it out of my jacket pocket. 'Now, get hold o' the man's body and prop it up against –' He searched the forepeak, his gaze finally coming to rest on the ladder leading down to the hold. There were the remains of an iron rail round it. 'Prop him against that. An' try an' avoid gettin' any of his blood on ye.'

It was a messy job, but he was dead, not screaming like that badly-burned pilot I had pulled from the plane he had crash-landed in a field near Shipton-under-Wychwood, the poor devil's nerves arching his body and his mouth open in an almost continuous scream. 'Ye'll have to hold him,' Iain said as the corpse sagged against the rail. 'Hold him upright. Make it look as though he's about to attack me. An' keep out of my line o' fire.'

He was holding the automatic in his right hand, raising it slowly, his left closing over the black glove, forefinger on the trigger. I saw this out of the corner of my eye as I wrestled with the limp body, trying to hold it upright. And then the bullet sang past me, so close I felt the displaced air on my face, the crack of the shot instantaneous and echoing loud in the iron vault, the body almost wrenched from my grasp.

'Okay. Ye can let him drop now.' He came over to where I was still standing, supporting the sodden, bloodstained mess. He turned to Belle. 'Where's his boat? Down there?' He pointed at the gaping hole below me.

She nodded.

'Okay, let go.' He raised his foot and slammed it into the man's knees. Slowly the body disappeared into the black rectangle at my feet, slithering over the rust-jagged edge and falling with a hollow splash.

'That's a bit of our story neither o' ye will forget.' He looked at us, smiling. 'In desperation he started to go for me, so Ah shot him. Not to kill, mind ye. Ah shot him in the shoulder. Ye both saw that – in the shoulder, in self-defence. Right?'

He waited, watching us both, making sure that his words had sunk in and that what we had seen was now visually imprinted on our memory. Finally he nodded. 'Good! Now we get somethin' solid an' heavy, strap it to his body, then take the bastard out and sink him in deep water, leaving his boat to drift. It's very easy for a man who's been shot to fall over the side o' a semi-inflatable, particularly if there's a bit of wind and the waves are breaking.'

He produced a small, high-powered torch and shone it down into the hold. I could see Seng's body, a crumpled heap draped over one of the ship's iron frames. There was no water directly below us. The angle of the beached hull was such that the sea did not reach beyond the foremast. 'Ah can see the boat.' Iain was halfway down the ladder, ducking his head under the deckplates. 'It's afloat, so the tide must be rising still.' He glanced down at his watch. 'Better get movin'. It's after four already an' we need to get him settled on the seabed before first light.' He clambered cautiously back up and stood, looking round the forepeak and probing with the torch. 'Some wire or rope,' he said, looking at me. 'See what ye can find.' He kicked the broken piece of iron ladder which had been her instrument of execution. 'Then get below an' strap this to the corpse. Ha' ye got gloves?'

'Woollen one, yes.'

'Put them on then. Ah don't imagine they'll go over an abandoned inflatable that's been pickled in seawater for fingerprints, but ye never know. Don't reck'n Brawdy anticipated anything like this when he was promoted to Detective-Inspector so he may take a deal of trouble over it.' He turned to Belle. 'So ye tell him straight out who the man is who dragged ye into his boat an' brought ye here. Okay?'

Her eyes widened, her mouth a tight line as she said, 'No, is not okay. I tell the polis nothing – nothing about what happen in Kampuchea. I don't know this man Seng. He is just an adventurer, a pirate, a Triad gangster who want ransom.'

Iain swung the torch full on her face. 'Either ye tell Brawdy or Ah do.'

'No.'

He ignored that. 'Ah think it is better if it comes from ye. An' there's Lange. Ha' ye though o' Lange? The boy was scared. Now we know why. He was goin' ter warn ye.' He looked at me. 'Isn't that right?'

I nodded.

'So ye tell him. An' don't let 'im have t'drag it out of ye. Tell him straight out.'

'No.' Her voice was crisp and cold, quite adamant. 'If I tell the authorities Seng is a Pol Pot patrol leader, if I tell them all the dreadful things he do, then they will find out what he do to me and they will start leaping to conclusions –'

'So what? O'course a man like Brawdy, a senior police officer, will draw the obvious conclusion, that somehow ye managed t'kill the man and that we disposed of the body. But he'll no' be able to prove it. He'll no' have a body even.'

I suddenly remembered that woman journalist, Snedden. What a break for her! 'Forget it,' I said. 'If Brawdy gets hold of Belle's background, that's too bad. But no reason why we should make it easy for him. And no reason you or I should know anything about Seng or what he did to her.'

He stood there for a moment, thinking that out. In the end he shook his head. 'It won't do. Once he realises she has been holding back vital information –'

'It's only vital,' I said, 'in so far as it provides a reason for Belle to have been a ransom target. Does Brawdy have to go ferreting about for her background? Surely –'

'Come'n. Let's go. We're wastin' time.' He picked up the section of ladder, using his right hand, and flung it down the hole. The clang of it landing at the bottom echoed through the hulk. 'We'll talk about it while we motor out into deep water.' He passed me his torch. 'Ye'll mebbe find somethin' suitable over there.' He indicated an ironwork table, probably for the use of the bo'sun in the old days. It had a small gas cylinder and cooker on it together with several plastic bags containing cartons of food and some rice. There was also a small reel of electric wire and a long-life battery. I took the wire and clambered down into the steeply-sloped bow section of the ship where the end of the anchor chain hung loose from the hawse-hole.

It was a sickening job, the man, so recently dead, oozed blood and bits of his innards as I dragged him down the slope, bumping him over the brown-rust of regularly-spaced iron frames. I flipped him into the inflatable and his head fell against a blue water-proof case with a carrying strap. It was a battery-operated VHF radio.

I took it up the ladder with me, thinking we might be able to contact either *Isvik* or the tug. But Iain shook his head. He was on his hands and knees, working at the bloodstains with a piece of rotting canvas. 'Later,' he said, and got to his feet, grinding the last vestiges into the rust of the deck plates with his seaboots. 'Time enough to contact them when we've got shot o' the body.' He turned to Belle. 'VHF – ye asked us to contact the tug on VHF. Remember? Back at Port Howard, when we were just leaving. It occurred to me then –' He shook his head. 'God! Ye're a schemer! Do ye play chess?'

'Sometimes.' She was smiling. 'Mah Jong also. And you – do you play chess?'

'Och aye, on occasions.' It was a ridiculous conversation in the bows of a hundred-year-old hulk with the water gurgling below, the oil wicks flickering and that battered corpse waiting for its watery grave below. And the two of them, smiling at each other, as he added, 'Ye'd make a fine business partner. Nothin' legal, mind ye. Everythin' *sub rosa*.'

'What is *sub rosa*?' And when he told her, she gave a laugh that was almost a giggle.

She seemed quite relaxed now and I wondered whether that had been his purpose. 'Right. We'd best get movin'.' He looked quickly round the forepeak, telling her to take the plastic food bags in case they gave a clue to the nationality of the ship Seng had come from. There was a torch on the bench, too. He took that and a narrow-bladed knife that had been half-concealed by an oil can that was empty and lying on its side.

'You want I give you this also?' Belle took a hand gun from the pocket of her oilskin jacket and held it out to him.

'Christ!' He took it in his gloved hand, wiping it carefully, using the piece of towelling from around his neck. He checked the magazine, then raised it and fired two shots at the base of the mast. The sound of them reverberated through the ship, the clunk of the bullets striking rusty iron equally loud and raising little clouds of red dust. 'That's another piece o' the story we must remember. Two shots, and then he fled in panic down to his boat.' The gun made a hollow clattering sound as he tossed it below. 'Glad ye found it,' he said and led the way up to the deck.

Our inflatable was afloat now, dancing around at the end of the painter we had made fast to the stump of the foremast. Iain paddled it round to the starb'd bow, where there was a great jagged hole like the entrance to a cave. He didn't take the boat in, but handed me a loose coil of rope and told me to get hold of Seng's boat and haul it out. It was an operation that took me a little time, for the beach, which had built up against the jagged bottom edge of the gap, was weed-covered boulder and very slippery, and once inside the hull, I had to work my way for'ard, probing with my torch, until I reached the boat.

It was very eerie down there in the bottom of the hold, the iron frames to clamber over and my body wet to the waist. The slop of the water filled the place with strange sounds and the slime-covered walls, gleaming with moisture, made it like the sort of dungeons, or oubliettes, one has read about. And the body waiting for me, laid out like a mummy the length of the inflatable and held there by the section of iron ladder I had lashed to it.

There were no paddles. I had to walk the boat out, stumbling as I felt for safe footholds. The weight of the body made it quite heavy and I had difficulty hauling it out. I threw the rope-end to Iain and he drew the boat alongside our own inflatable. 'We'll do a bit o' cleanin' up after we've slipped him over the side.' His torch was momentarily beamed on the body and for the first time I had a close look at the man's features. It was a rather flat face, almost pugilistic, and totally without expression. Only the hard line of the lips below the straight little moustache gave any sign of the sort of creature he was.

Belle had turned her head away, sitting very still. I sensed the tension in her, and then she said in an almost strangled voice, 'Let us get on with it for Christ's sake.'

I fixed the tow line and scrambled in as Iain started the engine. The wind had dropped considerably and we had a fast, fairly smooth run out to Harbour Island. We slid him overboard just beyond Shag Rock and I heard Belle say, a little over-brightly, 'So that is the end of that.' I think she would have liked to talk about it – she needed that sort of release. But she held herself in check, and all she said, in the same strangled voice, was, 'Do you think my mother and my father will know?'

'Forget it,' Iain said almost harshly. I think he knew better than I how close to the edge of hysteria she was. He got the engine going while I swabbed-up as best I could with the oily rag he handed me. Then we transferred back to our own boat and set the other adrift, its bows to the south-east with the outboard quietly ticking over. 'With the wind's help an' a wee bit o' luck they'll find it driftin' way south of the Bleakers.' He reached over and squeezed Belle's hand. 'Don't grieve for what's past. Ye can forget it now. Ye've paid 'em back, every one o' them, an' each accordin' to his deserts.'

She nodded. 'I know. But was I right?'

'Aye. O' course ye were. What else could ye do?'

'I was brought up a Christian.' Her voice was so low I could hardly hear her above the roar of the engine as we headed back inshore.

'An' done nothin' about them? Got down on yer knees an' prayed for 'em. That's no' in yer nature. Ye're a girl who does things.' He laughed. 'Very unfeminine. But there ye are. That's the person ye are.' He handed me the outboard's steering handle and unpacked the VHF from its case.

Black Rincon began to emerge, a dark shadow in the first cold glimmer of a grey dawn that was lighting a thread of sky low down against the horizon behind us. He called *Isvik* and Iris came on the air, sounding worried as she asked what had happened. But instead of answering her, he told her to make contact with the tug and tell them to alert the authorities that Miss Phuket was safe and unharmed, but that the man had got away. 'Tell 'em he's wounded. Ah had to shoot at him. If they get a search goin' right away they should pick him up somewhere off Bay of Harbours or Eagle Passage, mebbe south, or even east, of the Bleakers.'

They didn't pick him up, of course. Sid committed both the C-130 tankers to the search, as well as the SAR Sea King helicopter. We saw them take off in the dawn, just after we had weighed anchor, then watched them flying a carefully co-ordinated search pattern as we headed just north of east to the narrow gut of Bleakers Jump. The wind was still westerly, the Southern Ocean wave trains rolling up astern of us like mountains forever toppling. Looking aft one had a very heady, almost nightmarish sensation. First there would be the build-up as we sank into the bottom of the trough, then the stern's dizzy climb up the face of the wave, the roar of water falling off the crest, and finally the mad thrust ahead as the wind filled the sails with the bang of straining canvas and we careered forward in a surge of foam that went spilling noisily all along the deck.

It was my first experience of downwind sailing in this sort of an ocean and I found it marvellously exhilarating, like the first time I went through the sound barrier, or further back, when I was learning to fly and the instructor left me to kick the plane out of a tail-spin – exhilaration laced I suppose with fear. Up, up, up, and then the pause, the sense of hanging there, before the sudden spiralling down which was now a mad rush forward in a seething cauldron of white water, the towed inflatable nuzzling our stern and constantly threatening to come aboard.

A hand touched mine, fingers gripping tight. I was standing right aft, my back to the rear plating of the wheelhouse, and the grip of that hand seemed a part of the sea-mad trance into which I had fallen. And then a small, very clear, almost trembling voice said – 'Is beautiful. Like the stars, or a volcano erupting.'

I turned my head, looking down. It was Belle. Her fingers were laced in mine, her eyes sparkling with the excitement of the challenge of this huge, engulfing mass of water rolling up astern. She smiled. 'Nothing matter now. Just the great waves, and you – the both of us – and the sea.' Her fingers moved, a message that had my body suddenly tingling with the consciousness of her femininity.

And then, she reached up and kissed me.

I shall never forget that mad, impulsive gesture of hers, or my first reaction to it, which was one of shock. So many women, casual liaisons, violent sexual enthusiasms, and now here, on the edge of the Southern Ocean, half an hour's flying time from Cape Horn, with the waves piling their frothing crests above our heads, tumbling down around us, and this Chinese woman, almost straight from a violent killing, suddenly in my arms. And it was done so naturally, in a way that overwhelmed me with a feeling I had never had before.

A wave fell out of the sky, crashing down around us, and she was murmuring something in my ear, something about feeling safe again, or safe at last. She let go of me then and stood for a moment staring aft at the next wave building. Her eyes were alight with something, something that seemed to me also akin to wonder, and as the wave fell around us, she turned to me and said, 'Now I am like a new person. All this water, this sea, it is wonderful therapy. And so are you, my dear, good friend.' And she added, louder now as the sea frothed around our feet, 'Do you think now all is forgiven? Forgotten?' She was looking up at me. 'That is how it seem – as if I am reborn. Do you understand?' She was silent for a moment. 'Here, in this wilderness of water –' She hesitated as though searching for a word. 'I feel new. Nothing matter any more – nothing of the past, that is.'

She stared up at me a moment longer, her almond eyes tranquil now. Then she let go my hand. 'Thank you.' She smiled briefly and was gone, leaving me alone with the great waves, wondering about her, the sort of person she really was, and how much of what I felt had taken place between us was in my imagination. I felt confused, oddly unsure of myself, something that had never really happened to me before in my relations with women.

Shortly after that Pete called me to give a hand hardening in the sheets ready for gybing. Iris was on the helm, the low land that crooked the long, jagged finger of the Bleakers across the entrance to Adventure Sound coming rapidly nearer. On the crest of the waves we had a grandstand view of the seas breaking against it in a white mayhem of thrashing water. One by one we hardened in the sheets. 'Gybe-Oh!' The main and the mizzen came thundering across, the fores'l thrashing itself in a frenzy until I had hardened in on the starb'd sheet. We were round then, sailing fast in sickening swoops across the march of the waves with the quieter water of The Jump straight ahead.

We were sailing north then, and once through the gut the waves fell away, the wind whistling across the low land to port, driving us very fast over a flat calm sea. For ten minutes or so we had a wonderful high-speed sail and there were albatross wheeling, storm petrels diving. Then we were abreast of Adventure Island and turning towards Cow Hangar Cove. Iain was on the radio. We got the sails down, and by the time the deck was sorted out and everything stowed, we were in the cove and coming alongside the tug.

Cow Hangar House – it was not a settlement – was a fairly large clapboard building with a red tin roof built beside a stream on a little rise about half a kilometre back from the end of the cove. It looked in a somewhat dilapidated state, the white paint flaking and blackened in places where the wood had been patched with bitumen, and the outbuildings looked even more derelict. A wood and concrete jetty extended drunkenly a few yards from the steep, stony shore, a clear, freshwater lane running to it through the kelp that lined most of the cove.

One of the barges had already been hauled alongside the jetty and they had started unloading. The tugmaster greeted us laconically, his sharp little eyes roving over *Isvik* and then peering down at his half-submerged inflatable. 'You shouldn't have towed it.' The poor thing was full of water and looked a bit of a mess.

'Yer own fault,' Iain answered him. 'If yer man had been a little brighter –'

The altercation was interrupted by Belle. 'Where's Boss Mangan?' she demanded, her voice very different now, clipped and with a ring of authority.

'That your foreman? He's ashore, checking the unloading.'

She introduced herself and he helped her on to the tug's deck. 'Just about drained us of beer, that Aussie of yours. Anyway, glad to see you're none the worse for your ordeal.' And to Iain – 'You shot the bugger, that right?'

'Winged him, that's all. In the right shoulder. Stopped him firing at me.' He called to Barratt and the two of them climbed on to the tug. 'Can ye drop me ashore? Ah want to see Josh. An' there's a boy here, name o' Lange ...' I lost the rest as Pete needed help transferring the tug's inflatable. Once that was done, we let go our lines and anchored off. By then Iris and Nils had knocked up a comforting corned beef hash.

Lange didn't come aboard until the following morning. He had been out all night with Josh Reynolds searching for two llamas that had gone missing. Reynolds was one of those odd characters you meet up with in places like the Falklands. He was a small, wiry man with very sharp blue eyes and a left leg that was artificial from the knee down. From a minor public school he had gone straight into the City. I don't know what he really did there, he simply described himself as 'a number cruncher'. Two years of that was enough. 'The only life you can be sure about is this one, so better live it good and get some excitement out of it.' For want of anything better to do he had joined the Army and landed up in 2nd Para, losing his leg in Colonel H's suicidal dash at Goose Green. He had found Cow Hangar later, when revisiting the battlefield. 'I've always gone against the grain – it's a gamble, some you win, some you lose, but it gives a spice to each day of living, okay?' That was his reason for farming South American camelids and Scottish Highland cattle in Southern Hemisphere islands that were almost entirely given over to sheep.

All this was poured out over breakfast coffee suitably laced by Nils. A great guy, but lonely out here on his own, not even a wife. He had been married, to a nurse, a young Irish woman from Dublin who had helped him over the worst of his convalescence. They had had a son, but then she had left, taking the boy with her. 'Couldn't stand the loneliness, and the wind, that perpetual bloody wind. Gets you down in the end. Blows so steady there's times it'll hold your arse up like being seated in an armchair. You don't believe me, d'you, but it's true .'

He fell asleep shortly afterwards and I had a chance to talk to Bjorn Lange on his own. 'I was going to warn her. I really was.'

'But you didn't.'

'I don't get the chance, do I?' He seemed even more tensed-up than when I had met him by the war memorial. I think he must have been brooding over it all night as they searched for the llamas.

Seng had brought him in to land on East Falkland by the North Point of Bleaker Island and had put him ashore just south of Walker Creek Settlement where he had taken a small boat and crossed Choiseul sound to Mare Harbour. It was just after Seng cut the engine, leaving the inflatable to glide silently in to land, that he told him why he had offered to bring him ashore. 'He knows about my father, how he had killed himself after his company is taken over. That is why he take me ashore.' He had been wondering about that ever since Seng had approached him on the Korean fishing vessel. But it was only after they were in the inflatable and heading for the land, that he began to realise the sort of man he was.

'He has a gun, and two knives. There is also a VHF radio, which he listen to at certain times.'

I asked him how Seng had known about his father and the KLME Company, and he said, 'There is a place in Paris, a restaurant, where rich Chinese from South-East Asia go. I know somebody who work there.'

'The Dragon Rouge?'

'*Ja*. The Dragon Rouge.'

What Seng had wanted him to do was to contact Ward and tell him the Chinese lady would no longer be worth calling Belle if a ransom of half a million pounds sterling was not paid into a Singapore bank account within twenty-four hours of her disappearance. 'Bits and pieces of the woman would follow with each day of delay.' He sat there for a moment, staring at me, his blue eyes gone blank, his mouth actually trembling at the recollection. 'It was horrible. Not because of what he intend. It was not that. It was because I see he is having pleasure at the thought of it. He is psychopath, and what he will do to her gives him intense pleasure.'

'So what happened next?' I asked him. 'Didn't you try to do anything?'

He shook his head, sitting at the table, dumb and miserable at the memory of that night. 'What can I do? He has a gun. And those knives – I knew then what they are for.' And he added, 'He is a very dangerous man.'

'So you just crouched there in the inflatable until he put you ashore. You didn't even –'

'I was going to warn her.'

'So you said. But you didn't, did you? You could have told me, or Ward, or gone to the police.'

'They would not believe me. Mr Ward would have known it was true , but not the police, or you. That is why I don't tell you. I thought if I can get myself here, to Cow Hangar, then I can talk to Mr Ward ...'

All this time I had been conscious of an outboard coming nearer. There was a slight clang of metal against hull plates as it came alongside, then the murmur of voices raised in argument.

'He tell me I can come on *Isvik*,' Lange was saying. 'He does not seem to mind now that I come with you the whole voyage. Why does he change his mind, do you know? Before he ...'

I was barely listening, my ears tuned to the voices, which were above us now, in the wheelhouse. 'Don't be a bloody little fool. He'll take it from ye. If Ah tell him he'll be suspicious an' jump to the conclusion it's some sort of a cover-up.'

'Why? Why should he do that?' Belle was halfway down the companion ladder and she turned, looking back up at him. 'I don't understand. It is the truth. And he can check. Somebody must have written a report of what they found in that village.'

'Aye. But there was so much goin' on. Reports like that ...' Iain shrugged. 'You tell him –'

'Tell who?' I asked him.

'Brawdy.'

They had just heard over the tug's radio that Seng's inflatable had been spotted. Not by the three aircraft flying a new search pattern, but by the guard destroyer's Lynx on a routine flight to MPA for the TriStar mail delivery from Brize Norton. The pilot had come down to about twenty feet as he approached land, flying up the Bleaker coast, then across to the Triste Islands and Lively Sound. 'It was wedged into the rocks by Prong Point at the southern tip o' Lively Island. If he had'n bin flyin' so low Ah doubt he'd've seen it in the welter of breaking water.' Iain hesitated, glancing across at Iris as though for support. 'Brawdy wants us to make Stanley t'night so he can interview us tomorrow mornin'. The three of us,' he added, looking down at Belle.

'I tell you I won't go.' She had stopped at the foot of the ladder, standing very still and tense. 'I will not be ordered about by a –'

'Ye've no choice.' Iain's voice was harsh.

'All right, I go. But I tell him nothing. Not about the past. You tell him.'

He shook his head, his eyes darting round the room, realising that he couldn't argue freely with her now the others were present.

Seeing the frozen state she was in, I found it difficult to keep my temper. 'Do you seriously expect her to tell him the whole story of what happened in that village, to go through it all again for a policeman who hasn't the faintest idea what it was like? If he has to know, then why don't you do as she suggests and tell him yourself? You say you were in Kampuchea –'

'No.' His gloved hand came down on the rail, his grey eyes gone hard. 'He'd suspect –'

'Why? What would he suspect?' I had risen to my feet, suddenly very angry. 'Why shouldn't you tell him? You know her story as well as I do.' I was remembering every word she had said in that candle-lit private room, the look on her face ... 'Why? For God's sake why? Why should she be forced to go through the hell of it again –'

'Ye know damn well why.' He was off the ladder now, coming towards me.

'No, I don't – I don't see why you ...'

He reached out, gripping my arm. 'It wouldna' work. He wouldna' believe it, not from me.'

'Why the hell not?'

'Because of what I am.' He was glaring at me, the steel fingers of that gloved hand biting into my arm, his whole being willing me to leave it at that.

And suddenly, without understanding why, I nodded. 'All right,' I said. 'I'll tell him myself – just as she told it to me.'

He nodded, beginning to relax. 'Good boy.' He smiled. 'That's what I was hoping. It'll come better from you.'

I looked at Belle. She had seated herself at the table beside Iris and she had that blank look on her face again. Iris put her arm round her and she gave a brief smile.

'Well, what are we waitin' for?' Iain's voice, brisk and determined, sounded almost light-hearted. 'Let's get movin'.'

IV

ICE

ONE

'That's all very interesting, sir. But what did you do with the body?'

I was sitting facing him at his desk, just as I had been when he was questioning me about Lange. He would already know Belle's background, some of it at any rate. A woman like that, head of a mining outfit that was running seismographical surveys over two areas of his territory – they would surely have some sort of a dossier on her. 'Well?' He was leaning forward, elbows on desk, watching me intently.

His shock tactics had thrown me off balance for a moment. I hadn't expected him to play it so rough and I shied away from answering him, seeking refuge in what now lay ahead of me. 'You know why I'm here,' I said. Ever since we had made it into Stanley at first light and anchored off the jetty, I had been conscious that now I was on the verge of departure into the ice of the Weddell, and at the back of my mind was the thought that the abandoned C-130 might well be the end of me. Contemplation of a nasty end really does concentrate the mind. It put Brawdy, and that unexpectedly abrupt question, into a sensible perspective. I nearly told him to go to hell and let me get on with the things that really mattered. 'We leave in just over a week's time,' I told him. 'I've got a lot on my mind.'

'You haven't answered my question.'

'Not much point, is there? You've already questioned Iain Ward.'

'Right. But now I'm questioning you. I'd like your version, sir.' He was watching me, waiting. 'You went on board the hulk at what time?'

'I don't know.'

'An ace pilot and you don't know what time you landed on target?'

I was trying to remember. 'Is it important?'

He gave the briefest of smiles. 'No, not really. Mr Ward said just after 02.00 he thought.'

'Yes, about that.'

'And you landed on the deck. Did you go below straight away?'

'We had heard noises.'

'What sort of noises?' He had picked up a ballpoint and was beginning to write.

'A scream. Somebody in pain.'

'Thank you, sir. Let's start from there, shall we? Just tell it to me as you saw it – in your own words.'

'What's that supposed to mean?' I asked. 'I can hardly describe what we saw other than in my –' I stopped, my eyes locked on his as I realised what he was getting at.

'Just your own words, sir. Then we'll talk to Miss Phuket. Between the three of you we should get a pretty clear picture of what happened.'

So I told him what we had agreed between the three of us, how Seng had grabbed a small automatic out of his pocket and had then started firing.

'Did he say anything?'

I hesitated, realising there were a host of little details for which we hadn't prepared ourselves. 'He may have done.' I shook my head. 'I'm not certain. All I remember is the shock of seeing the bullets flying out of that little hand gun of his.'

'And then ...?' He was watching me again, his pen poised over the notebook. 'Did Mr Ward say anything before he fired back? Did he warn him?'

'For God's sake! The man was shooting at him. You don't start a conversation in those circumstances.'

'So he fired straight back?'

'Yes.'

'Where did he get the gun from?'

I shook my head. 'I don't know – his pocket, I suppose.'

'Or an armpit holster?'

I didn't answer that. And then he put a really awkward question to me – 'Which hand did he use?'

It was a trap. However I answered it he would almost certainly get a different reply out of Belle. 'It all happened so quickly,' I said. 'I think he used both hands.'

'So he's a trained marksman. Is that what you're saying?' And when I told him I knew nothing about Iain's background, he said, 'Never mind about the actual firing of the gun. Did he pull it out with his right or his left hand?'

'His left, I suppose. His right hand –'

'Yes, I know about that. What happened then?'

This seemed to require some sort of a graphic description, so I told him the bullet had hit the man somewhere up by the right collarbone, the force of it half spinning him round. 'Then he seemed to recover himself and dived for the bulkhead ladder leading down to the hold.'

'And Mr Ward, didn't he try and stop him?'

I shook my head. 'I think we were all a bit dazed.'

'He didn't fire again?'

'No, I don't think so.'

'He let him get away.'

'Yes.'

'You and he, you just stood there doing nothing while an injured man manoeuvred a semi-rigid inflatable out through a hole in the wreck's hull, got the outboard going and disappeared into the night?'

I felt the chill of his trained, logical mind. Put like that it didn't sound convincing. 'It was dark down there in the hold. We couldn't see anything and we were in a state of shock.'

'You may have been, but I can't see Ward being in shock. No way,' he added, smiling to himself. 'And that was the last you saw of Seng?'

'Yes.'

'You went up on deck. The three of you?'

'Just Ward and myself. Miss Phuket was –' I hesitated. 'Dazed I think would be a right description.'

'And what did you see when you were back on deck?'

'It was a very dark night. It had started to rain again.'

'You didn't see the inflatable.'

'No, but we could hear it.'

'Where was it headed?'

'Eastward. Out towards the Bleakers.'

'So you launched your own inflatable and went after him?'

'Yes, but when we started our own engine the noise of it drowned the sound of his. So we lost him.'

He nodded, his pen moving fast over the page of his notebook. 'Anything else?' He was looking at me again, silence hanging in the air so that the sound of a ship's siren was able to penetrate the double-glazed stillness of the room. 'Are you sure there's nothing else you can add, nothing you feel you ought to tell me?'

I shook my head.

He was silent a moment, staring across the desk at me. Finally he said, 'Then that's it.' He closed the notebook. 'If there should be ...' He waited a moment longer, then added, 'I'll get this typed up in the form of a statement. If you'll be good enough to wait outside, sir ...' His eyes were still fixed on me intently. 'I'd like you to read it through, and if there's still nothing you wish to add, I'll ask you to sign it.' He nodded to the door. 'Perhaps you would ask the Chinese lady to come in.'

But when I passed on his message Iain put his gloved hand over hers, restraining her. 'Sit tight. Ah'll deal wi' this.' He got to his feet, his face set as he pushed past me, storming into Brawdy's office in such haste he didn't close the door properly, or perhaps he intended to leave it ajar.

I couldn't hear what was said at first, but then suddenly Iain was almost shouting: 'Ye canna do that, not unless ye arrest us. An' if ye do arrest us, there's a woman called Snedden over at MPA would just love it ...' His voice dropped away, and then it was Brawdy speaking, too softly for me to distinguish the words.

'No, ye know dam' well she's not.' It was Iain again. 'She's a French national. Yu tell that to yer Superintendent, an' ye can also tell 'im, if he starts makin' wild accusations, Ah'll see that the Quai d'Orsay hears of it. Then he'll have the Foreign Office on his back and he'll wonder ...'

He was interrupted by Brawdy, but again I couldn't make out the words. Finally Iain said, 'Ah appreciate all that. Ah also appreciate that he's new here. He'll be wantin' to make his mark. Rape, vengeance, murder, a young Chinese woman and a shadowy character like me, plus a pilot who's been a wee bit too wild for the brass, an' Snedden just waiting out there at MPA with her mouth open ...' He gave a quick bark of a laugh. 'Och aye, it's a wonderful scenario! But Ah'm warnin' ye, the Governor isn't goin' ter like it – scrambled messages flying back an' forth, the whole thing blowing up in his face, an' that journalist woman just waitin' to light the fuse.'

There was a pause, then Iain went on, 'Well, what are ye goin' t'do? After what ye've said to me, ye canna expect any one of the three of us to co-operate further. If ye wish to continue with this interrogation, then ye'll have to arrest us an' do it properly, the interview taped. An' that, of course, means formally charging us. Wi' what?'

By shifting my position I could just see Brawdy's face. His lips were motionless, his face impassive. I suppose he was thinking it out, but then he must have realised the door was ajar, for he suddenly got up from his desk and next moment the door clicked shut. I looked at Belle, her face in silhouette, the skin grafts showing like blotchy birthmarks. Why in God's name they'd called her Belle I can't think, and yet . . .

I tried to think how I would have behaved if I had done what she had. But that, of course, wasn't possible; my reactions, my whole behaviour would have been entirely different. I probably wouldn't have had the guts, anyway.

She turned her head and smiled. There was a strange serenity about that smile, so that I suddenly felt I was looking at an older world in which vengeance, justice, call it what you like, was a matter for individuals. The calm of her damaged features made it obvious she saw no wrong in what she had done, and it occurred to me then that she would be impatient at any attempt at interrogation, simply stating the facts and the reasons for her actions. I started to explain what would happen if she did that. Brawdy would play it by the rules. It would leave him no alternative. But then the door suddenly opened, wide this time, framing Iain's bulk. 'Ah think ye're very wise.'

Brawdy didn't say anything. He was standing now, his face lit by a fleeting shaft of sunlight. He was staring at Belle, his expression a mixture of curiosity and, unless I am mistaken, a glimmer of admiration.

It was Iain who shut the door behind him. 'It's all settled now.' He said it with a smile and a droop of the left eyelid. 'He accepts our version o' what happened, so we're free t'get on wi' what we came out here t'do. Okay?'

Brawdy's decision not to interrogate Belle, and to accept the validity of the statements Iain and I had made, was almost certainly due to the French connection. I was told later, I think by Sid, that his Superintendent had been picked for the job because he was the most politically aware policeman available, a very important qualification, given that our relations with the Argentine were delicate to say the least of it. Added to that was the ethnic mix of the squid fleet, some three hundred vessels and around eight thousand men, licensed to operate close in to the Falklands from early February. He would hardly relish his Detective-Inspector involving the French in a murder case that Snedden, or the resident journalists of *Penguin News*, the *Teaberry Express*, even the Forces PR set-up, could turn into a media *cause célèbre*.

Charlie wasn't around when we arrived in Stanley. The Upland Goose said he had gone fishing over by Teal Creek. He had, of course, failed to leave any specific address or telephone number where I could contact him. In fact, he hadn't gone fishing at all. He rolled his fat arse along the quay two days later, a smug grin on his face and looking the worse for wear. He had been living it up in the Mount Pleasant Naafi, dossing down in a spare bunk in the RAF quarters and drinking far too much.

However, he hadn't wasted his time. He had met an old chum in the resident C-130 detachment. The Hercs were parked over by the control tower and the Met Office was close by. He had not only been able to check out the Herc maintenance details with a stripped-down engine in front of him, but he had also obtained detailed interior measurements of the fuselage with rough drawings and specifications of the fuel tank securing brackets.

In addition, he had familiarised himself with control tower emergency procedures. He even wanted to charge me for the drinks he had stood several of the air controllers. 'Not that I haven't the greatest respect for you as a pilot, Eddie, but I thought you might like to have the latest radio information, call signs, wave bands, the lot for the nearest bases with airfields, just in case.' And he added, 'The American base at McMurdo Sound remains the best option, of course. It has helicopters and workshops. I had a talk on the radio with one of their engineers. They can just about rebuild a Herc. All we got to do is get ourselves there.'

Something else he had done: he had spent several hours talking to the Met Officers and looking over the latest weather maps. One of these, taken from the satellite in almost cloudless conditions, showed the break-up of the ice extending almost the whole length of the Ronne Ice Front. It was definitely early this year, the pack only closed up against the ice cliff front at the Shelf's western end. This was confirmed by a Landsat pic he had photocopied.

We were almost two weeks getting ready for the voyage down into the ice. *Isvik* had done it twice already, the second time only the previous year when she had taken Iain on what appeared to have been a recce. Neither Iris nor Pete would talk about it. Nor would Iain, of course. But it meant that the drill for preparing the ship for a voyage, which could in certain circumstances result in her being locked in for the winter, was fairly well established.

On that voyage she had had a well-known round-the-worlder on board as well as an ex-Royal Marine with Antarctic base experience. Now we would be sailing with a much less experienced crew. As a result Pete had decided on several adjustments to rigging and gear, nothing drastic, mostly concerning ease of sail-handling in case the main engine packed up or the prop was irrevocably damaged. Also he had the yard weld lugs for'ard of the mainmast so that a heavily-cocooned snowmobile could be firmly lashed to the deck. The spacing of those lugs was to measurements provided by him, and when they were in place he checked them himself.

Apart from this, preparing the ship for sea was so much a routine to Iris and Pete that the work progressed with a degree of efficiency that left me in admiration of both of them. There was so much to do, and the work so organised, that we had neither time nor energy for the development of personality clashes. Only once during that whole fortnight was there any real argument, and this was over Belle's decision to sail with us direct to her company's old Ronne base instead of taking passage on the icebreaker supplying the BAS base at Halley Bay as Iain was doing.

I was on the open steering platform at the time, checking out the electrical wiring. There is a straight up-and-down voice pipe to the wheelhouse immediately below and, just to make certain it had not become clogged, I lifted the cap. I was about to blow down it when I heard Iain's voice: '. . . can't be serious. She's no experience.' And Iris saying, 'So what? She's tough and she's got a quick brain. She'll learn.'

'The answer is still No.' The short fuse of Iain's temper was there in the tone of his voice.

'It's my decision, not yours.' There was a tremor in Iris's voice as she went on, 'I'm not asking you, Iain. I'm telling you.'

'Look. Don't be a fool, girl. Ye've already got the air crew, both of them novices. An' that brother o' yours hasn't done any sailing since he was a kid. That leaves you an' Pete, an' young Lange. Ah don't know whether he's good or not, but anyway ye should be thinking about shipping an experienced hand, not cluttering the ship up wi' a woman who has never sailed a ship in her life and who will probably be retching her guts out –'

'You forget she sailed an open boat across the Gulf of Siam from Kampuchea –'

'Och aye. But that's no' the same as the Weddell Sea.'

'Two-fifty miles and entirely alone? That's good enough qualification for me.'

'For God's sake! This is a much heavier vessel. Give that berth to a man who can pull his weight. Ah've a nice young laddie in mind –'

'No. I'm taking Belle.'

'You'll do as Ah say.' The snap in his voice was followed by what sounded like a cry of pain. 'Apart from the voyage, Ah need an extra man on board.'

'I'm taking Belle,' Iris repeated flatly. 'She's in a state of shock. She sees this voyage as a way out, something that will take her mind off –'

'Ah'm not in the business o' providing mental therapy. She knew what she was doin'. She planned it – quite cold-bloodedly. So she's no reason –'

'Just leave it at that, Iain.' Though still under control, her voice had become a little strident. 'I own this boat. I run it. And I'm taking Belle.'

'You own it? God damn it, girl!' The crash of his steel hand on the instrument panel came loud up the voice pipe. 'You own nothing. Nothing until that court case ye're bringing in BA is finally settled.' And he added, his tone less violent, 'Ah found *Isvik* lying in Ushuaia. In Tierra del Fuego, the Beagle Channel. Remember? Ah bought her wi' money Ah'd saved from runnin' truckloads of arms through Turkey to Iran and Iraq in their eight-year war. All right, it was bad money, but it bought me the right ship, an' Ah don't intend she should be sent to the bottom of the Weddell Sea in some howlin' ice blow just because ye've shipped an inexperienced woman instead of Gary McShane, who crewed for a friend round the Horn and landed up here. Now just be sensible.'

'And you – you be reasonable, Iain. Remember that Australian girl, Go-Go, we took on the first voyage. Half-Aborigine and a totally unknown quantity. It was you who insisted she should come.'

'Only because we needed her husband as radio operator. Ye're short of a radio op right now, and as it happens, McShane . . .'

But she wasn't listening. 'Never mind your reason,' she went on. 'You shipped her and she turned out all right. So will Belle.'

'No. Ye're not taking her. That's flat. She's booked her passage on the icebreaker, same as I have. Just tell her to stick to her original plan.'

'If that's what she wants. But if she wants to come on *Isvik* I'll take her.' And she added, her voice suddenly pitched higher, 'It's my ship. You gave it to me. Never mind why. Just remember, I hold all sixty-four shares and I choose my own crew. Is that clear?'

There was a long silence. Finally Iain said, 'Och aye. Ah just hope ye dinna drown in the ice regretting that.' The crash of the door as he slammed it shut was very loud. He was on the deck right below me then and I heard him mutter 'Bloody wimen!' as he went for'ard to the gangway and stumped off down the quay.

We saw very little of him after that, and on the occasions he did visit the ship, he steered clear of any reference to Belle's intention to sail with us. So did Iris. But Belle herself had no such inhibition. The Sunday before we were due to leave she came on board for lunch. Iris had planned it as a pleasant, relaxed meal, a winding-down after the pressure of work that had kept us at full stretch all week. *Isvik* was as ready for the ice and all eventualities as she could possibly be, given the limitations of facilities and spares in Stanley for her sort of vessel.

Then suddenly Iain appeared, sliding down from the wheelhouse. I don't think Iris had invited him. He just turned up. 'What's on the menu, girl?' He didn't wait for an answer. 'Mutton. Bloody mutton. Ah can smell it.' He sat himself down at the saloon table and reached for the bottle of Scotch I had got one of the RAF boys to bring me from the Naafi. He pulled some typed sheets from his pocket and passed them over to Iris. 'Instructions for ye in the event ye arrive at the KLME ice station before me. Well, here's to us all.' He had poured himself a large slug and downed half of it at a gulp. 'You and

Pete, read that through, see if there are any queries ye want to raise an' Ah'll do my best to answer them.'

Iris pushed the papers aside. 'It can wait,' she said coldly. 'This is a going-away lunch, so no business, please. If you wish to join us you're very welcome.'

He stared at her. 'On your terms. Is that it?'

She nodded, and I could see the pressure building up in her. So could he and, quite deliberately, with no smile to soften the bluntness of it, he said, 'Per'aps Ah should remind ye that, apart from the fact that Ah gave ye the ship in the first place, ye've been under charter to me for the past week.' A long, deep silence followed this. He had sat himself down directly opposite Belle. 'An' you.' He was being deliberately rude. 'Ha' ye made up yer mind yet?'

'Of course.'

He waited, the two of them staring at each other. Her face was impassive, and her eyes on his were quite without expression. She had a stillness and composure that reminded me of statues I had seen in Buddhist temples in the north of Pakistan. She knew, of course, what he was after.

'So what's the answer?' He was clearly in a foul temper.

'Iris told you.'

'That was on Wednesday. Ye've had four days to think it over.'

Belle nodded, smiling at him sweetly. 'I do not think you have much knowledge of the sort of woman I am. When I make a decision –'

'We don't have room for passengers on this ship.'

'Mr Ward.' She was suddenly very formal. 'As I was saying, once I make a decision it is final. I don't change.'

For a moment I thought Iain was going to lash out at her. But her tone, her whole manner, had been so implacable when she had said 'I don't change' that he just nodded. 'Aye.' He sat back in his seat, smiling. It was not a nice smile. 'So ye'll be sailing direct to the Ronne Ice Front in *Isvik*.'

She nodded.

'Then ye'll be hot-bunking wi' a laddie name o' Gary McShane. I hope Iris warned ye about that.'

'Perhaps you explain what is hot-bunking.' Her voice was steely. 'No, you don't have to. You wish to make it difficult for me. You don't want me here on this ship because you are afraid I already

224

know . . .' She stopped there. There was no conversation at the table, everybody silent. She got abruptly to her feet. 'I think Iris needs some help now.'

He caught hold of her arm as she pushed past him. 'Know what?' he demanded.

She looked down at him, smiling, but without expression, a cold, fixed smile. 'The reason you are here. What else?' She stared point-edly at the gloved hand gripping her arm and he let go. 'I think it is better that we don't travel on the same ship. Perhaps by the time we are both at the Ronne ice station co-existence will be possible. But then, of course, you will be away to that old ship and its macabre remains.' Her voice, and the way she said it, that slight accent of hers . . . Iain was staring up at her and I saw him flinch. Or perhaps it was my imagination. I glanced at Pete. The reference to the *Santa Maria del Sud* and the dead bodies that were her cargo had turned his face pale under the dark wind-tan. He caught my eye and I knew what he was thinking, both of us conscious that this lunch marked almost the final stage in the countdown to departure.

Iain stretched out his left hand for the bottle, but I got there before him. I had bought it for the whole ship's company. At the same moment Iris dumped a wooden platter in front of him. On it was a large leg of mutton still steaming from the heat of the oven. 'Now you are here per'aps you make yourself useful, Iain. Will you carve please?' Nils was leaning over my shoulder with a carafe of red wine. The table seemed to relax.

There were nine of us feeding there that Sunday lunch time, and if we shipped the young Irishman Iain had found, then we would still be nine for the actual voyage. 'There will be no hot-bunking,' Iris said in a small, tight voice as she took the plate Iain had just piled with meat and ladled out boiled potatoes from the stew pot on top of the stove. 'If McShane comes Belle can share my cabin.' Both the stern cabins were fitted with two-tier bunks.

The atmosphere in the big saloon thawed as the red infuriator they had shipped in from Ushuaia weeks ago by a Chilean fishing boat went the rounds. Faces flushed. Tongues loosened. Nils began crooning what he claimed was a saga set to music. Bjorn Lange sang the town song of Bergen. 'Every Norwegian town has its own song.' He sang it softly, a hint of nostalgia in his voice.

And then to my surprise, and I think everybody else's, Iain began singing, '*Full fathom five* ...' It was a most inappropriate choice, particularly as he sang it looking straight across at Bjorn ... '*Those are pearls that were his eyes* ...'

'Plees.' Belle's eyes were pleading for him to stop and Bjorn leapt to his feet.

'Och aye.' Iain waved him back. 'Ah'll sing somethin' else from the *Dream* then, somethin' a little more countrified.' And in the same deep baritone he switched to '*Where the bee sucks, there suck I* ...'

The clock on the for'ard bulkhead was showing 16.12 as he reached the last line – '*Merrily, merrily shall I live now, Under the blossom that hangs on the bough.*' A big jug of black coffee had appeared, Nils smiling as he filled the mugs Iris was handing round. Bjorn took his in both hands, tipped it up, spilling some of it down his sweater as he drank, then lumbered carefully to his feet to deliver a long speech about care for the environment in the frozen world we would be sailing through. 'Everything impinge on the envir'nment – it is zo fragile, zo prec-riush. You get caught short on the ice an' your shit shtay there for years. Your footprints, too –'

'Si'down, man. Si'down an' shu'-up.' Charlie's eyes were bulging, sure sign of a belligerency build-up. 'You shit on the ice down there an' it gets covered in snow in no time. One winter an' it'll be like that Herc we're supposed to fly out – all covered over.'

'You know nothing about it.' Bjorn was leaning down, glaring at him. 'The further inland you go, the less snow. The great central mass of Anta-a-arkika is a desert.' He was beginning to stumble over words as the nervous tension in him, always close to the surface, threatened to break out.

'You don't know what you're talking about.' Charlie looked as though he was about to get to his feet and I saw Pete half-rise, ready to intervene. 'There's an ice dome covers the centre and it's a mile or so high. Solid, impacted ice. Where the hell d'you think that came from? Snow, boy. Lashings of storm-driven white stuff. Killed Scott, didn't it? And Amundsen ate his dogs.'

'It's too cold for snow up there. It's powder ice crystals, wind-driven by great storms. That dome of ice has taken thousands of years ...' He seemed to lose the thread, falling strangely silent for a moment. Then he said, 'Nunataks, peaks of rock, poke their snouts through the glacial surface. It is so colossal that dome, so heavy, the weight of it has flattened the polar surface of the earth.'

He stopped there, leaning his weight on the table, staring wildly round at us, nobody saying anything, all of us watching him. 'Antarctica eez a laboratory. Eez unique. A frozen research place. The holes in the ozone layer. That is discovering down here in Antarctica base.'

'Don't be daft, man. We got satellites what survey the upper atmosphere.'

'*Ja*, but they don't believe what they see. Fifteen, no, more, years ago, NASA haf the holes on their satellite, but the computer say No. It is something abnormal and the computer is programme to reject abnormalisms. It is BAS who find and alert the world to those holes. Your British Antarctica Survey. I tell you –' his fist thumped the table – 'there is no other such place in the world like it. Ve haf so much to learn from Antarctica.' He waved a hand at us in frustration. 'Ach, you don't understand.'

Standing there, swaying slightly, the fair skin of his face flushed and his blond hair on end like a brush, we were all of us silent, even Charlie. 'None of you understands. You 'ave rape the whole world now. Everywhere. Only the Antarctic is left.' He flung out his arm, a finger pointing at us. 'Now you come. The scientists first, then the minerologists. It is like the way it was when the sealers and the whalers follow Cook.' He talked of some twenty nations scratching around in the ice. 'All very good people – scientists, learning new things all the time. But scientists have to eat. They have to be kep' varm; glaciologists, minerologists, all with their bases, their back-up.' He leaned down towards us, face intent and very flushed. 'You know, there are about seventy bases in the Antarctic. Russia alone had over a thousand men and women working down there. Over forty of these bases are open all the year. Now you come. Not for science, but for greed. I tell you, the environment down there is so fragile . . .'

He went on like that for about five more minutes, his voice getting more and more slurred as the contents of lectures he had given or attended poured compulsively out of him. Finally his voice trailed away and he subsided back into his seat, reaching for his glass and gulping down the rest of his wine as though he hadn't had a drop all day.

I turned to Iain, but he had slipped away.

I don't think Bjorn knew anything about Eduardo's background, for he started talking again, loudly and at a great rate, this time about overwintering in Antarctica, something Iris's brother knew far more about. However, his Greenpeace voyage, and the winter he had spent at the BAS under-ice base at Halley, covered a wider perspective, so that, like the others, I found myself listening almost spellbound.

He was talking about real episodes now, an eye-witness account of a tracked vehicle being driven fast in a white-out over crevassed ice. 'The silly bogger want to get his team to the next observation point before the light go. There is always that danger. If you are too cautious you don't get very little done. But if you go at it too fast, cut corners, take risk, then you get much more of the work completed, but . . .' He shrugged. 'Maybe he don't realise the ice we are crossing is heavily crevassed. There was clear snow ahead. I don't know how fast we go – twenty, twenty-five miles per hour.'

He shook his head, laughing and held out his glass for a refill. 'Perhaps it is fortunate we are going fast. The snowmobile dig its snout into the far side and we hang there – just long enough for us to scramble out. We save our skins, but we lose the vehicle. Also we have to walk, with nothing for food – unless we eat each other.' He roared with laughter again. 'Fortunately we have a little UHF radio and the helicopter is able to pick us up.'

He went on about his experiences, his face getting more and more flushed, his voice louder, until suddenly he passed out and was violently sick.

The following day, Monday, we motored round to the FIC jetty, where we moored alongside to take on our final stores, all the fresh food – a lot of fruit, oranges and bananas chiefly, joints of mutton, most of it already cooked and frozen, eggs which had to be individually wrapped, a time-consuming job, potatoes and green vegetables, groceries of all sorts – rice, a lot of rice, and spices. Everything had to be marked and carefully stowed. Iris, with Belle to help her, took a great deal of trouble over the stowage, so that, whatever the weather, however much we were being thrown about, we would be able to lay our hands on what we wanted without having to search the ship.

Gary McShane chose this moment to join ship. He had a very erect bearing, close-cropped hair and one of those solid-looking heads that run straight down into the neck. A pongo. I could tell that at a glance. And an ex-NCO from the way he behaved. He dumped his kit and got stuck in right away, mostly giving me a hand. He turned out to be a Geordie, stolid, dependable and almost totally monosyllabic.

Fortunately it was a fine day, so we were able to pile sacks and packing cases, all the cardboard boxes, on deck and feed them down from there. Even so, it took time, and in the midst of it we were asked to vacate the jetty to make room for an incoming vessel. We moved out to the mooring Pete had laid the previous year. This was close to the hulk of the *Charles Cooper*, near where the s.s. *Great Britain* had once been moored and almost opposite the cathedral.

It was past seven before any of us were clear to go ashore, and later that evening, sitting with Charlie in the bar of the Upland Goose, I discovered what it was that had put Iain in such a foul temper. The machine he called the 'mole', ordered from England, had been off-loaded by mistake at Punta Arenas. This meant the departure of the icebreaker had to be delayed until the next boat arrived at Stanley, something nobody was pleased about, least of all the Halley Base. Thank God, it made no difference to our own departure, which was scheduled for Wednesday. I wanted to get on with this now, and so did Charlie.

A flight lieutenant, one of the Phantom boys, came into the bar and handed me a note. It was from Sid inviting Charlie and myself to his home for a farewell dinner the following evening. Iain was invited, also Iris and Pete. Belle Phuket, too. He would send transport down for the six of us, ETD from the Upland Goose 18.30 hours. What he didn't say was that his wife had invited Cynthia Snedden to balance up the sexes.

When we got there, a little late, having squared everything up so that we would be all ready for our departure next day, she was already there. She smiled at me sweetly, but her eyes were watching for Iain. He checked at the sight of her, then walked straight past her to pay his respects to Wendy. I think he would have made his apologies to the Mackenzies and left if he hadn't needed Sid's co-operation in transporting the 'mole' when it arrived from the Port Stanley jetty to the icebreaker at Mare Harbour.

The Station Commander's house at Mount Pleasant is a standard design job with a glassed-in entrance, everything very practical with

MoD furniture. Being all on one level, however, there seemed barely room for all of us as we sat down to dinner, or perhaps that was an illusion. Both in physical bulk and in personality Iain Ward took up a lot of space, and with Snedden placed directly opposite him, the walls seemed to close in around the two of them.

There were other women on the station Wendy could have invited, so I guessed Snedden was there to satisfy Sid's uproarious, but sometimes odd, sense of humour. He kept an eye on her all through the meal and I got the impression he was waiting for the moment when she would get out her mental notebook and start interviewing Iain. He hadn't even realised that the story she was really after concerned Belle rather than Iain. She had her eye on her all through the meal.

She left it until the cheese was on the table, and then, instead of a notebook, she took a small tape recorder from her handbag and placed it quietly on the table between herself and Iain. 'You don't mind, do you?' She didn't wait for an answer, but went straight into her first question, which was not about the machine he was waiting for and the use to which he was going to put it. It was about Iris's brother. 'Why?' she asked. 'What was the purpose? And to fake a funeral – I would have thought that was an illegal act.'

Iain reached for the butter, ignoring her. He raised his glass, taking his time. He took his time, too, over his selection from the cheeseboard. But he couldn't go on ignoring the questions she kept throwing at him, leaning forward across the table, breasts bulging out of her close-fitting black evening frock, a glittering artificial diamond necklace sparkling against the twin mounds of flesh, and her eyes like gimlets, her voice hard and insistent. 'You can't just cremate non-existent cadavers. Who gave you permission?' She looked across at Sid, apologising. 'Sorry, but this is important. Was there a body in that coffin?'

Iain didn't answer, his steel fingers clenched round his glass, anger boiling up.

'Or did you just cremate an empty coffin?' She waited. 'Oh for Christ's sake! You're not dumb, are you? How did you get the Church to agree? You can't just cremate any old body and say it's Eduardo Connor-Gómez, then turn up in the Falklands with the real Eduardo and have him pass himself off to Immigration as Ferdinand Barratt. And a D-Notice. There was a D-Notice, wasn't there? The ship, that old frigate, his return to England – we weren't allowed to write a line on it.'

The table was silent, all of us listening, and Iain sitting, hunched and furious, his body tensed as though about to spring. 'If you were a man . . .' he growled.

'You'd leap over the table, I suppose, grab me by the throat –'

'No.' He was smiling. 'Ah never play it rough unless Ah have to.' And he added, the smile stretching to a sort of grin, 'No, Ah'd probably do just what Ah'm going to do now.' The gloved hand, lying black like some large insect on the table, suddenly pounced, grabbing her wrist so that she gave an involuntary cry as the steel claws closed. Then he reached his left hand out for the tape recorder, picked it up and flicked the switch to fast rewind.

Cynthia Snedden snatched her hand out of his grasp, watching, furious, as he slipped the cassette out of the tape recorder and put it in his pocket. 'And what about the Chinese lady?' She turned suddenly on Belle. 'What happened, dear? After they had set fire to that village and the leader had raped you while the bodies sizzled in the flames. That was some years back. What happened?' She was leaning forward, staring intently at Belle, all of us silent. 'All right. You don't want to talk about it. But now, here in the Falklands, you got him cornered in that old hulk –'

'How do you know who is hiding in the *Suzie Whittaker*?' Belle's eyes were wide and staring. 'Do you speak with the police? Is that where your information –'

'No, I faxed a whole list of questions to my paper. It seems incredible, I know, but you can bounce any message you like off the satellite from here. Look!' She produced a tight bundle of papers from her bag. 'A few hours and they came back with this. All sorts of information – about the fake cremation, about your experience in that village. Even your birth. You're not Chinese, not wholly. Your mother was Chinese. But your father was half-French. And it seems almost every one of that Pol Pot detachment who gang-banged you in Kampuchea is either dead or irrevocably damaged. A messy end in some cases. And now Tan Seng, the leader of that detachment . . .' The inevitable question hung in the air as she leaned towards Belle, the rabbit teeth showing in a nasty little smile. 'What did you kill him with?' She snapped the question out, enjoying herself, certain that by goading her victim she would get the story she wanted so badly.

And she wasn't the only one who was enjoying this. Sid was sitting there at the head of the table, his teeth showing white under that ginger moustache, his eyes riveted on the two women. And Iain – he was leaning back in his chair now, his eyes gleaming. The bloody bastard was enjoying it, too.

That was what got me. The two of them thinking it was fun, a hard-bitten woman journalist tearing the guts out of another woman, who had been through hell and was in no state to defend herself.

And then that wretched little Snedden bitch switched her line of questioning. 'According to this fax message, you had an operation. You want children, don't you? And your innards are all to hell. But a gynaecologist, with her eye on your bank account, says she can open up the blocked tubes, that there's still a chance. And just before you leave Paris you have a final examination.'

'No. No, please.' Belle's voice was a strangled cry.

'Have you heard the result? Is that why you killed him? You believed the gynaecologist, and then, when you knew she'd just been playing you along for the money –'

Something inside me snapped at that. I reached across my hostess, caught hold of that bright, artificial necklace and yanked at it. The white of the metal setting was hard as stainless steel. It held, and I pulled her upright out of her seat. 'You dirty little gutter-crawling bitch!' My face was bent close to hers. I could see the hairs on her upper lip, the fillings at the back of those prominent eyeteeth as she opened her mouth to cry out. Then I hit her, with my open hand, of course. First on one side of her face, then on the other. And I put all my strength into those two slaps.

She started to scream and I hit her again. Then, still holding her by the necklace, her eyes almost starting out of her head as I came near to throttling her, I dragged her to the door, across the passageway and through the glassed-in entrance, where I opened the main door and flung her out on to the wind-blown gravel.

Back in the dining-room I found them all sitting like mummies, a stunned silence hanging over the table. It was the sort of unhappy silence that follows a joke that has gone unmistakeably wrong. Only Iris was standing. She had gone round to Belle, her head bent to

232

that sad, set face, hands moving at the back of the neck, massaging gently. She was whispering something, but I couldn't hear what, and Belle just sat there, frozen in her seat, no flicker of an expression.

'A drink?' Sid held the bottle out to me. 'You deserve a drink after that. I thought it would be our friend Ward here whose skin she'd get under.' And he added, 'Lucky we don't have any brief-hungry lawyers here in the Falklands.' His wife said something to him, I forget what, but he suddenly seemed to sober up as he looked across at Belle. 'I'm sorry, my dear. It never occurred to me she'd have a go at you.' He pushed the bottle towards her. 'Have a drink. Seems your need is greater than friend Eddie's.'

Wendy got to her feet and went over to the coffee, which was bubbling quietly on the sideboard. She served it in little cups that had no handles, the sort you buy in Arab *souks* with bright gold trimmings on rim and base. The malt, a twelve-year-old Highland Park, passed rapidly round the table. Conversation was muted, most of us – Sid in particular – thinking about what that wretched little tabloid woman would do to get her own back.

We left shortly after ten, Pete having arranged to clear Customs and Immigration at 09.00 the following morning. We planned to take our departure about noon. We would then have the comfort of the big lighthouse on Cape Pembroke astern of us to give us a positive back-bearing.

It was nearly midnight before we were back on board with *Isvik*'s tender swung up into its davits. I was asleep the instant I hit my bunk. I can usually do that, whatever is going on in my mind. But two hours later I was awake, nature calling and what I thought was the sound of footsteps on the deck over my head. They were gone by the time I was fully awake. I decided that at this hour of night Port Stanley would hardly be awake enough to mind if I relieved myself over the side, so I went up top.

There was hardly any wind when I slid back the starb'd wheelhouse door and stepped out on to the deck. I could hear somebody's snores through an open porthole. There was no other sound, apart from what I was making myself. The night was very dark, the cloud base low and a slight drizzle falling. I stretched and started on a slow amble round the deck, the steel of it cold and wet under my bare feet.

It was when I paused in the bows and looked back down the

length of the ship that I saw the muffled figure standing motionless by the wheel on the upper conning platform.

Moving quietly, and with care, I worked my way down the port side until I was hidden from view by the bulk of the wheelhouse. I was about to ask who it was, but the stillness and the damp took me back to that scene on the *Suzie Whittaker*. What if that silent figure on the wheelhouse top were one of the Pol Pot gang, or even Seng himself? Pure fantasy, of course, but at dead of night . . .

I looked round for a weapon, but there was nothing immediately to hand. I thought of rousing Pete or Gary McShane, but in the end I started up the ladder on my own, climbing cautiously. When my head was just above the roof edge I stopped. The figure had moved now and was standing above the starb'd quarter, staring out towards The Narrows. There was something familiar about the size of it and the absolute stillness, the way the arms were folded over the anorak, hugging it close against the cold that was creeping in from the south . . . 'Belle?'

She started, turning abruptly. A torch flashed on my face. '*Ah!' C'est toi!*' Her voice sounded breathless. 'I thought for a moment –' She switched the torch off. 'My mind was far away.' And she added, 'It is hot in my cabin, so, I come up here for some good air.'

I hauled myself up on to the platform. 'It's nearly two,' I said as I joined her at the rail. 'Why couldn't you sleep?'

She had turned away and was staring out again at the ethereal outline of the Stanley waterfront. She didn't say anything.

I repeated my question and she shook her head.

'Are you scared?' I asked her. 'Is that why you couldn't sleep?'

'Of the ice? Of the voyage ahead? You think I am scared of that?' She turned her head, looking up at me, her face round and pale under the black hair. She looked strangely vulnerable.

So it was that scene in the Mackenzies' dining-room that was worrying her. She had been silent all the way back during the drive from Mount Pleasant. 'Don't let that Snedden woman spoil your sleep,' I said. I had had some experience of reporters scrabbling for a story and I hadn't enjoyed it. 'She works for a tabloid,' I told her. 'She was needling you and Iain to get her story, and if either of you had responded –'

'It's not that.' She had turned away. 'But thank you – for what you did.'

Over in Stanley a dog was barking. That was the only sound apart from the wavelets slapping at our bows. The air was so damp it was almost a drizzle and there was a chill in it, though there was hardly any breeze. 'How did they find out?' She said it so softly, so hesitantly, I barely heard her, and it took me a while to realise the implication.

'You never lost your memory. Is that what you're saying?' There was a slight movement of her head – a nod. Then suddenly she turned to me. 'That's between ourselves, just the two of us. Plees.'

'Of course.' I was thinking of the bureaucratic problems such an admission would now cause.

'You promise?'

'Yes, I promise.' She had done it, of course, so that she would be treated as a refugee, and to gain the sympathy of that Australian TV unit. Once having done it she was committed. 'How did Seng track you down?' I asked.

She shrugged. 'Does it matter? He is mixing it with the Triads. That is what I hear.' Then, flatly, but very firmly, as though to convince herself, she added, 'But he is dead now. Finish. All of that part of my life is finish.'

'But you couldn't sleep,' I said.

There was a long silence, and then she said, 'It was something else that woman say to me.' She was speaking in a whisper so that her words were almost lost in the slap of small waves against the hull as a light gust of wind swung us towards the shore. 'Do you think she knows something I don't? She is telling me my gynaecologist is a –' She hesitated, her hand on the rail, gripping very tight. '*Charlatan*. Is that right? She thinks Eloise Donon don't tell me the truth – that there is no hope for me having a child.' She stopped there and I waited, certain now that she wanted to talk.

After a while she went on, 'I have nobody, you see. No family. No relations. All dead.' Her hand gripped hold of my arm. 'Somehow I can talk to you, I think, but you still cannot know what it is like. I have nobody. I am alone, *absolument*. I have a business, people, but they do not belong to me. I have nobody who belong.' Again that whispered declaration of her loneliness. 'I need to start a family of my own. I need children – desperately. Do you understand? No, of course you don't. How could you?'

I nodded, not saying anything, and she went on, 'I should have heard by now. The gynaecologist – she said I must be patient. The assessment would take time. She would let me know the instant she had the results of the various tests. And then that woman … Had her newspaper office talked with Eloise, do you think? Is she holding back the result for fear I will do something desperate like trying to kill myself? That is why I cannot sleep. I am so afraid –' She hesitated. 'I am sorry. This is a woman's matter and I am talking to you. But somehow –' Her fingers gripped my hand. They were very cold. 'Thank you. To talk to you … It has helped. Thank you,' she said again, and then she turned quickly and went down the ladder.

I heard the wheelhouse door slide back, then it closed and I stood there for a while longer trying to imagine what it must be like for her, all the people who had been close to her in the formative years of her life gone … Alone. Totally alone. I shivered, the cold seeping up from my feet. And nothing anybody could do for her. She had fought her way up from nothing. Even her name was her own invention. But now she had money, power, a whole raft of people working for her – and all she wanted was children, proof that her shattered body could still do what the humblest peasant girl of her native Cambodia took for granted.

To think about that was to start probing into the nature of the human species, the meaning of life. Poor woman! She wanted a kid, and I just wanted to get that stranded Hercules airborne, both of us with limited horizons, and both of us in God's hands. My thoughts were becoming far too deep. I shied away from them and went below to my bunk, where I lay till sleep overtook me, wondering what she would be like in bed after all that had been done to her. Did she hate all males as a result? But if it turned out she could have children, a male would be essential. Was I destined to offer my services as a stud male? It was with this thought in mind that I drifted off …

Dawn came with the sound of waves and shafts of sunlight between black clumps of cloud racing in from the south-west. It was blowing twelve knots, the barometric pressure down to 986 and falling. 'We'll have a fast run for starters,' Pete told us over breakfast, which was eggs, bacon, lamb chops, the whole works, in fact, with lashings of coffee and a nip of Nils's special with which to toast the ship and drink to a good voyage. '*Skarl!* Boddom's up!' Everybody was in a state of subdued excitement, which not even Pete's report of the forecast could dampen. He had been up since 06.20. 'It'll be a full gale by the time we're clear of the Falklands' lee.' He said it with a certain relish. 'Good thing really, a reminder this ain't going to be no picnic.' He was smiling. 'Here's to the voyage!' And he raised his glass to Iris.

We went alongside the Public Jetty and cleared Customs and Immigration from there, Bjorn having by then been issued with temporary papers. Iain came down to see us off, playing the barrow-boy turned Antarctic adventurer with the Glasgie accent switched on full volume. Watching the performance, I found myself thinking of Kirsty Fraser, wondering how she would have dealt with him, for it was all a front put on for our benefit. He was whistling in the wind and I suddenly knew he really had risked his all on this venture.

Sid said goodbye to us by flying a Phantom low over the harbour, then spiralling upwards right over us in a vertical climb, flipping almost continuously. Word had got round and there was a little crowd to see us off. I saw Snedden there, but she kept in the background. Jack Simmonds came over from the Secretariat. The Governor had asked him to wish us a safe voyage. 'He won't be coming down himself for obvious reasons.'

Iain picked him up on that. 'Ye mean he daren't. He's afraid that Snedden woman, or one of the local journalists, might report back to London he was givin' official support to a private venture in the Antarctic. Is that it, man?' He thrust his great bull of a head close to Simmonds. 'Well, ye just tell 'im from me, he'll mebbe think himself lucky to 'ave bin Governor 'ere when that Southern Continent . . .' He checked himself, and then on a quieter note: 'So far, that barren desert of ice has cost us dear an' yielded nothin'.' And then, just as he was turning away, he added, 'When Ah come back in a few months' time Ah'll expect 'im t'have 'is feathers on as well as the town band t'greet me.'

He didn't stay to see us haul in our mooring lines and move out into the open water of the harbour. After a last-minute discussion with Pete and Iris in the saloon, mainly about communications between the station on top of the Ronne and a ship afloat on the sea below, he called me up into the wheelhouse. 'Ah'm relyin' on ye, Eddie. Get that C-130 off the berg an' on to the Ronne. Everythin' depends on that.' He looked at me hard, then clapped me on the shoulder. 'Good luck!'

He wished the others good luck and a good voyage, shaking each of them by the hand. To Gary McShane he said. 'Keep in touch. Down here communications are everything. Okay?' And McShane said, 'Yes, sir.' And I thought for a moment he was going to stamp his feet and salute.

'See you all at the Ronne.' He raised his gloved hand in a farewell gesture as he went over the rail and jumped on to the jetty, pushing his way through the crowd. He didn't look back.

It was ten-forty-two local time as we cleared the jetty, heading for The Narrows under engine. From now on we would be on Zulu time for navigational and radio purposes. There was something very final about that switch of time. We sent down the warps, cleared the deck and checked the lashings, and after passing through The Narrows and making the turn to starb'd that would take us down Port William and out into the Southern Ocean, we hoisted the number two jib, then the squares'l with the triangular raffee above it.

I had never sailed with squares'l and raffee before. It was magic. We were on an easterly course, with the wind almost dead aft, and the foremast's gable-ended pile of bellying sail hauled us along like a locomotive. Even when we had passed the Cape Pembroke lighthouse and were into the wave trains coming up from the Horn, the ship remained surprisingly steady with none of the yawing there would have been if we had been flying a spinnaker.

Throughout the late afternoon and early evening the wind increased steadily, until by nightfall it was blowing gale force. By then we had taken down both raffee and squares'l, and changed to a smaller jib. Eduardo had gone to his bunk, his face deathly pale and mumbling something about it always affecting him at the outset. Bjorn didn't look too happy either.

'You all right?' Pete asked me as I took over the wheel.

I wasn't at all sure, but I said I was. It was like the start of an op but things happen a lot faster in an aircraft. Here the time factor stretched endlessly ahead of us, the movement becoming wilder, the roar of the seas breaking a constant cacophany of sound. 'We'll be a bit short-handed till they get their sea legs,' he said.

'What about McShane?' I asked.

'He's okay. Wolfed a plateful of stew and went straight to his bunk. He knows his heavy-weather drill.'

We went into watches at 20.00 hours. The barometer was then 982, but falling more slowly. Gary McShane and myself were in Iris's watch, Eduardo, Charlie and Bjorn in Pete's. For the time being Belle was left to assist Nils at the galley.

In the early hours of the morning we had a violent thunderstorm, hail like damp cubes of sugar and the wind gusting over forty knots. It was like that for almost three days, the wind blowing a steady force 8 with occasional storms, the waves building up to somewhere around thirty feet, a bumpy ride, and very tiring. Nobody talked much. We stood our watches, grabbed soup, stew, coffee, anything hot that was going, then took to our bunks. And all the time the foremast sails hauling us along at between eight and nine knots.

It was a rough introduction to Southern Ocean sailing, but with both wind and current with us we were knocking off around two hundred miles a day, so that by the third day we were halfway to South Georgia. I was seated in the driving seat at the time, the wheel quite steady in my hands, and I knew nothing about the Convergence. Gary was dozing on the settle behind me, Iris down below, the wind was dropping steadily so that I was beginning to wonder whether we ought to be setting the squares'l again.

What made me hesitate was that it had grown quite dark, the cloud base almost flat on the deck, visibility poor and worsening by the minute. There was a strange, unpleasant look about the weather. The digital time display on the control panel showed 16.22. It should have been full daylight. Instead, a dark heavy greyness clouded the sea.

Alone at the helm in charge of a ship in bad visibility was not unlike powering an aircraft through storm clouds. The mind plays tricks, dreaming up all sorts of fanciful horrors. I think perhaps if the seas had still been breaking heavily I would have been too occupied keeping *Isvik's* stern square-on to the giant combers to start seeing icebergs and rocks as ghostly shapes coming at me out of the murk. But the waves weren't breaking. They were being smoothed out, and I remember thinking the surface of the sea had that glassy, unnatural silkiness of water just before it slides over the rock ledge of a great fall. Our position was then about 54° South, 45° West and we were approaching the area of the Shag Rocks.

The sea ahead looked a mess and I didn't like it. I called Iris up. She stood looking at it a moment, then slid back the starb'd door and went out to stand at the rail peering down into the water. When she came back she went straight to the chart, the finely-chiselled features intent in concentration, the raven-black hair glistening with tiny droplets of water. 'The Antarctic Convergence,' she muttered. 'It has to be. *Si*.' She nodded her head several times. 'I have crossed it before, but all we noticed was the change in temperature.'

She called Pete up. He had been through it in similar conditions once before. Then, as now, he had been headed for the Weddell Sea. That had been the voyage when Iris had been away in the Argentine dealing with legal problems and Iain Ward had been on board. Coming north at the end of that trip they had encountered very disturbed wave conditions at almost the same position we were in at present.

We hoisted the mains'l, sheeting it in hard. This steadied the ship and with the larger jib we began to make headway again. There was considerably more movement, of course, but Pete was taking no chances with the wind. We were in the Convergence area for all the rest of that day, for we were passing through it diagonally. Once clear of it, and on the Antarctic side, the waves became more regular. But it was, of course, very much colder.

Chafe was our main concern during this part of the voyage, something that was brought home to me when the starb'd outhaul of the raffee suddenly parted, leaving half the sail flogging so violently it would have been in tatters if Gary hadn't rushed for'ard and eased off the hoist. The weight of the wind in the sail was such that it took three of us to get it down, and by then some of the stitching had been torn out. That was my first introduction to operating the heavy-duty sewing machine, and volunteering for the job in the near-gale conditions we were again experiencing was something I came to regret.

With the wind speed indicator oscillating mostly between twenty-five and forty-two knots, the wave trains marching up behind us were constantly breaking. Apart from the movement, which was a dive and swoop, like an aircraft with a trainee who will never make it as a pilot at the helm, there was the noise. The wave troughs, though long, were deep, and at the bottom, blocked from the wind by the wave coming up behind, rigging and sails flapped and banged, then up, up, up, the stern climbing, tipping us forward, the sails filling with a great clap and the roar of the wind-broken wave tops, the hiss and seethe of the sea flooding white along the ship, the whole deck as far as the bows under foaming surf. For two days it was like this, with no let-up. The wind direction did not vary, nor did its weight. We were averaging almost nine knots through the water. Add to this the wind speed being fed down to us by the anemometer at the top of the mainmast, the true wind speed we entered in the log then became thirty-four, up to fifty-one, knots. We were constantly having to venture out on deck to check for chafe, taping rags round sheets and standing rigging where the wind was flogging rope against wire. And when it became necessary to haul a sail down for repair, or to get to a chafe point above deck level, it usually required both watches on deck.

Navigation was increasingly a problem. For five days we had to rely on dead reckoning, sun, moon and stars being totally obscured by a massive cloud cover, which periodically thickened, lashing us with rain or hail, even snow on one occasion. We were all of us becoming more and more tired. Tempers frayed as little things got on our nerves. It wasn't only exhaustion, there was the worry of not knowing exactly where we were. Ahead of us, and hopefully well away to port, was the towering glacial bulk of South Georgia. Both Decca and Loran were non-operative in these waters, and satnav unreliable. What Pete wanted was sight of a star, something to give him a fix, but he didn't get it, and anyway the seas and the movement would have made it difficult to get a steady horizon with the sextant.

It was during the early afternoon of the fifth day that the clouds began to lift and thin. Quite suddenly they were gone. The wind had died some time ago, leaving an awkward, lumpy sea, the wave trains reduced to a long downland swell. Now a slight breeze was coming in from the north, where visibility was shut off by a band of fog. It had become much colder. At 15.30 Gary, who had climbed the foremast and was ensconced in the crow's nest above the squares'l yard, shouted, 'Land-ho!' He was pointing about 40° off the port bow.

I thought for a moment he was hallucinating, for none of us saw it at first, our eyes being fixed where, but for the fog, the horizon would have been. 'Up there!' His arm was jabbing at the sky, and suddenly I saw it – a great white peak glistening spectre-like in the frozen sunlight. Mount Paget. It couldn't be anything else, so high, so white – and more glacial mounds appearing round it.

That was my first sight of South Georgia. It looked very near, but that was a trick of the light, the extraordinary clarity of the atmosphere, for our radar, set for close range, showed nothing. Only when we switched to a sweep double the distance did the bleak southern coast of the island show as a long, jagged line stretching half across the screen in a south-east north-westerly direction.

I watched the sweep hand for some time, trying to estimate the contours from what Iris and Pete were telling me. They saw it, of course, from the point of view of sailing people on a very hostile shore, while I was looking at it from the standpoint of a pilot. This would perhaps be my only landfall between the Ronne ice station and Mount Pleasant, and if I had to make a forced landing ... 'You can't,' Pete said. 'There's nowhere you could put down. Not that I know of.' And Iris agreed.

That was when we first saw it, a blip on the screen just south of Cape Disappointment at the extreme south-eastern end of the island. 'Probably our naval patrol vessel. We have a destroyer on guard duty that does a periodic sweep of the Falkland Island Dependencies, just to check there are no Argie scrap dealers, like those who sparked off the Falklands War by raising their flag at the whaling station at Grytviken, or one of their pseudo-scientific expeditions.'

'Could it be the icebreaker?' Eduardo asked. It had sailed the day after us, the 'mole' having been delivered by a small and unexpected cargo vessel very soon after we had left. But Pete said, 'No.' He had been in almost daily touch with the icebreaker by radio and she was now well ahead of us and a good two hundred miles further south. 'The blip we're looking at is probably headed for shelter. Keep watching it. My guess is she'll turn Cape Disappointment and go into Drygalski Fjord. If it's the guard destroyer, then she'll continue on round South Georgia, check on the northern inlets and head back for the Falklands, or she might even continue eastwards to the South Sandwich Islands.'

The blip did none of those things. It began to move south from Cape Disappointment, heading in our direction. We speculated about it for some time, wondering whether it was the Korean ship that Sid had referred to as patrolling just to the east of the 200-mile Falkland Island Outer Zone. It had been one of the larger fishing vessels, but it hadn't been fishing at the time one of his Phantoms had dived over it on a recce. It had been lying a'hull, screws barely turning, as though waiting for some other ship to join it. A brief radio contact with the master had elicited the information in very broken English that one 'mechanismo was caput for renovations'.

'It will be a joke if that sheep is the one I haf been on board of come to look for me,' Bjorn said as we sat over our evening meal, but he did not laugh. Nor did the rest of us. By then Gary had reported its presence direct to the duty destroyer and late that night, when we switched the radar on, there was the blip halfway between us and the outline of South Georgia. It was still there next day, and the next. Its bearing was about 290°, almost dead astern of us.

It began to dawn on us then that we were being followed. But why? 'If it is a Greenpeace ship,' Bjorn said, 'I can understand. But a Korean fishing boat ...'

The wind had eased off, the movement less, so that we were able to linger over our coffee, speculation about the mystery ship gradually switching to reminiscences of the sea area we were just leaving. Both Pete and Iris, with Nils of course in charge of the engine, had crossed the Convergence line quite a few times, running expense-no-object charters to South Georgia.

TWO

I shall always think of South Georgia as I saw it that afternoon, a very strange, disembodied land with a glint of glistening peaks high in the sky above a grey band of ectoplasmic mist. 'When we come back,' Pete said, 'we'll try and show you some of the fjords. Maybe take you to Albatross Island and show you this year's brood. They're the only birds, I believe, whose chicks spend all their first winter with the parent birds.'

Iris opened a cupboard at the back of the wheelhouse. It was stacked with books. A very catholic collection, particularly the paperbacks, which ranged from Conrad, Waugh, Joyce and Hemingway to Fleming, Forsythe and, something that really surprised me, that little flying classic, *Sagittarius Rising*. 'People leave them with us for others to read.' She pulled out a fattish volume with a very dirty, torn jacket and handed it to me. *Antarctic Isle* by Niall Rankin. 'All about South Georgia. An expedition he did shortly after World War Two.'

I took it to my cabin and was lost for the next few hours. It was 14 December that he had first landed on Albatross Island: *I came over the top of a ridge to be insulted by a Stinker, which vomited a pinkish flood all over my boot, and there, not five yards away, sat a huge albatross dozing on his nest with beak beneath his wing. The Stinker's outburst woke him up, when he slowly turned himself round in the nest so as to face this strange new arrival. I advanced slowly, thinking he would naturally leave the site, but stretching up his neck he greeted me with a gentle snapping of his bill, clop-clop, clop-clop, eyeing me suspiciously but making no attempt to move. In a short time I was able to stroke his wing and finally the superb white softness of his head and neck. Eventually we became firm friends.*

This, and a Greenpeace book on Antarctica, filled the few

occasions when I lay sleepless on my bunk. Mostly I was too tired to read. And when I was on my feet I spent most of my spare time wrestling with the intricacies of astral navigation. Pete had got us too far north and unable, because of the constant cloud layer, to get a fix that would confirm our position, he became very touchy about his navigation. For myself I was glad of the error. It had given me that tantalizing glimpse of South Georgia. But it meant, of course, that we were now headed well south of east so that both wind and wave pattern were hitting us on the starb'd quarter.

It was like that for seven days, wind coming and going, sudden storms of sleet and hail lashing us, then dying away to leave *Isvik* rolling violently. Sail changes became a way of life with too little sleep for the watch off duty. We were all very tired and tempers were short. The sextant episode was typical. The men were all on deck, even Nils, lowering sail in a hell of a hurry. It was night, so it took longer than usual. And then, when we had got her stripped to bare masts, the wind fell light and the wrack of louring cloud thinned. Suddenly the overcast was gone, swept away as though some wind god had pulled a heavy curtain back from across the sky.

I don't think Pete noticed the stars showing. He was too busy arguing with Bjorn about what sail to hoist. Ever since the white peaks of South Georgia had dropped below the horizon astern of us we had had thick cloud over us with visibility in the repeated storms virtually nil. And now that we were headed about south-east and getting closer to the pack-ice it became increasingly important to fix our exact position.

I was hauling a sheet in that had slipped over the side, cursing the seawater that was almost freezing on my hands, when I looked up and saw a figure standing at the upper steering position on the wheelhouse top. It was Belle, and she had Pete's sextant in her hand. I remember thinking it was a hell of a time to start fooling with such a vital navigational aid. Pete saw her at almost the same moment, yelling at her to take the sextant below. But the wind had come back and a wave top broke right across the deck. It was storm jib then and two rolls in the main.

It was half an hour at least before we had the ship properly balanced and riding the waves with some degree of comfort. By the time I had worked my way from the bows, where I had been checking the set of the number three jib, and was back at the wheelhouse,

Belle was standing by the single sideband radio with Pete balanced effortlessly in the middle of the wheelhouse telling her bluntly and brutally that under no circumstances was she ever to touch the sextant again. He was very tired and almost beside himself with anger. 'If you had dropped it –'

'But I don't drop it, do I?' Her voice was very calm, and she was smiling.

I think it was that smile of hers that so infuriated him that he began shouting at her. Iris was at the wheel, and without turning her head, she said, 'For God's sake, Pete, shut up. No harm has been done.'

'No harm! That's the only sextant we have. You remember the other was broken –'

'I have a spare sextant,' Belle said quietly. 'I bring it with me.'

I don't think he heard. Certainly he didn't take it in, and I must admit the implication of it only dawned on me gradually.

'Pete!' Iris's voice was sharper now. 'Let it rest.'

'No. If she insists on coming with us she must learn to behave –'

'Do you know where we are?' Belle asked him. But we all knew Pete hadn't been able to get a fix since South Georgia had been blotted out by that storm.

Eduardo said facetiously, 'Per'aps we consult the bleep.'

It produced a quick laugh, but Pete remained deadly serious, and Belle said, 'That is exactly what I mean. You know roughly where we are, but not the exact position.' She moved to the chart table. 'We are there.' She pointed with her finger. 'I have mark it on the chart for you.'

'You've no right –' He stopped there, for he had noticed the almanack and the tables spread out on the chart table. A storm of hail rattled at the starb'd window. The clouds were back, no sign of any stars now. 'You mean ... you understand how to take a sight, how to use the tables and work it out?'

'Yes.'

'But how? It takes a lot of practice to understand –'

'No, not so long. I like figures. I am good at them.' And she added with a little shrug, 'That is why I am a good businesswoman.'

'But the time. You have to know the exact time. How do you do that when you are on the upper steering platform where there is no chronometer?'

'With a stopwatch, the same as any single-hander. There is a watch in the drawer there. I use that to count the seconds till I get back to the wheelhouse and can enter the ship's time less the difference between that time and the time I take the sight and start the watch.' And she added very earnestly, 'Plees understand, Pete – and you, Iris, plees – I know what I am doing. So, I think you find that position correct. Or per'aps I have to say as correct as the movement of the ship will allow of an accurate horizon. Okay?'

Pete strode to the chart table and stood for a moment staring down at the position she had pencilled in. Then he picked up her sheet of calculations, his hands gripping the page of pencilled figures so tight his knuckles showed white. I thought for a moment he was going to tell her they were wrong and tear the sheet up. He was so obviously almost blind with suppressed fury. But then, to his credit, he put it carefully back on the chart table, standing there for a moment, very still and quite silent, rubbing gently at a livid bruise on his forehead got from the swinging block of the main sheet. Suddenly he burst out laughing. 'So we have an extra navigator on board.' He patted her arm. 'Just don't drop the sextant in the drink, that's all.'

After that he let her take sights whenever she was on deck and there was a break in the overcast. And then on the fifth day after our sighting of South Georgia, the sky cleared on the tail end of a near-gale, the sun came out in a milky haze and the wind died away to almost nothing.

Gradually that milky haze became so blindingly white we broke out our sunglasses. It was the ice blink, sure indication that we were approaching the pack. Our speed was down to less than three knots and within an hour we were among stray pieces of brash bobbing about like white seabirds. The blink was over the south-western horizon, and as darkness fell our watches included a bow look-out and we were steering from the upper platform.

Morning, and the pack all to starb'd of us, a wonderful sight. Not a cloud in the sky and I had the dawn watch. The sun came up as a great flaming ball dripping fire along the eastern horizon, colouring the sea to the west of us, particularly the pack, with prismatic beauty. The temperature increased rapidly. No wind, no sea, and all to the south and west a great plain of ice broken up into islands by long leads running generally in the direction we needed to go. With the strengthening power of the sun the ice blink became blinding, and the leads were mirrored in the sky, long dark threads, some of them ending abruptly or leading into polynyas, large ice-girt patches of open water, most of which seemed to have no exit. Navigation by ice blink through the leads was like finding one's way through a giant maze with the aid of an enormous looking glass. And the sea damped down by the weight of the ice, so that there was only a shallow swell and all the bright, white world *Isvik* was slipping through a frozen stillness, the water gurgling at our bows virtually the only sound.

For the first time since leaving Port Stanley we were able to relax. I hadn't realised until then how tired I had become. I felt utterly drained. Nobody spoke very much. We went about our habitual chores in a sort of daze, eating without enthusiasm, then falling into our bunks. That evening, when I was alone at the wheel with Gary at the single sideband making his routine calls, I suddenly heard him say, 'Okay. No need to wake him. Just tell him when he wakes the albatross has left us ... Yes, that's right. The albatross. It went off the radar screen –' I didn't hear the rest of it because I had left the wheel and was out on the side deck looking aft. The bird had been with us ever since we had passed South Georgia and I was damn sure it hadn't left us.

He was off the radio when I returned. 'That bird is still with us,' I told him.

He was starting to descend the ladder to the saloon, behaving as though he hadn't heard me. 'Who was that message for – Ward? You were talking to the icebreaker, weren't you? McShane!' Rapping out his surname like that stopped him in his tracks. 'I asked you a question.' He was staring at me dumbly, his head now almost level with the wheelhouse door. 'What do you know about that ship? Codename Albatross. That right?' And then I asked him what her real name was. 'Why's she been following us? And now, disappearing off the screen. What's she up to?'

It was a mistake, asking him too many questions all at once. 'You ask Mr Ward, sir.' That's all I got out of him. But I was certain he knew the name of the boat, her nationality and the reason she had been tailing us. 'Is she Argentinian?' It was a shot in the dark and his head jerked up, his eyes fixed on mine. 'Ask Mr Ward when you see him,' he repeated, and with a set face disappeared below.

It was Pete who took over from me at midnight. Having spent most of the afternoon asleep, my mind had become much sharper. Something Iris had said as we lurched through the gale-swept waters south-east of South Georgia niggling at me. And the memory of Travers describing the scene in that bunkhouse as the opening crevasse tore it apart. 'Two years ago,' I said, 'Iain Ward chartered *Isvik*. Iris was away in Buenos Aires, but you were with him, weren't you? You went down to the southern reaches of the Weddell Sea. Right?'

He nodded, and I sensed, rather than saw, that his body had tensed. Something else I remembered now – that feeling I had that McShane already knew Pete when he came aboard. Not only that, but he had known where things had to be stored. He had known what sails to break out, where the radio connections were, the routine of the ship, everything – 'McShane,' I said. 'He was with you on that trip, wasn't he?'

He didn't say anything.

'And when you got to the Ronne ...?'

'You have to ask Iain about this.'

'And McShane was with him when he went across to explore the Ice Front. Anybody else? He did go across to the Ice Front, didn't he?'

'You talk to Iain,' he repeated. That was his final answer – for the moment. He was tired, the skin of his face pale under the wind-tan. We were all of us tired, suffering from the muscular ache that comes of near-exhaustion. If I questioned him further I thought he might suddenly fly at me. We were not lacking in food, or even in sleep. It was the movement, the constant battering of wind, the roar of wave-top surf breaking along the ship, and the undercurrent of fear as we had moved down to the ice and the unknown ahead of us.

And then, after two days of dawdling through the leads of the pack-ice in bright sunshine, what a difference! The tension drained out of us. We became relaxed and much more tolerant of little personal habits and foibles that are so apt to drive people to the edge of madness when they are living in such close proximity to each other. Eduardo had an annoying habit of sniffing, Bjorn was a nail-biter, Belle was constantly scratching at her scars, Iris chattered incessantly under tension, and I – 'For God's sake!' she blazed at me suddenly. 'Stop picking at those wind-burn scabs on your ears.'

249

Until then I had no idea I had any. Only Nils and Gary seemed devoid of any irritating habits, going about their work in the same placid manner whatever the conditions.

Dawdling fairly describes this section of the voyage, the wind speed indicator never higher than twenty knots, sometimes falling away to almost nil, so that there was a good deal of sail changing to do. Also a watch could be kept from the foremast, particularly at night, when of course it was cold. Allowing for the wind-chill factor the little crow's nest was probably registering minus two or three degrees.

The second night of pack-ice sailing we were crossing a polynya that was so vast it was more like an ice-bound sea. Our speed was nearly six knots at times, the wind variable, gusting up to force 4. I took over the helm just as Gary relieved Eduardo, who came down from his half-hour stint up the mast, stamping his feet and blowing on his fingers. 'Iain is now arriving at the Ronne.'

'Everything all right?' I asked him.

'*Si*. Gary talk to him on the radio. The weather is good down there. They will be climbing the Ice Front in the morning, then they get the first of the flubbers ashore and the pipeline, so by the next day maybe they have gasolene on the remains of the Shelf camp and can commence to clear the runway for you.' He paused there, sniffing several times. Then he suddenly said, 'You like Belle, don't you?'

'She's got a lot of guts,' I murmured, not sure what he was after.

Another pause, longer this time. 'Guts, yes, I think so. But she is dangerous, don't you think?'

'Why do you ask?'

He shrugged. And then, abruptly, he blurted it out – 'Because I think he do a deal with her.'

'What do you mean, a deal?' I asked him. 'What sort of a deal?'

Again that slight shrug. 'That ice station, all the equipment there is belonging to her company. He needs it, so he must either buy it from her, or else cut her in on the deal. And since she is here, on this voyage ...' He paused for a moment, as though wondering whether to go on. 'You know he goes down to the Weddell Sea two years past? Peter says he goes straight to the KLME station, which is just then being finalised following work in the previous season. Then, some time after that, the crevasse split open. It is very lucky they don't lose some lives.' He shook his head. 'I have been thinking very much about that.' His hand gripped my arm, his voice urgent. 'You like Iain?'

'I hardly know him,' I said.

'But you are risking your life to get him that aircraft.'

'That's for myself,' I told him. 'I'm not doing it for Iain.'

'But if you succeed, you will land it on the Ronne. And then –' His dark brown eyes were staring at me and I saw then the likeness to his sister. 'What you do then?'

The silence that followed was punctuated by the rattle of wind in the rigging. In the end I told him the truth. 'I don't know,' I said.

The grip on my arm tightened. 'Do you trust him?' he asked.

That was something that had been bothering me ever since we had taken off from Brize Norton. Did I trust him? 'How the hell do I know,' I told him. 'I barely know the man.'

We stared at each other a moment longer, then he let go of my arm and turned away. I watched him as he descended to the saloon below, my mind in turmoil at the doubts he had put into it. Doubts that had already been there when I had first met the man. If Ward had known about the crevasse, if he had chartered *Isvik* and gone down to the Ronne with the intention of blowing the ice station apart ... It opened a new and very disturbing aspect of the man.

But by then other thoughts were in my head. The male libido is an odd animal dependent almost entirely on the output of surplus energy. I had been living now for the better part of a fortnight with two women in very confined and intimate circumstances. But it was only now, after two days of relative relaxation, that I began to feel again the stirring of sexual attraction. Probably because of my Service upbringing I have always made it a tenet of my off-duty activities that you don't fool around with another man's girl. It's stealing. More important, it's bad for morale. A pilot who's lost his girl has temporarily lost his pride. He's either gone limp on the squadron or else his reaction becomes a maverick one of not giving a damn, and that's much more dangerous because it affects others.

With her Latin blood I thought at moments I might make it with Iris. I caught her looking at me once or twice with a speculative expression in those limpid eyes. But she and Pete were in this together, shipboard partners. I was remembering his reaction when I had first come on board *Isvik* in Bold Cove and had caught them

251

virtually *in flagrante delicto*. And there was her brother – an odd, probably incestuous relationship going back to childhood. That left only Belle.

I watched her covertly during that second day of sun and dazzling white, and I found I was strangely uncertain of myself. It was a challenge, particularly in view of what had happened to her. And I had certainly never made love to a woman who was capable of killing another human being. She spent a lot of time alone on the upper steering platform and I was uneasily conscious that my relationship with her would have depths that I had never faced with any other woman. In a sense, it added to the excitement – that, and the knowledge she had killed one man for certain, maybe others. She was dangerous game. With that jet black hair, and those eyes and that strange, scarred face, the feeling that if she wanted something she would pounce on it conjured up in me the memory of the female spider I had once watched devouring its mate after copulation – or had it been a stick insect? A species of locust perhaps? I couldn't be sure, my mind still numb from ten days of being battered by high winds and huge waves. Dangerous. That was the word Travers had used to describe her.

All the rest of that day I found myself thinking about it, a process that suggested I was becoming almost obsessed by her. That evening, as darkness began to close in on us, and the moon showed a pale, almost luminous streak along the horizon to the east, I suddenly made up my mind, hauling myself to my feet and stepping clear of the saloon's table that was still full of food and dirty dishes, the coffee pot almost empty and only Nils and Pete still there. She had gone up about half an hour ago and I knew where I would find her.

I shrugged my arms into the sleeves of my anorak while climbing the ladder to the wheelhouse. Eduardo had just handed over the wheel. It was his turn to stand look-out on the foremast. He took the cordless phone and went out. I followed him, waiting until he was fully occupied climbing the ratlines to the crow's nest before going quickly up the ladder to the upper steering platform. She was standing at the port rail. 'Do you see?' She must have sensed my presence behind her, and she knew who it was without the need to turn her head. 'Moonlight on ice.' She was staring out across our beam. 'It must be mountains. Far inland. Far. Far.' Her voice was a murmur of wonderment. 'To see the ice on the mountains the visibility must be crystal – we are looking much over a hundred kilometres.'

'It's beautiful,' I whispered. And it was, the moon a great round cheese in the sky and that jagged, undulating line of brilliant white lying along the far horizon. 'It is also cold,' I said, and I laid my hand lightly on her waist.

'What is a little coldness when you have the privilege of a night like this? You turn your head, and still there is colour in the western sky. And this side there is no colour, only the dark of the sea, the pale movement of the pack, and out there, on the edge of nothingness, that white, moonlit ice streak.' She was looking up at me then. 'You read poetry?' She smiled and shook her head. 'No, I don't think. You are all action. I don't think perhaps you have that sort of imagination, you don't see what is in a poet's words, in his eyes, or his head. For plays the French is per'aps best. But for the poetry, there is no language like English. What do you think?'

I was barely listening, for I had tightened my arm around her waist and she hadn't protested, hadn't even attempted a shift of position.

'You don't answer.'

I moved my hand down to the round of her buttock and she gave a little, tinkling Chinese laugh, brittle as an icicle falling.

'Why do you giggle like that?' I asked her.

'Why do you think? I am embarrassed.'

Embarrassed! I felt a flutter of excitement deep inside me. Her hand had moved to mine, but not to remove it. Her fingers, cold to the touch, were gently stroking the back of my hand.

We stood like that, neither of us moving, for I don't know how long. It seemed an age, for we were very conscious of each other, and all the time those fingers of hers gently caressing. 'It is so beautiful,' she murmured. 'So coldly, so impersonally beautiful. Sometimes I hate the beauty I see around me, the world so cruel, so much unhappiness.'

She let go of my hand and moved away, and I didn't try to hold her back. I had advanced a step and I had not been rebuffed, and now I felt the need to step back and think about what it all meant, what, above all, was her relationship with Iain Ward.

She had walked over to the starb'd side, standing at the rail and looking out at the last of the daylight lying like a faded band of palest green along the opaque glimmer of the pack. I joined her, but I didn't touch her. Instead, I leaned against the wheel and asked her what she thought had caused the seaward half of the KLME Ice Front airstrip to break away. 'Did you know there was a crevasse there?'

'Of course we don't know there is a crevasse there.' She said it sharply, impatient at the stupidity of my question. 'If we knew there was a crevasse we don't site the airstrip there at all. It could have been much further along the Front to the west.'

'Did you know Iain chartered this vessel and actually took the rubber boat over to the Ice Front below your airstrip? That was shortly before half of the airstrip broke away.'

She gave that little shrug of hers. 'Probably it break anyway. But remembering what you say Travers tell you, that he sees a ship like this one in a flash of lightning and afterwards there is a clap like thunder, I think perhaps it is not exactly an accident.' She looked at me, smiling, and gave that little tinkling laugh. 'Okay. Maybe he do give that crevasse a little nudge.' And she added, not laughing now and her voice much harder, 'It would be in character. What do you think?'

What did I think? It was such a monstrous thing to do. 'Have you spoken to Pete? Or Gary?' I was thinking of the little Welshman who had been with them, wondering whether I could persuade Gary to talk. If I could get Nils to produce one of his hoarded bottles ...

'I asked you what you think.' She said it quite sharply.

I told her about the Welsh miner then, but she already knew. Iris had told her. 'But why does he need help? He has had practice, I am sure.'

I nodded, thinking now about the future, my future. If he really was connected with the SAS, he would have been on killing and demolition courses. In that novel of his, Pete had had him using that metal arm of his to slam an Andean Indian over a cliff into a gorge, and later, much later, in the iceberg-protected area where that old frigate lay like an icing sugar decoration on a wedding cake, he had had him thrust that angel-faced killer into the hold amongst the anthraxed dead and slam the heavy hatch down on him. If there was any truth in what Pete had written the man was a killer, and quite ruthless.

Belle was on the ladder, climbing back down to the deck. I think she said *au revoir*. But by then my mind had switched to the two women I knew in his life. Barbara, separated from him, but still in love with him. And Kirsty. Kirsty Fraser would know much more than Barbara – about the business side, about the real nature of the man. Ruthless he might be, but the killings I knew about, or suspected, they were both of them justified. And the way he had gone to Belle's assistance ... If she hadn't killed Seng, he would have killed him.

And I was going to land a C-130 on the Ice Front airstrip with virtually no fuel in the tanks. From there I couldn't fly anywhere unless he stuck to our agreement and allowed me to tank up from his flubbers. It was a sobering thought, and at that moment Eduardo, standing up in the crow's nest high above me, began shouting and waving an arm in sweeping gestures left to right across the bows. He was yelling into the cordless. 'I-C-E.' The word came floating down to me, and suddenly the deck was alive with bods, Pete clambering up to join me and seize the wheel.

We could see it then, right across the horizon, a solid wall of white lit by the moon. It was whiter than the chalk cliffs of Sussex and Kent, a dazzling, sparkling barrier that stretched in a north-south direction as far as the eye could see.

The Filchner Ice Front.

We would have picked the Front up much sooner if we had been using our radar, but it wasn't effective for threading our way through the pack. For the last two days, ever since we had lost our shadowing vessel, we hadn't switched it on. No point in running down our batteries in search of a blip that was lost among myriad ice blips scattered over the screen like chaff. The last time we felt positive about its identity, because of its movement relative to the others, it had been swallowed by the rebound from what we suspected to be a group of icebergs calved off the Filchner Shelf.

Bjorn explained to me that ice shelves like the Filchner and the Ronne are colossal great tongues of glacier ice, some covering an area almost the size of France, pushed out from the land, the whole tongue going afloat, thrust seaward by the weight of the two central ice domes he had talked about. The end result, of course, was that finally the tip breaks off to become yet another flat-topped iceberg. In one year thirty thousand of these tabular bergs had been counted in an area of four thousand four hundred square kilometres, some of them over three hundred kilometres long.

I went to my bunk that night thinking how very, very small was the tabular berg on which my Herc was marooned. But it didn't keep me awake and the next I knew was the watch on duty shaking me and the sun colouring the deck above my head. 'Your tea, sir.' I blinked my eyes at the light streaming in through the little fixed porthole window. It was Belle holding a mug out to me. 'Come quick pleez,' she said. 'It is –' she hesitated – '*incroyable*! There is no other word for it. Pete has brought us in close and the whole Front of ice is hanging right over us.'

I dragged my anorak on and, clasping the hot mug in my hands, went up to the wheelhouse. There was nobody there. The watch were all on the upper platform, Pete at the wheel steering parallel to an endless cliff of ice that was leaning outwards and looked as though it would calve at any moment. I suppose we were two or three hundred metres from it and Iris, Bjorn and Eduardo were all taking photographs. Belle, too, up in the bows.

'Bit close, innit?' Charlie whispered to me. 'I seen a satpic of this Front at the moment the whole cliff-face of ice is crumbling and sliding into the water. Hope he knows what he's doing.'

So did I. But there was quite a wind coming down off the Ice Shelf and *Isvik* was tramping along in sparkling calm water at something over seven knots. If it did calve, we would probably have enough way on us to pull clear. Beyond the bows, the Front went on and on, headland after headland of ice, the whole endless cliff-face mirroring the changing colours of the sunrise. And seaward, calved-off tabular bergs glinted in glorious spectrum colour as far as the eye could see, hundreds of them, quietly edging their way into the distant pack, layering it in great slab-like heaps.

And somewhere, over that beautiful, but menacing, horizon was the vessel that had produced the blip on our radar screen for most of the days we had been running down from South Georgia.

Pete was already edging away from the Ice Front, using the katabatic wind streaming down the Filchner Shelf from the glaciers born of the great ice dome that was feeding it. It was tricky sailing, for we were into the edge of the pack, bits of ice keeping up a constant knocking on our steel hull. There were bergy bits and the occasional growler that necessitated abrupt alterations of course.

That evening Iain came on the air very late, asking for Belle, his voice loud and clear. He was up the ice cliff and on the Shelf itself, radioing us from the old KLME office, which was still intact. The remains of the bunkhouse had disappeared, but the rest of the camp was still usable, he said, once the drifted snow had been dug out of the hut interiors. They had a hoist rigged and equipment and stores had already been off-loaded. The flubbers were in place, also the single line pipe, and they had just started pumping the AVTUR (Aviation Turbo Kerosene) fuel into them.

He had had a word with me after he had finished talking to Belle, but only briefly. They reckoned to complete the transfer of cargo by midnight at the latest, and with full darkness virtually non-existent now we had reached latitude 77° South, the icebreaker would then proceed north-west to locate the present position of the berg with my C-130 on it and do their best to break through any pack there was, so that we could sail or motor right up to it. 'Ye'll be on the flight deck this time tomorrow. Guaranteed, man, as the Welshman said to . . .' There was a sudden shout, 'Hell! Hold on a minute.'

I waited for what seemed an age, and then his voice came crackling back, thick and furious. Somebody tugged at my sleeve and thrust a pencilled note under my nose just as he said, 'That was the icebreaker. They've just picked up a weather forecast, an' it's lousy – westerly winds reaching storm force at times with hail and some snow. Tell Pete to watch the pack. Skipper here says it could move fast, might even close right up to the Ice Front.' And he added, 'Have fun! Over and out.'

The information was the same as had been scribbled on the piece of paper thrust in front of me. We started shortening sail at once, and as soon as I was out on deck I realised the wind from the west was already overriding the cold katabatic airstream. I have been frightened in the air – quite a few times. But that was in my own element. This was different. It wasn't just the wind, and the speed with which it increased in weight to storm force and beyond, it was the way the pack began to move, the ferocity of its behaviour as wind and sea broke it into slabs that reared up, piling themselves one on top of the other.

By then we were riding the wind under bare poles with the engine ticking over and the Ice Front still quite clear on the radar. It was about twenty miles away, straight over the bows. We were close to nil visibility, despite the fact that, theoretically, it was still daylight, the sun time being 20.42.

Conditions steadily worsened, the wind increasing to over seventy knots in the gusts with sudden bursts of driving snow, the movement of the ship abrupt and violent, but only intermittently. Most of the time she was remarkably stable, only dipping her bows to the wave troughs then climbing the back of the next. The sound of the storm in our rigging, the crash of the seas were mind-destroying. In my case, to the physical exhaustion was added the growing pain of a headache, the cause of which gradually showed in brilliant discharges of atmospheric electricity.

Eduardo had taken to his bunk. 'Call me if you have need of my help, okay?' He wasn't scared and his face showed none of the pallor of seasickness. He was just behaving sensibly, nursing the warmth of his body and conserving his energy. Iris did the same, giving Pete a quick hug of encouragement before disappearing below. Periodically Nils emerged from below. A quick check of the engine and navigation instruments, then he would take up his stand beside Pete, the two of them balancing easily to the unpredictable movements of the wheelhouse. Once I heard him say, 'You turn soon,' and Pete had nodded.

'*Ja*, more room northward, eh?'

Bjorn appeared once, and a glance at his face told me he was scared. He checked our course, glanced quickly at the chart, then stood with his eyes glued to the radar. Finally he turned to Pete. 'Is closing on us.'

'What is?' Pete answered sharply. 'What are you talking about?' His voice was on edge. He knew damn well what Bjorn was talking about.

'The pack, man. The Ice Front is only nine and a quarter miles away.'

And the pack not three miles astern of us. It was something that had been nagging at me for the last hour. But it wasn't for me to tell somebody like Peter Kettil, a man in his own element, what action he should take. 'Go back to your bunk.' I could only just hear his words in the sudden devastating clatter and crash of a hail storm, great pebbles of ice banging at the steel shell of the wheelhouse structure.

Bjorn started to argue. He was literally trembling, desperate to make Pete understand. 'You turn. You must turn. Now!' His voice sounded almost hysterical. 'I haf been one year at the Halley Base. I watch the movement of the ice, and always the gap between pack and shore is better the further north –'

Pete turned on him then, his voice thick with anger as he told him again to get back to his cabin. 'Get some rest. We'll turn when I say. Okay?'

'No, not okay. Turn now. For God's sake –'

Pete's hand reached out, gripping his arm, thrusting him off balance towards the ladder so that he almost fell the whole length into the saloon below. Only a sudden gust heeling us saved him. He seized hold of the handgrip at the top, shouting, 'You're crazy. *Ja*, crazy, man. If we get caught between the pack and the Front –'

'We're not going to get caught. Just understand that. If you were a real seaman –'

'I tell you, man – '

'Go to your bunk! That is an order.' Pete had him by his shoulders, forcing him back towards the companion ladder.

'You don't know what you're doing,' Bjorn screamed. 'First you get your navigation wrong. Now ... You'll kill us all.'

I think Pete would have hit him then. They were both of them so tensed-up, so certain each of them was right, and Bjorn was younger, bigger. I was just about to move in, hoping I could handle it, when Belle's tiny figure emerged from the shadows behind me, her heavy, fur-lined parka making a slithering sound at a moment when the ship and the sea had become strangely quiet. 'Pete!' The way she said his name, making of it something almost musical, seemed to quieten him. 'Why don't you explain, instead of yelling at him. Just tell him what your plan is. Don't fight him. Plees – he mean it for the good of all. Just tell him.'

'Tell him what?' He was staring at her, surprised and fascinated.

'About the convergence of the different air currents, the effect of changed temperatures.'

He stared at her unbelievingly. 'What do you know about it? How the hell –?'

She laughed that tinkling laugh of hers. 'You don't think I come down into – what shall I say? – this neck of the wood –' the tinkling laugh again – 'without I prepare myself. Before ever I set up that

259

ice station on the Ronne I read up on Antarctica – *South*, *Worsley*, *Bellingshausen*, everything of which I could get my hands on. It is the katabatic ice shelf wind, isn't it? That is what you are relying on.' They were silent now, both of them, and she was staring at him, smiling. 'So why don't you tell him it will be okay?'

He hesitated, still gazing at her with that dazed, almost incredulous look on his face. And then suddenly he blurted out, 'Because I don't know it will be okay, do I? I can't be sure. I've read about it, like you. But reading of somebody else's experience is not the same as experiencing it yourself – physically.'

'You never experience it before?'

'No, never.'

'How many times you come here?' She said it quite innocently. 'I mean as far south as …' The roar of a wave breaking along the deck drowned the rest of her words, and neither of us heard his reply, but I did notice his momentary hesitation, so I think did she. Silence again and the sense of waiting, all of us tense. The storm world outside our wheelhouse shelter was intensely black. It was a blackness that was intensified by the abundance of electricity with which the storm was charged, resulting in brilliant flashes that showed the cloud base right on top of us, also occasional glimpses of great piled-up masses of roiling vapour. Those flashes gave a visual dimension to the storm that was far more frightening than it would otherwise have been, and for myself, and I think for most of the others, the high intensity of the electricity in the atmosphere played hell with the nerves. All of the six or seven hours the storm was with us I was conscious of a growing pressure in my head as though a billion skyborne devils were tightening a tourniquet around my brain.

Then, suddenly, *Isvik* was brought up all standing, the ship trembling as though in the grip of some terminal metal fever, the foremast visibly shaking, all the rigging shivering in a frenzy. Pete switched on the crosstree deck lights. That's when we realised we were in the grip of the strange phenomenon he and Belle had hinted at, the sea all round us flattened, as though a heavy weight were pressing it down, and the water itself boiling and bubbling as though we were in the midst of some frightful cauldron. And it was cold, suddenly it was bitterly cold.

I saw Pete's hand trembling as he reached out for the engine control lever and slammed it into maximum revs. I felt the ship respond, a surge forward. The sense of thrust and power was there as the big Mercedes marine diesel gathered speed, but though it was right under my feet the vibration of it was lost in the violent trembling of the ship, just as the sound of it was lost in the uproar from outside as two violent wind patterns fought for supremacy.

It was like that for perhaps ten minutes, maybe half an hour. I didn't look at the clock. I just stood there, paralysed into immobility by the immensity of it. I remember Nils bursting into the wheelhouse, demanding to know what was happening, reaching for the engine controls as he yelled at Pete that he would rip 'the fucking *skrue* right out of the shaft'. They were almost fighting over the lever when Charlie appeared, his hair standing on end with electricity, his eyes watery as they practically swam out of their sockets. 'You're pissed,' I said. It was a ridiculous observation in all that mayhem.

'O' course Oi'm pissed. You'd be pissed if you'd had as much sense as me an' hid a coupl'a bottles ...' His mouth opened as he caught sight of the trembling mast and its standing rigging lashing back and forth, the heavy duty wire beginning to fray and break under the strain. 'Cor', stone 'em.'

'Plees, I don't understand.' Perhaps it was the bone structure of her partly-Chinese features, but they showed no sign of tension. She seemed, in fact, genuinely interested in Charlie's reversion to his native Cockney. 'Stone who?'

'The crows, o' corse.'

'But why you want to throw stones at crows? There are no crows here.'

Charlie's brows wrinkled. 'Corse there ain't, missy. A manner o' speakin' as you might say. That's all. Cor, stone the crows! Biblical I 'spect. Wot they did to the Israelites or the Malachites, all them that transgressed. Adulterers, thieves, forni –' He stopped there, for a sudden silence had descended on the ship. The mast was no longer shaking, and the rigging – those wires that were still intact – was no longer frantically trembling. Pete heaved a sigh, and it was so quiet now I actually heard the expulsion of his breath. 'That was the down-draught area we've just been through,' he said, quietly, as though explaining something as ordinary as the tidal effect of the moon's monthly passage around Planet Earth.

'Ye mean it's over?' Charlie's voice was trembling on the edge of disbelief. 'We're okay now?'

Pete nodded. 'I think so.' And then he was explaining that the down-draught area we had just motored through was the point where the cold air sweeping down from the central ice dome of Antarctica met the relatively warmer westerlies head-on, and then, because the cold air was heavier, it slid underneath the westerly airstream, down-draughting sharply. 'That's what we've just been through. Now we're into the cold glacial air and the storm winds are being forced up over our heads. At least, that's the theory of it – I think.' He reached out for a piece of wood and touched it. 'I hope.' He was grinning then. And suddenly Iris was there and she was hugging him.

My head ached and I was still trembling, reaction setting in. A hand gripped mine. It was small, the grip of the fingers fierce. 'Every day we learn something.' She was smiling up at me, her eyes bright, and I bent down to her, touching my lips to her forehead, my arms on her shoulders. That's when I discovered that she was human. Her body, like mine, was trembling.

Everything was relatively quiet now, all of us in the wheelhouse, not talking and very still, as though bludgeoned into a daze by the immensity of the forces to which the frail steel of our vessel had been subjected. We could still hear the storm winds, but only as a distant, grumbling roar, and the sea was quite smoothed out. But beyond the storm there was something else, a crashing, impacted, scraping sound – the sound of the pack astern of us.

It was there on the radar screen, a faint, uncertain line in a welter of wave and spray chaff, and behind it the blips of ice-floe sections that had calved from the Shelf and were now floating tabular bergs. They were so numerous at the limit of the radar screen that they merged into an almost solid blur of light.

Pete was writing up the log. Looking at it later, it was almost impossible to decipher, his hand was so shaky. I heard Iris telling him to get some rest. He had been in the wheelhouse since before yesterday's dawn. It was now 03.52. He nodded vaguely, but he didn't move, standing motionless, staring out towards the bows through the snow-clear circle of revolving glass. The ship was ghostly grey under a thin coating of ice dusted with powder snow.

'Get some sleep,' Iris said again.

'Okay, your watch then.' He threw down the pen and rubbed his eyes wearily, then started for the ladder. 'You'll have to set a bow look-out now. There'll be bergy bits and growlers between the tabulars.'

'Of course.' She turned to me. 'You too. Get some sleep. You'll need to be fresh for what you're planning to do.'

Down below in the dimly-lit saloon Pete was standing in a daze, reaction setting in. 'Tea or coffee?' He looked dreadful, and then, as I started towards the galley, Nils appeared balancing a tray loaded with steaming mugs. '*Kaffe*,' he said, 'and somezing to make you sleep gud.' God knows where he'd found it – a bottle of twelve-year-old malt.

Pete collapsed on to the for'ard settle and for those few minutes, before Iris had sorted out watches and duties and the saloon was invaded by the others, I had him to myself. Once again I tried to get from him the truth of what had happened the last time he had been in these waters. 'You hove-to off the Ronne Ice Shelf, right?' He nodded vaguely. 'Who was on board besides you and Iris? McShane?'

'Not Iris – she was in the Argentine.'

'McShane?'

His nose was buried in his mug, hands tight round it, warming. 'Gary McShane,' I said again. 'Was he with you?'

A slow nod as he gulped at the malt I had poured him. 'Gary and two others.'

'Ex-SAS?'

His eyes snapped open, looking at me warily as he muttered something about asking Iain.

'You hove-to off the Ice Front. You were right opposite the KLME station.' His eyes were sliding away from me. I leaned forward, the gimballed table swinging under the weight of my elbows. 'They took the rubber dinghy, Ward and who else? How many besides Ward – two, three?'

'Two.'

'Semtex? Had they got any Semtex with them?'

He started to get to his feet, but I gripped hold of his arm. I had to know. I had to know what sort of a man I was dealing with. 'Iain Ward, Gary McShane and one other. How long were they gone?'

'I'm tired,' he mumbled, struggling to get to his feet. 'Bloody tired.'

'How long?' His eyes were closing. 'There was a moon. Did you see where they landed?'

'Ask Iain. If you want to find out what happened – I wasn't responsible. I was on board, standing the ship on and off, waiting for them.'

'For how long?' His head was nodding, his eyes half-closed. 'Were you close in to the Ice Front when it calved? How near were you?'

'Later,' he mumbled.

'Were they back on board then?'

'Of course. We were several miles away. Talk to Iain.'

Eduardo tumbled down the ladder from the wheelhouse, Charlie close behind him. '¡ *Dios*! Is cold.' They had been tidying up on deck.

'Bugger off, she says, just like that.' Charlie dived into the galley, came out with the coffee pot and refilled our mugs. ''Struth! 'E does pick 'em don't 'e. Tol' me ter get into me scratcher, an' that's just wot I'm goin' ter do, right now.'

That was the last chance I was to get of talking to Pete alone. I got my head down and was out right away. The ship's movement now was gentle as a rocking horse, only the occasional clang resounding through the saloon as we hit a bergy bit or the slithering clatter of brash ice sliding along the steel hull to remind me I wasn't snugged up in my RAF quarters.

They let Charlie and myself sleep on and it was almost midday before nature finally forced me to roll out of my bunk. The wind had gone, cloud down on the deck and visibility almost nil. Iris was at the wheel again, jinking *Isvik* through a litter of ice. We had a storm jib and tops'l up to steady us, the engine pushing us through the water at just over four knots.

'Since daylight it has been like this.' Her eyes were dark-ringed, enormous in a face that was drawn with weariness, the olive skin almost white. 'Not your sort of weather.' She smiled at me.

'No,' I said, thinking what it would be like stuck on that berg, the Herc all ready to go and no bloody vis. I could take off – maybe. But if I did get myself airborne and the Ronne station became fogged in … Where the hell would I go? On to the Ice Shelf, I suppose, burying my nose in a nice soft snowdrift, if I could find one. Nasty thoughts like that were rattling round in my mind, and then suddenly Iris slammed the engine into reverse and I saw Gary's arms were raised above his head. Something grey beyond him, becoming green as we neared it.

We were on maximum revs, the ship gathering sternway and Gary turning to face us, jabbing with his hands as though to push us out of harm's way.

'Iceberg,' Iris said in a small, tight voice. 'That is the third we have to back away from in the last hour.'

Pete stirred from the couch at the rear of the wheelhouse where he had flaked out. 'All right?' His voice was full of sleep.

'*Si*. Go to sleep.'

'Another berg?'

'Of course.'

The radar was hard to read, a litter of blips with the outline of the berg ahead beginning to take shape. 'Is Gary still on look-out? Don't leave him . . .' His voice faded away.

'How long has he been out there?' I asked her.

'Just over the hour now.'

'I'll relieve him shall I?'

She nodded. 'Please.'

I was almost two hours up there alone in the bows, wearing all the cold-weather clothing I had been able to lay my hands on, my eyes watering with the cold as I peered and peered into that grey curtain, shadows forming, imaginary shapes emerging, watching the water ahead for growlers, and waiting for somebody to relieve me, the warmth of hot cocoa becoming increasingly urgent. That was how it would be if anything went wrong and I was still alive to feel the cold. The sound of the water gurgling below me as the bows slid down the Weddell Sea, our course veering more and more westerly, was like a lullaby, my eyelids closing, then opening with a jerk as I fought for consciousness.

Why? Why had I been fool enough to get myself involved with Ward and this bloody C-130? I didn't have to be here. I hadn't had to accept the challenge. The cold, the sea and that infernal wind – ice, ice, ice. This wasn't my scene. Better an aircraft and a mountain straight ahead. A quick end, not this lingering misery.

Then, suddenly, everything began to change – a glow in the mist that slowly coagulated into a pale, round disc of enormous size hanging in a greenish sky away to my right. Ahead the sea was turning white, brash everywhere, and three tabulars in a row almost blocking our way. A little warmth crept into the air, and with it a return of my usual optimism. Why imagine what could go wrong when we hadn't even seen the Herc yet or checked that broken scrap of runway ice that was now a berg. Over a hundred and fifty metres. It would be all right, and if I hadn't the lift, then the ditching touchdown would leave us floating and *Isvik* could pick us up before we sank.

That evening Iain came through on UHF, his voice very different from the faint, static-disturbed reception we had had previously on the single sideband. And he sounded cheerful. There was still a little open water between the Ice Front and the pack, the gap beginning to widen as the ice was pushed northwards. The big icebreaker had lost a full day, unable to locate our particular berg in the welter of up-ended ice slabs and other bergs. But now their INMAR-sat had produced a clear picture of it and they were headed out into the pack to break a way for us. 'It's no' yur problem, laddie, but chartering icebreakers is big money and that wee storm has cost me a fortune. So, Ah'm movin' everythin' forward. Instead o' landin' here, ye'll go straight for the berg. Okay?'

'No,' I said. 'Not okay.' Did he really expect me to land that Herc on a glacial ice field I had never had a chance to recce? All right if I'd been full of fuel with alternative landing places. But the only alternatives were MPA or McMurdo, and I would be just about out of fuel. 'No,' I repeated.

But though I explained it to him in simple terms, all he did was yell at me: 'Ye dinna seem t'understand. The delay in Stanley, and now this storm – Ah'm jist aboot skint. And there's this bloody Argentine ship. INMAR-sat showed it quite clearly sitting there, waiting for us just clear o' the pack. That's wot Ah'm up against. Time laddie. Ah'm gamblin' on creamin' enough off the top o' that pipe to pay me creditors an' set meself up. This is me one chance. Ah'll never 'ave another like this.' His voice was slurred, but whether with tiredness or drink … 'Everythin' Ah got Ah've sunk into this venture. And more. Ah'm in hock to the bank. Ah didn't realise when Ah started out on this 'ow much it'd cost. That mole alone was almost eighty thousand by the time they'd got it t'Stanley. An' shippin' the stuff out on that icebreaker – Jesus Christ! D'ye know wot it cost me to charter the bloody thing from Halley to here?'

I interrupted him then. 'You're on loudspeaker here. You can be heard all over the ship. Probably on the icebreaker, too, and on that Argentine ship if they're listening out.'

'Bugger them!' he said. 'Bugger them all! Ah don't care who hears wot it's costin' me. But Ah'm talkin' ter yu. Ah bin thinkin'. It all hinges on yu an' that plane o' yurs. If ye don't get it off an' flyin', then phu-ut –' clear over the air was the snap of his fingers – 'Ah'm bust. An' so are yu, laddie. We'll both of us be deep in the shit so fer Christ's sake get it airborne, okay?' A moment's silence, as though he were waiting for his words to sink in, then in a thick, hard, suddenly sober voice, he told me to pass the mike to Pete. Once again he ordered him to make straight for the C-130. 'No time ter lose. Ye understand? Follow that icebreaker. Captain Rijsberg will've cleared a way for yer thru the ice.' He had the position of the berg now and Pete took it down. 'Ah want yer there first light tomorrow mornin'. Ah've told the icebreaker to wait for ye. Their crew will get the bulldozer workin'. The runway should be clear o' drifts by the time ye arrive. Now move it, laddie. Every minute the vessel is delayed costs money and I want Eddie to check that the berg-top runway is clear for him to take off as soon as the plane is operational.' His voice was fading. 'We'll be in reg'lar contact.' There was a sharp, metallic sound as he dropped his mike, then silence.

Pete plotted the berg's position on the chart. It was less than fifty miles away, even allowing for the fact that we could not sail to it direct, but had to pick up the path the icebreaker had cleared for us through the pack. I tried to persuade him to land me at the Ronne ice station first, so that I could check the state of the runway there, but the terms of his charter were that he follow instructions absolutely. And when I pressed him, he said he was sorry, but they needed the money.

Money! Down here at the bottom of the world it seemed it was money that ruled the lives of all those who were not employed by governments. They all needed money – Pete and Iris, the icebreaker owners, Iain, myself too. Were we building something for the future, or was it greed? That was what Bjorn called it, lecturing us on the importance and the fragility of the Antarctic 'laboratory' whenever he could. And it always came back to the fur seal and the fin whale, the horrific manner and extent of their slaughter. And when Belle told him he was wasting his breath, reminding him that four of the people present were doing no more than providing a transport service, he backed away into an argument about sea and air transport being the vehicles for an invasion that would finally destroy the world's last untouched land mass.

The fact that Belle had been seeking minerals, that big companies were sniffing round for oil reserves, only had the effect of infuriating him further. Mining and oil production required an infrastructure, a larger than usual infrastructure because of the hostile nature of the territory, and tourist vessels he regarded as instant pollution of the environment. I remember, in a quiet spell a couple of days back, he had suddenly lashed out at me. 'On target, on time. Isn't that one of your Service catch phrases? Target this, target that, bombs, destruction – and now target Antarctica.' He almost screamed the words at me. And when I reminded him the C-130 was a workhorse aircraft that had delivered thousands of tons of famine relief supplies round the world he shouted, 'It also carry lethal loads, troops, fuel for warplanes. You were a fighter pilot. Why don't you stay a fighter pilot? Instead you use the skills your taxpayers' money has taught you to grab this stranded Herc and put it at the disposal of a man like Ward, and this woman here –' he jabbed his finger at Belle – 'neither of them caring a damn what they do to this untouched slice of the world.' And he had added, with extraordinary venom, 'I hope you don't get it off that berg. I pray God you crash it – into the ice or into the sea, I don't care which.'

His words were fresh in my mind as we approached the edge of the pack on a north-westerly course. And during most of that night, remembering his words, I lay sleepless in my bunk. The fur seal almost wiped out, the fin whale reduced to barely one hundredth of its original numbers, and I was a member of the species that had done it. Did I deserve to die? Dreaming, I think I saw the whole human race packed into that C-130's fuselage and myself watching from the flight deck as it tipped over the end of the iceberg runway and plunged into the sea.

THREE

We had just finished breakfast. The wind was off the Ronne, very cold, and we were under sail, heading straight for the blip on the radar screen we had decided must be the icebreaker lying close to a berg. There were blips all over the place, but this was larger and brighter than any of the others. The pack was moving away north-westward, so that *Isvik* was still in open water, battering her way through the brash ice debris left by the retreating pack.

Sunrise had brought with it a sea mist that was almost as blinding as a white-out, visibility so poor that Pete was relying solely on the radar to steer clear of the occasional bergy bit that lay across our path. Charlie and I were below, at the saloon table, poring over the cold weather handbook included in the pack George Saddler had passed on to us at Brize Norton in what seemed another age. We were just beginning to discuss the problem of fuel when Belle called down to me. 'You should come up I think. We are getting close and the mist is thinning.'

Charlie was then into the problem of stale fuel. 'Condensation,' he said. 'The tanks are bound to have a certain amount of condensation water in them. We'll have to be sure, when we drain off to reduce the load to the minimum of around four thousand pounds, that we get every bit of the condensation out of the system.' He was also worried about minimum fuel load. 'If there's any atmospheric moisture left in the tanks . . .' It didn't bear thinking about. It would have been sensible to carry an extra thousand pounds as a reserve. It would give us ten minutes extra flying time. And we had planned to cut the wing-relieving fuel to a thousand pounds when the correct minimum in the outboard tanks to relieve wing stress was fifteen hundred pounds.

'Eddie! Plees, you must come, quick.'

The urgency in her voice sent me hurrying up the companion

ladder to find the wheelhouse flooded with a blinding light. The mist had all gone, eaten up by the sun, and there was the berg, a flat table-land of ice that was green and blue with the white of snow crusting the top of it. Just visible on the far side of the berg was a white hump that must be the remains of the bunkhouse with several smaller humps beside it. Through the glasses I could see figures moving, black against the opaque glare of the sun. They were shovelling snow from around the KLME units, and on the line of the runway two machines were moving back and forth.

It was the smallness of the berg that struck me so forcibly. It seemed at that distance a mere block of ice, like a sugar cube.

As we sailed nearer we could see alloy ladders pinned to the near-vertical side of it like a staircase, two ant-like figures moving laboriously up it, carrying a length of hose between them. The icebreaker was a monstrous great brute of a vessel, the hull painted a brilliant orange-yellow and the superstructure bright red. Their launch, a big semi-inflatable, came out to meet us with an invitation for Pete, Iris and myself to join the Captain in his cabin. I asked Belle to come with us. While the icebreaker was here there was a chance I might get help with clearing the ice and snow off the top of the under-ice hangar. If we could get into it before they left, Charlie could check the aircraft over, and if there was anything damaged, we might get a replacement out of their stores, or made up in their workshops. Belle could be very persuasive, and she was quick at spotting any deficiency.

The Captain's quarters were three decks up in the bridge housing. We went up in a lift that served no fewer than seven decks, for this ship was not just an icebreaker, she was a tug, a workshop, a lab-oratory, at times a rescue ship complete with mini-hospital. Captain Rijsberg proved to be Dutch. Not being from the coast, but from inland, close by the German border, he offered us Schnapps. 'I haf very little time I can spare here, but vee do vot vee can. The runway iss clear for you, Mister Cruse. To our surprise the leedle bulldozer that is parking beside ze huts work okay. No problem. Vee give it fresh fuel and voof, away she go. And vee haul a small JCB of our own up the ice cliff. Vee are now clearing the huts – there is part of a sleeping quarter with beds, but is full of snow. That vee clear. There is a toilet place separate and what we think is office-cum-laboratory.'

I thanked him and asked him about the state of the runway – was the surface of it ice or impacted snow?

'You see for yourself. When you finish your drink vee go up and you see for yourself.'

'What about the aircraft?'

'Vee do not touch that of course. There is powder snow naturally.' But he did not think there was any likelihood of damage. 'I haf look under the exterior covers, but vee do not remove them. Is cold down there like a tomb and there is ice.'

I asked him about de-icing fluid. I had insisted Iain send out as much as would be needed to clear wings and fuselage, and keep them clear until I was airborne. But he couldn't tell me whether it had been included in the stores they had off-loaded and manhandled up the crazy scaffolding of ladders. 'Vee check with my Stores Officer. He is up there now. The whole crew is up there helping to clear the vinter snow.' He glanced at his watch. 'Vee are due to leave in just one hour and a half, so now vee go up on the berg.'

It was unfortunate that *Isvik* was now lying off to the north-east, secured by two ice anchors to a large unbroken section of the pack. I would have liked Charlie to have been with us, but Rijsberg insisted on heading straight for the ice quay they had hacked out at the base of the berg. The alloy ladders were steep and slippery, the berg top 'sixty-nine metres above sea level'. In other words, the berg was just over two hundred feet high. That's all the air space I would have between take-off height and bellying into the sea. I asked him if he had had the runway length measured. We were in shadow then, close to the top of the last ladder, and he turned, looking down at me. 'You vill not like it, I think. There has been crumbling at the point where you vill start your take-off. You vill see.' And he began climbing again.

A moment later we were out on the trampled-snow top of the berg and I could see the whole sweep of the cleared runway, a narrow band of ice gleaming with surface melt in the brilliant sunlight. Close beside us was the gantry they had rigged to hoist the stores up. Flubbers, fuel, all the things Charlie and I had so laboriously worked over back in England, were piled beside the remains of the bunkhouse, which was now almost clear of snow. I just hoped Iain had not forgotten anything. My eyes strayed back

271

to that shining blade of ice that was cut off so abruptly. 'So what's the length?' I asked Captain Rijsberg.

He was staring down the ice hangar ramp to the crouched bulk of the Hercules. It looked like a giant beetle about to emerge from its burrow. 'How long?' I repeated. 'How much of a run have I got?'

'My Chief Officer do the measuring. Is one hundred and thirty-seven point three metres.' And he added, 'Mister Ward was most insistent vee measure it exactly, so you vill know the worst and can plan ahead.'

'A hundred and thirty-seven metres!' I stared at him, appalled as my brain calculated. 'That's only about four fifty feet. I need five hundred minimum.'

He shook his head. 'I am sorry. You vant to speak with my Officer?'

'No.' There was no point. We'd measure it ourselves as best we could just to be sure. But looking at the beastly strip, gleaming so brightly like wet tarmac, I knew he would have got it right, for it looked even shorter against the immensity of sky and ice that surrounded us.

A whistle blew, shrill in the cold, still air, and the boomed-out orders from a loud-hailer came to us across the ice. The bulldozers turned, clearing ridges of ice as they came towards us. The Captain pointed to the smaller of the two. 'That is yours. Where do you like it parked?'

'By the slipway to the ice hangar.' And I explained that we would need it to tow the Herc to its start position. 'Have we got a towbar?' I was looking round at the pile of stores and equipment they had hoisted up from below.

'Ja.' It was the Chief Officer, a short, bearded man with bright blue eyes and ash-blond hair, who answered. 'You haf towbar, fuel line, hose from flubber to wing tank, everything you order. It is all there. I check everything myself against the list.'

By the time they had lowered their bulldozer into the work boat, dismantled their gantry crane and were ready to leave, the metal plates covering the Herc's winter quarters had been stripped bare of the build-up of snow and ice. There was still a lot to do to it, but Charlie had been brought over from *Isvik*, Gary too. They had gone down into the ice hangar, had got the fuselage door open and were already checking over the electrics. The charger had been hitched up to the batteries and was running flat out. Gary reported radio and electronics all working. Charlie's inspection was inevitably superficial, but at least he was able to reassure me the aircraft had sustained no obvious damage as a result of its exposure to the Antarctic winter.

But then, just as I was saying goodbye to Captain Rijsberg and was thanking him for all he had done, Charlie rushed up to me. 'Fuel,' he said breathlessly. 'We have flubber pipes, but I can't find a pressure pump. There should be pressure pumps.'

I suddenly felt sick in my stomach, the bottom dropping out of my world. The fuelling point was low down on the port side, just aft of the undercarriage recess. It is even called the pressure refuelling point. God! That should have been enough to remind me. We would have to send *Isvik* across to the Ronne base to pick up a pump from the old KLME stores.

That was when Charlie dropped his final bombshell. He had already contacted them on VHF. The KLME store hut, with all its contents, had disappeared into the crevasse when the outer section of the shelf had broken away. 'There's no way we can load clean AVTUR through the pressure refuelling point.'

'Then we'll have to gravity-feed it through the over-wing refuelling points,' I said. This meant hauling cans of fuel up to the top of the wings and pouring it in by hand. Primitive, time-consuming, and exhausting. The C-130H had eight fuel tanks, two main tanks in each wing, two auxiliaries and two external tanks bolted on under the wings. Fully-loaded, that gave her a range of over two thousand five hundred nautical miles.

'By hand.' Charlie nodded. 'Only one snag, mate, we ain't got any suitable cans that are clean enough. Maybe the Chief Engineer ...'

If I reduced my wing relieving fuel in the outboard tanks to one thousand pounds and allowed only a thousand pounds to give me start-up and manoeuvring margin plus two thousand for take-off and the flight to the Ronne base – four thousand pounds to be loaded by hand via the over-wing fuelling points – 'Don't do it, plees.' The voice behind me was saying what my nerves were screaming. 'You can never lift that huge plane ...'

I turned away from her, hearing that strange tinkling voice of hers tempting me like a little devil to give it up. Forget about it, sweep the streets, be a traffic warden or a security guard, a hotel doorman, anything rather than try and fly up into this icy sky and fall like Icarus, but into a frozen sea.

I turned on her, in fury at myself, rather than her – 'You know nothing about it. That aircraft is designed to take off on a pocket handkerchief.'

I was whistling in the wind. Pocket handkerchief be buggered! I needed five hundred feet, and the fuel load had to be exact – less, and I wouldn't make it, more and I wouldn't get airborne. I wondered how quickly *Isvik*, acting as stand-by boat, would be able to get us out of the water.

But while I was going over in my mind all the worst scenarios, Charlie had scrambled down the ladders and caught the Chief Engineer just as he was getting into the work boat. The result was a promise to send over three clean five-litre cans. 'All we got to do,' he gasped, his fat belly heaving with the climb back up the ladders, 'is weigh each can empty, then weigh it full. The difference will give us the weight of the fuel alone. Five litres weigh about nine pounds –'

'Christ!' I said. 'That's around four hundred and fifty bloody cans of the stuff we've got to feed into the tanks by hand. Why the hell didn't you remember?'

'Why the hell didn't you, mate?'

We were suddenly yelling at each other. Which was pointless. Bloody pointless. We'd both forgotten about it. We were both of us to blame. God! How stupid can –.

The Captain's voice close behind me cut into my recriminations. 'This liddle lady of yours ask me if my sheep is strong enough to push the runway end of this iceberg round some forty degrees so it face directly to the Ronne.' I said nothing for a moment, just stared at him, wondering what he was getting at. I was so appalled at my failure to think of a simple thing like a pump for the fuel hose that for a moment my mind was incapable of switching to this new line of thought. 'That is where the vind is most likely to come from, *ja*?' The bright blue eyes were staring at me. 'You don't understand? But if you haf vind ahead of you, then you haf more lift, eh?'

As simple as that, and it was Belle who had thought of it. While Charlie and I had been at each other's throats, she had been thinking out a possible solution and acting on it. 'Can you?' I asked, feeling small and very stupid, faced with this giant of a man. I looked

274

along the length of that glimmering runway, guessing at its present bearing. About 240°, and the Ronne I knew bore just on 200°?. 'Can your icebreaker really push the end of the berg about forty degrees anti-clockwise?'

He shook his head. 'I don't know, but I can try. I do my best, okay?'

I thanked him, thanked him for all he and his men had done to help, and we stood there in the bright, cold sunlight, Belle and I, watching as they fetched their anchor and began to move across the icescape to the north of us, a towering mass of red and orange against the white of the pack and the multi-spectrumed icebergs. Very slowly the icebreaker approached the south-westerly end of our berg. There was a slight, trembling jar, and for what seemed an age nothing happened. We could hear the straining roar of the ship's engines, could see the froth of water emerging beyond the berg's rim.

Then slowly, very slowly, the bright blade-edge of the runway began to move against the distant pencil-line of white that was the top of the Ronne Ice Front glistening in the sun.

The work boat appeared, heading across the cold bright sea towards us. Charlie disappeared down the ladders to the ice quay. By the time the runway was pointing straight at the Ronne he was back again, grinning all over his face and waving a metal tap with a dial on it in his hand.

The icebreaker was backing off now, the work boat being hauled up into its davits. A froth of water at the big ship's stern and it began to gather speed, crossing the runway-end and heading north, the noontide stillness of the day blasted by a farewell from its foghorn.

It was hot that afternoon as we worked to clear the remainder of the snow, and such was the clarity of the air that it was past 1500 hours before we finally lost sight of that dwindling patch of red and orange. By evening the remains of the bunkhouse were habitable, and *Isvik* moored to the ice quay at the foot of the ladders. Once we had taken a VHF set to the top of the berg we had contact with the Ronne base, something I came to regret for Iain was so tensed-up that his voice began to play on my nerves. He was through to me every half-hour or so, wanting a progress report.

'Ha' ye got the engines runnin' yet?' This was about an hour after we had lost sight of the icebreaker. I had already told him Charlie and I had decided the only safe way to play it was to empty the tanks, bleed all the fuel lines, then fill up with fresh AVTUR.

'What's wrong wi' the fuel you already got in the tanks? They told me they were pretty well full when they abandoned the iceberg.'

Once again I went over the reasons why I needed fresh fuel, why it had to be measured out as we loaded it. 'Ye'll save the old stuff? Mebbe we can use it. Think o' the cost, laddie. T'fill that bugger wi' gas down here at the end o' the world costs a bloody fortune.' That was what really worried him, the cost of it. He didn't care about me. I was expendable, except that the whole operation, his operation, depended on my getting the Herc airborne. That's what silenced him, but it didn't stop him from belly-aching about it the next time he came through. I suppose it was the Gaelic in him. He got so violent at one stage that I thought he was going out of his mind. 'Ye're a cringin', cowardly bastard,' he yelled at me. 'Get on the flight deck an' start those engines. Call me back when ye've got them goin'. An' move it, laddie. Bloody well –'

I started to explain once again, but it was no use. Everything he owned was sunk in this venture and the whole thing depended on my getting that Herc into the air so that the mole and all the equipment could be lifted to the mining site. He was still yelling at me, talking about how he'd planned to drop the JCB they had off-loaded from the icebreaker into a snowdrift, parachute a couple of men in and clear a smooth patch of ice so I could land. 'There's men an' gear, living accommodation, a big generator ...' It poured out of him, a wild mixture of plans, accusation, even pleadings.

'You go to bed,' I said finally. 'Get some sleep. You go on like this and I'll drop the whole crazy operation. It's my life that's going to be at risk. Not yours.'

But all he said was 'When? When're ye goin' t'get movin'?'

'When everything's ready,' I told him.

'Ye're scared.'

'Of course I'm scared.' I cut him off then and disconnected the set, so that he couldn't come through to me during the night. But I couldn't sleep anyway, so many possibilities running through my mind. And it was cold.

Next morning we hauled the Herc gently up the ramp and out of its ice-cold quarters, and I stood there, staring at the old familiar shape of the beast. So cumbersome-looking on the ground, like an enormous grey slug, the body so large and the wheels so small it looked as though it wasn't designed to fly. It was ugly. Nothing beautiful about it at all, not even in flight, when it looked a bit like an old flying boat. But to handle – it was a dream of an aircraft. And this one was mine, my very own; not the property of some government, but mine to do what I liked with. All I had to do now was fly it off this berg and land it on the Ronne.

It took us virtually all that day to prepare the C-130 for take-off, clearing all the vents, drains and breathers of ice, cleaning out the landing gear oleos with hydraulic fluid, draining condensation from fuel, oil and hydraulic sumps, and finally running over the whole fuselage, particularly the areas in shade, with anti-icing fluid.

Unfortunately, I had to guess at the amount of extra fuel I needed for a test run-up of the engines. No snow had penetrated the fuselage or the flight deck, but the whole interior of the aircraft had the cold dankness of a tomb. The moon began to lift above the white line of the horizon just as I had finished checking everything and we started engine tests. They were Allisons, all four of them, and when the first one coughed and caught, I could hardly believe it. 'Told yer.' Charlie's voice, chirpy with glee, came through on my headset. 'Told yer, did'n' I?'

One by one the engines caught and he slid into the seat beside me, his hand closing over the engine-control levers, boosting them slowly up to maximum revs, both of us with our eyes fixed on the gauges. It just goes to prove what a marvellous, almost indestructible workhorse the C-130 is, everything still apparently working okay after a winter in the Weddell Sea.

After manoeuvring the Herc back into its ice hangar the others had gone down to the ship to sleep, but somehow, having got this far, Charlie and I couldn't bear to leave the aircraft on its own for the night. We broke out a bottle of Scotch, had a good slug to celebrate and slid into the cold-weather sleeping bags we had laid out on the bunkhouse floor. And I slept like a log. No nerves, no worries, and when I woke a thin layer of mist lay like an ectoplasmic mantle over everything, so that we couldn't see the runway-end and the C-130 looked even more like a great burrowing beetle crouched there in its hole, only the black of its snout showing.

If the Ronne had been clear, I think I might have risked it. But Iain reported the mist so thick on the Ice Shelf that the limit of visibility was no more than forty-seven feet. He was in a foul temper, for he had measured it, and though I think I really would have risked a take-off – anything to avoid the nerve-rack of waiting – a landing on the Ronne was obviously out of the question. And so the weary hours dragged by as we waited, going over and over again all the things that could go wrong, checking and double-checking the instruments, eating, dozing, playing cards, anything to pass the time and stop ourselves from thinking. It reminded me of the Gulf War, waiting for the order to scramble, and always the possibility of a missile striking first.

It was just after eight in the evening when Gary, who had gone out to relieve himself, came running into the bunkhouse. 'There's a breeze. Not much, but the mist is thinning.' Almost immediately Iain came through on the VHF. Over on the Ronne the mist was being torn apart by a sudden breeze. 'Go!' he shouted. 'Once ye're airborne ...' But I was already diving for the door and Gary was running for the bulldozer which we'd left with the towbar hitched to the aircraft.

I don't think it took more than ten minutes to get the Herc in position, as close as we dared to the broken-ice edge of the runway's start. I even got the engines started. We were all ready to go and I was arguing with Charlie. He wanted to come with me. 'You need somebody to nurse those engines.' He was obsessed by the fear I wouldn't have enough fuel and I was obsessed by the extra weight on take-off. 'A hundred and sixty-eight pounds, mate, that's all I weigh, and you've over four thousand pounds of fuel on board. I'll save you my own weight in fuel in the first twenty miles.' He got up and closed the door. The loading gate at the rear was already shut. 'Okay,' I said. 'Let's go.' No point in wasting more time with the light beginning to fade. And then, just as we began to speed the props up with the brakes hard on, Iain's voice was suddenly loud in my headset: 'Hold it, Eddie! Hold it! The bloody fog is back.' And a moment later: 'We're closed right in now. Do you hear me? Abort take-off.'

We shut the engines down, my body in a cold sweat at the thought of how near to death we had been. If Iain had come through a few minutes later, just after I had got us airborne, then there was no way I could have put the Herc back down on to our tiny iceberg runway. Soon we were shut into our own dank void.

It stayed like that all next day, the fog thick and grey and cold, no sign of the sun, Iain's voice hoarse with frustration on the radio, my own sharp with nerves, my mind obsessed with fuel weight calculations, and Charlie's chirpy Cockney nature totally subdued. We badly needed a drink, but that was out of the question, with take-off so imminent, and time dragging, the damp cold seeping into us.

I was asleep and I hit the ice. We had rolled off the runway-end, no lift and a slab of pack rushing towards me, a soundless crash, then a hand shaking me – 'Wake up, boss! Wake up! The Ronne's clear. Scramble!'

Scramble! Only somebody who knew the jargon ... I opened my eyes, half-blinded by a shaft of light. 'The sun's breaking through, boss.' Gary's face hung over me, his usually phlegmatic manner bubbling with excitement. He thrust the radiophone against my ear and I heard Iain's voice yelling, 'Eddie, for Chrissakes move it. Go, go, go – while you have the chance. Vis is infinity up the Shelf. Move it, laddie.'

'Okay,' I called back. 'We're on our way. Maintain contact and report weather at your end.' I was already scrambling out of my sleeping bag. Charlie was over by the window, gazing out at the runway. 'Come on, skip. There's a breeze. In a few minutes the fog'll be –'

'What's the flag doing?'

'Drooping like a lazy prick.'

I rushed to the door, the cold hitting me as I looked out at the strip of bunting we had hoisted by the Herc. It lifted briefly, pointing away from the Ronne end of the runway.

'No hurry,' I told Iain. 'There's a trickle of a southerly breeze. If it strengthens –'

He started to yell at me again. 'Ye've got a window, grab it, for God's sake. If ye sit there waitin' for it to blow harder ... it could die on ye. The fog'd be back then. Or it could shift direction.'

I told him I'd go when I thought it was right. Not before. 'I don't take chances,' I said. 'Not if they're avoidable. That way you stay alive – you hope.'

He got very excited then. 'Ye got a chance now. Take it. If ye can play the fool with bridges ye can take a chance when the good Laird gives it ye. Now go!'

279

'I'm flying the bloody thing,' I told him. 'You're not. So the decision's mine.' He started calling me names then, but I wasn't in the mood for a battle of words. I tossed the radiophone across to Gary. 'All I want from his end is continuous weather reporting.'

We dressed and went out to the aircraft. The breeze was strengthening and I didn't hurry. There was no point – except to soothe my nerves. My whole being cried out to get it over with, but I forced myself to walk slowly, deliberately. I had already called up *Isvik* and by the time I was clambering on to the flight deck Pete was reporting he was under way. It would take him almost a quarter of an hour to get into his stand-by position about two miles south of the berg. No hurry, take your time, check everything.

Charlie shut and clamped the door to the fuselage and we took our seats on the flight deck. The bunting was lifting a little higher now, the breeze still strengthening, and while Charlie concentrated on engine checks, I ran through the control checks, exercising the ailerons, checking flight instruments, ADI Comparator, Flight Direction System, all things that came naturally to me and were, therefore, run through very quickly. The only trouble we had was with the brakes. We had to scramble out and clear the oleos again with hydraulic fluid. After that we sat there, in the cockpit, silent, waiting.

Those last few minutes were the worst. Waiting. Waiting. And even Charlie not saying anything. It was bitterly cold, damp too, yet his face shone with sweat. I was sweating, too, sweating and shivering at the same time.

Then at last Pete's voice came through announcing he was in position. 'Good luck!' And then another voice, very faint; something about Belle. But once Pete had reported *Isvik* on station nothing really registered, for we were starting up the engines, our minds tuned to detect the slightest hesitation as we ran them up, a comforting roar of sound, wings and fuselage trembling as the lumbering beast strained against the brakes.

Suddenly I felt it start to slide. But before we had lost any ground Charlie slammed the two inboard engines into reverse thrust, and so we ran them up, two by two, until they were all four fully warmed. Charlie looked at me, and I nodded. Then all four of those big Allison turbo-props were straining against the brakes again. Once more we began to slide.

Things happened very fast then. Brakes off, engines up to full power. No time for nerves now. We were committed, moving faster and faster, the ice slipping away under us and my eyes on the lip of the berg, the runway-end rushing towards us – forty knots, forty-five, fifty, and still no lift. Then suddenly, at just over fifty – well below the normal sixty knots – I had rudder control. But the wheels were still glued to the ice.

I felt the sudden sag as they hit plain air, bracing myself for the smash of the tailplane hitting the edge of the berg, and at the same moment I sighted *Isvik*, bows on, and a small growler, directly in my path and coming nearer as the Herc sank down towards the ice-spattered surface of the sea. And then, miraculously, my hands sensed solid air and I eased back gently on the controls, feeling for lift. And I got it – just. A whale spouted, so near I could see its blowhole. I swear I flew through the vapour of its venting I was that close to the sea's surface, but by then we were lifting, the brash ice slipping away beneath us, becoming smaller as I climbed.

Charlie shouted something, a wild release of tension. And then, my God, he started on the Battle Hymn of the Republic – *Mine eyes have seen the glory of the coming of the Lord, He is trampling down the icicles the bergs of Hell have stored* ... He was still improvising when something moved beside my seat. I saw it out of the corner of my eye, a figure come to stand between us, and at the same moment Iain's voice loud in my headset shouting something in Gaelic, a cry of emotional intensity. 'Ye've done it! Ye've done it!' He kept on saying that. He could see us on his radar. 'Forty-seven miles. That's all. And ye're clear to land. No sign o' fog and the wind's from the south.'

I didn't hear him after that, for I had turned my head. It was Belle standing close behind us. What the hell! Her extra weight ... I was suddenly beside myself with anger, a release of pent-up tension, I suppose. I called her all the names I could think of, cursing her for endangering our lives. First Charlie, now her – the weight of two extra bodies, enough on that miserably tiny runway ... 'Why? Why, for God's sake?' And those dark eyes of hers staring down into mine, her hand on my shoulder –

'You don't know why?'

She turned away then, staring out at the white-flecked sea and the distant line of the Ice Front. She had risked her own life. That was what silenced me. She had slipped on board quite voluntarily, hiding away in the cold, empty interior of the fuselage. She must have lowered the loo bucket and crouched behind that. There was no other way she could have concealed herself.

'I think I can see the power light now.'

I thought my eyesight was good, but it was several seconds before I caught the pinpoint gleam of the light Iain had said he would rig to mark the beginning of the runway. 'If I remain with *Isvik*,' she said, 'I do not know when I am able to transfer to the Ronne. I am in his hands. This way he will have me watching him all the time.'

'You were taking a hell of a chance,' I said. 'If we'd gone into the drink ... I don't even have an extra lifejacket on board.'

'So?' She laughed. 'Then you are gallant and give me yours, eh?' It was said lightly, but her eyes seemed to be sending a more personal message. 'Anyway, there was no danger. I know you will fly the plane off, and I am such a little extra weight.'

I told her to take the navigator's seat and strap herself in. We may have got off the berg safely, but I had still to land the aircraft on an ice strip that had only just been cleared and was almost certainly flanked by solid walls of frozen debris and well below the minimum recommended width of a hundred feet. The chance of a skid was high, particularly as I was not certain, from the way the machine was handling, that the CG – the centre of gravity – was positioned correctly.

I don't know why, but I came in a little too low, so that I had to lift the plane over the edge of the Ice Front. My speed was then faster than I would have liked. I can still see that runway, a too-narrow blade of black ice streaked with snow like a white-barred venetian blind. I had the flaps full down, the engines cut back as far as I dared. We were damn near the point of free fall. The wheels hit with a crash that jarred, a nasty jump, then another thumping crash and we were down and starting to slew. Drops of sweat were trickling down my nose as I corrected, but nothing happened. Charlie did it for me, boosting the starb'd engines, and that's how we went thundering up that rough ice track, playing the engines, not daring to touch the brakes. Fortunately, coming in from the north, the 'runway' ran uphill. Soon I was able to throw the props into reverse thrust.

Guided into position close to the bulging, whale-like flubbers, we hauled open the fuselage door to be faced by Iain and his mining team, all cheering like mad. He came forward to greet me as I stepped down on to the ice, his gloved steel fingers fastening like talons on my shoulder, his other hand slapping my back. 'Marvellous! Marvellous!' And then he was asking what he could get me – 'whisky, rum, vodka?'

'What I really need,' I said, 'is a hot bath.' My body was freezing as the wind-chill cooled the sweat to ice. To my surprise I heard him say, 'Can do. A bit spartan –' He nodded to a series of three container units bolted together – 'Bare boards, no frills, but hot water, aye.' He was grinning, pleased with himself for being able to meet my need, pleased with everything because it had all gone according to plan. And then he saw Belle and his eyes narrowed. 'There's a message for you,' he told her and turned on his heel, boots crunching on snow, head thrust forward, shoulders hunched. 'Why the hell d'ye bring that woman along?'

I don't think he believed my explanation, but it didn't matter, his mind already leaping to the next phase. He sat on the edge of the galvanised iron bath, words pouring out of him as I lay there in a lather of soap. First we had to locate the area where the old frigate lay with its ghastly load, then drop the bulldozer into a snowdrift, parachute a small team in to dig it out and clear an ice landing strip. After that it would be up to Eduardo – 'It's a wee bit o' a gamble an' Ah'm bankin' on his memory bein' unimpaired. Also on his desire to see his sister provided for. He's in love wi' her, ye realise that.'

He said it as though a love affair between brother and sister was the most natural thing in the world, his mind going straight on to the problem of locating the diamond pipe. 'We don't know whether it covers a small area or a big one, whether there's just the one pipe or several. Eduardo was dragging the bottom for molluscs at the time he brought up that first bucket full of blue-ground rocks.'

It was only while he was talking that I gradually realised I was the actual owner of a C-130. I had salvaged it. The Herc was mine. But when I started to talk about salvage terms he got to his feet. 'Later, laddie. Later. An' don't forget – 'he jabbed his gloved hand at me – 'Ah provided the back-up, the fuel, the icebreaker, all the things you needed to get that Herc airborne. Ah'll talk about charter terms when Ah got some spare cash. Right now Ah don't have any.'

Too tired to argue, I fell asleep. I was absolutely drained. Only the cooling of the water woke me. So many things to do if I were going to fly a recce next day. But the plane was mine. I had bought it as junk for next to nothing, and now it was out there on the Ronne station runway, no longer junk, but a serviceable aerial workhorse, and it was mine.

I couldn't resist it. As soon as I was dressed I went out to look at it – to gloat. It was still early, the sun low over the north-eastern horizon, a great ball of red against a pale blue sky. And the Herc was no longer drab. It gleamed with the reflected red of the sun, its wings spread like a fat-bellied moth just broken from its chrysalis. Mentally I hugged myself. I had done it. I had a plane now. I was no longer grounded, no longer unemployed and on the scrap heap.

'Bravo! *Félicitations!*

I turned to find Belle looking up at me, the scarred face radiant in the frost-clear light, her eyes bright with some inner sparkle of excitement. 'This is our day, Eddie.' The way she said it made it sound very personal. 'You have your aircraft, and I have news from Milano.'

I thought it must be business at first, but her hand was gripping mine. Then she stretched up and kissed me, her lips warm and soft against mine. 'That is for your good pilotage, for your success. Now you kiss me, plees, for the way my world has changed.'

I put my hands on her shoulders and asked her what the hell she was talking about.

'That first time we meet. We have dinner together. Remember? The next day I am flying to Milano.' She paused, her eyes on mine, her face alight with the bubbling of some strong emotion. 'That is not a work trip. That is for an operation to put my insides together again. The gynaecologist don't know whether it work or not. And just before I come on this expedition I go for X-ray. Look!' She held a slip of paper out to me. *As far as we can tell there is now nothing to prevent you leading a normal life. All you need is the right man. Good hunting! Alberto.* 'That means I can have children after all.' And the way she looked at me, the pride, the excitement, the longing, her mood matching mine ... I hugged her, murmuring my own fel-icitations. But at the back of my mind I was wondering what sort of a relationship it was that we were drifting into. And once again I found myself thinking, was she casting me in the role of stud male?

V

FULL FATHOM FIVE

ONE

In the seventeen days that followed, Iain's Phase Two was succeeded by Phase Three. Such a short period, but it was during those seventeen days that I grew up and learned the hard way what it was like to be outside of the Service and operating an aircraft of my own, only Charlie and a rudimentary workshop to keep it going. Iain's energy and drive pervaded the whole camp. He was a furious organiser, but all the time on a short fuse, his temper barely controlled. It burst over me in a flood of abuse when I refused to fly the reconnaissance without some form of agreement between us.

He guessed, of course, that it was Belle who had put me up to it and he turned on her in a fury. We were standing in the sunshine beside the Herc, now fully tanked-up from the flubbers the ice-breaker had fuelled. The JCB and all the equipment had been loaded, and Charlie, with Gary and two others who would parachute in if we found what we were looking for, were all within earshot. Belle faced him, tiny and quite impassive, the burn scars showing like daubs of dark paint in the bright light as she let his words roll over her, saying nothing.

Early that morning she had been in touch with her Paris office by satellite. I had glimpsed her at the radio, a different person entirely from the one who had kissed me the day before. Now she was the businesswoman again, the blank immobility of her features finally silencing his outburst. She jerked her head towards the office container unit, suggesting they discuss the matter in private.

They were gone a long time, and when they finally emerged Iain walked straight to the aircraft, his face set as he ordered everybody to embark. Belle handed me two sheets of typed paper for signature. 'Is not perfect,' she said, 'but is the best I can do. At least now you have a charter contract. But –' she pointed to the last paragraph –

'you only get paid if the venture is successful. He cannot do anything without your co-operation. That is your safeguard. He has no money left now, so you must accept a percentage. It is as though you are a shareholder.'

I signed both copies and she said she would keep them safe. 'If I can contact my people in the Falklands, then I dictate the Agreement so that it is on record and filed in my office. Okay?' She wished me luck then, adding, 'What is that funny Scots phrase he use? Gang wearily.'

'Warily,' I said.

'Yes, warily.' And we laughed.

Those two sides of her – the hard business brain and the emotional nature that made her at times seem so vulnerable – were in my thoughts as I flew the course I had mapped out from the position Iain had given me. Distance 372 miles, flying time just over the hour, and I was wondering what the children would be like. I flew at two thousand feet, which gave us a wide enough field of vision without losing clarity of detail. All ahead of us was pack-ice, broken and slabbed where the tabular bergs had driven into it. Could I really manage a single aircraft charter business? I was flying automatically, my mind flitting from one thought to another, a kaleidoscope of looming possibilities.

Away to the west the dark of open water showed as a narrowing band against the land-gripped ice. To the north the sea passages became more and more fragmented. Finally there were only thread-like leads opening out into occasional sea lakes, or polynyas. And then there was no more open water. Visibility was incredible, almost infinity. All ahead of us, as far as the eye could see, there was nothing but ice and the remains of degraded bergs. A hand gripped my shoulder, Iain's voice shouting through the intercom: 'Change course! Ten degrees right ... Don't argue. Do it. Steer three-forty.'

He was so urgent I banked quite sharply, and as I straightened up on the new course, I saw it, a ship way over to port, snugged up against the north side of an iceberg. 'Waitin' for us to show 'em where they got to go.' He said it was the Argentine ship that had dogged us all the way from South Georgia, adding, 'Ah just hope t'God they didna' get the bearin' we started on.'

He was convinced their intention was to blow the frigate up and so destroy the evidence of their attempt to infect the Falklands with anthrax. But that wasn't what worried him. It was the fear that they would see what he was doing. 'Next thing Ah know they'll muscle in on Eduardo's discovery.'

He called up *Isvik*, gave Pete the ship's position and asked him to keep an eye on it. 'It's movin' out of the lee of the iceberg. Ye'll be able to pick it up on radar any minute now. Let me know where it's heading. Exact bearing please.'

The waiting had him fidgeting impatiently, and when Pete finally came through it did nothing to calm his nerves. The ship was steering three-O-five degrees, which was the bearing we had started out on. He sighed and told me to get back on course.

On his instructions I was keeping to a fuel-economy speed, so that it wasn't until the sun was almost at its zenith that we reached the target area. For the last hour or more the pack below us had been an endless plain of ice with only the occasional berg to cause slabbing as the pack layered under pressure. But, as we neared the Weddell Sea's western coast, patches of sastruga showed below us, the slanting sun dramatically shading the windblown corrugations. I was bloody glad to be flying over it. The thought of trying to get through those violently-sculpted waves of piled-up snow and ice on foot appalled me.

Iain was leaning forward, checking his watch against distance flown. 'Well, that's it. Better start a square search. An' get a wee bit higher.' He was peering ahead through his binoculars. 'There should be at least half a dozen grounded icebergs dotted around wi' fairly flat, unbroken pack between.'

I flew due north, climbing to 3,000 feet, then to 4,000 as I flew the same distance west. 'Down there! D'ye see it?' The excitement in his voice was transmitted to his steel fingers which were fastened on my shoulder. I altered course to the direction he was pointing and began to lose height in a long, shallow glide. 'Christ! What the hell?' I could see the icebergs, no longer tabular, their tops degraded by summer melt into fantastic shapes, crumbling spines and pinnacles undermined by caverns and arches. They were grounded. That was obvious. Otherwise, in the time it must have taken for all that ice erosion to occur, the northward drift would have carried them almost up as far as the Graham Land Peninsula.

But it wasn't their grounding that had excited Iain. It was the ship, the old wooden frigate where he and Pete had met up with

Eduardo and rescued the poor devil from his two years of solitary imprisonment in the ice. I was remembering the description in that book, how they had walked across the ice and climbed aboard. The masts had been stumps then, the hull held fast in the pack, but still on a level keel. Now the frigate was standing on its stern, bows pointing skyward, a burnt and blackened wreck, the ice all melted by fire. And beyond it, there were great holes in the ice with smoke, or maybe it was steam, coming out of them. 'Fumaroles!' He was looking wildly round. 'Over there. That flat stretch. Can you land?'

'No,' I said. 'Not unless I know the thickness of the ice.'

'For God's sake! Think of the time it'll save. Go on, land the bugger. It looks solid enough and Eduardo told me it was two to three metres thick where he was dredging. Go on! Land the bloody thing. One metre thick that'd be enough, surely?'

'No,' I said again.

He called Gary forward, asking him what he thought. The bastard didn't hesitate. He was all for landing. It would save the risk of damage to the JCB, and he wouldn't have to jump. There was cold-weather gear and bivouacs on board, rations for ten days, a sled and an inflatable.

'Okay, we land.'

'No,' I repeated. Having just got myself a valuable transport aircraft I wasn't going to risk it, and possibly my life, just to save time, or for the sake of a JCB.

'Land, dam' ye!' He threw the bridges at me, all the damn fool things I had done, and when I still said No, I felt the leather of his artificial hand against the nape of my neck, steel fingers groping for the arteries. There was only one thing to do then. I threatened to turn the Herc upside down. I glanced quickly round, looking up into his face. It was dead white. Nervous tension, I suppose. And his eyes – they were quite blank. 'And don't think I won't,' I yelled at him. I felt I had to shout to get through the blank look in those cold grey eyes. 'Don't be a fool!' I was suddenly scared, knowing what the man was capable of – 'If I black out. . .' The aircraft lurched to port. I was still gazing up at him, not watching the instruments, and I yelled at him to let go my neck. I could feel the controls going slack as the wings rolled over. I was very near to losing control.

His eyes lifted away from mine. Now, thank God, they were in focus again, and slowly the grip of those hard fingers relaxed.

'Ah believe ye would, too.' And then, in a voice that was no longer Glaswegian, but pure Eton, he said, 'Straighten her up, Mr Cruse, if you would. I've no intention of causing you to lose consciousness. That wouldn't do either of us any good. Now straighten her up, please.'

I remembered how surprised I had been when he had pleaded like that once before. It had the same effect on me now as it had had on me then. I turned my attention back to the instruments, got hold of the Herc again and began to circle the up-ended, burnt-out frigate, both of us peering down at the smoking vents of the fumaroles. 'We're on the edge of the Peninsula here – all part of the Andean chain.' He was talking to himself. 'Mount Erebus.' Mount Erebus was a 13,000-foot active volcano over by the Scott and McMurdo Sound bases in the Ross Sea. 'Don't go too close,' he said. I was down to little over 500 feet. 'Head back over there.' He nodded in a south-westerly direction. 'Over there,' he insisted, 'you'll be all right there.' And when I started to argue again, he said, 'Oh, for God's sake! Give it a try, man.' And he added, smiling, 'I don't know about you, but I could do with a pee.' It was true , he was actually smiling. 'And it would be good to stretch our legs, eh?'

He wanted me to land as near as possible to the point where Eduardo had dredged up seabed rubble with diamonds embedded in it. 'Seven of 'em, one of 'em as big as eighty grams. Uncut, of course. The quality and size equal to the top end of the Kimberley finds. One of the best cutters in Amsterdam assured me he could get a superb white water gemstone of sixty, mebbe seventy carats out of it. That's a quarter the size of the De Beers diamond. If there are more like that ...'

He was talking very fast, I think to cover his own nerves. But then he stopped, indicating where he wanted me to land. It was bang in the centre of a half-circle of stranded bergs. They must have acted like a breakwater, for the area between was flat ice, much of it scoured clear by the wind of all but a light dusting of snow. The most southerly berg was almost due east of the wreck. No gas or steam venting from fumaroles here. I flew close along its gleaming northern flank, a prismatic fantasy shape of spectrum colours, brilliant in the sun. A quick glance, that was all, my eyes glued to the windswept ice streaming away beneath me.

It looked solid enough. There were ridges of packed snow, but with luck . . .

'What's the matter? Why didn't ye put her down?' Nervous tension in his voice, and I didn't reply.

A sharp turn, circling the berg, then I was back on the same run, dropping the engine revs with the flaps down. The wheels touched, began to drag. Full power again, the wheels still dragging, the plane ungumming itself reluctantly from the mushy surface, a bumpy, unpleasant take-off. 'I'll try further out,' I said.

'Get on wi' it, laddie, fer God's sake.' There was sweat on his face and Albertini was being sick.

Toni Albertini was a mining engineer from the Brazilian diamond fields. He had come out on the icebreaker with Iain and I had met him that morning at breakfast, a dark, very volatile little man who knew the blue-ground pipes of South Africa, particularly the De Beers mine at Kimberley.

I tried a second landing, just to the north and west of the berg where there was a build up of wind and the surface dusting of snow was moving faster. This time I put the Herc down hard, ready to lift off on the bounce if there was any sign at all of the ice cracking or the weight causing a wave effect. But it was okay. The surface was hard, the ice solid. I braked. It was only the slightest touch, but it was enough. We slewed, and in the end I had to let her run until I could use reverse thrust. Shattered by the jolting of wheels on ice ridges, we came to rest facing the burnt-out wreck of the frigate, and less than a mile away to our right the first of the fumaroles was venting white vapour. There were several others just visible like old-fashioned steamers hull-down on the horizon.

We had come to rest much nearer the wreck than I had intended. Iain would have liked to have been closer to the berg. They needed its shelter for their camp. But he didn't press the point as a bitter wind drove into the interior of the fuselage. They had already opened the rear door, so the loading ramp was down and they were unlashing the JCB.

We were there just over two hours, long enough for them to unload and for Iain to take sun and moon sights and check the resultant plot against the position Eduardo had given him, which was based on bearings he had taken over two years ago on leading edges of three of the grounded icebergs. They didn't match exactly, but near enough. A flag was set up and we took off, leaving Albertini behind on the ice with Gary. I don't think the poor little fellow had ever seen ice before, except perhaps on a mountain-top. The snow ridges, which were across the direction of the wind, were frozen ice, hard as steel rails. I was glad the JCB was now on site and that it had a blade on it. Much more of this sort of treatment and the whole airframe would be metal-fatigued.

The take-off was uneventful, but after I had retracted the undercarriage the controls seemed heavier and there was a tendency to drift off course. It could be the tailplane, or the rudder, maybe the starb'd flap was not fully retracting. As we closed the Ronne I called up *Isvik*, got her position and flew over her low enough for them to see if anything was wrong. They were all on deck, waving and pointing as we doubled back, passing over her almost at masthead height.

Then Pete's voice on the radio, loud and clear: 'Starb'd undercarriage door swinging loose. Watch it when you land. And something else. Is Iain there?' His voice sounded ill-at-ease.

What Pete reported left him speechless for a moment. Bjorn Lange had taken the inflatable and headed out to the berg behind which the Argentine ship had been lurking. But then I suddenly heard Iain's laugh in my headset. 'Serve the bugger right. He'll have a verra tirin' yomp over the ice if he goes with the demolition party. But Ah doubt they'll let him ...' The Ronne began coming through with a weather report: *Vis still okay, but wind speed now 36, direction 190–195.* Straight from the Pole and almost certainly katabatic. *Some ice-crystal drifting. Watch your brakes – very slippery.*

The Ice Front was growing larger by the minute, and then, Belle, who was standing beside Iain, suddenly said, 'There's the ship. A hand's breadth to your right and bows-on.' It was the Argentine ship all right. I dropped down to have a closer look. There was the Argentine flag. And dangling from the derrick hoist on the port quarter was an inflatable. Our inflatable presumably. I tried calling them up, but either they weren't listening out on the usual channel or they just didn't want to know us. We passed over them at less than a thousand feet. We could see several of them standing on the deck staring up at our underbelly with the undercarriage door flapping about. If I lost it in the turbulence we would undoubtedly experience as I came in to land I wondered how it would affect the Herc's performance.

We hit the turbulence almost immediately after passing over the ship. It knocked us down virtually to sea level, so that I was climbing against it at almost full power. It was bad right up to the Ice Front, the wings flapping, the fuselage being thrown about to such a degree the plane was almost unmanageable. I caught a glimpse of *Isvik* right below me. She was snugged up against the white, jagged cliff-face with mooring lines out to the landing place where the ladders had been set up to reach the top. Just a glimpse, and then I was skimming the lip of the front, and the instant I was over the runway I slammed down hard, not thinking about the undercarriage, thinking only of the fact that the width of that cleared blade of ice was much less than the recommended hundred feet minimum. The wheels hit the concrete solidity of ice with a shattering bang. No bounce. We stayed down and I let it run. Nothing else I could do with piled-up walls of frozen snow either side. Gradually the wind and the upward slant of the runway slowed us sufficiently for me to use reverse thrust.

That night Iain broke out a bottle of eighteen-year-old Highland Park. The Herc was already serviceable again, undercarriage door fastening repaired, and tanks topped up. I now had two runways. Even if the Ronne field reported fog closing in and I was in the middle of my flight back to base, I had an alternative landing field less than two hundred miles away.

The next day we uncrated the mole, got it working and then tried to fit it into the fuselage. As we had expected, the brackets of the old fuel tank were the trouble. We had to shorten them with a torch, then drill holes to take the mole's securing wires. It was a lengthy, finicky job, and it wasn't until after the evening meal that we finally got the machine loaded and secured with all its surface control gear packed round it. By then there was very little room left for all the stores and equipment that still had to be airlifted to the mining site. It meant another supply run, and however carefully I nursed the Herc along, she used a hell of a lot of fuel when fully loaded.

Take-off was scheduled for 04.00, but when I poked my head out visibility was virtually nil. The fog had closed in on us, no wind and a dark, cold world, very still, very silent, and the sun, presumably just tipping the horizon to the north-east, tingeing the white opaqueness with a pale, rosy glow. By midday it was a white-out. And it was the same at the camp on the ice. Only for them, with just the one tent, the cold, damp rawness of the fog was eating into their bones. They wanted to get on with it. And so did Iain, of course. With nothing more to do, nothing to occupy his mind, he sat over the bottle of malt, playing chess with Eduardo. Stew for lunch. Stew for supper. And the fog worse than ever. I began to think it would never lift, that I'd be trapped here for ever, or until we ran out of the endless packets of dehydrated soups, stews, veg and fruit. Prunes! My God! We must have shipped in enough dried prunes to keep our bowels open till we ran out of stews and quietly faded away, or did an Oates and walked out into the fog, never to return.

It was just after I had finally got to sleep – at least it felt like that – when one of the ex-SAS boys (Bob, I think) let out a yell. *Rise and shine! The wind's back and the fog's gone.* And then Iain's voice on a note of excitement: 'Och aye. Good for ye, laddie. Eddie, Charlie, Eduardo – let's go!' Just the four of us. Anything to save fuel. Dawn was breaking and it was clear right away to the north and west. Wherever we looked it was clear, and the bitter wind off the ice dome was drifting powder-dry ice crystals across the runway.

I took off in a hurry, not bothering to make contact with the boys at the ice camp. By the time the sun was fully up I was on the long glide down towards the feathery plumes of steam rising from the fumaroles. By then we could see the blackened hull of the up-ended frigate and the men we had left on the ice were standing outside their tent, beating their arms and waving to us. 'Ah wonder where that ship is? D'ye think they'll make it across the ice with a snow-mobile weighted down wi' a ton or more of explosives?'

'All those Antarctic bases,' I said. 'They've a lot of very experienced men.'

'Aye. Ah s'pose so. Two hundred miles, Ah reck'n. That's what Pete and I had to face. An' goin' back, we had to drag Eduardo. Wouldn't want to do that again.' And he added, 'On the way back we'll have a look-see for that ship. Mebbe it's got strengthened bows, and the ice melt could be better this year. They might only have to trek a hundred miles.'

But I was barely listening, my mind concentrated on the dark line of cleared ice coming up fast. Bang, and we were down. No crosswind, no rails of frozen snow. They had done a good job with the JCB.

The unloading was done at speed, the mole coming out down the ramp as though the Herc had been designed for it. We were away in just forty-three minutes, flying low over that blackened wreck. Iain was working the radio, switching bands. Suddenly, loud and clear, came a jabber of Spanish. 'No, Argentinian.' The claw hand slapped me violently on the shoulder. 'That's her all right, an' I got her on the direction finder. Turn on to one-eight-five.'

That was a near-thirty-degree turn to starb'd and I began to argue. I didn't want to waste the fuel. But he was insistent. 'Ah must know what time we got. If they're working their way north along the coastal leads . . .'

But we had begun to hit turbulence. If it wasn't fog, it was wind. With the fuselage empty, the plane was being thrown about quite violently. It didn't seem to worry him. He sat there in the co-pilot's seat, his eyes glued to his binoculars, and all below us was solid pack-ice, broken and up-ended in slabs where the occasional berg had ploughed through it. 'Look!' He was pointing away to starb'd. 'A polynya. And there's another, dead ahead.'

That was where we found them, the ship stationary with ice anchors out and men moving around like Lowry stick insects on the ice, landing a tracked vehicle, and inflatables ferrying stores. 'Ah'll murder that Greenpeace bastard if Ah ever get me hands on him again. That's our inflatable.' He was jabbing his finger at a big rubber dinghy just leaving the ship's side. 'An' the little sod is driving it himself.'

I banked, setting a course that would take me direct to the Ronne ice station. Iain was checking distance flown since take-off. 'One-five-six, that's wot Ah make it. One hundred an' fifty-six miles they got t'trek, an' some of it looked pretty rough.' He reckoned they would make it to the frigate in three, at most four days.

'Depends on the weather,' I said.

'Aye. These katabatic south winds leave a void that sucks in the warmer sea air from the north. It comes in over the colder air, freezes and drops into the katabatics to produce blizzards. We're bound to have one sooner or later, and when that happens . . .' He and Pete had been stopped for three days. But I wasn't thinking about blizzards then. I was fighting the katabatic wind. That was

296

quite enough as the empty Herc was thrown all over the place.

To my surprise I had a smoother landing than before. No fog this time and the prefab hut with all the stores loaded very fast, so that we were away again in less than an hour. The wind was astern of us now, and though it was extremely difficult flying, it was far less turbulent, and in the latter part of the flight I had time to consider the implications of Iain's decision to take on board Bob and Paddy, the two other ex-SAS boys.

They had come aboard at the double and fully equipped – camouflage white over flak jackets, white helmets, lightweight automatic rifles with telescopic sights, ammunition pouches, grenades, pistol and knives belted round their waists, and massive great packs on their backs. They were battle-ready and my heart began to pound. Gary was already on-site and he had off-loaded the same sort of equipment bundled up in white, heavy-duty tent material.

I would have refused to take off, but Belle had come running across to me. Somehow she had guessed what was in my mind. 'Don't!' she hissed. 'Don't do it, Eddie! He is armed.' And when I told her I knew that, she had said, 'You don't understand. He is very desperate, that man. Everything he has ever made, his whole life, is in this venture. Neither you, nor those Argentines, will stop him.'

By then Iain had been yelling at me to get started. He was very tense, living now on his nerves. So much at stake. Belle's hand was on my arm, her fingers gripping tight as she pushed me away from the undercarriage door I had been checking towards the flight deck entrance. 'Don't go across him, plees. He can break under the strain. I have plans for you and that plane of yours. He is ver' dangerous now, and all these next days. Gang wearily.'

I had corrected her, and we had both laughed as we had done before; then I climbed aboard, the tension gone out of me for the moment.

But now, as the fumaroles and the blackened wreck came into sight, I knew I was scared. By accident rather than design I had got myself into the sort of situation I had never had to face before. Death in the sky – it's all so remote. Ground targets, too. They're not people. Not at the moment of firing, or when the bombs drop away. They're just targets. Enemy targets. But Iain and Gary, those two other SAS-trained lads in the fuselage, they would close up on the Argentine ice-trekking team and gun them down without a thought. And then what? Murder on the ice and the Argentine ship waiting for men who would never return. They would report the presence of Iain Ward's mining group, might even be capable of sending out quite a large group of armed men. Or would Ward try to pre-empt such a move by calling on me to parachute his killing team in at night to board the ship.

God! How the imagination runs away with one! And Himself standing there behind Charlie's seat, the steel-gloved hand clutching the back of it and the face, that heavy, jutting jaw, that hawk nose, all his features set and immobile as though sculpted in granite. What was he thinking? What was going on in that bull-like head of his? Automatically I began the long glide down to the wheel lines we had scored on the ice, calling on them to stand by for landing. That was when all thoughts of Iain, and what he was planning, were pushed right out of my mind. The Ice Front base was reporting cloud increasing and occasional flurries of hail.

I was in such a hurry then to get back to base that, as soon as we were down, I began braking. I just didn't think. The Herc started to slew and again it was Charlie who saved us from hitting the frozen bank of snow on the port side by reaching over as I applied right rudder and slamming three of the four engines into reverse thrust. The rear door was up and the ramp down almost before I had brought the plane to a standstill, a bitter cold wind sweeping into the fuselage.

They had the plane unloaded in record time and we were away, leaving Eduardo to check over his bearings before they drilled through the ice and sent the mole down to chew up the seabed. The cloud was thickening rapidly and before I had reached the point of no return, snow was coming at us in flurries. To keep in visual contact with the pack I was forced lower and lower. Soon it got so dark I had to rely on instruments alone. I didn't like it. Nor did Iain. But his only comment was: 'It's no' verra nice.'

Wind and sleet thrashed at the windshield, the sleet turning to hail, the sound of the engines almost drowned in the thunder of ice crystals hitting the fuselage. I tried climbing above it, but it suddenly ceased. We had run out of it and there was the pack below us, a slanting shaft of sunlight giving it an unearthly glow, cloud piled ahead of it and very black. I tried diving under it, but then I was into snow again.

We had snow all the way to the Ice Front. I don't know whether it eased up slightly, or whether my eyes had adjusted to the strain of peering through the grey murk, but suddenly I could see it – a white cliff of ice straight ahead of me. I lifted over it and hit the runway hard. I don't think I have ever been more relieved to hear the rumble of the wheels, even if it was on ice. And then, when I went into reverse thrust, I was blinded by the snow and ice the props slung at the windshield. Even when I just let the aircraft run I could hardly see where I was going. And when it finally came to rest and I had manoeuvred it round, the camp container units were lost in the driving snow. God! We were lucky.

There was only Belle to signal me into position, and when I stumbled out I could hardly stand. My legs were trembling uncontrollably and the wind was blowing with demoniac force. We chocked the wheels, strapped the aircraft down to the steel pegs we had sunk deep into the ice, and fled to the shelter of the container mess, by then barely visible in the driving snow.

That was one of the closest shaves I ever had. We had no talk-down facilities. A few minutes later and I would not have been able to see the Ice Front or the runway. Either I would have crashed into the face of the ice cliff or I would still be circling round in nil visibility, waiting for the moment when we had emptied our tanks and I crash-landed somewhere on the Ice Shelf. Perhaps we would have survived dug deep into the snow and ice, but probably not, for this was a full-scale Antarctic blizzard. It lasted for eighty-seven hours, the wind speed rising from thirty-five to over seventy in the gusts, and the noise of it gradually lessening as the snow built up against the containers, and all that time we had no contact with the pack-ice station or with the outside world. The radio was useless.

We were all asleep when the wind finally stopped. We woke to the sound of voices. Then a door was forced open and Pete and Nils suddenly appeared in a beam of light from a window they had cleared. With *Isvik* hooked on to the ice quay at the base of the Front, the storm had passed over their heads. They could hear it, but there was no sea and very little snow.

The plane was now a humped-up drift of snow. I wished we had been able to get it into the ice hangar. It would have saved us long hours of snow-clearing. The aerials were down and we had to set them up again before we could make contact with the mining party out on the pack. They seemed in good heart, reporting very little snow and wind speeds no higher than twenty-six, so that they had been able to work throughout the period we had been snowed in. The mole was on the seabed sending up trial samples, and this very morning, in a position approximately three hundred metres south-west of that given by Eduardo's bearings, samples taken from 4.8 metres depth showed they were at last into the blue-ground.

The effect on Iain was almost magical. From being in a mood of near manic depression, he was suddenly like a schoolboy given a present he has long been coveting. Gone was the worried, almost distracted look. His step was lighter and he threw himself with enthusiasm into the snow-clearing operation. We had all those on *Isvik* up to help, but even so it took a full day of exhausting, back-breaking work to clear the C-130 of snow, get the little bulldozer working and start clearing the runway of drifts. We still had to clear one of the flubbers and tank up with fuel. How much to carry? I now knew how quickly the weather could change here on the Ice Shelf and this was a question that kept me awake for what seemed hours. In the end I decided to restrict the fuel load to double that required for a single return flight. By morning it was snowing again, but only fitfully, a nice, crisp day with occasional gleams of sun.

It was just after we had begun refuelling that Iris, who had been having coffee with Belle, came running out to say Gary was on the radio reporting a dozen men at least with a snowmobile and sleds were moving northwards across the ice towards the wreck of the frigate.

We took off just as the sun began its slow emergence above the north-eastern horizon, Iain full of a sort of suppressed excitement. 'Everythin's comin' t'gether now.' That was after we were clear of the runway and climbing to my economical cruising height. He said it again, after I had levelled off and the engine noise had dropped to a steady drone, clapping me on the back, a grin all over his face. 'Eduardo.' He almost shouted the man's name. 'Eduardo called me up. They've found the first stone, a big one – as big as the largest he brought out with him. And there's a mass of small stuff. Industrial. Easier to sell these days than the gemstones.' His hand banged at my shoulder. 'Everythin's fallin' into place. We're in luck.' He was then literally rubbing his hands together and I wondered whether that was a gesture he had picked up from the old man who had sent him to Eton. I could just see that elderly East End barrow boy rubbing his hands together after selling a piece of stolen silver at the full Sotheby auction price. 'In luck –' And suddenly he was singing, something about a beautiful morning.

Later he went on to elaborate: the volcanic pipe found, the Hercules salvaged and Belle and himself planning some sort of partnership. 'Ah did her an injury, but reck'n that's squared now. For the future we'll be workin' together. An' there's Eduardo an' Iris, an' *Isvik.*' He was even regarding the Argentinians as being part of his luck. 'They'll blow that frigate up an' that'll be that – no reason for any maritime museum, or other semi-official body, to come pokin' around down here lookin' for a prime exhibit.' The last thing he wanted was publicity. 'They destroy that frigate an' that'll be the end of it. No reason then for any Porton Down, or equivalent scientific body, to send an expedition to examine the entrails an' produce another learned paper. Jus' think what the tabloids would make of it with no D-Notice and us down here screwing a fortune out of this shallow-water seabed.'

Shortly after that exchange we got our first sight of the fumaroles. This at a distance of over forty miles, the air crystal clear and visibility almost infinite. Soon we could see the reared-up bows of the frigate. There were several tents in a huddle by the waist where it dipped under the sea, and figures moving about on deck. Away to the right was our own camp, the square box-shape of the hut we had flown in in sections standing out very clearly.

There must have been a slight surface thaw for once I had put the C-130 down on the ice it was like gliding on silk, the surface dark with a dusting of powder snow that blanketed all sound from the undercarriage wheels. The first thing Iain did after we landed was to open up a coffin-shaped box that contained weapons and ammunition. 'Just in case,' he said, handing me a short-barrelled machine pistol. 'Ah'm takin' no chances with those boys.' He nodded over to the frigate, where they now had a hatch cover off and two of them in full biological warfare protective clothing, masks over their faces, were descending below decks. He was convinced that, once they had set their charges and blown the whole ship to pieces, they would turn their attention to us.

The mole, powered by the generator we had flown in, was now grinding out blue-ground volcanic rock, feeding the rubble into its metal belly, and from there it was hauled to the surface through a hole blasted in the ice. In one section of the hut was a small, rather primitive pulverising machine and a separation table. An old bucket was already half-full of what the Brazilian had identified as material of value. Two or three pieces of rubble had been set aside for display and we were examining what Albertini said was the largest uncut stone they had brought up so far, when Gary called to us to come quickly.

After the dark of the processing cubicle, the light outside was so brilliant I couldn't see anything, only the glare of sunlight on pack-ice. Beyond the shadowed outline of the frigate was a berg radiating an eye-searing spectrum of colour. It was like a huge diamond, crystal-brilliant and shot through with colours, red, yellow, blue, green. It was against that huge lump of blinding ice crystal that I gradually made out the shapes of men running to seek shelter behind their snowmobile and sleds. One of them had a reel under his arm and was slowly turning it, paying out wire. But I couldn't see the wire, only guessed what he was doing by his movements.

We watched in absolute silence as they all sought cover. The last man to reach the shelter of the snowmobile, with its piled-up heap of gear, was the one with the reel. There was a pause then, and now that my eyes had become accustomed to the glare, I could see heads peering over the top of the sled loads, one of them standing and looking back over his shoulder. He raised his arm, then dropped it, turning to face the direction of the frigate.

For a moment nothing happened, everything very quiet as though the whole frozen world was dead under a blazing sun and a cold blue sky. Then – Boom! Boom! Boom, boom, boom! The charges did not go off all together, but in sequence, the wreck of the frigate disintegrating before our eyes, planks, bulwarks, stumps of masts flying up into the air, the wooden sides of the hull folding outwards like a film of one of the more unusual fungi opening its strange shape to the world.

The sound of that destruction lingered in the still air, echoing back from berg to berg. Then, finally, all was quiet and the demolition crew came out from the shelter of their sleds, those with protective clothing walking cumbersomely back to what little was left of the wreck. 'Looks like they're experts at that sort o' thing,'

Charlie muttered, and Gary said, 'Navy. They just been talking to their ship – in clear.'

'So you speak Spanish,' I said.

He looked at me sharply, his eyes gone dead and his mouth a tight line. It was Iain who answered for him. 'Ye don't imagine Ah'd bring a man out here who could only make himself understood in English, do ye?'

Remembering how rapidly the weather had changed on our previous flight I suggested we make a move back to base. Iain took no notice. He had his binoculars trained on the Argentinians, who were grouped around their sleds, all except the inspection party over by the dark heap of smouldering ship's timbers. But they weren't examining the debris. They were staring out at something they could see, but we could not. 'Somethin' goin' on there,' Iain muttered. And then – 'Christ!'

At the same moment the Argentinian inspection team turned and began to run, waving their arms. One of them threw off his protective clothing in order to run faster. The others did the same, looking over their shoulders – southward, towards the iridescent rainbow sparkle of the iceberg. 'What is it?' Iris asked. 'What is it, Iain?'

He didn't reply. There was no need. The glittering iceberg was beginning to tumble, and at the same time I felt a slight shiver in the ice under my feet. There was a grating, rumbling sound. Iain yelled at me to get the Herc started up. 'We got to get out.' He was running for the hut, shouting to the others to get on to the aircraft.

Nobody asked why or what it was all about. We all knew by then, for the ice was literally trembling under our feet, the grating sound of plates grinding deep down under the seabed getting louder. Out of the tail of my eye, just as I was swinging myself into the Herc, I caught a glimpse of that scintillating berg just as it disintegrated. It stopped me for a second, for it didn't just disintegrate, it literally disappeared, and in its place an explosion of seawater, ice crystals, the red of liquid rock, magma from deep down, rose into the air, a great cloud of ash building in the terrible clear blue of the sky.

I flung myself into the flight deck, grabbing at the controls, yelling to the others to get in and close the bloody door. Iain was last aboard. He had a bucket in his hand, his face bright red with running in his cold-weather clothing. A crack opened up where the mole was still grinding away at the seabed. The hole they had blown in the ice was opening up, a crack growing wider as it came snaking towards us. I had the engines running by then, but I still heard the noise of the seabed's four-metre-thick coating of ice being torn apart. The door clanged shut and I eased off the brakes, swinging north-eastward, away from the line of the crack that was now a mini-crevasse.

It was just as I turned on to our makeshift runway that the second volcanic eruption occurred almost at the position where the frigate had been. By then I was building up speed, committed to take-off. Away to my right I saw the Argentinians trapped by the breaking ice, cracks all around them. And then suddenly they weren't there any more. The widening ice mouth of a newly-formed crevasse had swallowed them completely. Their snowmobile was the last thing to go into that cold, gaping maw, and as though it were some sort of detonator, red hot lava began spewing out on to the ice, clouds of white steam hanging in the air.

A crack had now opened up right ahead of me. If we had been fully loaded I would not have made it, but with only the nine of us, and no other cargo but that bucket, I pulled her off just before the wheels reached the crack, and then we were into an updraft of hot air and steam as more of the seabed was flung into the air.

Suddenly we were clear, nothing ahead of us but the pale blue of the sky. I banked to look back at what we had so narrowly missed. Already it was a great billowing cloud of ash mushrooming out from a thick column that rose out of a dirty mix of seabed and ice. It was beginning to take on the shape of an atomic explosion, getting blacker by the minute, and violent stabs of lightning forking through it.

I looked back at Iain. He was standing close behind me, his body, his face ... I can't describe it. Haggard is not quite the right word. He looked absolutely shattered, the face very pale, almost white, and there was a ghastly tenseness about it that made him appear suddenly much older. Iris caught at his arm, trying to comfort him, but he shrugged her off. 'Ye don't understand.'

'I do,' she cried. 'I do, I do, Iain.'

'And the Lord said unto Satan ...'

'What are you talking about?'

'Job,' he said, his eyes blank, seeing nothing, only the disaster that nature had flung at him. 'I feel like Job,' he muttered. 'Afflicted of Satan, poor sod.'

'What do you mean?'

'Nothing, nothing. *Man is born into trouble as the sparks fly upwards.*' He closed his eyes then, his mouth clenched shut, and I turned back on to my course.

Behind me I heard Iris asking him what he was going to do, but he didn't answer for a moment, then he muttered, 'Get drunk, Ah s'pose. What does any man do when his whole world blows up in his face?'

09056.484848

SILVER. ~~Grey~~   teal
    Pink ~
514 . 794   796